D0935901

The

SKIN

and

ITS GIRL

The

SKIN

and

ITS GIRL

A Novel

Sarah Cypher

EMMA S. CLARK MEMORIAL LIBRARY
Setauket, L.I., New York 11733

BALLANTINE BOOKS

NEW YORK

The Skin and Its Girl is a work of fiction. Names, characters, places, and incidents are the products of the author's imagination or are used fictitiously. Any resemblance to actual events, locales, or persons, living or dead, is entirely coincidental.

Copyright © 2023 by Sarah Cypher

All rights reserved.

Published in the United States by Ballantine Books, an imprint of Random House, a division of Penguin Random House LLC, New York.

BALLANTINE is a registered trademark and the colophon is a trademark of Penguin Random House LLC.

Grateful acknowledgment is made to the Mahmoud Darwish Foundation and Nada Sneige Fuleihan for permission to translate five lines of "We Travel Like Other People" by Mahmoud Darwish, © Mahmoud Darwish Foundation. Translation from Arabic to English by Nada Sneige Fuleihan. Translated and used by permission.

LIBRARY OF CONGRESS CATALOGING-IN-PUBLICATION DATA
Names: Cypher, Sarah, author.
Title: The skin and its girl: a novel / Sarah Cypher.
Description: First edition. | New York: Ballantine Books, 2023.
Identifiers: LCCN 2022038974 (print) | LCCN 2022038975 (ebook) |
ISBN 9780593499535 (hardcover; acid-free paper) | ISBN 9780593499542 (ebook)
Subjects: LCGFT: Lesbian fiction. | Novels.
Classification: LCC PS3603.Y67 S57 2023 (print) | LCC PS3603.Y67 (ebook) |
DDC 813/.6—dc23/eng/20220829
LC record available at https://lccn.loc.gov/2022038974
LC ebook record available at https://lccn.loc.gov/2022038975

Printed in Canada on acid-free paper

randomhousebooks.com

2 4 6 8 9 7 5 3 1

First Edition

Book design by Caroline Cunningham

For Nagy & Millie Kanaan

We travel like other people, but do not return to anything. . . .

We have a country of words. Speak, speak, let us see an end to this journey.

—MAHMOUD DARWISH
(trans. Nada Sneige Fuleihan)

AN ORDERING

———•—•—

PART I

---·---

Soap

(Ages 0–1)

Q: What speaks with no body?
A: The wind, Auntie.

Q: What grows larger the more you take away?
A: A hole, Auntie.

Q: What tells the truth by telling lies?

I was going to say a novel. But in my life, the first answer to that question is you, Auntie. Tonight is one of your birthdays. Persephone-like, you had two of them, and here at your stone in the grass, out in the cold San Francisco fog at the nadir of the year, I put a cube of soap down and ask for your attention. I'll speak in your native tongue—lies and fables braided with the truth. It is like those dreams where I can fly or just open my mouth and sing on key: realizing how easy it is to address the dead and expect an answer.

Postmortem

———•—◦—•———

I magine this. In the final hour before dawn, the doctor pulls a baby through an incision under a woman's belly. Everyone is doomed to this first unhousing, one way or another. And as he lifts me from the dark warmth of my mother's body and unwraps the cord from around my neck, everyone here begins to work as hard as they can. They work for several minutes, until the outcome is obvious. Someone looks at the clock, announces the time.

My mother might be to blame—she refused to push—or the doctor, so hard on himself, so ready to take responsibility for real and imagined mistakes. All their medical instruments agree: this is not a beginning, but an ending.

When my mother has been taken away, her blood still marks the floor, the room's metal surfaces, and the doctor's gown. He and the nurse, who have stayed behind to clean the body, are angry—at my mother, yes, but mostly at themselves because they made promises to her and to the adoptive parents that my birth would be routine.

But at this moment, my skin is a pallid version of my mother's wheat-colored complexion, fading to the flat yellow-gray of death. Blood vessels ruptured in my face during asphyxiation by the cord, and now, fine blue filaments around my mouth cause the doctor's hands to shake as he wipes the waxy film from behind my stiff ears. The nurse hands him another rag. When their work is finished, they will swaddle my body and offer my mother and the adoptive parents a chance to speak with the hospital's chaplain.

The doctor checks the time of death with the nurse but gets no answer.

"I said, was it six thirty-eight?"

The nurse is staring at my body with a frown.

Imagine their surprise: a vein pulses on the crown of my head. And imagine, as I have many times, the strangeness of what they see happening to my face. It is turning blue. No, not an airless blue. Like a fine network of roots, cobalt filaments are wiggling outward from lips and eyelids, webbing together under the skin across cheeks and forehead. The broken blood vessels seem to multiply with every branching. They grow in density, too, coloring my face. Down my neck, across my chest, underneath my fingernails, and between my toes. Soon my entire body is an even, lustrous blue like a creature from a fairy tale.

The nurse asks the doctor, "Have you seen anything like this before?"

Later, in his report, he will make a fuller description which will be filed away and forgotten among the handful of other strange cases in the hospital's history, reread only by me a few decades later when the hospital is about to purge its archives. But just now, he can only stare, stranded between curiosity and shock.

The nurse sets the bell of a stethoscope on my bare chest and says, "There's a heartbeat."

The doctor ignores this observation and gropes for the EEG leads. Yet no doctor in the world needs a machine to prove what anyone's eyes can see. My whole body is alive and blue: the pure cobalt of a gas flame. The color is most brilliant on my thighs, belly, and cheeks. On a normal baby, the pattern would indicate a healthy flush. My blue eyelids twitch, my blue limbs move, and I sneeze.

My birth comes over two centuries after our family first exalted the glories of the color blue, Auntie, but you taught me a few rules of interpretation. Everything depends on context. I will get around to why I am here at your gravestone, but first, let me try again to understand how you came to my bassinet on my first day in this world.

You taught me stories so old they were last repeated when today's aunties' aunties were still small enough to run barefoot around the soap factory. The curse of the despicable woman, they said, is to give birth to stones, to puppies, to a piece of cannibalistic dung. In that world, there are crones and magic rings, red-eyed ogres and water-dwelling djinn. Back then, everybody knew that Aladdin meant the Glory of Religion (Ala' ad-Din, if you want to break it down) and that every tale is an allegory.

To be clear, ours was no longer that world.

Yet we found ourselves one day with an uncanny pure thing on the top floor of a middling Portland hospital. Here we had, somehow, me—a blue baby—and, soon, three fairy godmothers.

Births in the Rummani family had always been newsworthy, so it was unusual, that morning, for only one blood relative to attend: my maternal grandmother, Saeeda Rummani. During my nine months in utero there had been a divorce, the resurgence of a mental illness, the decision to give a baby away, even a lie about a miscarriage—nothing to be proud of. The birth deserved no pomp, and Saeeda had left her husband in the care of his home nurse and gone, without much optimism, to her daughter's bedside the way she might attend a shotgun wedding before a justice of the peace.

In the hospital courtyard, under a metal saint splattered with pigeon dung, Saeeda unknit seven rows of a baby blanket she was making, searching for the error. Harried, she stuffed the project back into her purse. Her daughter had embarrassed her. Fighting her labor, fighting the doctors, monopolizing everyone's time and worry. Bra-zenly making a scene, until it turned into a big emergency and the doctors evicted Saeeda from the bedside and exiled her to the waiting room and adjacent garden. Now she made the doctor wait at the doorway a long time as she gathered her things to come see this baby, because her hands did not seem to be working right in the morning cold. She apologized a dozen times on the way, but it was as though this doctor didn't even hear her.

She did not know I had died and come back to life. Her daughter, my mother, was still asleep. And when they came to the delivery ward, not even the doctor could explain to Saeeda what had happened to make me, her granddaughter in the clear-sided isolette, such a dense shade of blue.

"She is on the small side," the doctor said, "but her weight is good. Oxygen saturation is normal. Apgar, eight out of ten. We can't say what's wrong. I mean, medically nothing seems wrong, but you can see . . ." He trailed off, assuming that this woman with the accent would certainly not understand what he was trying to say. He stood beside her, staring mutely at his newest patient, then promised her that the nurse would tell her when her daughter was awake.

Not many other machines were present, which reassured Saeeda. The incubator was an uneasy object, but otherwise, no one seemed to be paying me much attention.

The shock of a blue granddaughter: it felt like a counterargument from the old country. A silly tale come to life. After the doctor was gone, she pulled out the blocky little cellphone her husband had pro-grammed, in better days, with the short list of family numbers she was still welcome to call.

That her sister-in-law remained in the contact list was a matter of habit. Theirs was a mythically long and convoluted history, straining back to earliest childhood. Like a buzzard, both in her baldness and in her keenness for the scent of blood, this woman had landed on Saeeda's happiness long before Saeeda's first marriage and had been picking at its entrails long after the first husband had died. Remaining, technically, a sister-in-law. Seven months ago, she'd locked her talons into the family's newest pregnancy, but after my parents' marriage had come suddenly and spectacularly apart, the only thing Saeeda could do to chase the old bird out of her daughter's business was to tell her that Tashi had miscarried. Don't visit. Give her space. Let me do it, for once, because she can't handle a fuss right now. It was the sort of management Saeeda had not wielded over her daughter's life in twenty years, and it had given Tashi the time she needed to make a most unreasonable plan: adoption. Make the baby, like her marriage to my father, vanish. By Rummani standards, it was as terrible as what Saeeda had done when she had sold off the soap factory in Nablus, as well as all their land, to a rival family. Terrible, and also astounding, since her daughter was so unlike her in almost every other way: and what a trait to share, this propensity to make a mess when it is least expected.

The line rang through in Oakland. A flutter ran through Saeeda's stomach. As she held the phone to her ear, her breath fogged the glass between her face and the room where her blue granddaughter slept, curled up tight like a delphinium bud in the white blankets. She had seen the papers, too, the ones Tashi would sign to give this baby away to strangers. As best she could tell, the situation that had brought about this unreasonable plan was unchanged.

After six rings, the call went to the machine. How was it that at seven-thirty on a Friday morning, a seventy-eight-year-old misanthrope with no nuclear family and an increasingly housebound group of friends was somehow not at home? Saeeda left a message, one of the more startling ones in memory.

"Walek waynek? Yalla I need you in Portland. The baby isn't really dead. She's here and you have to stop your niece from giving her away."

Stories I would eventually learn in school: The earth emerges from a terrible flood. The man walks out of the tomb dragging his shroud.

The fertile female is resuscitated with a prince's kiss. I do not claim to know them all, but I believe none. Death is a one-way mutation, and, Auntie, I'm jogging your memory for the beginning of our entanglement because you too know death, and, like me, you must have no memory of the time before. Unlike me, to the best of my knowledge, you never woke up again, at least not in this world.

But I tell you, I recognize myself by death's mark, and for a time I imagined almost every day that it were different, that I could be anything other than impossibly blue. Ironic, considering that my grandmother feared I would be like an animal, a creature unable to imagine itself as anything other than what it is, even though she never imagined herself as anything other than a perfectly assimilated American.

My mother, however, was so much the opposite that she would see me as even more normal than herself. She was the second of my three fairy godmothers, let's say, one of my three furies, my three muses— my mad scientist and maker, Tashi Rummani.

When my mother finally woke, she was thirsty and her whole body shook with cold. She was on a railed bed beside an empty plastic chair. A wax-colored curtain surrounded her, holding her inside a dim solitude. A silhouette shifted on the curtain, busy with a task on its opposite side. She called out, "Mama?"

"I'm just the nurse," the silhouette answered, "but I can get her."

Under the lingering fog of drugs and twenty-six hours of labor, she listened to the impersonal sounds of the recovery wing, still feeling groggy. She couldn't remember why she'd believed that the baby needed to stay inside her, only that it had seemed like a matter of life and death.

A twist of unease: the nurse hadn't said anything about the baby. She tried to remember what had happened. The doctor had shouted more staff into the room, and then the oxygen mask was over her nose and mouth. What followed had been nothing like sleep; it had felt like a hole in the fabric of consciousness.

The lingering drugs took her down again, and when she opened her eyes, two nurses were pulling her bed into a sort of hospital penthouse with walls of windows. "The adoptive parents are downstairs," one said, "and they said to call whenever you are ready for them to meet the baby."

Tashi was too fuddled to trace her questions to their end. Stared out the windows. The whole city sprawled out beneath her, a gleaming promise pressed around a river, under a broken ceiling of clouds. The morning skyline was sharp and clear—more real than her body, which felt muted.

In the corridor, the staff elevator dinged and rumbled. Footsteps turned and squeaked in other directions, toward the nurses' station or into other rooms. Tashi braced for the extended family she'd remembered from her own childhood, the whole squabbling lot of them, before she remembered that no one had come but her mother. She hadn't even called her very recently ex-husband, who had signed away his right to know anything. The last few months of isolation and subterfuge had begun to seem driven by a mistake, something unanswerable, and—she was remembering now—it had made her labor terrifying. Unrealized dread of parting with the small human inside her body.

So when a cart arrived on quiet wheels at this most private floor of the building, guided to the bedside by a shy nurse, Tashi didn't immediately realize that her daughter was there, with her, right beside her bed.

"Ma'am, would you like to hold her now?"

"Oh!" Tashi peered into the cart. "Oh . . ." she said again, more tenderly, and reached up to settle the baby against her breastbone.

For the life of her, she couldn't remember how she thought a baby should look. This one, even wrapped in hospital cottons, was smaller than expected though heavy as a garden statue. But warm and mobile, scowling against the daylight. Tashi smoothed the fine, dark hair. Counted fingers and toes. Felt my skin's heat and strange firmness.

"Ma'am, just so you know, we checked the identity against the records, and she's definitely—"

"Mine, of course." Tashi didn't lift her eyes to the nurse, but felt the pressure of the woman's professional confusion.

"And the doctor will be wanting to stop by with some colleagues . . ."

"There's no need."

"Your mother is here now, but the adoptive parents are still—"

"Tell them to come later tonight. Just leave her with me now. She's okay. She's with me." Dreamlike, she observed that I was the purest blue, and the color was so much my own that comparing it to anything else would have diminished both the color and me. Her fear, that day and for the rest of her years, was of everyone else on my behalf.

The third woman who came out of the elevator and into my life that day was old and small. She reeked of what she called her *thinking tobacco*. She wore a layered pink sweater and dark lipstick, and yellow sunglasses the size of dessert plates. They held the heavy locks of a gray wig away from her face.

Saeeda caught her in the hallway. "I tried to call you twenty times. Why didn't you answer?"

"I've been driving since dawn. How come no one tells me that my own niece has been on her deathbed? I had to find out all about it from others—"

"Who did you talk to? The family? But I haven't told anyone!"

"Khalas!" The newcomer swept her hand through the air like a vulture's wing, with an attendant clattering of bracelets. "I'm the oldest of all. I know when and where I'm needed."

"Yes, you always get involved," Saeeda said. She'd rushed out of Tashi's room with her knitting when she'd heard that familiar voice asking for directions, and now she physically blocked her sister-in-law from leaving the elevator bank. No matter how wrinkled they got, no matter how gray and creaky, fighting with Nuha Rummani provoked a part of Saeeda that would never mature beyond age five, when she was sold into a betrothal and began to learn that this woman—impervious, unmarried—was an altogether different creature, a person of another species.

For her part, Nuha Rummani seemed to realize she was being held in place by a knitting needle. "I am here to see my grandniece. Let me pass."

Saeeda sighed. "What exactly have you heard?"

Nuha swept off her yellow sunglasses. "Walaw? I did not even know there was a baby until an hour ago. No one bothers to tell me. Step aside." She jammed the glasses into her purse and floated past Saeeda—the hallway was broad as a freeway—for just then, her venerable ears detected the sound of a crying baby.

In fact, the newcomer had heard no word of my birth at all. The news that had reached her was from Palestine, shocking news, and as she had explained to everyone within earshot of the elevator bank, she had determined that she needed to try to see the damage for herself. She'd packed three suitcases and locked her tiny flat in Oakland. Then she'd driven north intending to visit her favorite niece, my mother, leave the car parked at the apartment, and board a flight to Amman for as long as relatives needed her back home. But when she'd parked the car in the lot and rung the doorbell eleven times and finally shouted up from the porch like a buffoon, the top-floor neighbor told her that the lady who lived there had gone into labor two nights ago and had left a note to take any packages upstairs. Nuha asked for directions. It was one of the university hospitals, only a few steep blocks away.

Now here she was in the hallway, age-shrunken and iron-haired, wearing her war lipstick. Saeeda spoke a warning behind her, bejeweled and impotent as ever, but one piece of her information sounded outlandish. *Blue.*

Nuha stopped in the doorway. The hospital room was big enough to be a hangar.

The sight of my mother was the second surprise. The long hair Nuha remembered was gone—the tight black curls were now snipped hard against Tashi's temples and the nape of her neck. Tashi had always had Saeeda's fuller cheeks, but her face was thin and drained to the color of skim milk. Although she looked sickly against the white sheets and hospital gown, she held the swaddled baby not just with her arms but with her whole body, looking both as fierce and as befuddled as any new mother.

"Auntie!" Tashi's eyes filled first with relief, then tears.

Nuha washed her hands and rushed to hold the baby. She gazed down into the blanket. She hadn't misheard: there I lay, her little grandniece, exactly as Saeeda had said. *Blue.*

You, the formidable Nuha Rummani, stood at the bed looking down at me. Where my mother and grandmother saw only danger, you, Auntie, saw possibility.

I imagine my body, lying there like a blank sheet of paper. You reach down. Your hands are bones held together by tendons and loose skin, and as they make a solid cuff to lift me, the other women in the room fall away. You scoop me up to eye level, supporting me on your forearm. Soft black curls lie in rings against my scalp, where the almost-translucent skin pulses. And no, your old eyes aren't lying to you. I really am blue. You ask the most human of all questions, *What does it mean?* In the answering silence, your head fills with comparisons: blue as lapis, blue as certain Mediterranean evenings, blue as, yes, blue as you'd only heard in stories a young man once told you in an old city. The man and part of that city were now gone, but this blue girl—well, shout it from the hospital roof, I lived.

You'd brag about it for years, how I arched my spine and rolled my knobby shoulders back and shrieked. The cry tore out of the cavern of my small belly, mighty even then. And you just laughed your long, hooting laughter that was all joy.

This is how we entered each other's improbable stories.

"Oh, hush, Your Majesty, my little queen bee, come here . . ." From the beginning, you always spoke carefully to me, with diplomacy and a tiny bit of fear, as you would to real royalty. I fought against the blankets until I found the shape of your neck and shoulder. I nestled my head under your ear and went quiet. Perhaps the sensation of my moving torso, my beating heart, the appearance of immediate trust, reached down to the pit of your being. You shuffled to the window, making little shushes of comfort, and in our ghostly reflection, the two of us appeared to be wrecked against each other.

"What's the name?" you asked.

No answer, but the silence was a tension you'd have to poke at later.

"Fine. I'm calling her Betty." You peered down at me, your blue niece, whose tears were already drying. As the eldest in the Rummani family, old enough to have raised both Saeeda and Tashi, you saw you would need to take charge one last time.

"Ya, habeebti Betty, you better believe I am not letting you out of my sight."

That is why, Auntie, I am petitioning you now, on the darkest day of the year many decades afterward. I have not forgotten that in all practical and imaginary ways, you are still my author.

Coincidence will sometimes play a role in this story, as it does in all lives.

While a blue Rummani was getting ready to be born on the other side of the world, a formation of F-16 fighter jets had flown south from Ramat David Air Force Base along ancient mountains. They released a score of bombs in retaliation for some offense. These munitions exploded throughout the West Bank city of Nablus. In addition to the usual casualties, which had become as commonplace as lottery numbers, one of the bombs obliterated a six-hundred-year-old stone building that had once served as a soap factory. The factory housed disused tools and a round vat, several meters deep, which had been empty for decades.

Though no one could establish cause and effect, the Rummani
family always claimed authority over matters in which they were ignorant. And when my auntie stepped out to call Jerusalem, Amman,
London, Miami, and West L.A. to inform everyone of my unusual
blue skin, word of the demolished family soap factory was waiting for
her in twenty voices. The last of the Rummanis' history was gone.
They would never see it again, that building in which the aunties had
run barefoot for generations, whose soap had washed the bodies of
queens, emperors, sultans, at least forty-five popes, and every last one
of the Greek Orthodox metropolitans. It had been our factory many
years ago, before Saeeda's betrayal. And in an unwieldy web of long-
distance conference calls, they insisted that the loss of one and the
appearance of me must be related.

"Bismissalib! Esh yaani? Are you saying that the factory is gone
because the girl was born?"

One of the old brothers grumbled. "La'a, it would have to be the
other way around."

"The girl is the soul of our old factory?"

Someone laughed. "Wallahi, I had no idea buildings have souls.
Outhouses were lost in the bombing, too. What sort of creature do
you think was born from them?"

"Hush. The girl is half Rummani, yes, but no one has accounted for
her father. Surely the blue came from him."

"Impossible. He's Lutheran. And midwestern. They don't even put
spices in their food."

Indeed, how could they explain anything? The phenomenon felt
like a headstone for their losses. Then someone grumbled that maybe
I was actually a curse or half djinni.

"That's only for God to know," replied one of the cousins. "I wonder, has a date for the baptism been set?"

Back on familiar territory, the Rummanis in Jerusalem, Amman,
London, Miami, and West L.A. fell into a squabble of cross talk over
whether I should be baptized in the Orthodox Church or the Catho-

lic Church. No one bothered to consider my father's upbringing, be-cause, since the divorce, I was wholly theirs.

Even so, the family didn't settle on a cause for the blueness. In those days, so soon after 9/11, with Baghdad destined to fall within the year, in the heat of an intifada and the perpetual threat of apocalypse, I just seemed like a sign of the modern world. So what if a girl was born blue? Stranger things were happening all around.

An Origin Story

———•———

Listen, nobody can recite the *One Thousand and One Nights* straight through anymore, and neither can I. As you used to say, Auntie, a piece of yarn stretched out in a straight line is a waste of wool. And this one, like so many stories you told me, requires interruptions, divagations, a dash of rhetorical hypotaxis. My mother's love for me in the hospital on my literal birthday is a perfect example of how predisposed the people in our family are to go leaping sideways after their desires, abandoning one life to career into another. You know it better than all of us combined, so I'm at your grave site on your actual birthday desiring help, perspective, a story to follow through a patch of unspeakable confusion.

As soon as you saw the blank blue page of my body, you scrabbled to fill it with significance. In the Rummani tradition, ignorance was no reason to be shy: *Anyone with two eyes in their head can see exactly what this means,* you said to Saeeda. And to Tashi, *Anyone with two ears can hear the old stories come to life,* notwithstanding your inadequate hearing aids. You had a way of bullying, insisting that the body and its senses had anything at all to do with sensemaking.

But here is the problem, the sideways leap, the reason I stand here speaking. Tomorrow I'm to leave your grave for good. Someone loves me and wants a life with me elsewhere, beyond other borders, where other languages are spoken. To my shock I'd said yes, lit by the hot-faced enthusiasm always lurking at the bottom of a second boule-vardier; and when I woke up the next morning, I realized I'd meant it. The answer felt written in my bones, just as it must have when you changed every plan you had the moment you saw me in the hospital room, and grafted your story into mine.

But then I wondered, was this really what you would do? Depart family, abandon a safe little job in the out-of-sight archives of a minor museum, give up an apartment where the neighbors mind their own business? If I stay, my beating heart will leave the country in another woman's suitcase, unless, two generations after you brought us all to America, I submit to becoming an immigrant, in an untranslatable shade of blue, to live where anyone with two eyes in their head will stare at me as if I'm about to steal the silverware, and they will immediately begin to scrawl their nonsense ideas on me. Is that really what you'd do? What you'd wanted for me as well as for my mother, who sometimes still requires my help? It feels like rewriting much of what you gave me in a decade of your story-telling.

I confess, I did a cowardly thing. I agreed to go with my beloved, and I sat for a passport photo and purchased a ticket, yet did not get around to finding a subletter. Internet-walked the maps of our future neighborhood while telling my employer it was just a vacation. Found myself promising all the children of the family that I'd never leave them, and one of them is how my worsening ambivalence came to light. My beloved was furious, and last night we argued in the ugly way that happens when the language barrier becomes as high as the West Bank separation wall. No, I didn't quite lie to her: I was lying mainly to myself, because my desires are at war with each other. I realized that I inherited from you this ability to live with a foot in conflicting versions of the truth, and so I came up here to your grave to sort them out at the feet of the master.

Do I go, or do I stay? Do I gazelle-leap sideways or remain with family?

All the old stories talk about the Road of No Return, the Road of Good Fortune, and the Road of this or that, but I'm seeing that a woman is not fully in possession of herself until there is no road at all, and she must make her own way. That is the problem. I was born roadless, heavy and blue and happiest in one place—content to let you tell me how the world is, and to retreat from any further, disappointing discoveries of my own. But love is nothing if not a catastrophe, one that makes me second-guess gravity, history, the limits of my own person. Love is, might be, feels like, a kind of fairy tale too—one that can begin only once the story we thought we knew blows apart.

Our story together also started at a forking path. The first year after my birth began the way it did because you agreed that my mother was in no condition to raise a baby that year. It wasn't because I, the baby in question, was a blue-skinned, silver-eyed fairy-tale creature that so alarmed medical professionals. The reason for your intervention was my mother herself, underdressed, shoulders poking out of a blanket. Her skin was so pale that it borrowed its only color from the sunset, which was flaming off the plate-glass skyscrapers downtown. She was not a vision of maternal competence, not on that morning and at no time ever.

Right then, she lay in the hospital bed, ignoring a large sheaf of papers that was hidden under the sheet and digging into her hip. As you and Saeeda talked and talked, she gazed out at the sun-struck city as though all of it—its rivers, mountain, bridges, oblivious people—had sprung from her womb fourteen hours ago in the same rush of fluid that had brought a blue baby, new and illegible.

What had made sense to her two days ago was now gibberish. Before: my father had cheated on her and unraveled the whole story of their life, and inside the shrinking space that had begun closing around her, she had decided she was not equal to motherhood after all and could spare me from her nadirs, her bouts, her dislocations, the sense of doubt that plagued even simple tasks, like refilling her otherwise good medication. *Frantic self-revulsion,* he'd called it. His name was literally Adam, and like his biblical antecedent, Adam had set about naming her conditions, her problems, as if he knew better than her what her life contained. The papers at her hip were meant to be the solution. She had chosen to give me up for adoption because she wanted no part. Did not like the sense he and the endless psychiatrists had made of her life but had no concept for raising a child in its aftermath. This decision, made months ago, had not taken into account the soft, sideways tug of the present reality that I was an actual person about whom she felt unexpected, profound tenderness and curiosity.

The adoptive parents were waiting downstairs. She had created this fork in the path over many weeks, fully aware that even though she was a mother, she was still an ill-treated adjunct professor struggling through her thirties, and generally depressed and dreaming of her own death. She had confided these things to the couple over sandwiches at an upscale deli; they had listened skeptically, asking questions about her medications, the number and seriousness of her attempts, her history, her father's early death, things that, in all fairness to Adam, she had barely explained to him, using what might be called the mythological past tense. She had left that last adoption meeting, as she left all those meetings, feeling a complex jumble of resentment and relief.

Now the couple expected her to continue being self-aware and responsible enough to let them get on with their lives as an outstanding pair of parents, all by signing the sheaf of papers lying at this moment on the bed beside her hip. But those papers were hidden under the sheet because, Auntie, you still had no idea of the plan to give me away.

Maybe it begins here, the root of ambivalence, the forking of one path into two. Maybe I was soaked in division from the beginning, holding my mother's uncertainty inside me like arteries branching from the heart.

Yet when I imagine my mother that day of my birth looking out a plate-glass window at the city, seeing an illegible place full of strangers, or when I imagine myself as an immigrant in a land I've never seen, watching wars play out on the news as the children who call me auntie grow old enough to fight in them, I cannot help but wonder about the first branching, the primordial split. Not the Garden of Eden, you said—all of our problems began with a flood, and the first great demolition story of the Bible.

Long ago, all stories told only the truth, in a literal way, with no need to jump around and gather meanings piece by piece. This was because, you said, humans had been happy animals—and we remained happy for a short time after we had shed the last of our fur, when we still moved in tribes and answered our children's pleas for snacks in grammatically correct refusals, and we all spoke a single tongue. We humans fell in love, named our children, and migrated to new places without need of a dictionary or a map. Stories served no purpose but to tell exactly what happened. Lying, as a possibility, occurred to no one.

Then one day, it began to rain. "Quite a storm," we said to one another, the multitude of us, in our same language. "Better bring the washing in. Better bring the children, too." As we huddled indoors with our washing and our children and our worries, the skies poured, glaciers melted, and all the world's headlands and peninsulas turned into isolated knuckles of land. It wasn't as bad as the primary texts insist, but somewhere, a curmudgeon named Noah floated on a boat that reeked of animal shit, gazing across the floodwaters. The people who were drowning asked for help, but he pretended not to understand the words.

But we don't need to bother with his story anymore. The flood is the thing, and so is the authority he worshipped, and the origin of forking paths as the waters receded and revealed the land anew.

After the sodden earth began to dry, we all, the survivors, talked in our single language about who had died and what we'd lost and what we could have done better. And we decided that we should scoop clay and slime from the earth and make bricks and mortar of it: and we built a tower. High and higher. Look at us, working together, all to the same end! Our tower was miles wide, a stone hive of cities, tunnels, colonnades, and floating coliseums, an architecture of giddy excess (as it must be, Auntie, coming from your busy mind of many secrets). Anyway, when we humans were done, we climbed the millions of stairs above the waterline and stood on the roof, breathing the thinner air, and could see the rising sun, the white sea, and the incredible bounty of what remained. Under our feet was the earth's weight in bricks we'd fired and carried with our own hands.

But the god, the thing called LORD, still paid visits. You said to pretend the LORD was real, sort of, a spinning ball of ectoplasm with a temperament like your brother Zaki, worshipped by the animal-loving curmudgeon in his boat. We humans were assigned to its supervision by no choice we remember making, and when the LORD saw the tower, it felt we humans had gotten out ahead of it. Sputtering and spitting, it demanded to know who had authorized the construction, and did they have the proper permits? When we humans crossed our arms and said it was a joint decision and we surely needed no permit to enjoy our collective survival, the LORD blew our grand, uppity tower to bits.

Thus Babel became the predecessor of every faraway city that would ever be translated to a plume of smoke. It also became the point at which the human story begins to fork.

When we humans finally tore our gazes from the rubble, and our shock began to harden into outrage, the LORD noticed that there were a million of us and only one of it, so the LORD made some hasty decisions. It assigned us to districts and put up checkpoints and required ID cards to be stamped and counterstamped by approved stampers only, and it changed the colors of our skin and implemented a randomized system of worship requirements, and gave some of us all the timber and took away all the water from others, and for good measure, it twisted our words and consonants and vowels like putty—so that we peoples of the world spoke a thousand different tongues. We tried to say what had just happened, but now no one could agree.

Looking upon what it had wrought, the LORD said, "Good luck!" And that was the end of human cooperation. The LORD went home to rest.

But let me pause a moment and return to the hospital, where you began to poke, in your way, at that silence which had followed your very first question about my name.

You, Auntie, were willing to pretend to excuse Saeeda's six-month deception about a miscarriage because you were so thrilled by me. And when I regurgitated hospital formula down Saeeda's shirt collar, Saeeda blamed it all on you for exciting me with your too-big-for-every-room voice, and my mother lost patience. She begged the both of you to go away to her apartment for showers and naps, assuring you both that it was a good time for everyone to take a break, because she, for one, certainly needed a rest, some time alone. Saeeda took the key in a huff, and you promised you were right behind her, half a step only, just after you shared this *one tiny little idea* that had popped into your brain.

"Yaani just until Easter," you were saying now, cradling me. "I can sleep on the couch no problem. Anyway I wake up multiple times at night, like a baby. We could be up, me and Betty, while you sleep straight through the night. You'll thank me for coming to live with you."

My mother felt the sheaf of papers hidden beside her hip and was eager for you to leave. She said again, "What couch? What bed? You aren't listening to a thing I'm telling you. You really should rest, go with—"

"Anyone with two eyes in their head can see this baby needs two people in the home, at the minimum. When your mother was born, she had the entire city of Nablus coming in and out of your sainted grandfather's front gate night and day, traffic up and down the road, hooves on the courtyard, sunset to sunrise. The racket was so eternal that the owl who lived in our stable died of sleep deprivation by Epiphany." You shifted me to your other arm and tucked me farther into the folds of your sweater. Effortlessly, you went about this sense-making work, bullying coherence between past, present, and future. "Shu habeebti, what do you want to do? Yalla let me stay a bit with you and this very small queen of yours."

My mother wondered if dying of exhaustion would convince you to leave. After the divorce, she'd also pondered whether she was phys-ically strong enough to slit her own throat—she'd ring my father's doorbell, drag the knife across her neck, and bleed out on the yellow rubber welcome mat, the one that said *Hello* in fifteen languages, in-cluding misspelled Arabic. *Lest you interpret this as frantic self-revulsion,* she'd write, in a note pinned to her shirtfront, *no, I am just very tired.* If men could run whole airplanes into buildings just for spite, if he could go looking for his wedding ring in another woman's purse, if a blue child could come from her womb, then succumbing to fatigue . . . It seemed explicable, at least.

But the part of her brain that had been schooled by therapists saw these thoughts for what they were. She had resolved to do me a favor, surrender me to others. It surprised her, though, how much her body was arguing with her now. Here I was, myself, somehow easier than everything she had planned. She tried to keep the dilemma off her face long enough to be left alone, until she could look at the papers again. Certain promises said I was meant to go elsewhere, pushed out into the world like Moses, with a name and a new family. Escaping the misery upriver, I should soon be on my way toward everything that a loving pair of well-adjusted corporate managers could promise to someone they'd paid an astronomical amount of money to adopt. A whole pastel future, unfolding.

———

"Don't be embarrassed by your new place," you said. "We'll go to the thrift store me and you, and we will get what's needed and a bassinet for Betty!"

"Adam said he'd give me money for whatever I needed. That's not the problem."

"Have that cheating himar buy you a maid, then. A pair of them, why not? And a good guest bed for me while he's at it—just a little twin bed. You can go to work and I will teach Betty her letters. I will care for her around the clock, even on holidays. Nuha Rummani is a lifesaver."

"Auntie, you can't."

"Says who?" A girlish note insinuated itself into your voice. "I don't feel a day over sixty, and these two hands have held more babies than Baba Noël."

"You were going back to the West Bank till summer, you said. You shouldn't change your plans."

"So, she cuts me out of the child's life even before her milk has run dry."

"Auntie, stop it."

"She thinks, 'What does this fossil know about children? A retired teacher, this favorite auntie of three generations of Rummani children, clearly she belongs in a war zone instead.'"

"You *wanted* to go home."

"No, I was *needed* at home. But I am needed here, also. Or so I thought."

"Auntie, the thing is—" My mother crossed her arms tight under the blanket. "The thing is, Auntie, I'm giving the baby up for adoption. It's why, after the divorce, I didn't want anyone to know. The new family is already downstairs." She pulled the sheaf of papers from under the sheet and set them across her lap.

You didn't move or speak. Recognizing an old dilemma, you sat in front of Tashi and the papers like a figure on a tomb, expressionless and terrifying.

"Please try to understand, Auntie. I made up my mind. I can't do it.

I'm almost broke. I'm going to have to apply for jobs somewhere else, maybe Canada. My head isn't right again. I'm in—"

"No condition." You stood up. "Which anyone with two eyes in their head can see. You have not heard a word I said. I say give her to me if you are rejecting her."

"You're almost eighty years old." Tashi's voice got louder. "You're not going to raise a baby."

"Everyone knows that all the great queens of history were born with the cord around their necks. You can't just *give away* a queen." Your voice got louder, too, and I woke and began to cry. "And I have already announced her to the entire rest of your family."

"The attorney is with the parents, waiting for this paperwork. They're going to take the baby and give her a good life."

"I give you a chance to change your mind. I offer to live with you. You are too tired to hear me. Nurse!"

"I picked them because they have it together. I am a mess, as usual—"

"You're not thinking, as usual. Listen to yourself. You're exhausted."

"Yes! I am tired!"

The shift had changed, and the young nurse who responded to the emergency bell appeared in the doorway, looking fresh enough to haul her patient back from the gates of hell bare-handed.

"This woman needs to be sedated," you said. "She's having post-birth delusions."

"She's not serious," Tashi said. "I'm very sorry."

"I have never been more serious in my life! Whoever is here for this baby, tell them to go home. I'm here to make sure you do not do something stupid, and I will not move until you listen to reason." You lifted me from my blankets and thrust me forward. "Hold her. Look at her. This is your flesh and blood."

Tashi crossed her arms and looked at the floor. I had come out not as a generic baby, but somehow completely *her* baby. Bold, strange, the answer to an unknown question. Until yesterday she had expected to feel nothing, but now she felt me like a force field. Her skin tingled,

her breasts ached, her whole body was stupid enough not to compre-
hend why a person in a fragile state should not be trusted with a child.
And it filled her with dread: her body's stubborn clinging to a different future.

"Do you really want to give this baby away?" you asked.

"No." Her voice was a mumble. "But I don't know what to do."

"Ya habeebti, you do. Your own heart is telling you to let me fix
this."

Forty days and forty nights of chaos passed (or so your version of
Babel went).

After the destruction of our tower and the shattering of our common tongue, humans tried to get along. But necessity demands
sacrifice—a little raid here, a ransom there, an increasingly common
habit of price gouging all around, soon a bit of slavery to get work
done on the cheap. And still no one could make sense of what was
happening, because every word sounded like a lie to someone else.
Was it you who explained that "Babel" means confusion? We call it
the Tower of Babel only because we don't remember its name—just
the family tree that came afterward. The whole of human history
grew out of our demolished origins: a story in a mess of fragments.

But it's not all bad news, you assured me.

You cannot kill a tree simply by tearing off its leaves, and the LORD
had only scattered our words, not all that we desire to say.

Babel taught us to be tricky. Anyone with two eyes to see and two
ears to hear could go charging off in one direction or the other. We
would have to learn to speak sideways around the forking roads, in
feints and stories, if we were to get to the truth. Sensemaking was
subtle work, as it had to be when the truest thing to say had no words
of its own. I know I am going in circles, Auntie. But each time around
I pick up bits of memory here and there, a few old pictures, a box of
your effects. Nothing happens in a straight line, not life or love or
even time. This is the sensibility you instilled in me, and in Tashi,

whom you raised before me, and it is no wonder that we ended up the way we did, ambivalent, depending on you to fix everything for us. You were human, and your help came with a double edge.

There in the hospital, my mother preferred to delay the fight over my custody. Her whole life had been full of resistance to change. But when she told the nurse to ask the adoptive parents and their attorney to come back tomorrow, the nurse returned, embarrassed, and said that they were refusing to go. The couple had waited all day. They had spent tens of thousands of dollars. They felt they had a right to meet their baby.

"I can't," said my mother. She looked like she might hide under the sheet, denying the world until either she or it ceased to exist.

"If they want to be stubborn," you said, "we must be more stubborn. Either you declare the truth, or I will."

"Then I'll meet with them alone," my mother said, and tried to tell the nurse that I should be taken back to the nursery, out of sight.

"You'll do no such thing. Keep the baby here."

Tashi folded the pillow halfway over her face. "You don't understand." She'd already told them about her medications, about the times in her teens when she'd tried twice, halfheartedly, to end herself. About the divorce. About her failing job and mental health. All things that you and Saeeda were already aware of, having lived through them, but that were taboo unless Tashi made you remember.

"These people can make a giant fight out of it. I can't fight anyone else right now."

"If they must see her tonight," you said, "let them."

"No! They'll see there's something wrong with her, and they can blame me and get the court to put her with the state. And then they'd get her, anyway." In her eyes, she'd called down courts and lawyers and now there was no rolling these inexorable colossi back; their momentum would tear the baby away, normal or not.

You knew better. "Like I said. Bring them up." That night and in your better moods, you were a wellspring of faith that the underlying order of things was not, in fact, confusion—but simply a listening ear, the anticipation of a story that would explain everything in the best possible way for everyone. Tashi tried to object, but you settled me in my mother's arms and said, "Inshallah. We will show your child to these jackals, if they want to see how she looks. You told me to fix this, and I will. But we have to be clever. Clean yourself up a little, first, because you look like Halloween."

You followed the nurse out of the room at a slight distance. The plan was to get a look at these pushy adoptive parents and decide where exactly to insert the scalpel. How dare these people? It would be a bloviating man and a grasping woman, here to sign a receipt for their new baby. Wasn't it incredible, the nerve of certain people when imposing their designs on the future? Slicing up people and families and whole maps because the authorities tell them they are allowed to take a Rummani baby home with them. And Tashi—almost ridiculous, this girl's ability to tie herself up in her own shoelaces. Her father had been the same, needing someone to go along behind him, unbungling his messes.

This unbungling project was working out fine until the nurse sped up in a long hallway and took a shortcut through a restricted area. As the metal door clapped shut, you found yourself out of breath with a sore foot and stranded in an unmarked wide hallway. Nothing to do but lower your bones into a wheelchair left by a water fountain, then wait for the quarry to come back through.

Or maybe they wouldn't. If they returned another way, that would mean sitting out here like a boob while Tashi signed over a Rummani baby to kidnappers.

Yes, it was so easy to get lost. A fricative, directionless anxiety was mounting behind your eyes, the sort you always despised. It had aged into your life with the arthritis and the forgetful moments, all symptoms of a brain turning into a saltine cracker from boredom, no better than Saeeda's demented husband. Tashi was wrong: being almost eighty didn't mean a person couldn't handle a baby. On the contrary, a task was good. The ladies would pass me around, take me to story circles, to the grassy side of the lake, and to birthday parties with the kind of hubbub everyone was forever trying to protect old women from for no good reason. Weren't these nice thoughts? Was it a bad person who tried to save her family? No, you didn't get through a war, a marriage, and a whole fruit bowl of cancer without an inkling that God was saving you for something special. So you'd just stay put and let your future come to you.

The concept wasn't totally wrong. The door eventually clapped open and brought the nurse and a party of three women. One was the attorney because of the blazer and sheaf of paperwork under her arm. But the young women in the nurse's wake were not the jackals you'd expected, and for a moment, your mind went blank. You abandoned the wheelchair. Trailed behind them along the waxed floors, squinting, not quite sure. The women's youthfulness had an odor: it was the smell of soft leather and the sweet, almost tactile perfume of coconut meringue. It wafted behind them, unfurling along the walls. Briefly, one clasped the other's hand. Between them was an ease so familiar yet so unspeakable that you could barely whisper it to the walls in the privacy of your own home.

Despite a day's purgatory in the waiting room, despite eating food out of lurid bags and receiving thirdhand news, the two women still possessed a twenty-something vitality, no trace of the threadbare impatience of middle-aged people. Yet they couldn't have been much younger than forty. It was the careful money in the quality of their clothes and the expense of adoption, but most of all the way their attention ranged in tandem, a shared couple-consciousness that forked out ahead of them, testing, searching, as the nurse led them to the doorway of Tashi's private room at the top floor of the hospital, a room they entered without surprise.

The room they had paid for, you realized. These two mothers had come together for a baby. They'd set all this up because Tashi, a mere adjunct academic, had only stingy insurance.

The one in the cordovan jacket ignored all of the adults, wanting nothing but a glimpse of the newborn in blankets. The other one radiated emphatic, obvious questions. How are you *feeling*? You got this room all to *yourself*? How lucky are we, seeing you again so *soon*? As if she hadn't just been making threats from the waiting room.

"Auntie," said Tashi, looking miserable, "can you bring her here? They are asking to see her."

You left the doorway, pulled me out of the plastic bassinet, and scooped me close. It was clear Tashi would be no help. At first, as you sat down, all you could think to do was keep your fingers fanned across the back of my head, breathing in the crisp, earthen smell of my neck.

"For heaven's sake," said the serious woman in the cordovan jacket, "can we finally get introduced to this baby?"

Something very old snapped awake: a dispassion that had seemed gone for decades, one that drew on a deeper pool of stubbornness.

"To which half?" you answered.

The fake-cheerful woman gave you a diluted smile. "I beg your pardon?"

"To which half of this baby would you like to be introduced?" You used your very best English, which you had learned in part from a rust-colored edition of Tipping's *Higher English Grammar*, already outdated in 1950. "I can introduce you to her top half or the bottom half, the right half or the left."

The women's attorney said she was very sorry, she didn't understand.

Speaking as though to a drunk, you said, "Surely you must know the story of Solomon and the baby. When two parties claimed the same child, the great king ordered it divided between the two of them. Therefore, one side should go with you. We will keep the other. I am thinking you will not want the whole thing."

Here you saw yourself being recognized as an obstacle, a role you had filled many times in life and relished.

"Adoption can bring out strong emotions," the attorney said.

"If you will be so kind," you told the nurse, "fetch us a bone saw?"

"What my aunt is trying to say is . . ." Tashi looked sick. "Maybe this is not the time for . . ."

"For what, habeebti?" You shifted your aim to the wives. "I propose for you two to take from the belly button down. You will be very sorry to miss her first steps, otherwise. Look." With a vaudeville showmanship, you began to unwrap my feet. The white receiving blanket still covered all of me, and your fingers were arthritic against the folds, fumbling. It gave everyone plenty of time to imagine a pair of disembodied legs taking steps across the kitchen floor, cheered along by their two mothers. But my actual feet were still hidden except for a hint of darker flesh in the white cotton.

"The very best time to cut them in half is now, before the bones harden. Or else you'll be stuck with the whole—"

"I'm so sorry," Tashi said. In her medicated exhaustion, she barely said it aloud. "What she means is that I'm not sure this is going to work."

"All right, okay, pause." The attorney clicked her pen. "Just cutting through any questions about propriety here, we have the father's relinquishment of paternal rights. We have a plan. But we could reconvene—"

"No." The woman in the jacket spoke. "The lady will stop messing around and show us now. We have been waiting all day."

Her command sank like a brick, grounding the billowing absurdity that had started to carry them off.

"Well, then. This is her," you said, "and she has a condition that runs in our family. There is no cure, and she will grow up to be an idiot." With no more fuss, you set me longwise on your lap and exposed my body.

Flesh prickling—the room was cool—I snuffled and kicked. I smashed my fist against my nose. The long preamble to my appearance had somehow amplified the oddity and the shock with which I landed: this business with four limbs and whose scalp flushed purple as I began to cry and my odor filled the room, an inorganic tang that recalled minerals and dry wind, not a living person. It was not the pink baby they'd expected. Not the whipped-cream confection they'd bought a set of knit caps for, nor hired a photographer in anticipation of, nor imagined themselves creating a family around. You and my mother both hated the way they looked at me. It was the look of discovering a house full of dry rot.

"What I decided is that I'd like to keep her," my mother finally said.

A look was exchanged, a few little nods.

The attorney said, "My clients are wanting a bit of time to talk to the doctors and discuss."

"Oh, the doctors don't know anything," you said. "They never will. But here, take all of her, if the law says you must. She's your idiot now."

"No, we can still put on the brakes," said the attorney, as her clients faded backward, toward the doorway. "The mother still has her right to say no. Nothing's carved in stone."

The mothers were gone. Tashi was crying. "God *damn* you sometimes."

"I fixed the problem. Your daughter gets to stay where she belongs. But now I am the worst person in the world?"

"You didn't have to be that awful to them. And you made a circus out of her."

"You didn't want a fight, and they would have fought you forever, with all your *maybe*s and *I think*s and *I'm sorry*s. It's good now—you have the baby all to yourself, not even her father to worry about, and these women can grieve the loss of their money and feel lucky it was not more. Nuha Rummani always does what she has to do." You crossed your arms, and your bracelets clattered. "But you, you could try to be less embarrassed of how Betty looks."

"You know that's not fair. And it's not true."

The nurse was uncomfortable. "Hon, the baby is due for a feeding. Tell me if you want to try, or we can take her to the nursery for formula."

Another lesson on breast-feeding sounded impossible to endure at this hour, under the circumstances, so the nurse took me away for the rest of the night. I was whole, and wholly a Rummani now, but maybe in the room's uneasiness was a premonition that something in me would always be divided in two.

And down in the darkness somewhere was a car with its wipers on. Women inside, deciding *no*. Their imaginations changing what they saw. It was like they'd seen a thing made out of mud, a deadness where life should be. My blueness was flat, chalky, all-consuming. An abomination. The attorney would assure my mother that she wasn't obligated to proceed and that the prospective parents were having second thoughts, anyway. The final correspondence, as it severed the women's relationship with me before it began, would cite my "uncertain medical needs beyond the scope of the clients' resources."

Just as well that the failed adoption was so carefully delineated. Otherwise, Tashi would have always blamed you for grandstanding. According to my mother, it was the only thing you knew how to do: to put yourself in the spotlight and get people upset. But because the reason was there in laser-jet ink on twenty-four-pound linen letterhead, so trim and specific and factual, my mother resented you only for several years, with a low-grade resentment that didn't prevent her from living with you from time to time, as during the first few months after my birth and before she began to hear her dead father's voice in a teacup. For some reason, she'd hang on to that letter for some years after I had learned to read.

But give us a moment before we hurry onward.

In the final hour of my birthday, a fog tumbled over the hilltop. It moved, sprawling toward the river, swathing first the hospital and then the floodlights in banks of vapor. Patients in their rooms moaned from their stupor and reached for morphine, and in the mortuary, in frigid lockers, corpses twitched and farted with the adjustments of decay. The night roiled with the sort of mist that had once settled over the Garden of Eden after the famous eviction, a mist that was not content to be in the background, but carried on until suitably ac-knowledged. And this fog had come far indeed, hissing down from the winter passes, over ice-bristled scrub, over borders east and west. Now arrived, it dissolved the hospital's edges and its bright windows, sharing the light evenly among itself so that it made a glowing cur-tain about the hospital, dull silver and strange, marking my first night on earth.

Nothing happened, exactly. Neither of you surrendered the argu-ment, but you both were tired. My mother drifted, half-asleep in the middle of a sentence, trying to figure out what time it was for the night to have gotten so bright. You retreated to the bed to get warm, and my mother let you in. You lay next to each other like sardines, seething, staring out at the weird fog as it nestled around the hospi-tal, each of you seeing whole worlds you couldn't speak of.

A Love Story with Bulldozers

———•———

My given name, the one to which I must respond if it is uttered by doctors or bureaucrats, is Elspeth Noura Rummani. My middle name means *light*, which my mother believed would cure all.

"Elspeth," repeated Tashi, who was American-born and for whom the letter *p* was second nature. The entire family would hesitate over it, sometimes blunting it into a *b*.

You, however, would keep on calling me Betty, proving the point that my mother always made things harder than they needed to be.

That spring and summer, in the first months of my life, the news showed multiple reports of tanks and bulldozers knocking their way through the heart of the West Bank city of Nablus. Stones, some laid a thousand years before America was even a glint in the European eye, came down in an hour. A family friend emailed pictures of the aftermath, a pile of limestone and broken tiles. The house had once been three floors of hidden courtyards, winding marble, and delicate mashrabiyya windows. And the old factory, bombed squarely, became a broken hole.

There is part of this story that will always be, mostly, a love poem. But it's the kind sung in a key you and I know so well: adoration galvanized by futility. The sweet apricot that is impossible to taste, the silver gazelle that is impossible to catch, the beloved with a one-way flight offshore—each could be a stanza in our own personal ghazal. So, I imagine how familiar it felt, for you and my grandmother, sitting in front of the laptop screen and those terrible photographs, feeling a new chord of love and its harmonizing grief. And not that you could tell by the pictures anymore, but our family's house and factory had meant more to our story than most buildings do. In more innocent times, they were extensions of the Rummani lifeblood, smooth of façade, parading the family fortune for hundreds of years before you'd ever laid eyes on them. Over the centuries, the estate had multiplied itself for new wives and scores of children. Found new rooms by encroaching on its inner courtyards and crawling up the slope of a garden, and then raising a new tile roof over this or that empty space. And the Rummani factory was just downhill along the road through the meat market, a stolid two-story cube of dark stone with huge windows open to the air, such that the towers of soap stacked inside could harden and be wrapped for export. The building had been busy and profitable for over six hundred years, and until the spring of 2002, it could have stood for another six hundred.

I've seen sepia-toned pictures too: a low ramp that led up from the street into the factory so the great barrels of olive oil could be wheeled inside. A little office overlooked that ramp, but our men would sit outdoors in the recess so they didn't miss anything in the courtyard across the way, near the mosque and clock tower, where one day a camera had been positioned. Behind them was the tall wooden door into a cave-dark space, which (you'd explained a hundred times) was wide open for storing the oil, with plenty of room for the great cooking vat and stairs down to the fire. Beyond what the eye could see in these pictures, I also knew from your descriptions that another staircase led up to the vaulted cutting-and-drying room, an otherworldly place of light, stacked soap, and circulating air. This, in other words, was the site of a shimmering process that turned olive oil into soap into money, into the orderly hive of stone rooms where the Rummanis lived and multiplied for hundreds of years, incubating a secret note of blue. It would take generations before the tanks and bulldozers went banging through them, breaking the structure open.

I don't mean to imply that the loss came as a surprise. There was the politics, yes, but also you had a reliable role among the Rummanis. You were used to your advice being sought during endings, used to mending heartbreak, grief, and confusion, because you were so good at making sense of a mess (just look at me now, Auntie, at your stone in the grass, asking which branch of a forking path I should abandon). But on that day in my first weeks of life, you and Saeeda enlarged these latest pictures on a laptop. Scowled through reading glasses, hesitantly touching the screen. "I think that was the staircase above the . . ." But at the end of your fingertips was nothing but empty air. Another place had been translated to a plume of smoke, leaving a residue of tales and memory, another Babel. Maybe, like mine, your confusion rested on a single question. Why was the end so good at making everything new? Maybe it baffled you and Saeeda as it still does me, this process of skinning of old maps away from the new, discarding the past into a subjunctive space where everything can be rewritten and misremembered infinitely. Imagination: it is the safest place for love to flourish, especially when it grafts itself onto fear.

But at that time, as you were imagining Palestine's past and present, I—an actual baby with a needy body—would not be ignored, fussing until you shut the computer. I demanded good American formula and the doting attention of my three squabbling muses. I had everything I needed. I was already growing at a heroic rate. In a month, I was just a little larger than most one-month-olds on the bell curve, but I weighed as much as a pail of cement—over thirty pounds, at least. I seemed alert to everything happening in your modest apartment in Oakland, deaf to everything else.

The agreement between you and Saeeda was to not talk about the intifada, not in front of my mother, because my mother had reentered a fragile state that impeded not just cooking and showering, but rising to answer my cries in the middle of the night. Saeeda and Nuha persuaded her to take her maternity leave in the Bay Area, relocating herself from Portland to be near good help. She took the bed in the office that she had once occupied for long stretches of her teens. She gave me hard baths and what she called *sun rests* at the window, on the thin hypothesis that light might change me.

"It will fade," she said. "I think it already is."

To your eyes, however, my skin was only getting darker, more opaque. And you said so. When the housework and laundry put a dull pain in your bones, you delivered screeds of advice from the bedroom recliner. It stunned you, my mother's ineptitude. There were tales about people who, by some spell, aged backward, but who were more whimsical than a mid-career divorcée. You flung your questions through the doorway: Are you going to get dressed today? Are you taking your medication? Do you have any money left? Do you know when your maternity leave ends? Do you know that your daughter vomits every time you lay her back like that? They blurred together, all these bewildered question marks, making the same accusation. *You know nothing about children.* And underneath that, *You are thirty-four years old and you know nothing about life.*

This is not to diminish the quality or amount of my mother's love, only her ability to need less help than I did. I've lived long enough to know that her form of resistance is to stop everything and go limp like an opossum. So, she just laid me on her lap at the window, letting my contentment distract her from your criticism. Growing more inert the louder you got. Sometimes, she put on her headphones and dabbed a little of her ivory face powder across my forehead because she liked the way it sparkled in the sun. There are simply women who are not transformed by motherhood, in whom those doors only open on a wall.

In the few pictures of my childhood you were able to save, Mama holds me in her lap beside the window. The film is overexposed. Half of my body is turned to the window, and the disposable camera captures her hand as though it is melted into my skin, making half our bodies a blown-out white. Her other hand, in shadow, is sharply pale against my blue flesh—you can make out each of her long-jointed fingers supporting my proud torso, as well as the paler scar that runs lengthwise inside her forearm. She wears the wan contentment of an amnesiac. It's the only picture where we look almost alike.

My fairy godmothers offered their care for those first several months of my life. Sang, told me stories. Dusted off the childhood tales and noticed after all this time how full of ogres they were—ugly, hungry, sneaky, and cruel, with great pelts of hair and long breasts. Not every story needs a monster, you said, and you told stories of clever children, of little queens, of stones that sang. You began the translation of a dark world into a brighter one, determined to raise an optimist.

But Rummanis are pessimists by nature. I howled for food, for light, for darkness—I howled for everything in a weird pipe-organ voice that sounded nothing like a child's. It was loud, like the sound of breath wailing across broken reeds. Every time I cried hard, it brought a round of broomsticks thumping the downstairs ceiling, and my mother would hurl herself into action from a dead sleep, grab me and swing me sideways like an airplane, or sprawl herself on the playmat to calm me down, to quiet me, to keep me in, to contain me. Her maternal energy had found a focus, after all: until she knew what to do about me, I would be raised in absolute secrecy under the umbrella of her own confusion. For now, my father didn't even know she'd kept me.

"Babies cry," my grandmother said.

And you: "The neighbors see the diapers coming in."

"We have no idea how people will treat her," my mother said, "but we can already guess." In her memory, over and over, the adoptive mothers in the hospital recoiled—this, from people who had been prepared to love me.

———

My grandmother Saeeda hired another caregiver for her declining American husband and drove up three days a week from her Palo Alto development in the South Bay to help. She had not felt so useful around her own daughter and her sister-in-law in almost twenty years, and along with her stout Rummani opinions, she brought what average people might call good sense to the situation.

For instance: "You need to have a doctor in town."

And: "What will you do when she gets a fever?"

But from the beginning, I was my mother's vulnerability, and thus ordered by her to stay hidden until she could find her way out of the maze she'd been lost in for months. New problems hit her voicemail and email messages every day. The doctors with their experimental trials, their increasingly desperate tone. Survey calls from the adoption agency. Friends inviting her to movie night and to walk, but they were people who liked my father better and were probably just nosy. And then my father himself, wanting dinner; wanting just to see how she was recovering; then wanting to know how it went with the women who'd taken the baby; then, still not having gotten any reply, wanting to know if their five good years counted for nothing. If she didn't call him, he said, he was going to send the police to make sure she was alive.

We will meet my father soon enough. In any case, she poured energy into hiding her blue phenomenon from the world.

"In my experience," said Saeeda, "people enjoy babies. Throw a party. A grand coming-out."

You gave a low moan of a laugh and drew on the cigarette butt so hard that your cheeks caved in.

Tashi opened the window for air. "Her *father* will come for her. He'll want to take her apart at the seams and look inside her. He pathologizes everything. And if you keep smoking like that, you'll give Elspeth an ear infection."

You crushed out the cigarette. "Betty has no seams. Betty has no doctor, either. Or friends. Or enough diapers to get her to Tuesday. Her father coming back with his big checkbook wouldn't be the worst thing to happen."

Saeeda waved off the smoke. "For once, I agree with you. He ought to pay. This baby is half his."

Tashi saw nothing of that man in me except for my habit of constant scrutiny. But my father did have money, so much of it that she feared he would use it on a lawyer to take me away. To study me, to steal me, and, most probably, to blot out his own nagging guilt for his affair by blaming my defect on her. He'd claim she had somehow ruined the promise of me with her frantic self-revulsion, proving that his ex-wife was some kind of monster undeserving of a child.

Every story finds an ogre, after all.

In the meantime, Saeeda stocked the kitchen with goods from her own pantry and continued to point out the obvious. "Yaani what are you thinking? You ran out of money and you are heading into big problems, with this girl in tow. How long do you think you can hide her?"

The man who owned the building we lived in at the time was a balding, long-haired behemoth who claimed to be ex–special forces. Yet he hulked around his properties in work boots and the funk of marijuana. He was in his fifties and had what seemed to be extra flaps of pale skin around his eyes that sagged like wax. One day, you came home from the convenience store and found him in the stairwell with a pair of black-suited men, conferring.

In the moment before he ignored you and resumed the conversation, his small, ice-chip eyes scribbled over the sight of you. It was the look he gave all the tenants in this least-visited property of his, the look that sorted through the lot of them, going, *Mexican Chinese Caribbean Filipino Korean,* until his slumlord pie chart hovered in his mind, its variety reassuring him that no one group of his tenants could grow large enough to become a bloc. Yet your unwillingness to speak to him and betray an accent, along with the frosted blondness of your new short wig, confounded his inability to match tenants' faces to the names on their rent checks. He sorted you into a nebulous slice of the pie labeled *Foreigners Who Hate Us for Our Freedom*.

His distraction ruffled the rhythm of whatever he was telling the men in black. Then you stepped into the elevator with a plastic bag of baby aspirin and orange juice, and the doors rumbled closed.

You went out again that afternoon to the dollar store for American flags and a pious doormat: "Here we show hospitality to strangers, for by doing so we might entertain angels without knowing it (Hebrews 13:2)." You had already brought inside the clay medallion with the pretty Arabic calligraphy—the very day the towers had fallen, in fact—but now you even went to the parking garage and scraped the Free Palestine bumper stickers off the car, tearing away their various entreaties in strips. For years the dirt would stick to the trunk in mottled rectangles that reminded both you and Saeeda of cracked soccer fields from home, or the mark left by duct tape that's been ripped away.

Saeeda noted without comment the disappearance of your bumper stickers, the proliferation of stars and stripes and the pious mat in the hallway. She observed that where Tashi created a margin of denial around me, you filled it with a chameleon skin of red, white, and blue. Noticed how both of you worked in a busy harmony at two different projects that gradually evolved into the same goal of hiding a blue baby in the apartment. And how every week, the air was staler and smokier, until the paint on the walls bubbled with distress.

One day you and she were filling the pantry with her extra Costco groceries, and she had not said a word since stepping through the door.

"What is it?"

"Take the baby outside at least," she said. "Betty is suffocating in here, hazeeneh."

Your eyebrows rose above your glasses. It was a look that could hoist its target up by the hair. "Is that how you would do it, ya ukhti?

Why don't we swap our burdens, then—you with Betty, me with your forgetful husband? I do not remember you letting him outside anymore. Hazeen, isn't he suffocating inside?"

"He loses his way home! This is no comparison."

He could not be left without a nurse to watch over him, not since he had tried turning the knobs on the gas stove to adjust the air conditioner and had nearly blown up the house.

"Then, ya habeebti, put away that tongue of yours and remember how much this old fossil is helping your daughter and granddaughter. I held you when you were a girl. I gave up a room of my home for your daughter all those years ago. And now look at me! The woman who brought all the Rummanis to America!" You hefted two jugs of dish soap from the bag, clutching them by their necks. "For this little bit of charity, you buy the right to insult me. If you can do better, take Betty home with you."

Silenced, irritated, Saeeda reserved her complaints with care. Practically bottled them up in brine and vinegar, so that when she poured them on Tashi the next time they spoke on the phone, they stung for days.

Tashi retaliated by pointing out all the bewildering concessions: the American flags taped inside the window, the doormat whose verse suggested that this apartment was a possibly Evangelical home. As gestures from the most cavalier woman to come out of 1950s Nablus, they were an anomaly.

"Five years ago, you had a whole dress made out of the Palestinian flag," Tashi said. "You and Mama gang up on me, but you're doing the same thing."

"This world has changed. We don't need to parade our identity on the car trunk."

"Okay, adaptation, yes. How is what I'm doing for my child any different?"

By lamplight, you stretched your wig over its mannequin head for the night and settled a panel of gray silk over your ruined scalp. Your hair had never grown back after chemo, and that was more than twenty years before I was born. As you tied the scarf at the nape of your neck, you met my mother's gaze in the mirror.

"You mean different, by canceling Betty's polio vaccine because you worry someone in the waiting room will recognize you and call her father?"

The walls of your four-room apartment in Oakland could not hold the world back forever. We lived in a so-called postwar building, one whose various televisions had broadcast between four and twenty-two American wars since 1945, depending on who was counting; and its construction was so thin that my unnaturally loud voice made my cries sound like air raid sirens. Then came the chorus of banging broomsticks and aggrieved notes on the door.

Neighbors thought I was a video game. A teakettle. Once, a dog—and that neighbor also reported us to the landlord. She lived upstairs, the mother of one of Tashi's old teenage rivals. She wrote, *You can't keep a howling dog here. The landlord agrees with me and you can argue about it with him.* Nuha pitched the note into the trash.

Saeeda had shown up with a camera that day. As she had for her own two children, she had begun taking pictures and arranging them in laminated album pages, since no one else was documenting my infancy. Most of that record would be lost or destroyed, but on one of those pages, I am sitting upright, bare-chested and shoulders back, like the warrior princess Noura of the vast Arabic epic *Sirat al-Amira Dhat al-Himma.* My eyes had changed color by then—their newborn quicksilver had faded, and they were just brown.

The picture's occasion is my first meal of solid food, and I've smeared it across my face and chest like the entrails of my enemies. Behind a soft plastic tray of pulped pear, my face is twisted in a glorious expression of command.

After Saeeda lowered the camera, I yelled—who knows why. Because it was fun, or because I'd grown bored, or because to this day pears are the blandest of all nectars. It is the fruit of Hera and a symbol of marital fidelity, the fruit of still-life paintings and subtle good taste. Maybe I was already skeptical of pears, as I am skeptical of all fruit names that cleave a thing from its flavor, and that day I filled my lungs and opened all the organs of my throat and gave a five-barreled cry that pulverized the mortar in Jericho and, more to the point, reached the ears of the landlord, who was standing on the sidewalk under the window with his black-suited real estate agent.

There is only one picture of me covered in pears because after I bellowed, my mother's hand shot out and smacked my shoulder and then clamped over my mouth. An argument, as they say, ensued. Saeeda had had enough of the secrecy and tension, and you were worried about neighbors and the landlord, and my mother knew that she had to go back to work in Portland in less than a week and leave me bouncing between aunt and grandmother until she could afford the airfare back to Oakland: a set of opinions the three of you voiced at exactly the same time and at a volume louder than my inciting shout.

And when the elevator dinged, we all went quiet.

We could hear everything: the squish of pear in my fist, the pillar of ash that tumbled off a cigarette into your coffee mug, the shuffle of the landlord's work boots as they approached the door. He knocked. My mother kept her hand over my face.

He knocked again.

You shut your eyes. If he were to open the door, what would he see? Three women still alight with squabbling, a mess of food, curtains and floors stained with two decades' worth of smoke and wear, the clutter of newspapers and a disorganized library, a carnage of lemon rinds and tea bags on the counter—not at all the dignified tableau of an American senior citizen in her golden years, keeping up with the housekeeping and peaceably spending her Social Security on crossword puzzles.

In this silence, we observed the silence itself, rolling off the most cavalier woman to come out of 1950s Nablus, along with the unfamiliar stink of fear.

The boots retreated for now. The landlord got back on the elevator and left us alone.

"I'm sorry, baby," said my mother, lifting her hand off my face.

I wanted to grow teeth so I could bite her. But I am not immune to example, and all three of my muses gave an imperative in triplicate to be silent. I didn't scream again all day.

"There is no law against babies in this building," Saeeda is saying. It is not long after the landlord's retreat. "What is anybody going to do? Arrest you? Arrest her? In fact, you don't even know what the landlord wanted because you are too afraid to open your door."

"I am not afraid!"

"We can't afford to invite people to pay attention to us," Tashi says. "We need to be invisible. We don't even exist. Or else somehow her father will create a problem."

You and Saeeda are looking individually dissatisfied. The arguing subsides. (Here, I imagine my grandmother wringing out the kitchen rag, and then all three of you settling beside one another on the couch and sharing an ashtray.)

After some consideration, you say, "I think these black-suited men, they must be CIA."

Saeeda bursts out laughing.

"This isn't that kind of problem, Auntie," says my mother. "The CIA is busy looking for terrorists."

"What do you think all Arabs look like to them?" you say.

My grandmother takes a drag off her cigarette and stubs it out. Behind your back, she has always called you al-Nakba, the Catastrophe. "Of course, dear sister," she says now, "it can only be the CIA. They have already bugged the microwave."

"Really funny. Then if you're so smart, tell this old woman who is it that's walking in my halls in dark suits and knocking on door?"

"Auntie," says my mother, "to be fair, the guys look more like Jehovah's Witnesses."

You release a flurry of smoke. "I saw them with my own two eyes multiple times. They are talking to the landlord. Hamdullah I still have eyes in my head. The suits are not here on God's business."

What the building's tenants would know soon enough: of course the men weren't Jehovah's Witnesses or the CIA, and of course it was our LORD's work, slicing up and dividing. The notices would start showing up on doors in a few more months.

In the meantime, you would tell it as a theory and a warning.

Saeeda would report the story of deep-state spies to her husband for a laugh, but by then he'd have lost too much of his mind to understand the joke.

My mother would think it almost funny, but as you had begun to fear, she was already being excavated from the inside. Pestering problems refused to stay buried—the doctors wanting to do research, the ex-husband's friends, the whole post-birth wreck of her body, the increasingly frequent calls from her ex-husband himself. She had to wonder if the adoption agency had maybe told him something. The thought of dealing with any problems of this size made her want nothing more than to lie down on the BART tracks, her head against the rail.

Don't you fucking dare, she'd begun telling herself, even as another part of her answered, *Or you put the silver barrel in the soft flesh under your jaw, angled a little backward, and pull the trigger.*

It wasn't worth sharing this invisible argument with anyone. Definitely not Saeeda, who was busy caring for a husband who became more babylike every few months. Definitely not you, with all your criticisms. My mother would deal with this herself, in her own way. She had to return to work, because after the failed adoption and the lack of promised payment, she was nearly broke.

———

And then my mother was nowhere. I howled. It was temporary to everyone else: a few months in her cruddy apartment in Oregon so she could return from maternity leave on time and keep her job. But I, still in California and only four months old, was new to losing a beloved. I thought she had vanished.

Calming children was one area in which Nuha Rummani was famously skilled. Interpreting catastrophe was another. You picked up your cigarette box and found it empty for the third time, brushed it onto the floor. You had practical, square hands so unlike my mother's and grandmother's long-jointed ones, and you fussed around until all that sat on the end table by the couch were a few of your inky little journals and an olive-wood carving: a mountain gazelle, *G. gazella,* gifted to you by C., that other endangered species in your life.

The absence of C. was a subtle thing: your lack of an answer when Tashi asked, the quiet phone, your restlessness in the evenings. Maybe you wanted to howl as I did for the person who wasn't there. You might have asked yourself the same questions I am asking you now: Who deserves the most love? How do we know? But muteness can be cultivated out of necessity. C. had her own family, her own sprawling tree to tend. Also, she knew you well and might have felt you gave the Rummanis too much. We come from an old and thorny shrub, Auntie, so dense that to wade into it is to be blessed only with scratches and blood.

So, you settled me on the center cushion and lay down beside me, your body scooped around mine like a wall against the world.

"Ya habeebti, I think it is time for you to hear a story of where we come from, and how we lived before our history was disappeared. The story before the beginning is always more important than anyone realizes. So, Betty, listen."

This was the very moment you escorted me over the doorsill between life and imagination. It was also where you began lying to me.

———

"Betty, there is no truth but in old women's tales.

"Before the beginning, our family, who call themselves the Rummanis now, lived for unnumbered generations in Nablus. Nablus! Where every timeworn building leans on the arm of the next, and every stone is cut from the shoulder of our mountains. Go far enough back, say two hundred years if you insist on counting, and there was one of our family, a boy named Jibril. Your mother's father was named after him, and we care about this long-ago boy's story because his fiery little heart was all aflame for the daughter of his uncle's business partner in Yaffa—and romantic love, when it shows its thorny face in this family, is usually somewhat monstrous. Anyway, this business partner traded soap for cloth, which Jibril's uncle traded for interest on the olive oil the peasants stored in wells in his factory. Never mind about all this, though. What matters is the boy Jibril, the love, and the soap.

"Jibril got only one single look at his beloved, a white cheek turned away from him, veiled by the shadows in her merchant father's carriage. In those days, if you were a boy, you didn't go striding willy-nilly up to a girl. Not if you both were from good families, and especially not if her family was even more respectable than yours. And besides, Jibril's uncle was a tyrant—you know what a tyrant is? Somebody who pisses on your shoes and blames you for it.

"Now, this uncle, he would have thumped Jibril senseless if he were caught sneaking out of his job, which was to wash and sweep the floors. Point being, Jibril was busy and had exactly zero chances of seeing his love again before her father went home—not after that one lucky glimpse. So Jibril went to church every Sabbath and kept every fast, praying for another chance, another glimpse. Maybe even an arranged marriage, if God was feeling generous. But God was drowsy that year, lazing in his heavenly abode with a bowl of butterscotch candies.

"Expect that from God, by the way.

"The kid only had his memories, and in them, this girl grew more

beautiful by the day. She was as fair as the morning light on the Nablus fields, as rich as all the oil in the district, and as elusive, he realized,
as a gazelle. Her face had been hidden. What did it mean? Does a
happy person sulk in their father's carriage? If she was sad, why? Did
her father beat her? Did she have a broken heart? Was she promised
to an Ottoman officer? It wasn't long before Jibril worked himself
into a damsel-rescuing frenzy, imagining all the tragedies she endured
over there in Yaffa.

"A sort of fever seized him. He had to let her know he loved her.
Even if he never saw her again, he had to send her something so
beautiful, so perfect in its making, that she would feel loved for the
rest of her life. Not just loved, but adored by him: by Jibril ibn-Umar
ibn-Yaqoub Rummani, in the Christian quarter near the city gates of
Nablus, the soap-making capital of Greater Syria, the richest wilayet
of the Ottoman Empire, and the whole world. Then she would sneak
away and come to him, and they would elope. The details in the middle were hazy, but he knew how to do one thing well: make soap.

"He began his plan in the vaulted warehouse room where the cy-
lindrical towers of cubed product aged. Behind these pallid towers
was a loose stone, a hiding place for his materials. First, he stole a jug
of olive oil from the barrel and bartered it for a cake of indigo dye
from the mute weaver. Then he pilfered enough powdered ash from
the storeroom and some more oil. After that, he set out to make a
small batch of his family's famous soap. Except instead of its plain,
ugly, waxy ivory color, it was going to be something new, a cake the
color of the sky over the mountains. A color like meadow flax. A
magical, pure, holy color.

"Yaani, he was going to make the soap blue.

"Women have been making soap in their homes for thousands of
years, he reasoned. So how hard can this be? He built a low fire on the
roof and stirred and stirred, waiting until the crusty golden concoc-
tion thickened. He tended his fire for days. In the last hour, he crum-
bled in the cake of indigo, and the liquid soap darkened to black.

"For a moment he panicked. He'd ruined it! But then the dye swirled and settled, and as it dispersed throughout the mix, the contents of the pot turned a dazzling, pure blue: a Mediterranean gem of a color. No one dyed their soap like this. No one had thought to. He was a genius. And someday, if he ever inherited the factory, he would make this soap its signature and become richer than the Abdulhadis, richer than the Tuqans, richer than the sultan himself.

"Next, he poured the liquid into a wooden frame and let it set. He pressed it flat, and when he stared into the hardening batch, it was like he was looking down a well into the realm of the djinn. He could almost see his reflection there, cradled in blue light.

"He dragged a blade across the slab, making sixteen perfect cubes. Finally, under cover of night, he borrowed the family mallet—yaani, it's like a wooden hammer that has the factory symbol on it, which for us was a halved pomegranate showing all its seeds—and he stamped each of the cubes so she would know where the soap originated. Then he stashed the sixteen cubes in the warehouse to age, like cheese.

"Patience is not the talent of most children. But, ismissalib, love does make you surpass yourself. Jibril waited until the cakes were hard as stones, smooth as glass, and ever so slightly fragrant—from what? The faint mineral odor of the powdered indigo? He wasn't sure, for this had never been done before.

"He papered the cubes, bound them in brocade, and paid a bribe of his entire life savings to his father's man to carry the gift with the next load bound for Yaffa. Eyes laughing, the man agreed to deliver the blue soap in secret to the merchant's daughter.

"And Jibril waited. And he waited more. Almost two months went by.

"And then one day, here comes a carriage around the mountain. Dust is flying, the mules are lathered, there is no slow caravan of goods trailing behind it—it's flying along like a divine chariot. Everyone, even the peasants in the hinterlands, drop their tools and water jugs to watch the crazed driver. Is the sultan dead? Is an army coming? Who is in the carriage? It churns toward Nablus, passes through the city gates, and threads the streets into the Christian quarter. Only then can anyone hear what the driver is shouting: he's shouting for Jibril's uncle. The carriage rattles to a stop before the factory doors and the driver shouts one more time, clearly, with the authority of a minor god, for Jibril's uncle to show himself immediately.

"His uncle appears in the doorway, flushed. 'What is all this about?'

"The merchant steps down, dragging someone behind him. From the carriage shadows comes his daughter, who's covered in a heavy veil. He demands they go inside to the uncle's office at once. Jibril sees the whole thing from the second floor and is thanking God a hundred times over. *She's in love with me. Her father is here to talk about betrothal.*

"A few minutes pass and his uncle calls for him in a voice that's black with rage. 'Jibril! You imbecile! Come here!' It chills his blood. He goes to the office door, quaking, and the two elder men are standing at the top of the stairs, looking at him like he's a two-headed pigeon.

"And between them is his love. Her skin is as blue as yours, Betty. From her high forehead to her straight nose to her fine-fingered hands and sandaled feet, the skin is shining like an indigo flower in the sun.

"'Your fool-headed soap stained my daughter, my Alissabat!' her father bellows. 'You ruined her wedding and her beauty! The groom was the archbishop's grandson, and the whole family deserted her on the day she was to be married.' He turns to the uncle. 'You. You owe me eight thousand piastres for her dowry and a share in the factory. Or instead of the share, make this whelp marry her himself, because it was he who ruined her.'

"Jibril's uncle let out a roar. To punctuate it, he whipped off his shoe and flung it at the boy.

"Jibril ducked. When he stood up again, his eyes were wide as coins. He should have been mortified. He should have been terrified, but all he felt was awe. *Alissabat,* he thought. Her name was as beautiful as she was, and he was to be her groom, and most of all, at last, she was looking directly at him and speaking to him with her eyes. She was both bored and amused by the old men's tantrum. A secret smile passed between them, and Alissabat gave him a tiny, one-shouldered shrug.

"'What do you have to say for yourself?' his uncle demanded, because the silence was getting awkward.

"'Uncle, this is a good alliance for you. And I think Alissabat is the most beautiful girl I've ever seen. Her blue skin will be the envy of every fashionable lady in the empire.' And he turned to her father. 'I would be honored, sir, if your daughter would have me as her groom.'

"And she did, and they were married the following week for a dowry of eight thousand piastres, and for the rest of her life she washed herself in Jibril's indigo soap; and though it never became fashionable beyond her household in Nablus, she insisted on her deathbed that the Rummani daughters be loved for their particularly pure shade of blue skin.

"To hell with everyone else. The end."

There was more. There is always more, even when nothing is left.

As of 1815

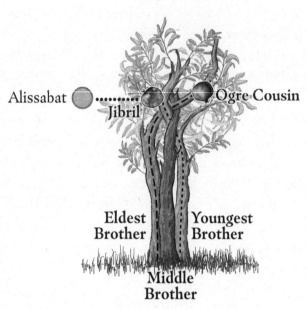

Alissabat

Jibril

Ogre Cousin

Eldest
Brother

Youngest
Brother

Middle
Brother

The Tenant's Tale

———•———

Here lies Nuha Rummani. I read the words a second and third time. Somewhere on the next hill the groundskeeper pushes a lawnmower between the stones, slow work that blankets the cemetery with its meditative, futile note. *Here lies.* It makes the most of a homonym, I realize for the first time in all the years I've been visiting. I could rewrite the words above the birth date, *Nuha Rummani is lying here.* Or, *Here she is, still lying.* And it would still cast a double shadow.

I'm not crazy. I know, with the sort of knowledge my mother made a career of, the *you* I'm speaking to is some bones in a box, buried under a slab of white granite. I don't believe Nuha Rummani lives anywhere in this universe, because she abandoned her body a long time ago. Maybe the wig is still in there, collapsed around the skull like a slub of grass, and all that is left of my great-aunt is what she called herself when she felt slighted: *an old fossil.*

Yet even when nothing is left, I go on living inside things she said, an eternal country I couldn't get out of my skull if I tried. It's for the philosophers, whether two people can live in the exact same place if that place is imaginary—or maybe a poet could tell me whether any set of words is sturdy enough, on its own, to duplicate an experience from one mind to the next. I have doubts (see: the history of religion, the history of politics, and the dismal success rate of long-distance relationships). I think the Tower of Babel story might be right. Even with the best of intentions, we humans use our words only for lies, because a lie may be nothing more than the condition of one individual speaking to another, across time and continents and also differences so small they ought not to matter as much as they do. It's one of the ways I've come to understand love—forgiving the misunderstandings between two imaginations.

Yet when two people imagine entirely different futures, they don't go on together for long; or when one person can imagine two entirely different futures, she feels, as I attest now, torn in two with dread. On one fork of the path, I break my promise to be like you, the fixture, the good relative, the aunt who remains. On the other, I break the one where I made myself the guardian of my beloved's exceedingly compassionate heart. Either way, I won't forgive myself for breaking a promise.

A more practical definition of love is this: liking the people you need. And I'm not sure if this is something I learned on my own or if I took it whole-cloth from someone I both liked and needed, marinated as it is in the sound of Nuha Rummani's deathless voice. So even when no throat or tongue or brain is left, something survives, even if the years twist the memory till it is almost unrecognizable. It's why I come to ask a pile of bones for relationship advice. It's why, after revisiting some memories and old mementos, I can still have doubts about exactly who I'm talking to at all. Is it really you down there? You'd lived so many secret lives, it's hard to know which one of you loved me, which one I needed; though I suspect it's the one who also lied the best.

Here I am. You're lying six feet down, but I'm still carrying some version of you around because you made sure I needed you this much.

———

Remember our Eden time, Auntie? By my first winter, I had a partial Stonehenge of teeth. I ate my considerable weight in pabulum and soft fruit. My body was the pure electric blue of a television-lit family. I babbled at the radio, I shouted at the voices in the hallway, I jabbed my fingers at the mortals on the sidewalk as they carried lumber and plastic sheeting into the building and began, by the bang and crash of it, to build another Tower of Babel.

We expected my mother back in Oakland for her October birthday, and then for Thanksgiving.

But here was my mother, instead—remaining in her cruddy apartment in Portland alone. The mess of papers was typical, a variation on homework, graph paper, a calculator between the pages, dilutions and all the other argot of a three-hundred-thousand-dollar education. I feel an old pride, thinking of her this way. My mother, officially Dr. Natasha Rummani, was, at the time of my birth, an adjunct professor of a respected medical school, a neuroscientist, a presenter at international conferences, a published writer, a holder of three very good degrees. She was not yet thirty-six, and she was now, technically, a working mother. Her life, written from just a half step sideways, was a golden chariot on an upward trajectory across the heavens.

But thinking of her this way, I also feel her terror and exhaustion. More than me at her side, what she thought she needed most was money—the stability of it, its façade of unassailability. So she set out to earn it, turning herself into an outwardly acceptable figure who appeared at faculty meetings on time, submitted correct paperwork to administrators, and fulfilled the duties of her job while, at the cruddy apartment, the hidden rafters of her life began to rain dust.

Ask anyone: she was a slob. And when my mother was young, Saeeda's domestic jeremiad was so familiar that it came to have the cadence of scripture, how any man would be appalled at Tashi's table manners, that monkeys were tidy in comparison, why would an employer hire a worker whose skirts had been peeled off the floor, that *people will judge us*—meaning their American neighbors. At first, it seemed to be the act of a willful child, this squalor. Then after Tashi's father had died, it appeared, to Saeeda and the rest of the Rummanis, to be an act of defiance. And then, feeling judged by her own family for having raised one human son and one ogre-in-training, Saeeda sent Tashi to boarding school in California, where Tashi's disorderliness was deemed unfixable and then pathological, once a shrink added it to her medical records after her first suicide attempt.

Do we need to cover this ground again, Auntie? Do you realize that I have been taking care of her for as long as you did? It seems so unlikely that I count backward through the years from the night you left this world to the morning you got her out of the hospital in Oakland, a messy-haired teenager with a medical bracelet on her wrist— that math adds up to about twenty years. But I am past the age my mother was when she had me, and I have been protecting her in small ways since childhood. For me, even putting my beloved aside for a moment, there is no decision to go anywhere without first reckoning with what my absence will cost my mother, given how fluently I can read her and how willingly she accepts help from me. It's not like what you and I had. With my mother, I've almost always been old enough to worry about her future.

Old families like the Rummanis inherit old problems. That is what I have come to understand from the history you gave to my mother and later to me: not only the timeless problems like madness and bad luck, but, in the late 1970s, the whole Rummani soap enterprise. When your little brother died in an accident, his widow, Saeeda, who had wed him out of obligation at sixteen, found herself in possession of the safe full of old deeds and records for the Nablus properties, whose key she fastened around her neck as if it were freedom itself.

Not long after, you invited yourself in a managerial spirit to the house outside Houston, having been nominated by the family to advise the uneducated Saeeda on what to do with her windfall. Jibril had been your favorite brother; you assured everyone that your guidance would be welcome. So you perched yourself in her formal sitting room between fireplace and picture window, noting how tastefully your sister-in-law had set up her house, despite its being a ranch home in a dull tract. Everything was clean, scrubbed free of grief and difficulty, as though by some glamour the inheritance of everything from the old country had been restored to innocence in the new.

The illusion wobbled in one place only: the now-fatherless Tashi, at just twelve years old, would not come out of her room. It reeked like a cave, wafting the scent of molding platefuls of food and stale laundry beyond its locked door. Saeeda said that if you really wanted to be helpful, you should gain entry and share with Tashi everything you had come to say about the proper use of soap.

You went to the door and offered this story, as you would offer it to me decades later.

"Tashi, listen. There is no truth but in old women's tales. Remember the blue soap?"

At your voice, Tashi cracked the door. She had heard the story a million times. Her father's pride in it was inexplicable. "I remember the blue soap, and that my father was named after the boy."

"Yes, your father's father's grandfather was the clever boy Jibril," you said. "And I'll tell you why the marriage of your mother and your father was such a celebrated union, if you want. The problem that he has left behind, now that he is with God, comes from empires ago."

My mother was impervious to your tales, honestly, but she cared for any world where her father was important and well regarded, since Saeeda did not seem to miss him enough. Tashi missed everything about him: the way he smiled with only one side of his mouth, his indifference to her messes, even the scars on his face from a child-hood fire—and especially his tales of the helpful silver gazelle who evaded Noah's ark and led humans to dry land. His voice had rumbled in his chest when her ear lay in the cup beneath his collarbone.

So she opened the door wider and let you take a place in the sour bed. She snuggled up to you, testing whether your cool, bony torso could suffice, and let your voice fill her mind.

"When your great-great-grandmother Alissabat finally keeled over, she followed Jibril into the grave after fifty years of happy mar-riage, and her indigo corpse turned the color of skim milk and almost looked normal in the funeral parade. But she died with a huge regret. She didn't see her daughters married. Yaani she made them wash themselves with that crazy blue soap forty years if it was a day, and the men thought the whole Rummani family was cuckoo. Or cursed. So there we have our factory, venerable as a castle in the heart of the city, caressed by drafts of coffee and apple-scented smoke, its windows open to the knocking cart wheels and the muezzin's chant, and its belly full of liquid gold.

"I mean the olive oil, chickpea. If you own a soap factory, you own a bank vault.

"So people are getting superstitious, working for these three pretty ladies who wash themselves blue. But yaani, do you blame them? These women are content, sitting on a hoard of money, with ninety-nine-year contracts for the olive harvest, and business connections across the empire. Don't ever forget the Eleventh Commandment: Make your own cash.

"Anyhoo, it is 1860 or so, and your ancestors are healthy, the soap factory is gangbusters, and the problem of an heir is a tickle in their noses, but they trust it is one that can be figured out from among their cousins. And yet God laughs at optimism. One day an ogre of a man stomps on their doorstep with the priest and claims he is the rightful heir to the factory, to the olive oil contracts, to everything. And what a horrible creature he was. Crooked of face, solitary of tooth, bald as a penis, and tattooed blue-black from neck to ankle. He snarls that he is a cousin, the son of Jibril's eldest uncle, and he had long ago run off to seek his fortunes on an Algerian ship. 'And now I am home to claim my birthright,' he growls.

"Funny thing about men is that they always assume things cannot work perfectly well without them.

"Now, had our ancestors been Muslim, the matter of inheritance would have gone to the Islamic courts, and the sisters' estate would have been safe. But the priest had the heart of a tribesman and the whole woman-hating history of the Church behind him. He tugs his beard this way and that, and flaps his robes, and says he just has no choice but to insist that the sisters allow their eldest male cousin to take the factory, the contracts, the oil, and the trade agreements, or else be excommunicated.

"So it was done. The ogre would have kicked the sisters out onto someone else's hospitality, but neither the leading families of Nablus nor the Cairene or Yaffa merchants wanted anything to do with such a mannerless beast. He needed the sisters to keep his business running. Five years it lasts, these three bluebirds in their cages, smelling their rightful fortune and freedom but no more of it to taste. And in the meanwhile, the ogre proposes marriage to a fertile female of the species—some fellahin girl from the hinterlands.

"Their wedding was like a nightmare, with the marriage crowns sitting on the heads of a pirate-ogre and some girl who doesn't know soap from a block of salt. The ogre and his bride clomped around the church in the traditional procession. The three sisters were the only witnesses. All the while, the priest is smoking up the church with enough incense to kill a person.

"Which in fact he did. The eldest sister keeled over dead in the aisle.

"Now, the bride was as greedy as her husband, and as soon as her pregnancy starts to show, she makes up her mind that the last two sisters are a threat—when the baby is born, one of them is going to count on her fingers and wonder why the wedding was only seven months ago. And the ogre is telling her that nothing, absolutely *zero thing,* can let the sisters get their factory back. He is the richest man in the family and he is going to stay that way.

"Well, the last two sisters are already making up their minds that the greedy woman must go, the baby must go, and the ogre must go. They want their lives to be normal again. So one winter day, when the woman is two months from popping, her husband the ogre goes missing.

"Nobody can find him. The goatherds in the hills don't see him, the peasants in the hinterlands don't know where he is, the rich heirs in their smoking parlors don't care, and the priest is secretly fretting because he is on the ogre's baksheesh list. All for nothing. No tattooed ogre. He's gone. Now it's spring, and the soap cubes are taken down from their pillars and wrapped for the caravans, and everybody is bragging that their color and texture are remarkable: bone swirled with faintest blue, with silken suds that smell of olive oil—but, also, a little whiff of the sea.

"And that's about when the workers find the skeleton at the bottom of the cooking vat. Big, gnarled bones like clubs.

"The priest was horrified. The wife was shrieking. The baby was laughing—his inheritance was sealed with murder soap. And a voice told the sisters to flee Nablus in the night. One was caught, and soldiers beheaded her. The other escaped and was scooped up from the road by a pair of mercenaries who pounded down on her like angels, and they carried her to Damascus, where an old friend of hers, a handsome gentleman merchant, guaranteed her safety, eventually married her, and took her to Haifa. But because love brings bad luck to Rummani women, her bloodline would not return to Nablus for eighty years, long after the British Empire had made a mess of slicing up the Ottoman corpse.

"So, Tash-tun, pay attention. There were two branches of Rummanis. One fled to Damascus after the murder. The other was the ogre's baby, whose bloodline stayed in Nablus. Your father, Jibril, was of the noble bloodline: a brave, exiled blue grandmother who felled a monster. Your mother, Saeeda, is the granddaughter of the greedy monster. Almost a hundred years later, by a very smart business agreement, your mother and father were betrothed by their respective fathers, and the rights and wealth of the Rummani soap factory were restored to the proper branch of the family. So, do you see why I am here now? Do you understand the dilemma?"

My mother's mouth had gone dry. She'd curled up with you for comfort, but it was as if you'd looked down inside her and given voice to a wrongness in her center, the rotten core of marrow she thought no one else could perceive. But no matter how warm your voice was, how natural you felt in the ancient pairing of storytelling and listener, Tashi could hear your question only as a demand for an answer.

"You all realized," she said, "that my brother and I are the products of incest?"

"Bad girl, no! Closer marriages are made all the time and no one bats an eye. My dilemma is that everything is slipping away again!" Your hand reached out as if to indicate all the lands to the horizon. "Your mother is inheriting everything, and she is having very strange ideas about what to do with it. Very selfish ideas. She must do the responsible thing and travel to Nablus as soon as possible, where she can learn the business operations of your birthright and our family can continue to make the world's best olive oil soap."

Like mine, my mother's life followed a political topography. She'd been born in '67, the year of the Setback, and now, following her father's death, those years on the cusp of 1980 were not a good time to think of packing up and following the family taproot home. Imagine trying to rediscover Babel. With munitions being shot back and forth among the Egyptian, Israeli, Lebanese, and Palestinian forces like a venereal disease, the factory in Nablus was already struggling. It took almost nothing at all to get arrested, and half the men of the city were either away, in a jail, or dead. The women of the city went to work, albeit for a pittance because they were women, and the families who still had a little money were organizing. When you said we needed to go home to produce olive oil soap, what you really meant was that friends were asking for help with a women's collective to provide childcare and handicraft work for the mothers who needed jobs to sustain their households. They needed your energy and Rummani money behind the venture, and Saeeda knew all this, too, because the women had made the same entreaties of her.

My mother was almost thirteen and, gathering a sense of the problem from snippets of overheard arguments, worked to appear "normal" at her new, enormous Texas middle school so her mother would choose to stay. Tashi selected exactly the right Trapper Keeper and tried harder with her hair, even when her father's voice began emanating from the cafeteria cups, and then the gymnasium water fountain, a singsong order to *stay inside, stay alive*. Scared, frantic, Tashi got excellent grades and insisted that school was great.

It becomes habit, smiling, when ants are pouring from the collapsing hill of your heart. But maybe it worked. Saeeda dismissed the first of your proposals to return, and then two more. Her pragmatic grief felt disappointing to you, because you'd always tried to have a relationship with her. Decades, emigration, children, and death had done nothing to erode her mysterious aloofness, and her expression still mirrored the one she'd given adults when she was a young child. She stared through any person who was speaking as if unplugging something behind her face for the duration of whatever they had to say.

"I already have plans," insisted Saeeda that autumn after becoming a widow, though she wouldn't admit what the plans were. These conversations were long, heated, and conducted at the dining room table, among Jibril's will and piles of stale-smelling records.

"The Israeli army put a fence around these orchards. We cannot enter to pick a single olive. What good are they to me?"

And: "What is in those warehouses now? Someone's filthy chicken cages—really? I should think carefully about robbing my children's college fund to pay taxes on a barn."

You took the tack you'd taken thirty years ago: Enforce family expectations. Be consistent. Hope for the best, as though Saeeda were still a child. It was not lost on you that the other Rummanis had been in Saeeda's ear since Jibril's death, too, reminding her of how much she'd inherit and that she must be generous with it. You opened your mouth and began to argue that the factory was not profitable enough to pay for an American education. But Saeeda stared through you as if she were staring past a bug on the windshield. The aloofness—it wasn't judgment. It was, for all this time, simple patience with trans-actions. Yaani, Saeeda had been legally betrothed to Jibril since she was five years old, and she had married him at sixteen as the contract had stipulated, and she had endured a wait, and now she held a for-tune in real estate, even if its business operations were paltry.

Saeeda craned forward even farther, peering at a pile of handwrit-ten records. "This pile of rocks. A factory . . . You're right, it hasn't seen a profit since before Atatürk's day. Even the venerable Tuqan family wants to turn theirs into a museum."

"We've owned it for centuries! People depend on us for the work." You jabbed a finger toward the hallway and the bedroom doors be-yond. "Your children are watching everything you do. Have a heart. If not for the factory, then for them. Your daughter barely speaks. She has no friends. She would be happier to grow up among her own people. It is selfish to keep her here, haram."

"*Selfish!* Ananiya, me?" Saeeda said the word a second time, in Ara-bic, as if to confirm that you knew what you were saying. "Is that what you think of me? You are not selfish? My husband, my dear, depressed, impulsive husband, was not selfish?" Her voice didn't rise, but it gained a cutting edge. "My daughter's curse is that she is like him. If you want to know what kind of mother I am, look to my son."

You had suspected coldness in Saeeda, but you hadn't guessed how dangerous a chasm ran through your brother's household. In the si-lence that followed, your heart began to turn toward Tashi.

"How could you, ya Saeeda?"

She had returned her attention to the documents. "Yes, how dare I keep my children here, safe. How dare I ask their teachers how much college costs, knowing how smart they are, but also that I have no job, knowing I am nothing, have been nothing, but their mother, who must provide for them? Yet here you are, another Rummani with an opinion, talking to me about something you understand even less than how to run a business."

You held your tongue long enough for it to become a reminder— you were Nuha Rummani, the eldest, to be respected. "You have family at home that would be happy to see you and your children again. That is all I am telling you. And just do as your husband did and trust the manager's judgment. It couldn't be easier."

"Yet I see no evidence of good judgment. My husband was a push-over. Walaw—he was like the fool from one of your stories, the boat-builder who made oars for the sultan's locomotive." She whipped her glasses off her face and pushed the long folders back across the table. "Whoever has the money," she announced, "buys Lux, Palmolive, this or that, as long as it is convenient. We can't even export what we make. It is time!"

"Then, ya Saeeda, buy your Palmolive." Your face felt like it was kindling in an invisible fire as you rose from the table, swaying like a pillar of flame. "Maybe it can wash the treason out of your betraying mouth. You have the money now to buy whatever you want, no matter what it costs your children."

The shock rattled around in your body as you packed your bags. Your reticent sister-in-law had emerged from these years as a creature unknown to the family's prim, traditional thinking. You should have recognized her stubbornness. You ought to have respected it. Our family once thought that women were only ever good for a few of their holes: their ears and the one between their legs. But after Jibril died, Saeeda took your example and opened that trickiest of orifices, her mouth, and she discovered that she liked the sound of her voice. With it, she announced her intention to sell off every last stone of the family's properties and give her two children the best futures Ameri-can dollars could buy.

———

So began the Time of Feuding. Rummanis don't forget a slight, let alone a disinheritance—and except for you, they no longer sent birthday wishes and holiday cards. A suffocating silence followed my mother between school and home. Black moods lasted for weeks, intolerable bouts of upset that made her itch to get out of her own skin. She lied to stay home in bed, to call you in private.

It was 1981 and Israel was bombing Palestinians in Beirut, but Saeeda shut off the news. She had quietly sawed her family not only from the Rummani tree, but from the entire world. The only visitor to the house was a tall, jowly American Saeeda had met at the school board meetings, a tattooed ex-marine who had shortened his good Arab name of Khalil to Kelly and who laughed like Muttley the dog. Around him, Saeeda smiled too much and seemed rather empty. Or at least this is what you suggested to Tashi when she reported how Saeeda allowed Kelly to wolf down six of her fatayer sabanekh pies, which he insisted on calling *spinach poppers*. He had somehow filled Saeeda's entire vision, and even before their small courthouse wedding, she made sure that it was his name on her son's ROTC applications and on the forms at Tashi's doctor's appointments.

"What does he want?" you asked my mother. "Does he know about the money?"

"Maybe. I don't know." She could feel your suspicions, your effort to align reality with the stories of an interloping pirate. "He already has a house and an ex-wife. He buys us things. He's doing okay."

"And how does he treat you," you asked, "this GI Joe who is invading my brother's family?"

"My stupid brother worships him, so I basically don't exist," Tashi answered. "Except he calls me Miss Piggy because of my room."

This slap confirmed in your mind that your niece would be healthier somewhere else. You knew how much money Saeeda had gotten from the sale. You were forming ideas, but because it was the Time of Feuding, you made no promises and did not yet confront Saeeda. It would be your scheme, eventually, for her to send my mother to boarding school in California, drawing Tashi closer to you. You were simply biding your time until Saeeda was desperate enough with the situation under her roof to ask for any kind of help, no matter how drastic.

(Maybe I'm exaggerating the degree to which you were conscious of your schemes. But it's funny, isn't it, how you made us all both like and need you? I think there is no exaggerating how desperate you were to be loved.)

You hung up, and Tashi listened to the dial tone for a long time, wrapping the cord around her wrist until her fingertips turned purple, until the dial tone turned to an urgent staccato, until the sun went down and the room was dark, until Kelly brought her brother home from a college visit, until her brother grabbed the phone away and said he had to make calls before dinner and would she *please* not leave her snotty tissues *everywhere, Miss Piggy, okay?*

That night, many nights, she sneaked out to go walking through the dark neighborhood while the three-person family that now excluded her slept. Other people's lit houses were soothing. And lately she had felt a thrumming in the house. No one else seemed aware of it, but its vibration made a tickling sensation over her skin. It wasn't something she could shout away or dig out of her body with her nails (she'd tried), or even outrun—though she had tried that, too. She knew not to speak of it or her mother would tell the doctor.

The sensation followed her, rasping in the palm fronds along the subdivision street, hissing in the dust through construction zones. When her father's voice had spoken to her from the water fountain at the school, it had been frightening—an encroachment, like someone sitting too close on the bus, a menacing stranger crowding in. This felt more like a beckoning promise of relief. She walked a dry cement culvert, then veered into one of the construction sites, and the change in the quality of the sound beneath her sandals alerted her to other sounds, too. The rumbling of thoughts was actually voices in her ears, coalescing into her father's voice, ordering her to sit inside the half-built house *until the air is gone.* And then *till her share is a song, where is it wrong* . . . Ringing in her head like a bell, its alien desperation tolling emptily in her bones.

Did it mean she was sick? Or separate from her terror of it, did it signify that she was capable of something no one else could understand—some unguessable feat that resided in her, like the power within dark matter? A wondrous intelligence, a way to discover what thread ran through all humankind and made them a single family, like that myth of the Tower of Babel you loved to tell? But this wasn't the world of your stories. Tashi would come of age in the decade of Prozac, and beyond the sawdust at her toes that night was only a heavy Texas sky, studded with the lights of distant aircraft. I picture my mother like this whenever I need to feel more tender toward her: a scrawny girl, bare calves with a fuzz of dark hair, crouched in a skeletal house with the mice and scorpions, astonished by a ghostly chorus. That night outside Houston, she'd scrambled to the top floor, wondering whether the drop to the foundation was enough to crack open her head and let the voices out. A few years later in boarding school, she'd try a whole bottle of Tylenol. And in college on the California coast, she'd wonder, What about a gun? In Portland, she'd imagine the sound of a single shot from that revolver softened by miles of pine forest. None of it would ever stop the phenomenon and its fixations. From that earthy Texas night onward, as nostalgia preoccupies the exile, death played in my mother's thoughts like the promise of homecoming.

The long-ago diagnosis was depression with psychotic tendencies, bound up with an adjustment disorder. This is the power of a story to shape the sense of things. It had rewritten a twelve-year-old's grief after she'd been made fatherless, overwritten her outrage at his being replaced by a know-nothing American; later, it footnoted the fifteen-year-old's homesickness, bullying, and adolescent hormones once she was swept away to school in California. It supplied an explanation for why teenage Tashi did not seem to get better, or want to, and it used her disorderliness as a damning detail—even though she just didn't care to clean and saw it as an obsolete performance of femininity. Under so much indelible ink, page-flagged by experts, my mother had spent so many years unable to quite recognize the person she was growing into, inside and out. Which is why she would want something entirely different for me, even if your intrusions seemed an uncanny repeat of her own childhood.

As a result of the expensive American education she had received from her mother's sale of the family soap factory, she was now paid to do neuroscience using rodent brains. It was *her work*, what she had used to justify all that time in Portland away from me. Yet even before her pregnancy, the sticking point was always here, on this commonplace framing of how she spent her portion of the family's properties. *Her work* implied continuity between what she did for sixty hours a week and having a belief that it was important. She didn't, and it wasn't. Not like her brother's striving corporate job in Singapore. She'd picked biology ages ago because it was the science of all life, but no one had warned her that every doorway led to a smaller and smaller room until she'd find herself nearly middle-aged, divorced, in a dark closet at eleven on a Friday night, squinting into a microscope at the indigo splatter of a mouse neuron.

In that closet, hunkered over an emulsified brain in the name of science, peering through a glowing aperture on her inheritance, Dr. Natasha Rummani, published writer and the holder of three very good degrees, etc., noticed how little curiosity she had about why her body had produced a baby like me. Instead she felt an old, immense relief—this proof that all these years at the bench and in this city, and even in her body and her family, were exactly as incomplete as they'd seemed.

So here was my mother that winter of my first year: returning to her cruddy apartment in Portland at one A.M. Sprawled on a futon on the floor, texting my father to evade yet another invitation to coffee. At her feet were her two pairs of jeans and three sweaters scattered around a large suitcase. Beside her shoulder, sitting on the tiles, was an electric kettle and one dirty teacup. Last week, its rippled porcelain had begun speaking to her again.

When her sleep was poor and she most wished to sever herself from life and the symptoms of her illness, her father's voice told her to find suicide and bury it. The week before, she'd found the idea emanating from a piece of toilet tissue full of fingernail clippings and hair. Then the real estate section of the Sunday paper. Tonight, a violent pillowcase. She had put a trowel by the back door for this purpose, so whenever an item announced itself as dangerous, she could obey. Now she got up and descended the stairs to the place where her building backed up against the public woods. She shimmied the trowel's blade into the dirt, deposited the offending pillowcase in its grave, and patted the dirt over it. The burying, it offered brief closure to a very particular distress, as if the cool soil were lying on her scalp, quieting her mind.

In the peace that followed, scrubbing her fingernails, she thought about how soon she could finish her part of the experiments and visit me. A month, two? As you had told her long ago, the Eleventh Commandment said to make your own cash. If she sent more of it to you for my care, perhaps it would buy time to sort herself out again. Find a better therapist, get her feet on the ground, get her mother off her case, buy the ticket.

She would not let herself fall into despair. She had accomplished an unguessable feat after all, found a path not just to the family taproot, but to infinite wonder—what she had craved since that night in the Texas heat, in a house with open walls. Through me, a door had opened onto another door onto another door.

Her plans weren't fast enough. When my mother didn't buy a plane ticket to visit her first-begotten and only begotten child for Christmas, Saeeda packed her matching canvas suitcase and carry-on lug-gage and appeared on her daughter's doorstep, at an apartment near the university where I was born.

She had almost talked herself out of coming. All these years, her chilly core of pragmatism had remained at her disposal, and she had been caring for Kelly, that deteriorating Second Husband, for so long that it was habit to remain at his side. Yaani, she loved him, and he had encouraged Saeeda to come. He had wept in one of those rare lucid spells for needing so much help. He sent her with a fortune in gift cards to give to Tashi so that I could be relocated to her apart-ment in preparation for a normal infancy, because some hopes for the future die hard.

The place was a difficult walk from the lab in a hillside academic slum—an incrustation of student dwellings that smelled of plywood and burnt fry oil. At present Tashi was out, but the door was un-locked.

It felt like a sort of halfway house for underfunded scientists. This scraped-bare space and its dirty windows finally epitomized my mother's inability to construct a domestic sanctuary, her state of mere tenancy inside her own life. Saeeda turned around once, taking in the stained tiles, the slanted porch, the plastic shower stall under a ceiling that sagged. There was nothing inside to steal because the rooms ap-peared already looted. The centerpiece was a futon mattress on the floor and a pile of three-ring binders gorged with papers.

Saeeda rubbed her pendant along her bottom lip, hoping maybe she'd misremembered and gotten the wrong place. The clothes draped over the suitcase looked like her daughter's. As she shook out the blanket she muttered, "Shu hal karkaba," then moved a dirty teacup to the sink and the binders to the countertop.

That was when Saeeda looked down the counter to the window overlooking the back porch and saw Dr. Natasha Rummani under the trees outside, burying something in the woods with a muddy trowel.

———

I don't know the worst of my mother's illness. I wasn't there for its untreated beginnings. You and Saeeda didn't speak of it, because it was embarrassing. And there are no records anymore. Tashi won't go into detail, because despite everything, she is still my mother and asserts maternal privilege when it suits her.

It's why I told my beloved yes while thinking, *Maybe,* and I sat for my passport photo hoping you might appear in the flash and snap of the camera, telling me what to do.

Mama would never force me to stay near her, but you know how she gets. It's frightening when she stops answering calls and locks the dead bolt, for which no one has a key except me. How does one turn that lock from an ocean and a continent away? For this quarter century since you've been dead, there is no one else she trusts to step inside her dark house. No voice she'll listen to except mine, telling her to stay.

Out of decorum, when Saeeda took her daughter out to dinner that evening, she pretended not to have seen the trowel or the burying. But she reported her discovery to three others.

Her husband's reaction (blessedly clear): "If she's doing that again, she needs to see a doctor." To him, Tashi would always be weak—the inscrutable teenager wearing a gown and a medical bracelet.

Your reaction: "First thing, who are you to snoop around in the business of your daughter? Then tell her nothing? This is very typical of you. Second thing, in my day . . ." You rattled and cursed a bottle of aspirin as you struggled with the cap. "In my day, nobody was 'sick.' They were either special or they were dying. People left you in peace to be the one or the other. Third thing . . ." You cast around, and finally just swore again at the pill bottle. It was a sad anger, not so different from what you'd felt years ago, hearing that Jibril Rummani had gotten himself killed while lighting a cigarette next to a bunch of refinery equipment. My mother, you had come around to admitting, was what Saeeda had said long ago: as cursed as her father.

And the reaction of my own father, when Saeeda got him on the phone, was to make a breakfast appointment with his ex-mother-in-law for eight the next morning, because Tashi was still, in his mind, someone with whom he had unsettled business. He had wanted to grovel, to make amends, to at least let her excoriate him—but since the legal proceedings of divorce and forfeiture of parental rights, the silence felt ominous. Saeeda's call punctured it, and so, life with my father began.

As of 1860

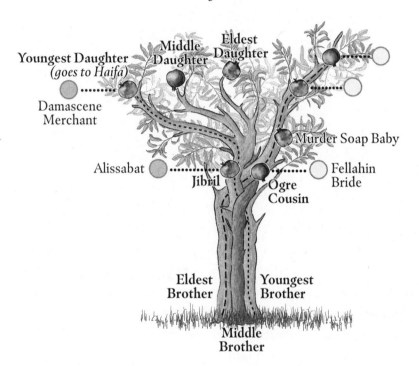

Youngest Daughter
(goes to Haifa)

Damascene
Merchant

Middle
Daughter

Eldest
Daughter

Murder Soap Baby

Alissabat

Jibril

Ogre
Cousin

Fellahin
Bride

Eldest
Brother

Youngest
Brother

Middle
Brother

In Which a Monster Is Discovered

———·———

While my mother was burying her feelings eight inches beneath the surface of the medical school's nature park, I had a valiant auntie in Oakland who penciled her eyebrows very dark, having emerged triumphant from a flu virus that ravaged half the building and almost, but not quite, required both of us to see a doctor. Now, on that soft, overcast February afternoon, you tied my head into a long-brimmed bonnet, got me into a corduroy shearling coat with over-long sleeves, plugged a stuffed toy under my arm, and steered the secondhand stroller from the building's elevator to the lakeshore. It was an urban lake, and people peered into my stroller and saw nothing but a bundle of clothes. They peered next at the severe face of the woman pushing it, and walked on.

We were halfway to the museum when a man caught up with us. His halfhearted pleas for attention finally became a nuisance.

"Excuse me." The sinewy man stood there, panting a little, glasses fogged. His left arm terminated a few inches above the wrist. When he saw his amputation being noticed, he returned it to the pocket of his coat. "You know me, Ms. Rummani."

"I should," you said, "but I'm old and forgetful. If you'll let me pass . . ."

He fell into step beside us. "That's not fair. You do know who I am."

Your heart began flapping around in your rib cage too wildly for a muscle of its age, so you steadied yourself on the stroller and shoved it onward. "You were the piano player at somebody's wedding, right?"

His legs were long, and it was no effort for him to keep up. "You can be that way. I don't mind." He kept that arm against his pocket, maintaining an illusion of a wrist continuing to a hand. "You know, I've called. I've talked to people in your building. I have been very polite."

You don't spend years in a walled city in a strategic valley without inheriting a sixth sense for the danger routes. In the Rummanis' case, it had always come from one of three places: the armies and refugees overland through the valleys, bombs from the heavens, or betrayal from within. Ever since the call from Saeeda, tattling on my mother, this day had been inevitable.

"You seem nice," you told the man. "Will you go down the road for a pack of Marlboro Lights? It's so far for this old fossil—"

"Try to see it from my end. That's all I'm asking."

You forced a laugh. "You know, I think that's almost the punch line to a very good joke I heard from my friend the proctologist. I think, however, you may have it backward."

"Ms. Rummani." Three long strides, and he put himself in her path. His shins were an inch from the tallow-colored soles of my rain boots. He seemed to forget what he was going to say. The wind across the water picked up a loose curl from his part and folded it against his forehead.

I should say, certain details survive in this story for the same reason everyone knows that Judas Iscariot sold his sweet street-preacher friend to the Roman army for exactly thirty pieces of silver and a kiss. Outrage is a stylus; its letters cut deep.

"You know," said Adam, my father, with a broken-sounding note at the back of his voice, "we both know, I am trying to help. Tashi won't return any of my calls. But the baby, Ms. Rummani, the one in this stroller, she is my daughter."

The wind pressed that trembling hook of hair between my father's eyebrows like the mark of Cain, and you considered walking away now, backward into the close rooms of my first ten months of life. But the wind was already inside the seams of our coats.

In January 2003, the ogre landlord had sold the building for $3 million and sailed away on a forty-foot yacht. A few weeks later, yellow slips had appeared on all the doors, stuck on with painter's tape. A real estate developer was renovating the units, but only as tenants moved out—and if they did so, they were guaranteed their full security deposit plus $500.

The grad students had been the first to take the offer. A handyman truck parked at the curb. Plastic sheeting went up over their old two-bedroom on the second floor. By noon, the men had dragged the tub onto the sidewalk and hammered the drywall to pieces. The next day, that unit was reduced to an empty socket covered in a film of respirating plastic. Within two weeks it emanated paint fumes, and the barrage of nail-gun fire fell off into the softer noises of workmen's boots coming and going on cardboard-protected floors. I didn't know it then, but it was the noise of a new city built on top of the old.

We didn't bother about the construction. At first, all we cared about was keeping tacks out of our feet, and the little dance we had to do at the elevator to get around stacked two-by-fours and buckets of sealant. In the weeks leading up to my father's first visit, however, the building's skin had seemed to peel back all over the place—revealing its dry-rotting bones and dust-felted conduits to the residents who'd had, until now, no intention of leaving. Elongated boards leaned down from ductwork and shadows. Peering out of them were nonsense surfaces that had not touched the air in over half a century. The building's innards were potent with the same smell that had been leaking into our apartment for a year: an intimate dampness, like river mud. I don't remember any of this except for the sense that once, before the beginning, I lived in a palace that seethed with holes.

Walking the hallway that first day, ducking slightly to avoid a board, my father took it in, making a little *hum* sound in the back of his throat.

"Tashi's mother told me everything. I swear, I'm just trying to do the right thing here." In the apartment, he was aswirl with words, said he would buy the cigarettes, came back bearing other gifts, too, including a single dahlia, with its supernova of petals. Mentioned clients in the area, was a torrent of gratitude, presented the flower for my wonderment.

He hadn't seemed threatening at the wedding five years ago, either. He'd been a nervous, solitary man in a gray tuxedo whose side of the wedding party comprised his lean sampling of athletes from the Twin Cities and the Bay Area, people who had known him when he'd still been a two-handed man with a fast bicycle and a faster motorcycle. Thereafter he had slipped from real life and retreated to being a mere character in Tashi's unhappy silences, a disenchanted man who had scooped out the heart from his chest to make more room for his intellect. You'd complained that he was like the English officers who had come and gone from the fine house you'd lived in during the British Mandate years, lizard-tongued men whose elite education and military commissions occupied their wandering talk endlessly. But the man squatting in the foyer, brandishing a flower because he was uncertain how to go about picking me up—this was a different sort of person. All your anger, therefore, was right now trained entirely on Saeeda, whose talent for unilateral action seemed to make her finally and perfectly American.

You hefted me from my stroller seat and offered me to his one good arm. "Careful. She's very heavy." Helped him get me situated against his hip, and he staggered back a step under my great weight.

It was true I'd gotten almost too heavy for a ropy, unsteady old woman to support. And it was also true that it took this much to see me: full physical contact, the weight of a body, the strong clasp of my fingers to the collar, the whisper of my oddly cool breath—all this was necessary to at last trust what his eyes were seeing. In the past months, as the workmen had opened the building's walls, my flesh had taken on more light, more firmness, so that even in the dim foyer my skin was as uncannily bright as the inside of a quartz vein.

But Adam seemed to blink it away, and after a moment of bewilderment, he fell into a dopey grin, and he laughed even as I slapped his cheek with my free hand. It took half a minute for him to brush away the tears running down his face from behind his glasses.

You watched as long as you could, weighing your words. "I am not sure I know what it is I can do for you." Unstated was that he was here while Tashi was absent, he was here at all, a man who had broken his wedding vows like a goat. But even as you tried to drag up all your familiar anger, the bucket was empty.

"Tashi's mom called me," he repeated, as if the conversation with Saeeda amounted to a letter of recommendation. "She worried me. I thought I could offer to help—whatever you need. Nannies. Doctors. Or stay with Betty and me in the house in Portland. You tell me."

"I wonder what it takes to worry a man who let his wife give birth alone."

He lifted his face enough that the light caught the tear streak on the left side of his face, and it seemed to cut his cheek in two, like an old scar.

"You don't need to answer," you said. "But you should think about this while you are getting out your checkbook."

Lest I seem ungrateful, my father's checkbook is important. Just as my grandmother sold the soap factory for her children's education, my father's fortune had also come from loss: his mother's life insurance policy when he was a young man, and then millions after a settlement from a trucking company whose driver clipped his motorcycle—a disaster that took his left hand before he met my mother. He still worked, but he didn't need to. And besides his checkbook, the other currencies he cared about were all soberly future-oriented: planning, reason, clarity of purpose. Together, they made him powerful. They also put him at an essential social distance from you, my backward-gazing aunt. So did the whole of his politics, the literal and political climate of his rural Minnesota origins, his lack of family, and his introversion.

Prior to my birth, you had only one thing in common with my father, that ever-lurking feeling of suspense around my mother's well-being. Then his dull, purposeless, and short affair proved my mother's conviction that no home was permanent, and your conviction that no Rummani woman was lucky in love.

But I am not here to probe my father's sex life. Like gravity, entropy, and hunger, it preceded me in the universe.

I am, however, here with certain questions. To tell a story well is to listen again, with an ear cupped against its walls to catch the background murmurs, now that I have the ears to hear.

The beginning of my parents, before they were my parents, was set in a three-story walk-up in San Francisco's Haight-Ashbury, during Tashi's postdoctoral fellowship and the first year of the consultancy my one-handed father created to occupy his time and his mind. He cooked for her. He left her an Easter basket of oranges in December. He sent a cleaning lady. He joined her on the fire escape on clear October nights, or at a wobbling table in Tashi's kitchen beside a bell curve of condensation, or in his bed in slatted morning light. They did the work of speaking a shared language into being. In return, my mother explained her research—and by the physical chaos of her life, we can ascertain, as we peer through this artificial window into those years, that she was having a good mental year.

No, of course we shouldn't decide on capability. There is literally no end

*to unanswered questions, questions we don't even know how to ask yet.
Living is doubting. Living in doubt is a good thing.* That was my mother's song of praise for her science in those months; it articulated
something Adam had always believed. He fell in love with her. And
she, as we have already seen, loved the calmness of being around him,
loved him according to her need—for his acceptance, for the gentle
rails he put around her disordered edges, for his patience, for his lack
of excessive dismay about her medical history. It is easy for a one-
handed man to understand remaking one's existence after a disaster,
and he basically believed her when she said her worst years were in
high school, and now they were done. The pills she took had leveled
the floors and ceilings in her mental house, nailed the trapdoors shut,
and created a trustworthy space in which to build a home.

Temporary, because everything is.

And because they are not just their names and birth dates and
government-issued identification numbers, but also my parents, there
is no ending to that story. Nor to the stories that came to my father's
mind when he stewed over the fact that I was alive and still with her.
For instance, he carried the story about my mother's miscarriage,
which he regarded as one beginning, because of the way she threw
herself into work to forget the toilet full of blood. Then the one about
the screaming tantrum in the car a few months later. Or the one
where she went walking, and he happened to find her the next morning, sleeping on a median off an Eastside thoroughfare. Or the way
she stared through him as he woke her up, as if they were strangers to
each other after all, and how incensed she grew at his fearful anger.

She'd been pregnant then, though they didn't know it. He would
have stayed loyal. He wanted to fix things. But after he confessed to
his stupid affair, he saw himself becoming, in his wife's eyes, just like
everyone else, and that was the moment he realized she wasn't his
wife anymore. They were just two people, speaking different languages, having lost a way to communicate with their future. So having seen all he'd seen, he thought adoption was a good idea.

But the future emerges anyway, never as expected. There I was, a blue syllable pulling their stories together again.

My mother showed up in Oakland three days after my father's unannounced visit like an avenging angel, spectacular and impotent. In her anger, she almost looked coherent. She did nothing but insist on holding me and, in general, spoiling me into being a terror. Deep in the freezer was a heap of lurid ice pops in plastic sleeves, which you said you were saving for the grandchildren of your friend Cecilia but which had been entombed in the ice since last summer. My mother and I ate so many of the grape ones that our mouths turned purple and I threw up. Babies throw up all the time, but you had been in the middle of my current favorite story—"Now, the silver gazelle wanted to steal a pomegranate from the queen of the djinn, so she sought entry to that realm from a spring outside the village of Maaloul"— but then I gave a retch and a *splat,* and there was yet another mess to clean out of the radiator vent. You squabbled with my mother for the rest of the day, and she was glad to leave for the conference she'd come to attend. This was not just an excuse: her work was truly going well, at the usual cost to her well-being.

Also, I had just taken my first unsupported steps alongside the circular coffee table. It was as if a mountain had discovered the excitement of motion. I uprooted myself and walked around and around the table, then scouted a path to the window, found challenging passes through the piles of junk, blazed a path to the kitchen and then the bathroom doorway. I was then, although I am more than that now, mostly a body—and without the distraction of being anything else, my body mastered the lifting of the knee, the setting of the foot, the collapsing of bed rails and gates not designed to contain an intelligent creature that was thirty inches tall and almost fifty awesome pounds. The ten-month-old god in diapers, a god with trajectories and whole unopened territories before her.

But—and I resent this now—something bone-deep began draining from you. Saeeda's warnings had stirred up dark, slithering worries. Had she been born in other times or places, people would have said Tashi was possessed. Her mental constitution was a delicate topic. Saeeda treated the trouble as your fault because it worsened during Tashi's school years, when you were most in her life. All these years later, speaking of demons was still taboo. But the pattern was obvious by now. Whenever Tashi's life seemed to be getting sorted out and orderly, she was most in danger of falling apart. And she *was* falling, again, into the kinds of silences from which one could not see land. Sitting in the window with me again, thinking the sun would bleach me; silently trying out her face powder on my forehead; walking all night; the purple ice-pop fixation. When her anxiety piled up on the horizon like thunderheads, it began charging her with strange ideas. And what if she soon needed more help than I did? Where was I to be? You added eighteen years to my age and thought about your own future.

Here, I swear, is an afterimage of a real memory. I can almost see you seated, perched for unmarked minutes on the arm of the couch as though about to rise—as though all willpower vacated whatever impulse commanded your limbs. Underfoot is my expanding conquest over your home. You had believed you knew what you were doing with babies; then here I was, ruining everything. My mother's child. Your dear Jibril's granddaughter. Child of cursed ancestors, drawing troubles to the surface, revealing all the breaks I had seemed at first to promise to fix. How much more might the future hold? Worse, friends had encouraged you, but then dismissed you after you took me on— and C. was a woman with her own horde of grandchildren to worry about. The phone rang less. The mailman brought little news, only holiday cards from the occasional Rummani. You had chosen this family, and pushed everyone away to hide me, and unthinkably, everyone seemed to have forgotten about you, even the one you loved. So what now? What road of the forking path had you abandoned, and could you live without it? You threw out the rest of those ice pops.

I've not come here to harass the dead. But in spite of my skin and my density and a lifetime of being stared at, I'm still human. I'm a woman with a beating heart in her chest, and last night, my beloved fell asleep with her ear in the cup of my shoulder, tears creeping down the bridge of her nose. And when I woke up this morning, she was already in the bathroom with her foot hauled up on the bathroom sink, cutting her toenails in the dissipating steam as if nothing were wrong. In our private language, it meant she was done arguing. The decision is simple: Leave or stay. Get on the plane tomorrow or don't. Our future is pressing in, and the more I listen against the walls of our history— mine and yours—the more I worry about the lesson of Babel: Anything can fall apart. Indeed, as my mother knows, everything is already broken.

Believe me, I've stepped back. I've had years. I know that being old and tired and proud creates its own reality, but shouldn't my peculiarity, my specialness, have merited more of your wavering attention? Shouldn't the whole world bend for someone such as me, or at least for love? Hadn't you learned to never again let anything interfere? You were a woman whose tenacity could solve any problem. And my father would have entertained any request, even one to have his most abrasive in-law come live at his house as a nanny. He would have either fled in terror or said yes. And I would not have had to grow up out in the unjust world, away from the tiny and completely self-referential universe inside your orbit.

But your sticking point was the apartment. Nuha Rummani, al-Nakba, decided not to be moved. Not again. And not for someone else's profit.

Even as the entire family crept around the edges of a realization that eighty was too many years old for raising a baby, workmen flayed the lobby floor of its carpeting. Despite the mildew this process unleashed, we refused four too-polite invitations to spend a weekend at my grandmother's house in Palo Alto, just as a matter of principle. Instead, because it was spring and I was now almost one year old and my mother would be returning soon, we propped open the windows, the apartment door, and the big window in the hallway that opened onto the fire escape, pulling a torrent of clear air through the building's upper stories. It was bath day for both of us.

Our tub was like a porcelain bus. Supported on four metal knobs, gleaming with chrome fixtures, and big enough for a woman and baby together, it was for Sundays only because it cost so much to fill. We laid our outfits on the bed and chose socks from the drawer. Standing next to the threadbare quilt, you leaned your hip into the mattress and climbed down out of a nightgown, peeling it off your mottled shoulders. One areola was a smeared purple scar. Skin hung in odd gills where other cuts had been made. As you stepped one foot and then the other out of snagged underwear, the obstructed light from the window cast your body in a faint murk. You wrapped it in a robe without looking at the dresser, where wigs sat with the backs of their heads to the mirror. Holding hands, we crossed the hallway into the room of warm tiles and turned off the tap.

I didn't like potty before bath time because it was oppression, and today, I got my way, because rules sometimes exhausted the adults who made them. You were out of the robe and immersed to your buttocks, seated on one of the two bath seats, where you helped me onto the metal stool, over the tub's slick shoulder, and onto the other bath seat. Facing each other, we smiled through the swirls and minarets of steam.

And out came the soap.

I have waited for so long to tell about the soap. For two hundred years, it had been the only pure thing in our fractured family.

Real Nabulsi soap comes in an immortal cube. Our cube was bigger than my fist and a little smaller than yours. People say pure soap is colorless and odorless. No. Open up the crinkly square of paper, and olive oil soap is the color of aged bone. It is hard, with sharp edges, but it has the most peaceful smell in the world. This fragrance expands in warm water. It is salty, pat—not unlike flour, but with an inscrutable life of its own, a beckoning pleasantness, as though the smell emanates from somewhere deeper in a house of many rooms.

"If your name was really up to me," you would tell me years later, "I would choose something softer, like soap. But I have no say in my own name either, ya Betty."

The last thing I will say about this cube of soap is that all its faces were blank. When soap is made, each cube is stamped with a hammer. Each hammer bears a family seal cast from copper. The image on the Rummanis' seal was the halved pomegranate. No more Rummani soap exists in the world, thanks to Saeeda. Not a single cube survives. We used the Tuqan family's soap, the one everyone gets as a souvenir, but it was still precious and hard to find, and even so, we would begin by wasting some of it by shaving the other family's crossed-keys logo off with a knife. As in so many of the broader conditions of life, an everyday task like a bath first involved cutting something else away.

But in any case, you were soaping your scalp when I shat in the tub.

Which made the injury that day my fault.

This is not a story where everything we do makes sense.

Splashing, wading, cursing, you couldn't make up your mind about who should come out of the soiled water first, yourself or me. You swore at Tashi. At Saeeda. At my grandfather Jibril. At the Rummanis all over the world, both the quick and the dead. It was the closest thing to a prayer I'd ever heard spoken in this apartment, as you were jackknifed over on a bad back and sending tidal waves of shit-water outside the tub and onto the floor.

Too apoplectic to just reach down and pull the plug.

That's when you decided to lift me, and you lost your balance. We fell.

So much begins in confusion and chaos. The corner of my eyebrow struck the corner of the sink. The wound opened with a burst of flakes, leaving a serrated dent above my temple. Light crashed through my brain. Somehow you were now facedown on the floor, out of my reach, one ankle still snagged on the tub, awake enough to be cursing floridly against the tiles. And meanwhile my howls were the envy of hellfire and hurricanes, loud enough to tear the tar paper off the roof and drive rats into the storm drains. In our gutted building, what the neighbors heard was a shriek announcing the end times.

It was the neighbor upstairs, Darlene, who came down first.

The cheap lock on the front door rattled, and then it banged free of the splintering doorframe. Wet, naked, bald, and strange, the two of us lay in all our glory on the bathroom floor.

"Come on, honey," said our neighbor, bending over. She took in only one thing at a time and went to the obvious casualty. "Easy now."

The wet tile was bloody and your leg was jointed wrong.

"I need—" You were unused to being this kind of spectacle. And your head seemed foggy. The sense of hurrying? A tangle of befuddling pains, someone's grasping hands. Someone in the bathroom. And the realization: *I have no clothes on.* It was the kind of thought that drowns out even a crying baby. *No clothes.* Under everything, dignity was perhaps your most unexpected virtue, and it made no exceptions.

The words came in a rush: "Out! Leave me alone!"

"Ms. Rummani, stay and I'll get somebody. You need the ambulance."

"Let me die! Get out!"

Darlene pulled down the robe and settled it in place.

As she dialed 911 on her phone, there was a blast of noise, a sort of howl. Her gold-flecked eyes, magnified behind a pair of glasses on a gemstone chain, finally took in the rest of the room. My cries seemed to be coming from everywhere.

The world is home to many kinds of people and many reactions to monsters. The two mothers in the hospital saw me as a lump of mud. When my father first laid eyes on me, he let the script of what you're supposed to do with a baby guide his reaction—in this, he was like my grandmother. Darlene—overworked, dressed for church, benignly taken advantage of by an adult daughter—experienced the scene in the bathroom through a tired little pinhole. One problem at a time dripped through. First getting a robe around the injured woman. Second dialing 911. And now in the puddle beside the sink, moving away from the toilet with a silver dent in her face, was a baby.

"What are my—" she said, and this is my first real memory:

Arms clanging with bracelets reach for me, and then a warm hand cups my forehead, pulling my head into a soft shoulder, and her voice rumbles against my ear as it states the emergency to a dispatcher. I feel her confusion in how her voice shakes.

"An old woman and a baby, right . . ." Even though I was crying, she kept saying I was cold, my color, I might not be able to breathe.

I saw through one eye the work of her other hand as it folded a towel into a thick strip; her long toes in platform-heeled jute sandals; her bright, body-hugging cotton dress wet with bathwater; the wrinkled skin along the sides of her feet as she kicked off her shoes, revealing a silver ring on her third toe. The hollow, copper taste of my own blood flaking. Her fear of me was in her busyness, as if by helping harder she could master it. As she hung up the phone, the towel and her soft rocking sifted the blinding white light in my head away until I was fully conscious of being comforted even as I was feared.

It was this kindness that still fixes those close, ratty rooms onto the impression of a larger dwelling, a hive of unexplored chambers where there was goodwill, the sort of peaceful Babel that preceded our more rotten impulses. This home of yours had become an alternative world, peopled and not fully malignant.

"I don't want the ambulance. They cannot come inside."

"You're hurt," Darlene said. "And they'll make you pay for it anyway, so just use it."

She helped us to the couch. It was dawning on her that I had been here all along. That the overloud bellowing and howling and wailing was mine. No, it hadn't made sense to bathe a baby that way. Yes, it probably happened all the time. No, this was not how any of it was supposed to go. The harder you tried to explain what you had been trying to do, not just in the bath but for the whole last year, the more convoluted your thoughts grew with shame. And the sound of an ambulance siren was growing louder.

You, no matter your effort, couldn't answer why you had Tashi's eleven-month infant but Tashi herself wasn't here. And where was this invading father who supposedly cared so much? Where was Saeeda, having lit another fuse and then retreated back to her own problems? Where were all the old friends who used to come and go from the apartment, whose lives actually looked like lives? Your fury, only your fury, focused you.

"Get my wig."

"Ms. Rummani," said the neighbor, "you gonna tell me about this child?"

You propped your one good elbow on your one good knee and let out a cough. It felt like finding whole lobes of your lungs you'd forgotten about. "Where to begin?"

When the paramedics arrived, they found the apartment empty except for you. The hospital provided X-rays, meds, and a sheet of instructions that would keep you ping-ponging between doctors until the swelling went down enough for an MRI. You came home by taxi with a walker, wanting nothing but to lie down and die of humiliation. Too tired to even weep.

In the meantime, in Darlene's apartment, neighbors had filed in to see me. They'd stood around in a circle, asking careful questions, as if I were a body washed ashore at their feet. The injury on my forehead was almost gone. A smooth black scab had grown over the divot, and the whole thing was smaller. Darlene had pointed it out many times to the crowd, saying that the color indicated some deeper wonder. Given time to take me in, they all agreed there was something oddly familiar about me, though they'd never seen anyone like me before.

Now she was helping you upstairs. In the forced privacy of the elevator, she said, "Ms. Rummani, I know this city. Somebody from one of the stations might come by. Like if the cameras are already here, then we show them how we're getting kicked out of our homes. Maybe somebody helps stop it, instead of ignoring us every time we call. We don't have a lot of options here, so think if the news can do a story on us where Betty's in it. I don't know, but people might pay attention."

"Yaani people looking at Betty this way . . . No."

"You have another idea, you tell me. Because right now, we are fresh out. You have a place to go if you lose this one? If I lose my place, I can't afford another one closer than Hayward."

She didn't push it further, stopping short of a threat. But it was clear that the neighbors had seen something to hope for in me, a freak who would command attention from the city's powers.

Our apartment was dark. You fumbled past the broken doorframe, saying, "This place is twenty years my home. Even before you. I'm not leaving. Where would I go, anyway? But I have to talk to the baby's mother before any big decisions like you are wanting me to make."

Big decisions for others was your forte, but you wanted to be left alone. And Darlene did leave. As you bumped the walker around the piles, lowering blinds, the piles seemed somehow neater. In the bathroom, everything smelled of bleach, and the porcelain had been scrubbed to gleaming with powdered soap. And the broken lock on the front door was fixed: not for good, but Darlene had explained that the handyman neighbor downstairs had come up and put a brass security lock across the unbroken section of doorframe, and she had given Nuha the new key. In the fridge was a plate of lasagna, along with milk and bananas.

You closed the fridge door. The humiliating fall had resulted in that ancient, accidental sense of community Saeeda had always wanted for all of us, and that was the moment you felt something inside you finally cave in.

———

My first birthday involved the entire building, plus my mother. Because Nuha's knee injury and the threat of eviction had inspired everyone with reckless generosity, I turned one year old with pink punch and yellow-papered tables set up on the courtyard's shaded concrete. I was dressed up in shades of gray and navy—not your usual baby clothes, but bespoke garments my father had shipped in a cedar box with a promise that these would "help the eye adjust."

The revelation that the noises in apartment 12 emanated from a human wonderchild had washed over the rest of the tenants, taking their suspicion and leaving a piercing curiosity. They lingered in a starstruck circle around my mother, granting her quasi-celebrity status because they knew so little else about her except for the outstanding accomplishment of my birth. All the while, she hugged me too hard against her hip, wearing a plastic smile of mistrust.

"Now, the blue . . ." That was Opinion Lady, who had been picking over her neighbors' behavior with zeal for the past eight years. She held the punch ladle across her lap so that no one else could hog it. "How is that again?"

"It's not anything," said my mother.

"And you call her . . ."

"Elspeth," you repeated, spitting the unnatural *p*. "But yaani, she comes to Betty." You leaned unsteadily on your new cane and dipped your cup directly in the punch bowl.

Opinion Lady tapped the ladle on her palm. "And she's been here a year? A whole year?"

Darlene breezed into the courtyard with her grandbaby on her hip, smelling of coconut lotion and sunscreen. "You always looking for problems, and it's rude." She gave my mother a one-armed hug. "Sorry, Tashi. You know how she is. It's good to see you." Her eyes lingered, looking for some sign of whether my mother had thought about calling the media.

"I heard you're living on your own?" said Opinion Lady to my mother. "Without your baby?"

"Now, what did I just—"

"It's okay," Tashi said, "really. Her father is going to get us every-thing we need."

"Uh-huh. He's feeling guilty as hell, I bet. If it's his dollar, you ask him for time off work, you ask him for a pedicure, you ask him for—"

"All right," said Darlene. "She heard you."

The older women were laughing, tipsy on the punch. Opinion Lady finally dunked the ladle into the bowl and handed a cup to Tashi. Her smile waned a little, and her look was sharp.

"If you already asked him for all that, you ask him if he knows anybody who can look into our situation here."

"Oh," said Tashi coolly, "we already know all about it."

The whole time, Tashi grew angrier. And back in the privacy of your apartment, she let loose. "When were you going to tell me you're all getting evicted?"

"I never see Betty this happy. Look at her."

"I'm not blind. I see this building. You told me it was a remodel, but Adam hired someone to research the plan. You're all getting kicked out."

"Nobody is evicting no one. Betty and I are okay. Especially if Betty stays with me. No one is going to kick out a little child and her old auntie. I'm not leaving until my body is in a box."

"I hear it almost was. My daughter was screaming and someone found you on the floor."

"It could have been you, if you were here."

"Don't you dare, Auntie. This place is filthy. It stinks. And it's un-safe."

You sucked your teeth once, sharply. "Eh yalla, then take your daughter and show me how it's done. You have done nothing but hide from every responsibility since you left your marriage. Lying about a miscarriage, holding her in your womb until you both nearly died . . ."

"That's unfair."

"Really? So you want what is fair now? You were wanting other women to raise her. Explain to me how you can give away your baby for others to raise yet you want fairness for yourself? You're not ready."

"Neither are you!"

"Look me in the eye and tell me, between you and me, that I am the disaster. You are digging holes to nowhere like a—"

"You have no idea how fucking hard I'm fighting." Tashi pushed a balled-up tissue against her eyes. "If you want to chain yourself to the stairwell, it's your prerogative. But not Elspeth. I don't owe these people anything. The best thing is to have her come back to Portland and Adam will help me. He bought us furniture and hired a maid."

"Just like that, khalas? Now you have a maid and a new couch and that makes you someone who will spend time at home and be a perfect mother? This is what you are proposing?"

"I'm not proposing it." Tashi sighed, shook out the letter she'd been holding back, and gave it to you. "She has to go live with her father. I'll visit when I want. I will get custody two days a week."

You snatched the paper Tashi held out. As you read it, a low sadness seeped into your expression, along with a new pang of guilt.

"His attorney sent it last week," said Tashi. The substance of the threat was that, yes, Adam had signed away his paternity rights during Tashi's pregnancy so that the baby could be adopted, but because the adoption never went through, and because Tashi had lied, and because the owners of the apartment building were evicting tenants and the air was full of mold, and because Tashi's own mother had attested that Tashi lacked the financial and mental stability to raise a baby . . . for all those reasons, he was prepared to sue my mother for full custody if she didn't agree to recognize his claim.

"Did you know about this?" asked Tashi. "Did you talk to him?"

You flung the piece of paper on the floor. "Your mother. She ruins everything. Coldhearted—"

"Auntie, what exactly did you say?"

You clutched the cane's handle and shut your eyes. "Your mother brought groceries after my surgery. He called the next day. I was just talking to him because he knows medicine, I was telling him how the accident happened, how heavy she was . . ."

Tashi folded her arms as if squeezing the heat back into her body. She looked more deflated than angry. "I can hire a lawyer, but I probably won't win. It says I don't have the resources to ensure the well-being of a *medically sensitive child*."

I was bouncing in my bouncy chair, buttoned up in the dull gray jumper from my father. A healthy baby, a baby invigorated by round-the-clock devotion. You had doubts, but never about my health—all the proof you needed was in the miracle of the healing cut on my brow and in the speed with which I emerged from viruses.

"Smallah look at her, she is all health and energy!"

But that was my mother's point. Other than us, no one else in the world would agree that I was fine. Saeeda had broken that wall wide open. Now the world was about to get in. It's what Tashi had been warning from the beginning, the perfectly lucid concern everyone had dismissed because she had been the one to say it.

She stuffed the paper into her backpack, and the abrupt movement knocked over a tower of your books. She knelt and began scooping them up, half-blind in the bar of dusty sunlight, and went on, almost to herself: "He will get tired of her, maybe, like he got tired of me, and life will go back to the way it was. Then someday she will grow up and make some therapists very rich, or go mad like her mother."

Not all stories end as we think they will.

I was asleep, or almost. Not really listening. You stood over my bassinet and my packed suitcases. Whatever came next in this universe of infinitely expanding possibilities kept you from resting. There is a whole genre of these agitated tales I remember only as a mood, whispered to the walls when family was elsewhere.

A voice, not yours, is giving me one about the silver gazelle. It works its way into my dreams, not as the rebel beauty who hung a djinni up by his hair and married the hero, but a nameless flash of hide in the darkness. *In the hinterlands between sea and mountains, in a hilltop village . . . A circle of colorful tents . . .* There is someone in the apartment with you this final night in Oakland, the clink of a glass in the sink. The presence feels familiar, as though on the occasional midnight, a piece of the wall sometimes turns inside out and a velvet-soft something stalks just beyond the edges of my sleep, and you go out to meet it. She has no face. No words of her own. Just a different perfume.

Cecilia once called you away from family, and you refused. You would not be moved. It was not the road for you, but you told its stories late at night and in little cardboard journals, in that tone of love galvanized by futility. As a younger woman, I used to think this was an operatically tragic decision, the loss of a whole late-in-life romance together, but I formed that opinion from a place of thirst for all of it—love, sex, care, the imaginary homes people can build for each other. And if a gazelle had come for me when I was young, I too might have caught her neck and let myself be jerked away from my life. But by the time she had made her offer, you were almost sixty, and then teenage Tashi moved in. You ended things rather than come out. You wouldn't show people who you really were under that bodacious attitude, even if it meant cutting out your own heart.

And my beloved, sometimes I can't tell with her. She promises a future together, but if I stay behind? She would move on. Cut her toenails on someone else's bathroom sink, borrow someone else's headphones and recipes. Moving on is survival. And she might not even waste any time doing it. The reason I refuse eye contact with her when we're making love is that, in fact, her eyes are not portals to her soul. There is often a door in the way.

On our bedside table is the wooden gazelle statue, taken from a box of your effects, a long-ago birthday present to you from C. that no one would ask after. Turns out that woman understood your stories better than all of us combined, and it was right there in plain sight, on long legs, with a proud chest and slender, sharp horns.

In the end, your late-in-life beloved was no gazelle. She kept showing up, even well into my era, even though it was not as often as you liked. In truth, you were primed to feel every emotion, even happiness, as a shade of abandonment—either past, potential, or happening right under your nose. So you clung to the apartment instead, that last bastion of privacy. You feared the loss of your dignity. You feared helplessness. You feared exposure. Yaani, you were a woman with fears.

I get that, Auntie. Really, I do.

But in that old memory, the small statue is in its place beyond the bedroom door, holding down a ring of sticky notes in the lamplight beside the couch. I blink heavily in the bassinet, half-asleep, separated from the doorway by small suitcases packed and ready for another future. You kiss the healing place on my forehead and tuck the blanket tighter around me. I will not see you for a long time, but for now, in this slice of time, you are still okay.

PART II

Salt

(Ages 1–6)

Q: Will you let them take me away, Auntie?
A: When the salt blossoms.

Q: Will you forget all about me, Auntie?
A: Sure, when the salt blossoms. Don't worry.

Q: Auntie, how about me, am I a salt blossom?

The universe didn't care if you had a fancy way of saying
never. In this cursed family, statements of impossibility
always amount to a challenge.

Look. Down in the coastal marshes, on hot days, I've
seen how the sun bakes the slime of the earth. A brittle
lace appears: intricate, fragile petals of salt. A whole rank
meadow of these unliving flowers.

Or there's you, the woman of two names, now a pile
of bones under Nuha Rummani's gravestone, with only a
few of us left to remember your mute winter birthday—
the one not chiseled alongside the death date. Or me,

right here, a woman out of a fable. The wind rips at my clothes and hair and dries the tears at the corners of my eyes into microscopic, crystalline flowers. The world is full of salt blossoms it schools people not to see, even when we are right here in plain sight.

The Lord's Tower Had
Many Fine Rooms

———•—•———

I took up residence in my father's house in the scorching green heart of a Portland summer.

His first task, as my mother had feared, was to establish the doctors. He got in touch with the obstetrician who had delivered me, an expert who wanted to run tests, and the hospital administrator who'd worried about a lawsuit. The studies began with a rope of blood drawn from my forearm. As the young man removed the needle, a chip of skin fell away, and my father ordered him to collect the spill of powder in a vial. He knew what the doctor would want because he, too, had been to medical school, before the accident that had taken his hand.

He prepared his house with operating-theater efficiency. I preferred your fuzzy housekeeping, but his weekly cleaning staff left the evidence of their work only in the absences: no salt grains on the counter, no smears, no laundry. We returned from the hospital's exam rooms and the house's very air had been shaken out and scrubbed. Its hardwood floors gave an amiable gleam, as though these rooms were friendly but kept forgetting who we were.

It was an enchanting house, though. A barnlike gambrel roof softened its crisp white eaves and porch railings, and it was full of hardworking windows. The walls hummed with indirect light. Honey-colored floorboards did their warm work with it, too, around the brazenness of a white living room rug. Only his furniture was old and personal. Its walnut feet were heavy like wolf paws, and under its patina, the vanity table in my second-story bedroom had a rippling muscularity, as though it might go padding through the house at night. He decorated with the family relics, including a pair of antique cannonballs.

He also gave me his mother's crib, telling me only that the row of tiny punctures along the rail were from her teeth. I stood on the mattress at night, feeling the teeth marks in the wood, tracing with my fingers everything I could reach. The caulking around the bottom windowpane was whiter and rougher than the caulking around the top. This room, in your storytelling, had achieved a kind of fame. But it didn't feel like the site where he and my mother had wept and shouted until she'd thrown one of the cannonballs through the glass. No, the room felt serene, even stable, like the surface of a frozen pond.

What to make of this all-of-a-sudden father?

He had squeezed so much material comfort out of his life by being cold at work, highly observant of and attentive to the smell of weakness, that when he directed a version of this attention at me, it was genial and quietly profuse. He watched and responded and researched. That first year, we spent hundreds of hours in his basement office, where the desk lamp was on ten hours at a time throughout his dim autumn workdays, spotlighting a mug and a drowned tea bag. The only other place for adults to sit was a deep chair in the corner whose arm held an open *New Yorker*. His law books and medical texts stood in ranks behind it and the desk, giving off the smell of glued leather. The air he breathed felt imbued with a promise of health and justice, the final order of the body in the orderly world. But this was the house's central enchantment: its hypnotic optimism.

My mother helped most evenings, driving down from the hill to show him what to do with the baby he'd excised so carefully for himself. She assisted with dinner and end-of-day chores, when Adam's phantom hand hurt the worst. She moved between the cutting board and the steaming pan, her face a mask. He sat with his wrist on the granite countertop, propping a small mirror against the flushed skin of his left inner forearm. He stared hard at the reflection of his right hand in the mirror as it played invisible piano keys, trying to convince his brain that its twin hadn't been crushed under a falling motorcycle and removed.

Those nights, even though my mother never set foot beyond the living room, kitchen, and small bathroom, he always turned on the tall lamp in the basement office, the room with the *New Yorker* magazine on the chair. Strange that the magazine was the only item in the house that never got put away; or more truly, it was in its right place already. The fold of its binding was almost gone, and its covers were rippled with disuse: a pastel map of "New Yorkistan." Its date was December 10, 2001, the week my mother had thrown a cannonball through the upstairs window and moved out.

I am uneasy giving the impression that I remember any of this.

You know as well as I do that there is a precipice between the senses and a feeling. My father's house is the actual place I lived for almost ten years, but it is also the place that it must have seemed to be at first. That's to say, I have no specific memories from those months but still dream sometimes that I live with women in an empty tower of rooms with hardwood floors and white rugs, and whenever I stumble out of the elevator, it is always in a part of the building I've never seen before.

Only it's tricky to make a story out of holes and impressions. We cover the holes with a mirror and insist that what we feel is what our eyes see.

———

My father's name was Adam. Like his biblical namesake, he was the son of an absent creator—a man who'd impregnated his wife after having been diagnosed with terminal cancer. But let's say this. Both Tashi and my father were haunted by absent fathers. In Adam's case, the ghost joined us for dinner: an extra shadow around the table or in the long china-cupboard mirror behind the good table, which my father seemed unable to see. The days my father and I were alone in the house, instead of him, I saw the back of a different man's head in that mirror—the same dense hair, but a great span of skull arcing between the wrinkled backs of small, sticking-out ears. Two massive hands maneuvered my sippy cup toward my face, instead of my father's weathered, dexterous one. This larger-than-life forebear, according to Adam, had been a clever engineer, a big-shouldered winter swimmer, and a churchgoing man with the wisdom of an Old Testament king. One who insisted on his genetic immortality after his corporeal death.

But for all my looking, I never once saw that man's face in our mirror. Only in my father's refusal to quit. Although my mother constantly entertained death at her midnight kitchen-counter meals, listening to Jibril's mumbling from her water glasses and teacups, my father was the one who had been raised to assert himself in every situation. Growing up in an iron-cold town in the middle reaches of a northern state, he was haunted by the man in the mirror his family and the congregation held up to him constantly. How could you not be haunted when your father was dead and every time people looked into your face, they were seeing not the first man, but his blurred second? So Adam was stubborn and bookish and future-focused, and it showed—in his patience with teaching me to say short words, in showing me the use of a fork, in the long and irritating process of introducing me to the house's toilets and their purpose. Also in his blindness to our occasional guest at the table.

Many years after my arrival, when I was old enough to ask him for stories, I would ask about the ghost, and he'd turn around and look at the piece of furniture holding the mirror and give me this sort of narrative instead:

"Do you see this knobby pattern on the edge of this china cabinet? It's a bromeliad. The same family as this pineapple." Between us on the dining room table was a plate of wet fruit squares, which he had been attaching to each other with toothpicks for my amusement. "The pineapple design showed up on furniture around the time of Queen Elizabeth I. Her explorers brought pineapples back from the New World and everyone went nuts for them. It's a common pattern on antique furniture." He stooped over his project again. The assemblage on the plate acquired a toothpick beak. "When you see it, think of a bunch of people in too many clothes who spent winters in castles, and then how a pineapple must have tasted to them. Like a bite out of the sun." He pinned two long pineapple leaves to the back of his creation. "So, what is a pineapple, kiddo?"

"A bromeliad."

"Excellent. Now look, it's a bird."

He spun the plate to me, my dessert. The fruit bird had a leaf tail and wings and a pointy beak. As I ate it, I would remember that you had once said that Queen Elizabeth had washed with Nablus soap. *Queen Betty*, you had called her, but I didn't tell him that, and so my father would nod approvingly as I polished off the fruit; because the more familiar we became with the factual world, he believed, the more of it we could claim as our own. And while he nodded, behind him in the mirror, the back of his own father's head would move up and down.

But that second year of my life, before ghosts and bromeliads, when the expert doctor called Adam with the results, she asked us to make the trip to the hospital to discuss the findings in person.

To her credit, my mother discovered a blouse for the occasion and was waiting in the frosted-glass lobby on time. Away from you, away from family, it was easier to see how much effort she spent on obscuring herself whenever she left the safety of your orbit—she became someone reserved and alert, a woman I didn't quite trust. The receptionist sent us straight back. I rode in a Ferrari carbon-fiber stroller that was my father's idea of a gas. Hidden, I rolled past six different pairs of waiting feet on the way to the inner sanctum. At the last moment I couldn't help myself: I ducked under the stroller's canopy and stuck my face out. People waited, bored and fumbling miserably with their little devices. A woman who was hunched in a damp red raincoat saw me right away, and as the others sensed alarm, more faces rose. Their attention seized on a blue baby staring back at them, my fatty cheeks and big eyes so nearly a reflection of what they expected to see that my color registered as a hypnotic deformity. Their shock trailed the stroller, even when my mother inserted herself in their line of sight to hide me.

Even more thrilling than this was the confusion around the first scale, then the second one to make sure the first one wasn't broken. I was twice the weight of a normal twenty-month-old but, size-wise, sort of small. I laughed at the tickle of the measuring tape as the nurse took the circumference of my limbs and torso and head. Her nitrile gloves were almost the same color as the flesh of my thighs. She put on a fresh pair to inflate the cuff around my arm.

My father sat in the chair and my mother lounged on the table, holding my body against hers. Goosebumps pebbled her skin because her blouse was sleeveless. A flutter of tension ran through her arms where they touched me, making the room feel dangerous and too bright. My father sat three feet away like he was running the show.

The expert entered the room in perfunctory business casual. She appeared to have braced herself for this encounter. Her handshake was warm but not domineering, and she had a rooty athleticism that grew all the way to the tips of her spiked black hair. Adam had selected her for her reputation as a researcher; and because anyone who worked in science assumed MD-PhDs were arrogant, the woman's humility was a surprise. As the expert opened her mouth to speak, both my parents detected a hint of disappointment in her posture.

"Stone-cold normal," she greeted us. "Let's get that out of the way first."

Tashi's muscles relaxed, but Adam was on his feet. He pulled my elbow from her embrace and showed off the chip in the crease of my arm. Since the blood draw, the rough notch had smoothed itself, but you could still feel the irregularity in the solid plane of skin.

"That's not normal," he said.

The expert was already nodding. "And we're talking it through now." Her clipboard was on her knee, covered by a blank folder. "Obviously, we all expected something else." Inside the folder were papers she shuffled around. "It took a while to get back to you because I ran extra tests. Different equipment, different assays. I even sent samples to a colleague's lab, blind." As she spoke, questions were dying in my father's mouth; the expert was somebody who briskly anticipated his reactions. "Nothing. He thought I was wasting his time. We can go through the results together and discuss what comes next."

He was still tugging my arm toward her, pushing his thumb into my skin. It hurt. "Feel it. Look at her." This crossed a line with my mother, and she swept my arm back into her embrace. "Obviously you couldn't have done the right tests," he said, towering over all three of us.

"Have a seat and I'll read you all I have."

My father didn't like to be on the weaker end of a negotiation, and he sat down, red-faced.

The expert began to read the findings aloud, handing off each page to Tashi as she got to the bottom, and Tashi took her time filtering them to Adam. His knee bounced with the effort of not standing up to look over a shoulder. The first two pages of the workup—organ function, cell counts, urinalysis, tox screens, all of that—were normal. The tests grew more desperate the further the expert waded.

Full neurological exam: normal.

Developmental landmarks: normal.

Cell cultures: healthy, typical.

Nothing unusual in the DNA markers.

Endoscopic exam of my vocal cords: all anatomical structures were as expected.

Bone density scan: normal.

Full MRI: same.

Spectroscopy of my skin dust, where the needles had damaged it: epithelial cells, typical.

"Oh, come on," said my father. "This is a sham. What else do you have?"

The expert glanced up. "The paternity test you requested, affirmative."

I felt the flinch go through my mother's legs, but she said nothing. The shock seethed around her. My mother had emerged from these several months of her family's scrutiny with a resolution not to do things that seemed unhinged—and that, probably, was why she stayed seated and quiet while she marveled at his nerve. The expert returned her attention to the folder and, finding nothing else but some X-ray films, handed the last page to Adam.

"Your daughter," she said, addressing both of them, "is healthy. Her weight is inexplicable, especially with the tape measurements, but further testing is too invasive."

"I can't accept that."

"Sure, no physician would say she presents as typical. We have to make some allowances. But so far, any measurement that would help science give us insight comes up as completely uninteresting. And I'm not giving her a spinal tap or bone biopsy or anything that will hurt, when every other test says her body is working and she is developing well. Behaviorally, she's happy and attached to you both. So here I have to default to doctor mode. If she's well, we can't fix her."

My mother bristled.

"Sorry, that's not what I meant." The expert's contrition was genuine. "I see nothing to fix. Regular vaccines are not contraindicated.

THE SKIN AND ITS GIRL   109

You can see your regular pediatrician to start getting her caught up. If anything changes, though, I hope to hear from you."

The appointment was over, and all their instruments agreed. I was stone-cold normal.

"I'm not *angry* at you," he said. "I'm *satisfied*. You're angry at me."

"You have some nerve to tell me what I feel about you."

(Was this what they said to each other? I can reconstruct the couplets of their fighting with an itinerant poet's ease. My father using the voice he used with clients. My mother's low, ferocious answer, an injured snarl.)

"You're satisfied," she went on, "but you asked for a paternity test? How is that fair? You just couldn't keep it in your pants, but you turn around and imply I'm the one—"

"You lied to me for a year. Kill me for wondering why you'd do that, even though it doesn't even touch the bigger question: Why are you still so ashamed to take her out in public? That's the real injustice."

(Here, maybe he gestured at me, where I slept on my blanket on the stiff new sofa. Or maybe I was still awake, getting fed Cheerios beside the new table in a high chair identical to the one in his house. Let's put him on a kitchen chair, his elbow propped high, the skin of his truncated forearm flushed purple, his face cut with lines of stress and pain. Let's put her beside her preposterous new toaster oven, ill at ease and shaking ibuprofen out of a plastic bottle.)

"Adam, before you claim the high road, let's pause there and remember how you gave me no reason to trust you. I did the best I could without you."

He frowned into his hand. "It was a short, stupid fever. It was wrong. I fucked up. But you were the one who said we couldn't come back from it, and I did everything you asked. The divorce papers, the adoption papers . . . Do we want to keep litigating the past or get the information to understand what's next?"

(Here, a hint of a détente. She was intent on attaining a better

future—one in which she was trusted with me. She treated the encroaching chairs and appliances he'd foisted on her as individual
questions on a complex and vaguely galling exam, all to prove she was
worth her two-days-a-week custody. But she set the pill and a glass of
water down at his elbow and touched his shoulder so he noticed.)

"Are you ashamed of our daughter?" he asked.

"I'm not ashamed of her. Good grief. The world is so unfair that
I'm scared for her. We both want what's best."

You, Auntie, were a woman with fears, too. Mostly in those years, they
were about losing your home. But when my mother turned thirty-
seven in October, you swooped down on Portland as the city's famous
roses were baring their necks in surrender to the season. Time's pas-
sage alarmed you, along with the news that I had spoken my father's
name for the first time, but not yours. At the airport curb, you directed the first cold spell at him, he who was there by himself on time
to chauffeur you to a room in his house: but instead of hustling inside,
out of the rain, you clutched a whole shopping bag of items you'd
wanted with you for the short flight, scowling into the SUV's cavern-
ous interior.

"Where are you taking me? What is this? Is too high. I want a
regular taxi."

"Tashi and Betty are at the house, waiting for you. I have Betty all
week, so you can spend every day with her. You've got my whole basement waiting. A room, your own bath—"

"Ismissalib, he puts me underground! Like a grave, for shame! No.
No."

My father, the great tactician when at work, stammered that it was
a guest *suite*.

"No one puts Nuha Rummani under their floor. And I cannot get
up into your car. Too high." You turned away, yelling vaguely into the
rain for a taxi. Mortified, Adam got out in the rain and begged you to

get in the vehicle, loaded the suitcase and shopping bag next to my empty car seat, and helped you clamber into the passenger seat, where your feet barely grazed the floor mat. As he merged into traffic, you muttered, "Or maybe this kidnapper is now putting an old lady in his *custody*. Walaw, he promises a bed in his basement, how could I refuse?"

In the before-times, your prickling would stop here, with the sorts of remarks that got muttered later between spouses in kitchens or with a snort between sisters on the telephone. Your protests were always enough to enforce respect, khalas. But now you hunkered in your big secondhand coat, hissing and bubbling with a new intolerance. This was the man who'd pried me away from you and then demanded a paternity test, the man who you said had no imagination but who came loaded with money and suspicions. I'd already been gone from you over a year, and time was going shapeless, sagging in on itself in the emptying building where you lived. Behind your sunglasses and war lipstick and coat, you struggled to sit upright in his passenger seat though the seatbelt cut into your face. When he tried to ask what sort of breakfast you'd eaten, you broke in to wonder whether he'd made a lot of money on his Halliburton stocks, and was he enjoying how well his SUV ran on stolen Iraqi oil.

My father was bewildered. "Let's not be unjust. I don't live in some Texas oil empire—this is Portland."

"Eh. You will survive it, habeebi. Money lives everywhere, like cockroaches."

Adam was not at all like the Rummanis, which is a difference that had long ago made him attractive to Tashi; but it also meant he had no understanding of the pure, accumulated hatred pouring from the other side of his car.

"How about tea?" he tried. The center console held a thermos and a baggie of lemon candies my mother had slipped into the vehicle before he'd left for the airport. "Tashi made it."

"My niece doesn't even know how to boil water. I don't want it."

Your pettiness disquieted him so much that he laughed. Behind the wig's immobile bangs and the saucer-sized sunglasses, you were expressionless as a sphinx.

The car turned in to the driveway.

I imagine your first sight of it, this house you had avoided for over a year. The honey-lit windows in the afternoon gloom, the sigh of warm steam from its chimneys, its trim bright above the muddy yard. Its bold *roominess:* two living rooms, dining room, four bedrooms, four bathrooms, laundry room, game room, attic, kitchen, porches, and detached garage. Another lovely, lifeless American palace. You got down out of the car and gazed upon my new home in disgust.

"I just decided. Betty and I will stay with Tashi all week, like always. Not here."

"But the guest room here is yours."

You waved him off and climbed the porch stairs, already calling for me.

Tashi tried to reason with you, but she had no better luck: *Auntie, aren't all the stairs to my apartment such a bother?* No, you were all health and energy. *But wouldn't the house be more comfortable this time?* No, it was too big, you couldn't relax. *So weren't the public woods and hilltop streets just as empty?* Was this a joke? The open air was always wonderful, and how refreshing to smell the evergreens! *But the apartment has no food for an extra person!* You needed but one tiny meal a day, surely my mother would not begrudge you a bowl of oatmeal. Firm in your strike against his hospitality, you perched on the side of the couch closest to the door, handing little bits of paper back and forth to me as I clung ecstatically to your legs.

"You seem to be teaching Betty all about exchanging paper," you said, taking another slip of crayon scribbles. "Trading with the skill of a banker, making her a good little capitalist."

My mother sighed. Adam's eyes were black and cold behind his tiny spectacles, and his face began to flush with helpless anger. "She tore up her deck of cards last week," he said. "So she made her own.

She thinks you're playing a game. I bet she'd love it if you stayed here."

Actually, I thought I was showing you family photographs, something you were so fond of doing at your own apartment.

"Auntie," my mother said one last time, "I'm asking. Stay here with Elspeth."

"I will stay with Betty and you at your apartment. I will not be moved."

Tashi looked sick. "Please. Auntie." She lowered her voice. "There's still a custody agreement. There are rules."

Adam leaned stiffly on the mantel of the lit fireplace, making a last attempt to smile. "Just this once. One night," he said. "And then you can either bring her back and stay here, or bring her back and leave."

You were invigorated by the victory. "What's the problem? Think. Finally I rescued your daughter. No kidnapper is smarter than Nuha Rummani."

My mother's hilltop apartment was a mess, and she was queasy with a deeper dread. "This is not how any of it works!"

"Who makes these rules? Him and his ilk, lawyering nice, fat knots in the hangman's rope? Never let them get away with it. Now you see how to win."

Tashi was going around the apartment stuffing work papers into grocery bags, sweeping at knee level for choking hazards, and in the process trying to find a missing knob for my playpen—anything not to look at you. The custody agreement was the single thread holding me in her life, and it had held for longer than she had expected. She kept her back turned as she filled the bag, shivering with tension even though the heat was on, wondering what this problem would do to her equilibrium and whether you had always been as unreasonable as Saeeda said. What she wanted right now was someone to shoot her with a tranquilizer dart, the kind made for elephants and gorillas, because raising a child across two households was already too much without an outsized, completely avoidable catastrophe landing in the middle of things. And why would you visit during a time Adam had custody? *Avoidable.* At this, her mind cleared.

"You aren't supposed to be here."

"Stinky-poo Betty," you cooed over the diaper bag, looking for a wipe, "your mama knows how everything works and where everyone is to be, lucky you, daughter of such an authority. It is not enough that I am here with you again."

Tashi finally stared you in the face. "Auntie, you said you were going out of the country for two whole weeks. You said the dates worked out, since you would arrive here for my custody weekend and not have to see much of Adam, like we always do it. Why are you in Portland so early this time?"

You hummed as you let me pick out my diaper, not quite able to hide a hesitation.

"Auntie?"

"Eh, a thing or two changed. I decided to not go on vacation. Not your concern."

My mother rarely pressed—but something in your posture shifted back, and she was angry. It was one of those disorienting moments where the habits of a relationship turn inside out.

"You don't want to travel? Now, while you have time? Go, have fun." This was the natural end of it, the place she should stop. But your presence suddenly felt unbearably claustrophobic, and she saw an opening. "Mama said the invitation was to Greece. She said you were looking forward to it. You don't want to see the Mediterranean again with Cecilia and her family?"

You engrossed yourself in struggling with the diaper tape. "I am old, I have my dignity. No one wants to drag a fossil along, ruining the family pictures."

Tashi felt a little rush of power. It was so much more than you ever said about that famously opaque relationship with C., and no wonder my mother mistook it for victory or, worse, permission to continue.

Maybe this was the trick, she was thinking—persuade you to talk about it and then convince you to take the trip, after all. Maybe it could all be salvaged—her week, her privacy—until you could come later, at a better time. She felt a floating sensation that might still be anger, as if striding out onto thin air.

"Auntie, that is a sad way of looking at it. Unfair, even. If I were Cee, I'd want to catch up on the time I'd missed with you. I'd want you to go along. Maybe it's not too late to spend—"

"Stay out of my life!" You spun around and flung the diaper at my mother. "Change your daughter! Do something you know how to do! Nothing has been so exhausting these whole long years but your total stupidity about everything! If you had your way, Betty would be growing up in some other house with a pair of perverts."

It was a shock. Tashi snatched up the diaper and shouldered you aside, though her hands seemed far away from her face, as if they were working at the wrong end of a telescope. Inside her mind a voice kept on shouting *your total stupidity* and *perverts,* hammering the gross error of mentioning the forbidden name until she felt convinced that she was about to be struck from behind, though she had never been struck. Had never even been yelled at by her favorite aunt, not like this, with loathing that seemed to come from the very bottom of the world. In the kitchen was the clank of cups shoved into the dishwasher, each clang and rattle sending its little stab through her chest. The sink ran at full blast, coughing out water, making the glasses ring. She snapped my last clean set of pajamas and wondered if she needed to sneak out, get away, maybe go far. At her temple was a little ringlet of hair that bounced with her movements, seeming to say, *Yes yes yes.*

"You are not allowed to say that he kidnapped her ever again," she said, striding into the kitchen and shutting off the water. "She goes back tomorrow. And you go with her."

"That house—"

"Used to be mine! My home! It is a *nice house.*"

"That house," you said to my mother, stabbing each word, "is where he cheated on you. It is where he took your kidnapped daughter. Where is your dignity? Your memory?"

"Auntie—"

"Open your eyes!"

My mother opened her mouth to answer but rushed out of the room, to me, and buried her face against my shoulder, tears stinging her eyes. The words she wanted to say came out as a whisper: *"If you hate it so much,"* she hissed, *"go home."* Her voice was tiny against my hair, stifling words she could not say to you aloud. They were too cruel to aim at anyone who had come far and could not return. Yet what disquieted her the most was how good it felt to say them, good as any curse.

Later.

You have threatened for two days to sleep in that coat. You have refused all food but dry toast. But we are downstairs at last, in my father's basement, surrendering. Your pride and dignity are not always the same trait, but here behind his closed door, you let out a sigh. The room is comfortable. Rain hits the high window. You sink onto the edge of the bed. I look sharply up at you from the floor. Heat from the vent swirls around me, and around you is a jet stream of wilder currents—anger, contrition, bewilderment. And shame, I realize now. Always shame.

You cover your feet in heavy socks and sit without speaking for several minutes as you scribble something in your notebook. It'll be decades before I read it, but you are recording that the sound of rain here reminds you of another place, another time, listening to the gurgle of a hillside spring under the shelter of a stone outcropping. This memory runs through you as you write, dislodging some of the days-long shame and irritation, washing it away with nostalgia for the past—a duller pain, since some of the injustices that separated you from your home were in many respects impersonal ones, originating beyond your power. Something to hide behind, even as you hated it.

Then you button the little notebook into your coat pocket. You tug my crib next to the mattress, finally take off the coat but leave on the socks, and put us both under the covers. "Betty," you say, "there is no truth but in old women's tales. So let me tell you why happiness is impossible."

Once upon a time, there was a gazelle. Her fur was pure silver-white and she was so beautiful she thought she could get away with anything. She trotted off one morning to steal a pomegranate from the queen of the djinn. But when she plucked the fruit from the tree and leapt the garden wall to return home, the queen flooded the whole world so that the gazelle had nowhere to go.

"Shame on you," said the queen to the trapped creature. "I will drain the waters and release you, but on one condition. The responsibility for that fruit is now yours." The queen explained that the pomegranate was enchanted, and each of its 613 seeds contained a single desire. "You cannot eat it. Instead, you must carry these seeds in your mouth and not let them fall, or else humans will know nothing but desire without satisfaction, and they will destroy the world again and again. Keep this promise, and I won't feed you to my lions."

After the queen drained the floodwaters, the gazelle went into the mountains so that she would not be tempted to talk to anyone, even though she was now full of desires. She swam rivers, leapt high into the rocky hills, outwaited the rain, and outwitted lions and soldiers. She watched in close-mouthed shock as Babel went up, then down, and cavalries came and went—David, Nebuchadnezzar, Darius, Alexander, Caesar, Constantine, Muhammad, Godfrey of Bouillon, Salah ad-Din, Genghis Khan, Selim I. Even though in the Surat al-Hujurat God said, "I created you into different nations and tribes that you may know and learn from each other," the armies learned only the arts of death and denuded the land behind them. The gazelle wanted to spit the seeds out. Could breaking her promise to protect the world from its desires make it any worse than people were already making it for themselves? Yaani, probably not, but she didn't want to be eaten by lions.

So, with her mouth still full, the gazelle tried to keep her vow. She drank carefully from a clear spring and slept in the sun, protecting the desires mutely under her tongue. Life became very lonely, but it would have gone on this way until the end of time if one day, a beautiful fellahin girl hadn't come to the spring and made the gazelle laugh. As soon as she opened her mouth, all the desires escaped except for one.

The 613th seed, which remained in her mouth, was justice, and because the gazelle has been running from the queen's lions ever since, this is why justice is so elusive.

"Sleep, my little pomegranate seed," you said to me in the dark.

You said it in Arabic, so the only word I might have understood was the word for pomegranate, which was *rummani*.

What Happened Was

————•————

You have to ask yourself, at some point, if the Rummani family is really so great, where were they in those years? Where were the relatives in Jerusalem, Amman, London, Miami, and West L.A.? Where was the clan, the cooperation? Where were Tashi's brother and nephews and stepfather? Where had Saeeda and everyone else gone, when one of them was a bright blue, stone-cold-normal blossom of salt right before their very eyes?

They were watching Palestine. Sort of. It's true enough, they had been watching it in the news for years, especially now that the second intifada was wearing on; they remembered that the house that collapsed in the bombing had wiped out an entire family, and the suicide bombing of a Jerusalem bus in 2002; and they watched countless funerals for years; they watched Mahmoud Abbas taking control of the Palestinian Authority in the spring of 2005, and then the Israeli settlers leaving Gaza under armed guard at the end of summer, an uneasy armistice. They were watching the resulting curfew and roadblocks and years-long strangulation of normal life throughout the West Bank, and they watched much of this in letters and on small internet news sites because no one but Arabs cared to watch so much complicated violence play out again and again on the main networks, which always got it wrong anyway.

Also, the Rummanis were watching their own children. Their waistlines. *The Sopranos*. The microwave timer. The soccer score. The weather. Office politics. The kettle. The lump in a breast, in the neck, in the wallpaper. The credit card balance. The Rummanis were a desire-ridden, anxious people, preoccupied with what was right in front of them. This quality served their business over the centuries, but emerged as a weakness once its members dispersed across the globe, out from under one another's noses.

As a result, their bright blue relative was, ironically, almost impossible to discern in the family emails, caught between your overstatements and Saeeda's understatements. I lived on this earth for two years, then three, and everyone ignored me or took me as abstract, like one of your stories. A certain kind of imagination had gone out of vogue, and when Nuha the Exaggerator and Saeeda the Betrayer told them about a bright blue cousin, they settled into believing it was some kind of put-on. They didn't want to bother with it. They had other things to worry about.

Also: my father came around to accepting a certain level of privacy. He and my mother agreed to an embargo on photographs and a limitation to traveling because somebody with an Oakland PO box address had written to him, directly and anonymously, and asked for my medical records. They wanted to confirm that I'd been poisoned.

Nothing else. Adam said it might be harassment. Or someone who'd heard a story thirdhand and gotten curious. Or maybe someone on either side of a lawsuit was fishing, because by then, half the tenants in your building had gone to court, including the ones who'd asked to put me on the news. You swore you knew nothing about it. Promised you'd try to find out who had done it and ask them to leave me alone. Many weeks passed without word, however, and at your next Sunday call, the issue of the letter was forgotten. You were visiting Saeeda because Kelly had taken a turn for the worse. At sixty-three, my grandmother had revealed for the second time in her life an openness to receiving your help, and at that late hour of your life, crisis was your lifeblood. Chaos was life itself.

Tashi took a second look at the PO box on the return envelope, frowned, and put it in her desk drawer at work.

No, chaos wasn't all bad.

Nor accident, error, or luck: *the building blocks of life,* Tashi had been told since middle school biology. And there they were, the combined edifice of those four bases, under a powerful lab microscope, manifested as the indigo splatter of a cell. The only Tower of Babel ever real to her—busy, diverse, triumphant, usually invisible.

That spring of 2006 she had the distraction and refuge of a new grant. She was grateful to be working among rodents and shelves of rank liquids again and, especially, to be doing it at odd hours. When the work involved just a microscope and a computer, she could do it at night, and in these hours she felt most like a mother, with no one watching or judging or comparing her to other women with children. Most of the experiments took a half hour to set up, and as she waited, she would then try to muse on what was bothering her. A scratching at the back of her mind, like a mouse behind the wall.

Since that terrible visit to my father's house, you'd visited other times, called often, sent handmade dolls—in short, delighted me— but something had changed between you and my mother, and to her, it still felt unresolved. My mother's therapist, whom she'd seen years ago all throughout her San Francisco postdoc, had acceded to resuming their old sessions by phone. In a call not long after the incident, she had asked her, when she thought of her aunt, what did she feel? *Disappointed,* she'd answered. It surprised her. The feeling had a deeper bottom than expected, containing not just the smarting wound of the argument but something she'd known much longer, surely since her mid-teens.

In my life, when I was the age my mother was when she'd skipped fourth-period trigonometry and swallowed an entire bottle of Tylenol in the dorm bathroom, ideas of suicide never tempted me because dying would put an end to my desires for love, for sex, for the satisfaction of curiosities—all those tensions that reeled me back to my living body. Where my mother and I differ is that I have always and simply been a Rummani full of desires. My mother is a Rummani with an incurable mental illness, and it has diluted her desires with an understandable amount of fear. When she suffered most, Saeeda told her to just try harder. And you, you thought you were being generous when you encouraged her to feel her feelings, but in notebooks, and to keep the notebooks hidden. It was the echo of that disappointment she felt now, trying to discern whether her instincts were trying to tell her something useful.

And, oddly, as Tashi shut down the microscope and locked the door, her thoughts went first to C. The woman you had hidden in your notebooks, the ones I now possess. It's true, you only ever refer to her by the first letter of her name, that overturned cup of the alphabet holding everything you didn't tell the family. But in Tashi's years with you, C. had come and gone, been an answer to an unasked question, the secret in plain sight. And as the years passed now, perhaps it was C. who had taken over your heart again. The woman knew you better than any Rummani alive, and she had stayed with you, even if at a distance.

How do I say this delicately? The truth is this: that request for medical records listed a PO box number Tashi knew by heart. It was the address Cecilia used. Tashi knew it the way she knew Cecilia's old phone number; she'd pried into the details of her aunt's life simply because, as an adolescent, she'd known it was forbidden. She'd learned only little things: teachers together, divorced, an adult son who caused trouble, a carriage-house apartment somewhere up in the hills. Whatever unsevered link had still connected you to Cecilia in the years after Tashi moved in part-time, it meant that packages you hadn't trusted to the building's mailroom were delivered instead to the PO box; it meant that certain notes on fine paper, beautiful stamps, books you enjoyed, and holiday cards were addressed to that PO box as well, often with a little inward-facing smile as you capped the pen. Tashi guessed that you kept this paper artery open because of its silence, the intimacy of a collage-by-post, a secret angle of yourself that was so unlike you it resisted attention. In fact, months could pass when she'd completely forget that the almost-clerical field of solitude around your home life was a lie.

Did Cecilia actually want my medical records? Of course not—you did.

In earlier days, Tashi would have let it go, but that old argument still washed into memory, bringing fresh anger and distrust. And in a way, she was more protective over me than Adam was. Cecilia, whom she'd met only a few times, might not welcome a call, but the lifetime holder of a post-office-box primary address should at least have more respect for other people's privacy.

At her desk, Tashi dialed the phone number from memory. She was prepared to crisply explain who she was, but the woman everyone knew as Cee made an *mm-hmm* of recognition straightaway. Only you called her Cecilia, drawing all the syllables into a kind of auditory calligraphy. But with everyone else, brevity reigned, and Cee was practical enough to know that this wasn't a social call.

"What can I do for you?"

Tashi felt every inch of distance in the phone line between Portland and Oakland. *What am I even doing?* With difficulty, she explained about the medical records request. As she spoke, she felt her anger giving way to awkwardness. The silences on the other end wilted her. She heard her voice thinning, becoming just another unwelcome intrusion.

"Okay," Cee said. "So your concern is . . ."

"I guess I wanted to know if you knew your address was on there."

Tashi repeated the PO box number. The woman, she recalled from their few meetings, was a slow responder. Words could hang in the air for long seconds before getting answered. That first day home from the psych hospital, for instance, Tashi had stood awkwardly in her aunt's doorway, with hair that smelled like vomit, in too-small shoes, asking if it was okay to change her clothes. Cee had waited for her to finish speaking, a tall woman with smile lines beside her eyes and in her cheeks, yet no actual smile, and said after a painfully long hesitation that Tashi could do whatever she wanted now that she lived here; and then she had put her purse on her shoulder and picked up a rather large duffel and left.

Now Cee sighed. "I had no idea. You know how your aunt is. I'm sure she's on to something else by now."

"Maybe. I hope. Do you know . . . She didn't say why?"

"I'm sure you're aware that she has been busy at your mother's since her birthday. You shouldn't worry. But good luck." Cee wasn't impolite. But it was the same as that day in the apartment. General warmth, specific chilliness. Or protectiveness.

"All right. I'm sorry for bothering you. Thank you." Tashi kept blurting out these phatic little conclusions until she realized that the other woman had already hung up the phone.

The whole thing bothered her so much that on her walk home through the miserable spring rain that night, she worried over the lie and what to tell Adam, if anything, and didn't bother to wonder for a moment why Cee had said *her birthday,* as if it had just happened. Your birthday had been all the way back in summertime.

For almost two months my mother had been in a liminal zone of never sleeping and feeling round-the-clock dead fatigue—a zone she was surviving by making midnight lists. She scrawled the tasks onto her hands, placed slips of paper on her bedside table, and added tasks whenever she woke up throughout the night. Phone calls, work emails, questions for Adam: she knew they had to wait for daylight hours. No calling him at one A.M. to make sure I was breathing and warm enough—none of that. Restraint was how to convince him she was a good mother and that the past was done.

Her therapist had encouraged being proactive rather than letting worries turn into anxiety, which sometimes turned into voices, so she put her shoes back on. She went out to walk the short loop down to the church door and back, wanting to clear her head.

What was worse? You, trying to snoop at my medical records—or her own choice, having trusted you in the first place to raise me for a year? Reporting the conversation with Cee to Adam would be the responsible thing; but also, withholding information could be judicious. Adam would be angry otherwise, and she had more than enough to deal with right now: research, managing grad students. Also her stepfather's inevitable death and how her mother would handle being a widow again. Her own health. The thorny question of whether to try daycare for me now that I was almost four. The lists went on and on.

A story you'd told came back to her, about a woman who became a flock of birds and broke the neck of one each night to feed her child. Diminishing herself one tiny body at a time. Is that what motherhood was—being nothing but a living list, self-disintegrating with each task that got crossed off?

Here, a longing to be null, to be suddenly done, passed over her like a vulture's shadow. *Walk to the river. Into the river.* She exhaled hard, made her attention go fully to the asphalt pounding under the soles of her bad-weather boots.

She couldn't end her life this year, knowing the looks people gave me—the postman, the driver in the next vehicle, the random dog walker. Their involuntary disgust and alarm. She had to stick around, protect me. Who could be there for me forever, besides Adam? And did she trust him that much? Certainly more than she trusted you right now. By the time she was striding back up the hill from the church, past the bus stop, past the parking lot, toward home, she was sweaty and upset but resolved. At the family dinner on Friday, she wouldn't tell Adam a thing about what she'd learned; too much going on already, no need to stir the pot.

It was unfortunate, then, that Adam brought up the medical records request again. "Have you heard anything more about it from Nuha? She said she would ask around."

Silverware clinked, a soft sound from the backyard patio, where they were eating dinner and I was smashing a biscuit against the tabletop. It was the sort of mess-making I'd almost outgrown, but Adam was too intent to notice, and Tashi was trying to cover up the kick in her heartbeat.

"She's been so busy at my mom's. Kelly isn't doing great, again."

"It seems like things are heating up with the apartment building fight again, though. I was wondering if I should send a lawyer letter to the PO box, just to scare them off, whoever they are. Or scare them out."

"Don't."

The force of her answer piqued Adam's attention. "Why not?"

"Why bother?" Tashi said. "It's a waste of aggression. And time. I don't even know where that letter is now. Give me another biscuit."

He shrugged and cut it in half for her and set the butter knife closer to her plate. It was new, the way they helped each other eat— they'd never done it when they were married, but a few years of having me around had created a shorthand for care.

Tashi shaved off some butter, thinking of you and Cecilia—exes too, of a sort. One foot forever in and one forever out. Cecilia had gotten divorced after her kids were grown, and she'd been with you since before Tashi had moved in during high school, but definitely never fully again after that. You had not been willing to come out to the family, and Tashi was still uncertain whether anyone but herself had even a suspicion.

The humps of two biscuit halves sat side by side on the plate until I loudly observed, "It a *butt*!" and my mother picked one up and buttered it. For some reason my parents seemed immune from the hilarity, smiling at me from their places at the picnic table, but seeming lost at different ends of the universe.

"Tash," my father said, "can you just ask her again? After that one bad visit, and then a lot of the other ones too, she could be doing more to mend the fence. We need to stand up to her sometimes."

My mother pushed her plate back. "Nuha doesn't see any fence, broken or otherwise. She'd club us with the fence post and make us a laughingstock if we tried to explain why she was in some kind of civility debt to us."

Adam sliced the air with his fork. "She is, though. That is a true fact."

"Don't debate truth with my aunt," she said, "or make her admit she's wrong. Starting an argument with Nuha Rummani is like rolling around in the mud with a pig. You both get dirty, and the pig likes it."

He resumed eating, focused on spearing a perfect stack of greens, chicken, and biscuit. The immobile muteness at the table felt dismaying, irritating, but calm—almost like a tiff in the best years of their marriage. Yet this new parental peace could be as uncomfortable as the silence between two gunshots.

"None of that is right," he said finally. "Except the last bit."

I burst out into squealing laughter. "Auntie a *pig*!"

"No, Adam, it's not right," she said. "It just is. Sorry my family sucks."

He didn't look at either one of us as he said, "Don't."

These small arguments, sometimes they cracked us a little.

After he'd said *Don't* at the table, no one dared speak for the rest of the evening, except for my mother's quiet goodbye to me as she slipped on her coat. *Don't ever tell Auntie I compared her to a pig,* she whispered, and then was gone.

After, my father and I lay on the living room rug, my head in the well of his shoulder as he paged through a storybook. In those years between things, my mother was still only a visitor. When a fight hung in the air, he was uneasy, as though out of the corner of his eye he really did see his father's ghost sliding across the walls.

"Where your hand?" I asked.

He pulled me close, too tired to redirect questions toward optimal educational value. He covered my eyes with his good hand. "Right here."

I grabbed his left arm, the other one. In the firelight, my blue fingers covered the scar tissue.

"I told you," he said, "it was an accident."

"Did you throw it away," I said, "'cause it was blue?"

"It wasn't blue."

"Throw me away?"

He snuggled his arm closer around me, buying time to conceal his anger. He would believe, for some years, that questions like this were because my mother and you had hidden me during my first year of life and my brain was already trained to think of my differences as shameful. "It was just my hand," he finally said, "and I would not have chosen to part with it under any circumstance."

He smoothed out my nightshirt so I didn't get cold, though I never seemed to feel the weather the way others did. He looked uncharacteristically tired.

"Did I ever tell you about the time I really did turn blue?"

"No." I buried my head deeper into the muscle of his shoulder. "Tell me stories."

And this time, he did. The one he told was about himself, which made it the first real story I ever heard outside the Rummani tale cycle, a doorway from my father's fine rooms into the possibility that the world was even more full of desire and mystery than it seemed.

Once upon a time, a doctor told a sick man that his disease would kill him soon, and the man's wife demanded a child. Nine months later, a few days after the man's coffin was put in the ground, his son was born. The mother went home to her father's house with the baby, and raised the child to boyhood.

One summer day the fatherless boy went swimming at a lake. His shoulders were narrow and weak, much smaller than his father's had been, but he had keen eyes. In the grass and muck on the bottom, his hands found a pitted cast-iron cannonball. Frantic with discovery, he kicked to the surface and brought it to his grandfather on the shore. The old man admired the cannonball from his fishing chair and told the boy how in trapper days, soldiers used to practice firing their cannons at the cluster of birch trees and cattails that stood in the middle of the lake.

The boy set the cannonball on his windowsill, and all through the rest of the summer, the beginning of school, and during the long autumn nights as the anniversary of his father's death approached, he imagined the soldiers' hands loading it into the barrel, their uniforms and drunkenness and carelessness, its eruption from the bore, its brief flight that splashed short of the island and sent the ball to the waiting mud. For two centuries, germinating.

And as the air got brittle with winter, an idea began to bloom. After school on a Friday, the boy put on boots and filled a sled with the ice-fishing tools, and went out before his mother returned from work. He'd decided already that winter was the best time to hunt for another cannonball.

Under five inches of ice, the boy reasoned, the muddy bottom would be calm. No wriggly larvae or blooms of algae. He'd auger a hole and chisel it open, then shine a beam straight down to the bottom, seeking the swell of iron in the mud. A quick dive, a change into dry clothes, a victory hike home. Last winter he'd been too small to work the auger, but now he planted his feet and began to crank it, making it bite through the ice.

As he worked, clouds sank and thickened on the edge of the lake, sending wind and pinpricks of snow into his face. He stopped to fumble his collar over his chin. At last he skimmed the last floating ice away, positioned the light at the mouth of the hole, and crouched down. Across the lake, the trees had disappeared in snow, but beneath him was a world of unearthly blue glass. The water beneath the ice was clear as a window.

Desire enchanted the boy. Every spell promises that if you want something hard enough, it will appear, dangling in front of you, dangerous, testing how much you really want it at all. And that day, he was lucky in the way only children can be: his flashlight beam cut through the water and struck its target. Nested in waving grasses beside a glinting beer can was the black egg of a cannonball.

He stuck the tip of his mitten between his teeth and tugged his left hand free. In his thick winter clothes, he knelt and tested the water. Forced his breath out in a hiss as the water came up to his wrist. After the first pain, it wasn't bad. It was cold, then almost warm. Then his bare hand didn't feel anything at all. It seemed his father whispered in his ear just then, saying this was the trick of being strong.

The boy swept off his hat. The wind froze the sweat in his hair by the time his coat hit the ice. His left hand didn't work, so he unbuttoned his flannel with his right. Excitement churned in his gut, a friction to keep him warm. He was Sir Edmund Hillary and Robin Olds and Lawrence of Arabia all in one. The wind gusted again, and his thoughts blurred.

All he could say later was that he dived through the hole to get warm.

As the water swallowed his body, the cold hit him between the eyes. It knocked his brain blank. He would try to doubt what had happened once he was out of boyhood, but it seemed so real—he swam down, like dream-flying. The lake under the ice rolled with a strange light. An eternity passed, and then the cannonball came free, and then it swam ahead of him on its own power, dragging him toward land of its own volition, shedding the mud of centuries, and on it were his two good hands, ten blue fingers clawing the iron for dear life.

Only in the coming days would his time in the strange blue world surface in his memory, crystallizing like shards of forming ice. His mother coming home and finding him gone ... His grandfather following the sled tracks to the lake ...

A white canvas, a red sled, the hole already frozen over.

A search party screaming into the blizzard.

The skeletal hillock of trees.

And on its bank, the boy slept. Behind him, ten yards out from land, was the shattered place from which he had crawled. He had turned blue and had curled against a birch trunk with the cannonball in his arms.

"Baby girl," he said now, "I promise you'll always have the two of us. Parents who stay for you, no matter what." He had helped me up to bed by now, and his hand rested on its antique headboard, gripping the wooden bedpost for emphasis.

Whatever coldness he'd dragged up from the lake that day, the last few shards of it frozen in the center of him had begun to melt. For years, tucked under my quilt, I'd stare at the two cannonballs that sat on the shelf, how they were caught between shadows and the silver streetlights like a pair of moons. I wondered which one my mother had launched through the window, and whether she'd understood that it, like me, was an artifact of something larger than the worst time in their marriage.

And honestly? Maybe something was recrystallizing between them—affinity that gathered a grain at a time. He could be generous. She could take better care of herself. They had done it long before me, until the bad period. My mother did not hate him, and she did not hate the house. She saw that he was not the enemy, at least no more of one than you. So there were times in the years that followed, putting me into my crib and then my high-sided little bed, in the months when the leaves turned their backs to the cold and every lit window in the world was an invitation, that I looked past my mother's shoulder to my father beside the bookshelf with his hand half-raised, frozen a moment before he let it reach for her.

Like the wind, the wanting in his face got loose and, after tracing over my mother's form, fled through the window and away. Yet for all her wandering, she always came back to the house. Sometimes she even slipped and called it *home*.

My father left for a week at the beginning of spring. He and some friends flew to the Southern California desert with over three thousand dollars' worth of new camping equipment to spend time in nature. My mother had wished for a vacation too, yet when he'd offered to drive all three of us to wherever she wanted to go, she'd realized that by *vacation* she meant only *sleep* and *a change of routine,* but she had insomnia and deadlines, so she'd told him to go have fun.

When she brought me to her office on campus at night, I slept. The giant building was placid in its emptiness. Revising a paper with me at her side felt almost natural to her, except it bothered her that other faculty members were free to drop by with their offspring at any time of the day, showing the babies off like chubby little celebrities, while most everyone forgot that Dr. Natasha Rummani had one of her own. It wasn't that she was ashamed of me, she didn't think; it was that she couldn't overlook people's awkwardness when they saw my picture at the bottom corner of her corkboard. Their reserve ignited something in her belly, an anger stoked by the disappointment she felt toward the rest of her family but especially at you: because for all your fiery feminism, your enduring advice had been to feel life's utmost feelings inside private notebooks. And here she was at night, not sure whether she was obeying you anyway or just being practical about what to do with sleepless hours.

On a night not long before my fourth birthday, her desk phone rang. The phone number was yours. She steeled herself, finished what she was doing, and called straight back. "I didn't listen to your message," she said. "What's wrong? Why so late?"

"You woke me up," you complained. There was shuffling in the background.

"You just called. It hasn't been twenty minutes. Is everyone okay?"

"I said I was going to bed." You cleared your throat wetly and turned on a faucet to fill a glass. "You're at work . . . Where is Betty?"

Inside the fancy little sleeping bag my father had bought me, I stirred, hanging on to a liminal awareness. It's a memory of late nights somewhere else, the murmur of a voice telling a story in a dark room. My mother's only stories were here: impersonal, microscopic, and resisting all but the concrete.

"With me. Doing a science lesson."

"At midnight. If you say so." The faucet turned off. "I spoke to somebody—you know Darlene from upstairs? She's saying she knows a person who is different like Betty."

Tashi spun her chair toward the clock. "I have twelve minutes, Auntie. Then I need to go check something in the lab."

"We were thinking, what if you bring Betty to the apartment to meet—"

"You know we don't travel with her, and I have deadlines. If you want to come up again, you can stay with Adam. Are you not at Mama's house?"

"Open your ears for five seconds! Darlene's person knows someone whose hair was fire. I cannot come to you because if I do they are sending the policemen to keep me from coming back in. I thought I left all that behind, but funny how your home-country situation catches up to you. Never mind, but you and Betty, you must come here—"

"Darlene was determined to put Elspeth on the news, once upon a time. Did you forget? It sounds like a trap." She wanted to also accuse you, but the pig comment hadn't been wrong—dragging you into the mud was useless.

"Khalas with your paranoia," you said. "We'll all have lunch and this person will tell you about a great-uncle or whoever who was different *like Betty*. Are you listening? Yes, I know, Nuha Rummani is an old fossil and lost her marbles and God forbid she believes Betty wants a childhood and not one continuous doctor's appointment, but ya habeebti, I am telling you, this is new. It is fact. Your daughter, she is blue, and she isn't the only one in the world."

My mother's lips moved, shaping the words as though exploring what they could mean. It seemed likely you had heard about the phone call to Cee, and Cee had given you some counsel. And this phone call wasn't an argument, so you must have listened to reason. The whole *like Betty* thing could be another dumb scheme, but you sounded uncharacteristically sunny, not at all mad. My mother clicked stray areas on her computer screen, wondering how Adam, the clever negotiator, would handle it.

"We agreed. She isn't to travel by airplane, and I don't have time to drive her down there right now. You just find out what you need to and tell me over the phone."

"You bring Betty here. This person needs to see."

"Betty has a right to some privacy, as you've told Darlene all along," my mother said, "which means she doesn't need to be continuously stared at in airplanes and at gas stations and by the police who you said are guarding your building—and, Auntie, is that real? That doesn't sound safe."

"The whole apartment is clean. Never been this nice in years. Darlene says this person is very old and would be happy to see a last miracle in their life."

"I'm sure that may be the case, but Betty isn't for show-and-tell. I'll ask her father. He's camping in Southern California, but he could visit. Could come see you and this person on his way home, since you say it is really important. Okay?"

The silence stretched. For a moment, my mother expected you to back down.

You coughed and said a visit would probably be pointless but yes, fine, you would make a small lunch to share, unless others wanted to come too, even though your knee hurt and you had to send out for groceries and it took you twice as long and twice as much money to make mansaff these days and it would probably all go to waste, anyway, if Adam was on one of his confusing health-food kicks. But yes, since Tashi was being so bossy, you supposed you wouldn't mind if he visited in two days, at promptly three in the afternoon, so you could all speak to this person and hear their tale.

Burning the Archives

———·—

[The tape starts with a click and a thrum. My father's voice, a soft baritone says,]

Hello hello hello. Test . . .

[The silence around him suggests Nuha's bathroom: unforgiving acoustics, unequal to the hard tile corners.]

When there is no other beginning but the broken middle of things, we find ourselves in a kind of limbo, in empty towers, following branching hallways, whispering to the walls. Searching for a chance to find others, to build sense out of similarity and affiliation.

I can't blame you for having gotten lonely sometimes, nor for trying to compete with my father in the hunt for an explanation. At stake were two futures: one where all the books of law and medicine behind his desk got to tell my story, where the world absorbed me, and another one where I kept being a wonder, an argument against the disappointing order of things.

Elsewhere I have mentioned that I work in an archive. My current work is for a minor museum—its specialty is money, but never mind that. Whether I hold a piece of scrip or a coin oxidized by the ages to the consistency of biscotti, so much of the story linking these pieces to other pieces depends on context. Often that context is full of excitement, as well as many holes. Only through great leaps of improbability does an event remain memorable; the rest is for the scholars.

Like my beloved, I have an unwieldy institutional employer, a fondness for extremely salty snacks, and the role of being a parental minder. These were the first things we had in common, in fact, when the context of our respective jobs brought us together. We also agree that the past is as difficult to discern as the future. She knows I have spent much of my life fearing and preventing a terrible obituary. She has lost friends to suicide, and she mostly understands, but she lacks the specific fears of our familial context. How much of my fear is overblown? What will happen if I do leave? The stories I know treat loneliness as a motivation, a cause of misfortune—but also, I just want to spare Mama from further pain.

And yet, Mama and I both know that I am causing pain for myself if I stay. We both know that this self-sacrifice is noble but means the undoing of future joy. We know how love tends to elude us Rummanis. She insists that she is glad I am in love with someone, has told me to please go, don't worry. She means it, which somehow only adds to the anxiety.

I went rifling around in her cluttered house and that is a major part of why I am standing here at your headstone, Auntie, with this bag of your notebooks, the closest thing I have to reading your mind. I also came upon a box of mementos, including this tape. I suppose I was looking for it; I am good at finding valuable artifacts in a mess. I set the bundle of your notebooks aside, because I am also trained to work methodically and simply wanted to hear your voice again. So let me shuttle myself back to what I had begun to say about their evidence before I reach into this bag of notebooks atop your headstone, warming in the midafternoon sun like a wrinkled basilisk.

The feast is special, as so many things are, only in retrospect. The family calls it the Last Lunch, for it was the last time Nuha Rummani would ever host a meal at home. Yet if I read the spaces in the notebook pages and in your irritable grumbling in the tape's background noise, you were feeling anything but gracious that day. You were still closely nursing a grudge against my father for his fruitless doctor's appointments. Outshining it was another anger, too—at Saeeda, not just for her role in what you still called my abduction but also for showing up in the morning, six hours early, with a plastic caddy of spray bottles and yellow gloves.

The nerve, the sheer inconsideration. The chemicals. Bleach by the cup. Foaming squirters. The apartment air was unbreathable as you grated your spices.

"Walek khalas, I don't know what I'm tasting anymore," you complained.

"Fazeea. You are impossible," said Saeeda, clearing the couch. "Why here? Why this place? All you had to do was ask me and we could have done this lunch at my house. My nice house, with room for everybody—"

"Next to the hospice bed, to be goggled at like strangers—"

"Haram aleiki. He's not as bad as that. Yaani, here is better? Your guests have to climb dark stairs or risk life and limb in the elevator and breathe this poisoning-me air."

"Poison you? You are poisoning yourself with those crap cleaners. I have a whole bag of good green soap under—"

Saeeda turned on the vacuum cleaner. Her own machine, for which she'd allegedly risked her life in taking the elevator. You plucked out your hearing aids and bent over a bloody shoulder of lamb, rubbing the spices in. A few inches above the hunch of your back, a sharp, straight column of light entered the kitchen window, igniting a frenzy of ash and dust overhead.

[My father's stubble rasps against the microphone.]

Interview with Frankie, last name unknown, March 30, 2006.

[The words echo a little—he has stepped out of the bathroom and into the hallway, heading for a swell of noise in the kitchen.]

Sometimes at the museum I have occasion to handle an object that is very old or very obsolete, and before the knowledge of it enters my mind, some other faculty takes over and the world around me dissolves. Sometimes an artifact brings its own context, a potent one that overpowers the real, diminishing the authority of the everyday. It's like, for a moment, I can feel the double shadow, a sense of everything the archives don't say, a catharsis I didn't know I needed. It all seems on the verge of making a complete, final sense. Then whatever it was fades like a mirage, and I'm still at the workbench under a buzzing light, holding a bit of copper or a little string of shells. A message light blinking on the phone, a toilet flushing in the breakroom . . . The only thing that has changed is a faint pang of absence.

I suppose you were craving that other kind of completeness when you invited Frankie to lunch, a desire I understand because that's what I was looking for when I went sifting through old boxes at my mother's house. And when I heard, in the background, your voice for the first time in twenty years, I sensed an imminent clarity: the real world beginning to bubble and fall apart, breaking away to reveal a longer truth behind it.

But usually epiphanies don't work that way.

The guests weren't the staff of *Better Homes & Gardens,* you'd insisted. Today was about answers. About discovering hidden order. Everything could change in a moment, if we let it. You knew epiphanies didn't work this way, either, but you could sometimes bully the world into making sense.

With less enthusiasm, Saeeda took the pictures off the hallway nails, revealing the twenty-year smoke stains. Then she set off through the rooms, pumping a mist of upholstery deodorizer through the air. An old grudge of her own: somehow her daughter had always preferred this hovel—and al-Nakba herself—to a proper home and mothering. This was not how a home was supposed to look, barricaded into a construction zone. She felt vindicated for having betrayed us to Adam.

Saeeda snapped a tablecloth across the scarred wood, reciting the litany of what was wrong. Currently, to induce the old tenants to leave, the new owners had tried hiring workers to do night labor; stacked towers of heavy paint halfway across the interior doors; entered private homes at unpredictable times, looking for violations; and when all that failed, last week, they'd filled the ducts with insecticide. It was only a matter of time before the other holdouts abandoned the place, and the police would come and evict anyone who still tried to hold on to their flat, so that all the units could be rented to different people for a fortune.

You knew this, but rather than think about what to do next, you hung out with Darlene. She was a good neighbor. She shared your desperation about losing a home. Also saw your loneliness and understood your sense of grievance against Adam. One day she made coffee for you and promised an interview with someone full of answers to an entirely different set of questions, and just like that, you were in. The idea to cook a feast had come over you like drunkenness. You arranged flowers under Saeeda's disgusted side-eye, humming to yourself. Saeeda didn't trust Darlene, and your eagerness seemed to prove a suspicion: maybe you were an old woman who'd lost discernment, ready to charge down any road that promised answers you already agreed with.

Arriving at the dimpled brass of the front door, my father entered the hated edifice full of pessimism. His phantom hand felt the size of a frozen turkey. During the drive from the airport, the pain had climbed his arm and into his shoulder. Now he fumbled for the banister, wanting just to stop and rest the invisible frozen turkey on the ground. Turn around, go home. Tashi would thank him for none of it, either way.

He had agreed with Saeeda since the beginning. Taking a baby out of this mess was a mercy. Long ago, after his mother had died and before the court released his inheritance, he'd spent a year in a bad place, sleeping behind barred windows and waking to needles in the hallway. Climbing the stairs, both then and now, he boiled with old anger. Places like this, he thought, were evidence that humankind was on a slow, deserved course toward suicide. We kept refusing to make living conditions like this impossible.

But just then, the smell caught him. Upstairs, pieces of meat had been stewing for more than an hour, diffusing the tang of garlic, spices, fat, salt, and a whiff of toasting bread. The smell overrode the sick-making reek of insecticide. He climbed to the scarred door on the third floor, not quite noticing that he was light-headed. Knocked. The full current of smells swirled out from under the door, and when Saeeda unbolted it, he was relieved to see her and not my aunt. The pain in his arm made him vulnerable, yanking on his nerves all the way into his chest.

"Excuse me, I—"

Oddly, when he stepped into the dense air of my aunt's apartment, his trachea wanted to crawl out of his throat, and that was how he realized that next to his hunger was a sudden wave of nausea.

"Come in, come in. Sit by the window. Breathe," Saeeda was saying. He tried again to greet her, but the churn in his belly was making the floor go slantwise.

"No, he needs to go wash up," Nuha intervened, trailing cigarette smoke. "Sleeping in the dirt for days, I hear. Cut his trip short because he wanted some good Arabic food. Well, if he wants it, he has to wash." A barb of silence—one of Saeeda's looks, probably. Nuha pushed him farther into the apartment, toward the bathroom. "You'll feel better if you wash. You know, when I moved back to Nablus in '48, there were thousands of people sleeping out in the dirt because the Israeli army had blasted their homes to smithereens. But, you know, now people camp outside for fun. America is a free country."

My father pushed the bathroom door shut. My aunt's monologue went on, muffled but refusing to be curtailed. He hung his head over the sink and blasted the water.

This damned place, he thought again. He'd gotten me out of it, but being done with it—that was a whole other story.

On the porcelain shelf beneath the mirror, he placed two items. The more valuable of the two was the silver tape recorder he had purchased for the occasion. He figured he should probably test it. As he reached, his face stared back at him from behind his reflected knuckles, gray-skinned and older than he thought he'd look at forty-one.

His other artifact was a square drink napkin. My father had thought about the interview on his flight from Palm Springs and had filled the square with his typical, responsible queries.

What is your full name?
What is your address and phone number?
Can you describe what you remember?
Can anyone else corroborate what you're describing?
Does any evidence exist, and if so, where?
Do you know of anyone else like this person?
What is their address and phone number?

Let me say that again. My father, whose DNA had produced a radiantly blue child who weighed as much as quarried limestone, against all laws of science, was about to encounter someone who claimed to know something about people like me. A firsthand witness to another miracle. And his best question, the one he wanted to ask twice for posterity, was for contact information.

It washes over me differently now. I first heard the tape in my teens, when he played it for me. I had already taken the relevant conclusions from the fact that I had no crushes but on girls, and had come out first to my unsurprised mother and then to my unflappable father. I had already found books about Palestine and queer kids and Krishna and the blue people of Appalachia; about migrations and colonization and neocolonialism and how language shapes the brain. I had learned that trees might communicate with one another and heard all manner of fairy tales, and for every new thing I learned about myself in the world, the world only ever became larger, my hunger for it keener. I was mad for it, in whatever form, and so the tape was only one more question adrift on a sea of tantalizing mysteries. But as the years gave me useful breakwaters in this sea of all that was possible—some way to order all the knowledge I will only ever halfway understand—the tape stands out. My father's unimaginative questions were, in truth, as good as any: because it's only the miraculous and the truly strange that resist all reason, reminding us of the tender limits of our humanity.

[A tree-bark voice cuts into the silence, roughing each word into scores of tiny syllables.]

My name is Frankie. I am ninety-four years old. My popo is the one you need to know about. He's buried in San Fernando Cemetery in San Antonio. Don't know the plot offhand.

———

Why *had* he come? He fully expected this meeting to be a load of horseshit, one of your fanciful and increasingly hallucinogenic tales from the phone calls to me. Gazelles! Fires! Fortune-tellers! The trip was an unkind way to humor you, a waste of everyone's time—and it was why this tape, no matter what it contained, would get chucked straight into a box in his office drawer, untouched for years.

Exhale. He made himself imagine that whatever had upset his equilibrium was now leaving his lungs. Picked up the bar of soap and inhaled. A blank smell. He twisted the crystal tap until just a trickle of cold water spilled out, washing over the sound of voices in the kitchen.

Why had he come, really? Because Tashi had asked. No, it was because when she'd asked, she had been jealous of the camping trip, which had surprised him and maybe meant something—he'd assumed she wanted nothing to do with his friends and would rather keep me all to her herself, hiding out in her hilltop crow's nest. But perhaps he had been guilty of caricature. He couldn't stay stuck in a sense of futility forever. Instead, he could cheerfully terminate the trip, show her that he could manage both her mother and her most difficult relative, be a master of both order and chaos. Maybe even try a family vacation soon. Be future-oriented, normal.

This is where his attention was, then. On a future with his ex-wife. Normalcy.

He balanced the soap on its tray and buried his face in a towel. Came up for air and searched his reflection one more time, gathering himself.

[Sound of coughing. An inward suck of breath, drawn over a saw blade.]

My address? He wants my address . . .

[Darlene's voice, younger by decades.]

It's okay, Frankie. Don't worry about that one. Just tell him what you came to say.

[The saw-blade voice again:]

Where is this baby? Somebody show me this baby . . .

"Come in, come in. Welcome. Please make yourself comfortable. Can I get you some tea?"

The guest of honor was a husk in blue polyester pants, someone whose complexion was a translucent gray but perhaps in earlier decades had been a delicate, freckled taupe. Her face was so age-slackened that it seemed almost genderless, a wooden mask over deep, small eyes. She set a little cardboard suitcase down beside the television.

"Some pictures for later." Her voice was like fistfuls of gravel. "How do you do?"

"This is my godparent," said Darlene, as she guided her to the table. "Frankie."

Under the bags beneath Darlene's eyes, a fan of veins stood out on her cheeks. Behind her glasses, her eyes bulged a little, given the exhaustion of still living in the building.

Limbering up to your duties as a host, you set a cup of tea and a honey bear beside Frankie's fine, wobbling wrist. "How do you do?"

"Is this coffee?" said Frankie. Her dark eyes, shrunken behind lids a size too large for her face, met yours only long enough to convey suspicion.

"Can I get you something?" asked Adam. "I'm the girl's father. Thank you for coming." He held out a hand to shake. Frankie was still looking for coffee. His hand was out there until it got awkward, and finally he settled on patting her shoulder. "Well, it's nice to meet—"

She flinched. Her deep-set dark eyes flicked over him, over his relative youth and bright hiking clothes and even his missing hand,

and dropped back to the teacup. "I thought there would be a baby," she said. "Who are you?"

"We can't travel with her on a plane. She's a conspicuous child."

Without looking up, Frankie blew a puff of air. "My popo took the train to Galveston the year he died. They didn't want to let him on, either." Like a winter draft, her voice was only a faint stirring of wind, but enough to raise bumps on the flesh. They all waited for more. She pulled her napkin onto her lap and patted the tablecloth for a spoon. Darlene squeezed her shoulder, asked her what year that was, but Frankie just looked confused. "I wouldn't know. It was between two wars . . ."

You had not felt young next to anyone for a very long time. You tried to see it as a good omen for the day. "Sit. Eat. We will not taste the food if we are talking too much. Sahtein!"

Yet after everyone had gotten themselves arranged around the food, you observed with some disappointment how your four guests looked more overwhelmed than delighted by the acres of lunch sprawled between them. And Frankie was still looking for a spoon.

"Sahtein," echoed Saeeda. "We might as well begin eating if we want to finish the salad by tomorrow."

[After another click, the tape jumps to the scrape and clatter of the feast.]

Born in January of the eighteen hundred and sixty-fourth year of the Lord, on a bloody corner of the plantation called Calvary Hill. You know Baton Rouge? Around those parts, once upon a time. But not that long ago.

[Something rattles and the saw-blade voice is suddenly right next to the microphone.]

Yes. Yoruba and Choctaw and Cajun and some other . . .

The recording ceases to be crisp. Even the high-end cassette player in the museum basement can't extract quality from the bleary recording that follows. It's present, but Frankie's voice, that cord of sound that was about to tell a living memory, becomes ambiguous enough to give the doubters their opening. I remembered its sounding clearer twenty years ago, but we all hear what we want to hear. My father and Saeeda weren't listening at all. Only you and the tape recorder sat there with open ears, and no one would trust either one of you. But even if it were perfect, an A+ artifact with affidavits and certificates of authenticity, most evidence still casts a double shadow: it reminds us that there is plenty more we don't see because we didn't ask the right questions.

My popo was born in January 1864, on the plantation called Calvary Hill.

He came into the world smooth as Jacob's chin. When the Union lost at Red River, his hair began growing in as coils of flame. Little baby sparks. And a tendril of an idea caught flame, too, in his mother's head: Escape from here.

Escape from Calvary wasn't impossible, but no one would travel with her because her baby's hair was bright as a signal fire in the dark. She, my great-grandmother, tried to extinguish him in the mule's trough—a baptism that nearly murdered him. Still he burned, and no one agreed to go with her.

She tried to shave his head bare as the day he was born, but he blistered her hands. So the band of travelers left them behind.

Then they were alone, just my grandfather's mother and his fiery self, on Calvary Hill, waiting for the Yankees to come with their dead eyes, with their greedy maypoles wanting a woman.

On their third night alone at Calvary Hill, the sky rumbled. A company of Northern soldiers took shelter in the house. The sun disappeared, and soon the skies poured rain that ripped the moss from the boughs. Even under that torrent, the boy's hair could not be snuffed. He burned and burned. When the dark came, a sentry's shout cut through the wind and rain-splatter. Mother and son were about to be found in the coop where they were hiding, and she knew that surely, as these things go, she would be passed around between men in the house, and they'd dash her child's head open on the hitching post.

But instead.

The nearby levee broke. And with the black night came a flood roiling and rising about the trees like an eerie new ocean. Silver froth lifted the boards where she and her burning child sat, bathing them in silver light, sweeping them up and out—over the fence, past the barn roof, west, terrifyingly onward. The bluecoat's wet uniform tugged him down; his lungs filled with the deluge. The last thing he saw was a woman floating past, clinging to boards bobbing at the water's surface. In his delirium and fear, she appeared cut from the night sky, draped in a fluttering dress, braced upright on the prow of a heavenly ship. She turned a fearsome gaze on him and drew a bundle of fire to her breast, carrying away the last light of his world.

So, one woman continued a westward journey by water that had claimed two million others.

The land dried, and the air dried, and the leaves went to dust underfoot.

Still she carried her child, my grandfather. She walked west after the sun, following its hot track across the sky. Remembered an echo of a story about a house like a great tower, and a road that traveled in a great circle from its doorstep of departure and return, the house of birth and death. Walked and walked, until a rancher took them in and married her.

He was built like a badger and clever enough to have deserted General Pedro de Ampudia's army before the rout at Monterrey, and he had gotten himself some cheap property in Texas that became their home. Maybe it wasn't true that all roads made a big circle, because this place felt like a long way from where she had started.

Her boy grew up there, happy. No hat could sit upon the beacon of his head. My handsome grandfather. Along the braided copper muscles of his arms and across his shoulders, his skin glowed with an undercurrent of fire. At night, he slept on a slab of Hill Country limestone that was hot as coal by dawn. He woke an hour before the other ranch hands to shave every inch of his body bare, or else his situation would burn off his clothes by noon and embarrass him. But there was nothing for his eyelashes, which were long and heavy, and they slid over his sleepy eyes. When he stood at the stockade knocking dust from his gloves, more than one of the townswomen felt a bit of answering heat.

We liked to say that he walked alone into all the county's infernos—into burning barns, wildfires, explosive silos, crackling farmhouses—and saved a thousand lives, but only in his tall tales did he have a fraction of his mother's mettle. For a young man born in horror, with shattered blood in his veins, the life he lived was routine and gentle. He became a very good storyteller and married a girl from town. As did his sons, who were very handsome and normal except for being so comfortable around fire.

On Independence Day every year, he'd let the children from town light Roman candles on his sideburns, until, in his old age, he finally went bald. The children of his life still got around him every chance they could to hear him tell his tales: the woman who sailed the stars, or the mother who turned into a flock of finches and killed them one by one to feed her children, or the strangest story of all, about the very big family in the very big house at the top of a road that went in a circle. He told it different every time, sometimes funny and sometimes sad, about how the family forgot how to speak to each other. The vowels and letters got all jumbled up in their mouths until, one day, no one spoke the same language anymore, and every time they left the house they lost their way home, even though the road began and ended in the exact same place.

My popo's only dissatisfaction in his long life was the mystery of his father, his blood father. Whenever he asked, the most his mother

ever said was "Your father was not a bad man. Don't you worry,
mijo." The final endearment always sounded a little foreign in her
mouth, but it was as good as any other, because she had come into
the world unrooted and felt like a stranger everywhere she ever
lived. She took the story to her grave.

I listened to the recording again at work, through headphones, and as I finished, my skin prickled. It was an alien sensation. My arms and the back of my neck felt lit by a mild current.

The story answered nothing, but it rhymed with what you used to tell me. The great house of humanity we all built together, and its ending in confusion—possibly you were right all along. Under everything that divided people, there was one common wire. And for a moment, it ran through me, sparking.

But you were dissatisfied with the Last Lunch for years. Adam and Saeeda didn't have the right attitude. Saeeda even poked a little fun after the guests were gone. *Why couldn't our Betty have gotten the burning head of hair?* She knew that your own mane, before cancer, had been a bonfire of buoyant cinnamon-colored curls—a physical asset so voluptuous and immodest that you used to brag of having to wear a headscarf the way other women wore blouses.

You ignored the gibe. Nobody had the right ears, and your feet hurt.

As for my father, he'd left in a good mood. Never mind that he had cut his camping trip short or that the building was oozing toxins from the vents, and all for a preposterous story. The point was, he could return to Portland as a bearer of good tidings, having had a pleasant solo lunch with Tashi's family and childhood neighbor: something he had never done even when they were married. He could tell her that the story was just more evidence that he and Saeeda were right to be concerned about what your building was doing to you.

His differing impression of the Last Lunch must also have been further tinted by what happened afterward. My mother was pleased with Adam's effort, and in the seasons to come, she began to spend some nights at the house.

And then there was Saeeda, still hanging around after everyone had left.

"Come with me," she said.

"Of course I'll walk with you to your car. Just let me find the topper for your leftovers . . ." You knew what she was really asking, but she'd made that irritating joke about the hair. You felt ugly, and the kitchen drawer was a mess, but somewhere in there was the perfect size of Tupperware.

"Yaani pack some clothes. This stuff in the vents. I still smell it with the windows open. How can you bear this?"

Out came a round yellow sunburst lid. It fitted perfectly over the mansaff. "Eh ya habeebti, the lawyers are working on it. Relax."

"The lawyers! Lawyers are working here, and they are working there, and they'll be working at the end of world. Adam fell sick, and he's in the prime of his life. You cannot think you are safe to sleep here. The room smells like death."

You tsked. "So, use better soap next time."

"Wake up and be serious," Saeeda said. "No lawyer is going to rescue you. It's time to leave. We have lots of space, and you can stay with us for good. Or until you find another flat. Come with me home."

But you just settled the Tupperware in the bottom of a plastic bag, tied the handles, and loaded the food into the walker you called your adventure scooter. "Remember what they say: if you insert yourself between an onion and its peel, you gain nothing but its bad smell. Do I look like an invalid to you? Yalla let me help you out to the car."

After Saeeda drove home alone, you caved in to your agitation. You propped open your windows and the big fire-escape window at the end of the hallway and dared anyone to come up and rob you. Nowadays, the worst that might happen was that some poor soul would wander in from the street and spread his bag on the hallway floor among the paint buckets. You locked the door but didn't fuss with the dead bolt, then went and lay on top of the covers, too tired to undress. You even tried scribbling in your diary, filling up a few pages between the grocery lists and shit lists. Yet somehow, you couldn't calm down. Hadn't the day been good? How could they not hear the similarity? Frontiers, conflagration . . . Not a one of us had a real home to go back to, and you recognized that your agitation was, in part, a dull fury. You'd been unhoused so many times. At least the fire-haired boy's family hadn't nagged him to leave a perfectly good apartment.

And here we begin to come to your inky notebooks.

You wrote that your very bones were crawling, as though previewing the grave and its vermin. You wanted to call Cecilia (always "C."), but that connection was as muddled as ever, and the hour was too late for old women to call each other and not incite a panic. You worried about this—panicking others—even as your breath shallowed, until your breaths seemed to leapfrog in your throat, stacking gulps of air, one on top of another, inside your chest.

Calm yourself. Calm thoughts. Exhale.

Once upon a time, when you'd lain on one half of the bed like this, my teenage mother had flopped down on the mattress and fallen asleep against your back. As Tashi's breath had lengthened, slowed, and deepened, steady as ocean waves, a habitual knot of tension between your shoulders had dissolved. It was the first time you'd ever felt like more than a convenient childcare solution for the Rummanis. That night long ago, you'd realized your new, powerful protectiveness over her. Felt a natural kinship with her awkwardness, defensive whenever Saeeda poked her to stand up straight, not walk pigeon-toed, and smile more. You recognized something deeper and gave her refuge.

Some people would never pass as normal, Cecilia had said. Just love them.

A shadow was dancing on the edge of your vision right now, like a floater. Rather than look straight at it, you sank into what seemed to hurt more: Tashi herself hadn't come. You were alone because some-how all that old love hadn't stopped you from being so hard on her now. Even Cecilia had given you a talking-to. What old curse made people bring out their worst selves, and so late in life? Turning over those age-spotted hands, the wrinkled and pitted skin, you didn't rec-ognize yourself anymore. An old estrangement repeated, like an echo, and it made your heart beat harder in its cage.

The questions I would have asked at the Last Lunch, had I been old enough, still float in the static before and after my father's tape ends.

Q: Was love possible because he didn't look back?
A:

Q: How many times do you need to lose everything before
   regaining your innocence?
A:

Q: Are strange bodies really the trouble? Or will humans
   find a problem anywhere?
A:

The Babel myth was your invention, Auntie, and I want to believe you were wise enough to wonder these very questions on that day. Perhaps you just lacked the courage to say them aloud—you were even more afraid of your sexuality than anyone knew. You barely even wrote about it, for shame. Although the body is the best source of information about bodies, archives are nearly immortal. They are a backstop on the endless second-guessing about the past, and a cor-nerstone of my work at the minor museum. I can't always trust that the artifacts are evidence of what they claim to prove, but they are a kind of body, an idea made physical.

I almost forgot to say: it was a kindness to know that someone like fire-boy existed. I can't say that it was useful, but it helped. After I heard the tape in my chaotic teens, one point of hard contrast between my body and the rest of the world softened. It was like when I'd come out to my mother by saying that after braiding my classmate's hair in detention we *might have* kissed, and that my heart was still butterflies, and my mother just put her arm around me and said, *It's normal.* And there were other experiences, too: the friendly curiosity when another Arab heard my family name for the first time. Or the joy of coming out to other queer people at work, saying *my last girlfriend* and feeling a lock slide open. All of it together was *trust,* a practice you never allowed yourself. Confession and reward. Even if the contents of a degraded tape were evidence of nothing except that you had a neighbor who saw your pains and wanted to offer aid, it makes me glad that you were seen and cared about. I am also sad, for you never quite knew the riches of your community. You'd already decided that there could be no reward big enough for confessing your secrets, end of story, let's move on.

A copy of a photograph from Frankie's cardboard suitcase survives, as well.

My father documented one of the pictures with his cellphone. The first image was a labeled portrait of Frankie's popo in 1914: stiff collar, stiff face, gravely staring into the twin lenses of a fine Homéos 35mm camera, whose early technology blurred as much as it revealed. A second image captured the careful label on the back. Sometimes I still study the white smears that mar the original portrait. Above the eyes, around the ears, across the top of the man's head is a halo that could be film damage—or, if Frankie was telling the truth, points of dire overexposure. Places where the open shutter was blinded by fire.

A Very Young Baby with

Enormous Wings

———·—·———

To support her excellent housekeeping, my grandmother Saeeda kept good records. During the early years of her husband's decline, she had heeded internet advice and noted what he was forgetting:

That he'd placed his wedding ring in his pocket, not by the sink.
That the laundry baskets were emptied yesterday.
That the word for butter is not *silky cheese*.
That the lemon tree died last August.
That he'd already gone to work today.
That his stepson lived in Singapore now.
That he'd received birthday gifts.
That the word for ambulance is not *mobile hospital*.
That the bathroom is not the corner by the kitchen sink.
That Tashi was alive; that all those years ago she had not succeeded in her attempt.
That his brother was not in the room, nor alive.
That all his family was gone, too.
Her name.

His doctor ceased to find these informative, and Saeeda simply watched this great caving in from a seat beside a hospice bed in the living room. For the first time in her life, her meticulous home began to feel truly empty. Even her legendary pragmatism couldn't banish the suspicion that no matter how often she dusted her collection of ceramic flowers or wiped the kitchen spigot, she was cursed to be surrounded by people who were losing their minds. And when you, Auntie, finally agreed to come to live with her a year after the Last Lunch, she was convinced that this curse was true. The court had upheld the ruling that you were trespassers in the building, and the law firm sent its bill, and the police posted a deadline for eviction. The world was tipped in favor of the disappointing order of things, and your home-country situation had caught up with you.

Sickness creates its own routines and sudden, new traditions. I had not traveled except once in my first four years of life, from your home to my father's, but the Second Husband's decline required Saeeda to stay home with him. Tashi and I drove to Palo Alto for Mother's Day that year, just after you moved in. You wrote in your notebook that the ambient crisis fostered helpfulness, and the usual tricky dynamics were forgotten. Promises were even made to repeat the visit next Mother's Day, inshallah. Meanwhile, the Second Husband hung on piteously. Inside the pages of a fresh notebook the following spring, you taped a California poppy. The label underneath it reads, *Spring 2008*.

I haven't kept all this to myself, you know. Mama remembers certain things. But she is angry about what the box from her attic contained. The anger is not what she needs right now, she said, and so she put the whole matter aside to focus on supporting me in whatever I decide to do. (*Nuha Rummani made enough trouble in her life and doesn't need to do it from beyond the grave*, etc.) But yes, she said, it is a pretty poppy.

What she doesn't say: she is now older than Saeeda was during these events, and like her mother that year, she knows she is on the precipice of a loss. Grief is simple. It comes whole, a stone on the heart.

None of it had been easy on you, though. You'd slept with your out-rage beside you, inside you. You had packed it into the moving boxes, held upright by one thick cable of pride, and had overseen its instal-lation in that guest room of Saeeda's Palo Alto house. It had sim-mered as you found a place for the wooden gazelle beneath the bedside lamp, and grown hotter as your longest friends and even dear Cee expressed relief that you were now living in a habitable space—relief, though you'd just lost your home of twenty years! They saw only a geriatric woman shuffled into a single-story home with safety bars and no-slip rugs and felt that a useless thing had at last been stored correctly.

Other Rummanis were no help. They all had their own troubles and were only politely interested in updates. Ah, the blue one, the Rummanis said. She isn't already in school? What is Tashi waiting for? Our family has at least twenty-four doctorates between us . . . And so on, as if they lived in a darkness knit from distraction and ego. Maybe they'd stayed away so long not because they hadn't forgiven Saeeda for selling the factory, but because by selling it, Saeeda had cut the family loose from its collective spirit—and then the bombing had crushed not just the stones, but the family's past. There was evil magic at work, you believed, causing them to move on from even those most important stories, until abandonment was the only theme that mat-tered.

For her part, Saeeda hadn't missed her relations in almost thirty years, not truly, but with second widowhood looming, she discovered certain regrets, a faint surprise that it had been so easy to cut herself off from a tree that had given her everything. You were in another bout of complaints and distress, no comfort at all. So, she summoned Tashi and me to please spend another Mother's Day in California.

Me, I had done what babies do. I paid almost no attention to time while it stuffed years of experiences in me, warped and disorganized like someone packing in a hurry. This was my second trip back to California, and I could not wait to show you how many new stories I could recite front to back without a mistake.

Adam drove us both to the airport. He had produced almost no objections to the trip, but Mama still kept casting suspicious little glances at him. *It was time,* he had said with a shrug as she'd stuffed the suitcases full; if a short flight was a problem, how could they continue to talk about school, or even normal life? I was a good car traveler. I would be fine in the air. And he had projects he couldn't reschedule. He promised to help make the dull ten-hour drive whenever it was time for her stepfather's funeral, when they were both free to share the work, and in the meantime we should just go have a nice Mother's Day, like last year.

Now, at the curb, Tashi clamped down on the quiver in her stomach and helped me out of the backseat. I wore a deep-hooded coat despite the warm day. She tugged my sleeves over my hands so that all my flesh would be hidden for as long as possible. "Coat off at security, back on when we're through, all the way to Sitti's house." The fear she had dared voice only once was that our Arab name would ensure a random screening. Adam had just shrugged again. *You aren't doing anything wrong.* Tashi had had to bite back the observation that he, not she or I, looked like the people who made the rules.

It was Saturday morning, and the travelers were mostly families. Looking around the expanse of concrete, she saw everyone busy with their own routines. Her hand closed around mine through the coat sleeve, and at her other hip was her suitcase and my miniature one. The door opened wide for us, sighing. On the other side, my mother searched for the counter with the shortest line. The airy, glass canopy sent fields of light across concrete and carpeting.

Awed, I flipped back my hood.

So many children! Never had I suspected that the world contained so many. All in warm shades from pink to taupe to brown, none of them blue, but one in alabaster and covered in constellations of orange freckles, like a songbird's egg.

A few faces turned to me. None smiled back. Adults' attention began to trail over me, too. Because they were in every direction, I didn't know who to greet first, so I stopped to let them all come to me. I thought to make myself a gathering point for so many humans on their migrations and pilgrimages.

My mother hissed my name in the tone that said I was in trouble. The hood came up roughly. Her grip now held it to my head, part talon, part steerer.

"Over there at the long line—let's go."

Two TSA officers ambled past with a dog.

We took a position at the back of the queue, but my mother kept shifting. Struggling, fidgeting. A strong wind seemed to push at her but no one else.

"Come on," she said, and left the queue with our bags. "We can just bring them on the plane with us. Let's just get on the plane." But my hood fell back again, and even after she tugged it up, little tendrils of attention still followed us. We walked fast. Then slower, then, where the corridor split in two directions, my mother seemed to grow roots. She was breathing hard. On both sides, more blue-shirted officers paced up and down the lines. One hundred steps in either direction, and I would have to take off my coat at the screening site.

On average, the apparatus in question cost more dollars than my imagination would ever understand, and later reports would find that ninety-five out of one hundred illegal things sailed through these checkpoints like wind through a tunnel. But even the staff's fog of indifference to everyone would surely make an exception for me. Her heart hammered.

The apparatus was security theater. The place where the real borders existed was in the mind, and my mother found herself caught on the wrong side of an invisible barrier as high as the West Bank separation wall. You'd told her this would be simple. You had counseled confidence, even defiance, and said that these nosy people would wilt if only she put enough steel in her spine. *Take a picture, it will last longer!* But my mother's upbringing had taught her only how to be quietly uncomfortable. Obey her mother, obey the teachers, and the doctors, and the academic advisers, as well as the unwritten rules, because the only sure thing about being from nowhere was feeling stared at everywhere.

You could argue, Auntie, that maybe this is why I think so hard about traveling now. I do remember this day. How people stopped walking to look at us, how my interest turned to doubt, and a sour feeling spread in the center of myself as my mother dragged me out of the airport.

Somehow my father's car was still waiting at the curb. Her distress found a target, and she was overcome with the certainty that this whole morning was a kind of demonstration, an event devised by Adam, as in the worst days of their conflict, to humiliate her. My mother ripped open the door, furious.

"Why are you here? What are you trying to do to me?"

His head jerked up from his phone. "My client called as you were ..."

Met with his bewilderment, Mama broke down sobbing. He tossed the phone onto the seat and got me into the car. When offered an embrace, she let herself fold against him, because he was the one person who felt utterly familiar right now. A policewoman had to blow her whistle and threaten a parking ticket before he would let her go.

"I just want her to be okay. I just want people to not look. I just want them to *fuck off.*"

But no matter how many times on the drive home he asked what had happened, she could only wag her head back and forth, in great heavy arcs of shame, because she already knew the truth. It wasn't everyone else. Not really. It was her. It always was, because of that rotten core in the middle of her where everyone else had a spine.

Sometimes she still asks forgiveness. I think it is why she refuses to show me anything but a brave face now: wanting to model a courage she didn't have that day. No matter that we flew the next day. It was fine, more or less. But underneath her performance of courage, nothing had changed. That is why my mother's brave faces are not to be trusted.

Saeeda's fussing about the state of the house had sunk barbs under your skin for weeks, but Tashi addressed the list with a concierge's patience. Helped choose a summer comforter for Kelly's bed, made tea with mint sprigs, supplied other notes of minor, placid companionship that offset Kelly's outbursts and comatose lapses. It all gave you a complicated feeling—Tashi and Saeeda, *working on their relationship*. Reminded you of their brief collusion to deceive you about the pregnancy. Reminded you that you'd never been anyone's mother at all. *Skim milk, never the real thing* was your self-deprecating joke.

Cee had long included you in her family's loose gatherings. Usually you skipped them, but this time you returned from a long day out, smelling of fresh air and with a handful of orange poppies. You carried them out to the patio on the copper tea tray.

"Hanoon," Saeeda said, naming the flower as she knew it.

"Almost the real thing," you said, "but little too small, and orange. Happy Mother's Day, Tash-tun."

"You aren't supposed to pick those," my mother said.

Saeeda gave her a look. "Beauty does not belong to anyone. God put them on the hillside, not in a museum."

"That's exactly . . . never mind." Tashi took a sip of tea and made room for you to sit down. "Thank you, Auntie."

The gossip turned to our cousin Hilwa, who had called that morning from Amman to ask about Kelly. On that call she reported that her son's sister-in-law's baby had been born with wings. Wet and gray, like a hatched goose. He died a few days after that.

"Wings?" you said.

"Naam," Saeeda replied. "Big enough to wrap around."

"Bismissalib!" You put your hand to your cheek. "What did he die of?"

"His heart, maybe. Honestly, does it matter? I am troubled by her call."

"Saint Michael tumbles out of a woman's loins and it's no big thing?"

"Ya Nuha, this woman never cared about me for anything. Not Kelly, not Betty, not babies who fly. What does she want with me after all this time? As if she was wanting sympathy from me."

Cousin Hilwa was a third cousin who floated through life on a soft cloud of Chanel perfume. Even in her earliest years, when she was still in lacy socks and braids, a few velvet-soft comments from her could rile the cousins in any direction that suited her.

"Her side of the family is losing a lot of money in the economy," you said. "Maybe that is what she wants from you. But why didn't we hear of the child sooner? That is the point of family—people who can't ignore you in a disaster like losing a baby."

"Hilwa only said that it was for the best. That tragedies happen all the time."

Tashi looked upset at this—not a new disturbance, but one that had already been lurking. You couldn't help it; you laughed.

"Walaw?" you exclaimed. "How many babies are dying around this woman as she goes to her salon and shops in Harrods and throws her parties? Watch out, children! Here comes Hilwa, angel of death!"

Saeeda set down her glass precisely, constraining her anger. "Hilwa did not mean the tragedy of a stillbirth. She meant the tragedy of deformity. She was referring to Betty. I believe Hilwa meant it to be a sympathetic statement."

"I don't understand."

"Bonding over bad luck," Tashi said, embittered. "Commiseration. Like there is something wrong with my daughter. Forget the blue-soap stuff, Auntie—no one thinks of it anymore. For the best if she had died? It's awful."

"Maybe she didn't mean that. Maybe she just wanted to understand."

Saeeda tsked. "The cousin I remember wouldn't know a significant piece of information if it hit her between the eyes. Khalas. Let Hilwa and all the rest of them go tile the ocean. I don't know what I was thinking, missing family."

The writing in your notebook presses deep into the paper, switching out of Arabic and into the unforgivable English. *It was for the best* when a problematic child dies? You were more committed to Rummani coherence and integrity than most of the family, because most of the children had heard these stories on your knee. You saw that Saeeda was hurt.

"Invite them," you said then. "When the time comes, give them a chance. Let me see what I can do."

I sat in the corner listening to you, my mother, and Saeeda talk about the winged baby as they sat around Kelly's bed. I was already six, un-schooled except at home, trained by then to sit with my fingers laced on top of my little-girl jeans and not to slouch, which made the whipping, red-hot thing inside my chest and behind my face even more of a mystery. It didn't matter that the allegedly winged baby was dead, never more than a rumor. It was like his wings had materialized inside my own skin, bruising the very meat of my being. For the first time, the attention in the hospitals and doctors' offices and now the airport seemed to align with a sense of wrongness. My mother's hands were the opaque pale tone of a halved almond and without a single callus; my grandmother's were pinker, usually from too much scrubbing, and busy with knitting; and yours were the comfortable color and texture of olive wood. Mine were blue, small, and clumsy. These details, until now, had all seemed of equal weight. But I looked again at my hands against my jeans—the color was wrong, somehow? Their color was the only detail people noticed? I felt helplessly full of the sourness from the airport.

Meanwhile the Second Husband made drowning gasps in his bed.

"Betty is a good girl," Saeeda said, "and she has everyone she needs. I don't want the Rummanis at the funeral. Let it just be us."

Nuha got to her feet. "Forget Hilwa, but bring other family. It is wrong to keep everyone away. You said you miss them, and Betty and Tashi need to know their people." Her attention seemed to recalibrate upon speaking my name, and sensing the confusion behind my extreme silence, she opened up the curio cabinet where Saeeda kept spare coloring books and crayons.

"Forget family," Tashi said. "I don't care."

Saeeda said, partly to herself, "I don't know. Maybe going back to Filasteen is what is better. Not people in my business, but feet on the soil. Wouldn't that make you happy more than Rummanis who don't know each other anymore?"

At first, the remark sounded like a dismissal—shooing you from the house almost as soon as you had unpacked. You hid your irritation by exclaiming over the various coloring-book options, trying to find one I might like. But I was looking away on purpose. Outside the window, the afternoon wind shoved the branches of a magnolia tree against the glass. The fragile blossoms shook loose, mantling the sill in fuchsia and white.

"A visit might be good," Saeeda added in a soft voice. "The situation is not so bad right now. Not as dangerous." She was staring away, across her husband's straining chest. She must have seen, on the other side and closer than ever, not the machines, but the empty rooms of her house and a terrible silence. "Though it could be a very long trip for women as old as us."

You set down the flimsy books and looked back at your sister-in-law in surprise. By the raw struggle around my grandmother's mouth, it was clear that she was actually desperate for a plan, a little prayer to the future, and she was speaking a sincere hope that the future included a trip with you to Palestine. She had chosen to love this man on the bed between them, this boring, dour, unmovable, occupying presence who had replaced your brother, who was as marginal in our lives as he is in this tale. And, after so many other losses, she had actually depended on him. Outside, the magnolia tapped at the window. Something in your heart recognized the terror of loss and sagged open, and a shudder went through you. Before you could batten the feeling down, your eyes were wet. Once upon a time, that's when you would have reached for me or Tashi, but your gaze went instead to my grandmother.

"Oh, it has been a long time since we went to the homeland, I suppose."

Saeeda gave the slantwise shrug that always indicated *home*. "We can try, iza Allah rad."

You reached across the bed and squeezed Saeeda's hand where it lay on top of her husband's. "We'll try when the time comes. I promise you. We can make a pilgrimage to visit family anywhere you want."

Saeeda's fingers gripped her husband's wrinkled, puckered ones, and she looked only at him. Though the journey was her idea, her hand did not seem to accept or even be aware of yours.

So, that was as much as was said about the subjects of travel, returning to Palestine, and whom to invite to the funeral, because to say more would have seemed like rushing a life out of the world. Or maybe Saeeda knew from experience never to trust your promises.

From where I sat, I did not understand that the Second Husband was dying. Only that on the reverse side of his face, if there is such a location in the body, the old man in the rumpled sheets was beginning to resemble more and more what I would say was a young Egyptian boy, smooth and elegant-featured. But also a stout, small-eyed grandmother from somewhere east of the European continent, but also a kind of jaybird, even though his external features did not change at all. I should say, more sensibly, that I was watching the invisible, inner surface of one person lose its form—like water running out of a vessel and into the sea.

I knew perfectly well that the rest of my family was unable to see him draining away. The way they carried on talking of their own sadness made me feel invisible, and I was sitting right there. To adults, the world was legible only in terms of loss, and separations and differences, too. But what was death to me, when it was my first act in life? Death looked like the house of the body opening, returning to a wider place: that place of confusion and strange beauty. I had the first inkling that some kinds of splendor were invisible to others. Were not *wrong*. And the solitude of this knowledge was wide and comfortable, a sort of imaginary palace.

We went home in time to meet hotter weather when it arrived. A fan of water swept over the backyard, wetting me on the first hot day, and my parents realized that they were still sending me outside wearing the same polka-dotted bathing suit I'd been given two years ago. I had grown heavier, but not much taller.

My father made another doctor's appointment. His face didn't change anymore when they said I was stone-cold normal; it was all they ever said, except for acknowledging my density and skin, and he had given up the expectation that their instruments would ever find evidence of anything miraculous. He didn't make a follow-up appointment and bought my mother flowers on the way home.

My parents had continued to lean, without quite realizing that in their fatigue they were leaning at all, on each other. And together they leaned on the matchstick tower of the world as it was. In America, there has never been any shortage of products for parents without answers; so what we gained were plenty of substitutes. Chain stores with storefronts entirely for children. Electronic games. Schools, camps, theme parks, a whole universe of pediatric experiences. My parents feared that if they didn't throw me on this world soon, I might never catch up.

I was a blue, eight-stone creature who should be entering first grade. You knew what was bound to happen next, which is why, every time you called, you asked me if I ever imagined what it would be like to live in the land of my ancestors, land of gazelles, land of wild thyme and mountains and cities as old as our ancient family. "I mean it!" you'd cry, "I really mean it!" as I laughed harder, sure that this was your longest-running joke, a monthslong lead-in to a story to tower above all others.

The women had been saying I was undersized, to be fair. It wasn't like no one noticed that the baby wasn't growing: strollers weren't meant for small bodies of nearly a hundred pounds. My father's antique furniture took the hit whenever I ran indoors. I broke my baby bicycle in two. They couldn't hoist me anywhere, and I cried when they pulled on my arms. I kept gaining density, reassuring everyone, but still I failed to grow into the school uniforms my grandmother had bought me, a hopeful gift. Perhaps I was, as the Rummanis once said, the spirit of that hulking soap factory come to life.

"If you send her to school," you said, "no one will want to be friends with a child in baby clothes. Americans want bigness. They respect size."

"Then they'll respect her," my mother said, "when she sits on them."

Tashi hung up the phone and sat for a long time at the kitchen counter, head in her hands. In all the human race, only you had this power to provoke sarcasm from her, and school had been a sore subject for months. After every doctor's appointment, for at least a day, Tashi would cancel everything and either retreat to her crow's-nest apartment on the hill or smother me with a panicked sort of attention, as if Adam had left me kenneled at the doctor's office overnight, like a dog. He outlawed ice pops but uneasily allowed her to gorge me on cartoons, which she herself sometimes seemed to enjoy. And if this was the result of half an hour in an exam room, what would she be like after leaving me for a full day at school? In one fight, Adam accused her of trying to ransom her sanity with my ignorance, and she accused him of trying to hurl me into a volcano—but somehow this remark elicited only a pause and him saying, *Actually, my evil plan was to leave our child on an ice floe somewhere,* and my mother paused, and the tension deflated. She said fine, they could at least look at a few schools to demystify the threat. No commitments.

My parents brought me first to a place I disliked, slightly uphill from the house, on the skirt of a favorite park, where a woman and her mother ran a day school for children. I rammed the butterfly garden fence with my body until the women were alarmed and said no.

They brought me to another place I liked better, slightly downhill and smelling of river, where a young teacher with a forelock of hair and inked arms met us with a clipboard. But my parents were the ones to object, and we left.

"Catholic schools are creepy," my mother said. "You can afford to hire a permanent tutor. That's my vote, if this is still a democracy." But his checkbook overruled her, and so did the entire field of child psychology, and we all drove outside the city to a cluster of low buildings, which you called, in private, Our Lady of the Wretched Sciatica School for Young Blondes. Actually it was St. Catherine's Joint School, after Catherine of Alexandria, the martyr whose decapitated body bled milk. This was the sole fact that clung in my head, raising my interest in a prospect that otherwise seemed to cause nothing but fights among adults—even though the first day of school was still months away.

That night, my father slid a mug of tea between my mother's elbows on the counter. "They'll respect her. She's a bright girl, and the school knows it, else she wouldn't be allowed to start first grade with the other kids her age. We'll make sure she has what she needs. We can't hide her from everything and expect her to be okay in twenty years."

My mother lifted her face and stared at him. "You know what's actually insane? Your optimism. Kids are going to tear her apart." She reached for me then, pulling me against her hip and then deep into her arms, until she was folded around me so tightly she seemed to have more than two arms, possibly ten or twenty squeezing me away from the lunatic world.

"We'll control what we can," he said, "starting with the clothes."

To prove his point, he hired a tailor.

The uniform was to be a navy-and-teal plaid skirt, a soft sweater, and a thick-lapeled blazer, hemmed small until it was sized for a doll. The old dressmaker who came to the house had a mouthful of straight pins and no lips as she smiled constantly at her working hands. Knelt on the floor while I stood on the chair. Later, playing with all the layers of new clothing, I saw that she had done all of my sewing in bright silver thread, in tiny glittering stitches only I could see.

I fondled the thread in the car's backseat as my father steered south onto the highway. I'd thought we were heading to school, but my parents informed me that this was to be the sharp outfit I would wear to my grandfather's funeral. The Second Husband had taken a long time dying, finally released from himself three months after we had visited. It was mid-August, and even though my parents were in short sleeves, I was happy in my little blazer. We had ten hours ahead of us, all the way down to California, which was plenty of time to wonder what it would be like to meet the man now that he was dead.

The Second Husband had been big. His casket was as long as an eighteen-wheeler, so I assumed that among Americans, he had been particularly respected. In Rummani style, I barely thought of him. I still had the impression of a very tall figure standing against the sun; and later, in a brown recliner, of a presence that had let the gusts of talk blow over him whenever we'd visited.

The funeral home was silent. It was not a home for anyone, as far as I could tell. There was no kitchen and nowhere to lie down, unless the coffin was for you. The place was more of an open house for vacant bodies. Agitated, my grandmother went out to her car for something and then had the funeral director put on a maudlin CD of Umm Kulthum. "That'll reel them in," my mother muttered to my father, who showed me that it was possible to laugh only with your eyes. We waited for others to arrive, standing in a small ring on the carpet despite the roomful of empty chairs.

"I spend fortunes on clothes for her," Saeeda announced. "She is still too small for any of them. What are you feeding her?"

Dazed from a sleepless night and the choice of subject, Tashi tucked her hair under its headband. "I feed her everything. She eats. You see her eat."

My grandmother's scowl was at odds with the pretty bouquets around the room.

"Betty," said Saeeda, "what did they feed you for lunch?"

You hadn't arrived yet, and I wanted only you. My mother kept saying you were coming down from Oakland, but it didn't make any sense. Everyone had made a big deal about never going back there. I didn't understand that you visited other friends, friends who knew a whole side of you the family didn't see.

"Do you need me to get you some crackers?" Saeeda said.

"Mama, she's not hungry."

"Did you ask *her*? Because you refuse to cook. Maybe she is not liking food because of you."

"Mama." My mother's face got dangerous. She raised her head just enough for her jaw to become sharp, and for a flatness to settle around her eyes and mouth like a warning. Usually it meant yelling and time-out. But she just put on her sweater and pushed her lips into a short line.

My father touched the small of Saeeda's back. "I noticed you have some muffins or something on your backseat. Do you mind? I'm starving, and maybe Betty will want some." Saeeda Rummani, as easy to distract as her ancestors and kin, let her son-in-law steer her toward the car, remembering that yes, the hospice worker had foisted a cardboard box of baked goods on her yesterday.

Their departure left my mother and me alone.

She sat down with her knees brushing the front of my school blazer. The casket was behind her like a low wall.

"Honey," she said. "You're going to meet some people. Relatives. Are you okay with a lot of people?" When she searched my face like this, her expression was the same as it was on those rare times when she looked in the mirror. Assessing. Measuring *is* against *ought to be*.

I sat down next to her. "I'm fine."

But it was one of those questions that wasn't what it seemed; it had no answer, just bent back around to her labyrinth of mental hallways. *Mama is not okay with me being in a crowd of people. She is not okay with her too-perfect brother. She is not okay with people who knew her during the bad time.* She and my father had talked about it for an eternity in the car.

She said now, "Do you understand that your step-grandpa . . . That's his body, but he's not here?"

We turned around in our chairs and looked over our shoulders as if he would sit up. But there was only the casket, its edges fancily bending our reflections into smears. In my view over the silk berm, there was the very tip of his nose and his rocky knuckles braided with olive-wood rosary beads. The wood and his waxy skin looked the same. And more than that, they *felt* the same. Dead matter, crafted to look familiar, but not.

This time, my mother was waiting for a response.

I thought about telling her how I'd seen him melting into other people, that what looked like his indifference to us had just been a brain clogged with the memories of everyone on earth. But I remembered I was alone and no one cared that a distant cousin of mine had been born with wings, gray wings big enough to wrap around. From you, I'd learned that it felt good to have a grudge—like a dash of preservative for all the beautiful things a person might bottle up and enjoy privately. I opened my mouth to ask why no one called him *step-grandpa* except her.

But just then, the noise of a commotion in the parlor's foyer tumbled through the rooms. The first wave of Rummanis had arrived. *My history,* you had promised on the phone, but still, you were not among them and no history seemed complete without you. Within fifteen minutes there were more than twenty people in here, from my mother's slick-haired brother and his family in from Singapore, to the phalanx of L.A. cousins, to old Zaki, whose name you never said without spitting. He was in his early eighties and leaned in the doorway without removing his sunglasses. He was Jibril's middle brother, the one who'd inherited the shipping business from the other side of the family, and he insisted that he was here only because he'd been visiting a friend in wine country.

People expected it to feel like a reunion. But children sense wrongness, and I sensed the Time of Feuding everywhere here. I crouched behind the casket, hidden by flowers.

The Rummanis weren't monsters. They existed, as I've said before, in a flurry of all the other things they were thinking about. It was difficult to discern their true attitude toward one another through the snowdrifts of polite conversation. What passed for polite, I mean, was that they came to the funeral home be-gouted, laden with new babies, with new hysterectomies, hypertensive, with responsibilities as the new varsity baseball captain, bearing photographs in folios and on the screens of the latest phones, on their way to vineyards, on the way to see the elephant seals, in the middle of selling a restaurant, carrying condolences, carrying on with that boy, enlisting in the navy because the recruiter promised a law degree. (The navy! We Rummanis are land-based, with a maximum distance of six nautical miles from shore—more than the Gaza blockade during those years, but still. I was given to believe we were not in favor of ships, arks, or other vessels.) They brought their complicated selves, unsure how to comfort a woman they didn't like and who hadn't invited them.

Oh yes. All this was your doing, and you weren't even here.

From my place behind the casket, I learned a lot.

"He was a loving stepfather," they said.

(He wasn't. He was cordial.)

"He fought for his country."

(I believe he'd mainly had a desk job.)

"He had eyes only for Saeeda."

(That was true.)

"She didn't cook. Made a lunch reservation. Ma'ool? Not surprising from Her Highness, Sit Balqis. She doesn't want us in her house."

Now they were on to the gossip. The Second Husband had always told Saeeda to ignore the relatives when they got to calling her the Queen of Sheba, because they were envious. Indeed, the guests murmured about how Saeeda was now wealthy as a queen, twice over—because there are some things that no one ever forgets, such as your having wealth they don't think you deserve. And isn't it telling, they said, that Nuha is not here? Organized the whole thing and does not show up, no doubt because Saeeda is impossible. *And Nuha always showed favoritism to our Jibril, God rest his soul, so how could someone like Kelly ever compare . . .*

"What do you think you are doing?"

The question cut into my thoughts. The figure now standing alone in front of the coffin was Saeeda, staring over her husband's corpse and straight into the flowers at me.

I hugged my knees. "Mom was nervous. I'm hiding for her."

"Come out. Now."

"I would rather wait for Auntie Nuha."

"Oh, you would rather?" All my grandmother's grief was compressed and focused into a sort of fury, and her stern expression sank into me like winter. "Is she the boss of today? Was she here early, helping? Is she greeting people at the door? Is she making food? No, your auntie's city friend makes her behave like she is no part of this family. But you are, and you're here, behaving no better than her."

She reached into the flowers and dragged me out into the crosscurrents of talk. The carpet felt miles wide, as big as a public park or a zoo. No longer an observer, I found I couldn't pull my eyes off anyone's shoes, not even as the hum of conversation changed pitch. By a degree, maybe two. Edging into my periphery were the tips of my father's black wingtips and my mother's shiny Mary Janes. My father's voice introduced me, herding me from one cluster of shoes to another. The voices and names blurred. I had never felt nervous before, and all I knew was that my ears seemed clogged with the beating of my heart. I know now that Saeeda was not herself that day, and that she spoke in anger, but the words wouldn't have hurt so much if they hadn't already felt a little true.

In each place, I was met with questions of a similar genre:

"How old are you?"

"Are you a good girl?"

"Are you starting school?"

"Did you pick out that snazzy jacket?"

I didn't feel like part of this family, true. Shyly, I showed off the silver thread. Yes, I responded to generic queries like a generic child. We are shaped by answering only the questions people know how to ask. But there, at the very beginning, without you to intervene or redirect, I was aware that I wanted someone to say that they had seen a baby with wings with their own eyes, that I reminded them of someone from a story. Something, anything, that stretched a thread between myself and the extraordinary; and because I still remember my disappointment—because I expected someone to admit to being surprised by my appearance, but not a single person did anything but what was polite—maybe the funeral was the first time I realized that I already knew that I wasn't like everyone else, and that no one would let me forget it. That I went into the world expecting resistance. Was flummoxed when it was there but hidden.

A second commotion, the one-woman kind, began to galvanize attention from the opposite side of the parlor. There was ululation, half in jest, and someone cried, "Ya Nuha, ya khalti!" It was powerful enough to release me from the discomfort of polite conversation with kin who were strangers, and I escaped to the last row of chairs, waiting for the tide of greeting to drain away from you. *Nuha Rummani.* Your name was honored so many times, this event seemed to be yours. Even the priest in his eternal robes sensed that the guest of honor had

arrived and embarked toward the front of the room with his censer
and altar boy. You settled in the front row. I crept to the chair behind
you and laid my cheek against your back, in the hammock of bone
and sweater that smelled of cigarettes and brunch and Cecilia's perfume. This, the ironic safe place at the center of everyone's gaze.

As the other chairs filled and the sweet ropes of incense crawled
along the ceiling, Saeeda sat down beside you with a glare that spoke
the unspoken.

I feared what she would hiss into the gap between her shoulder
and yours, what curse she would scald you to hell with. *Behaving like
no part of this family* or *Where were you?* Her fury trembled around her
eyes and turned her mouth down at the corners. On it went, this silent rage just a breath away from your cheekbone, while you sat in
stillness in three-quarters profile. Your breath was slow against my
ear, and your chest rose and sank with a soft sigh that somehow responded to her anger, then conversed with it, turning it over like a
bolt of bright orange cashmere. Saeeda's eyes filled with surprising
tears, staring hard at you until I knew I didn't understand the anger or
for whom it was meant.

The priest boomed the first line of the blessing that would fire the
soul of the Second Husband Who Was Not a Rummani back over the
walls of the kingdom of the Lord. Meanwhile, Saeeda reached over
and clutched your hand in front of the whole family. For that moment,
I saw her not as an old woman, but as all the ages she had ever been.

Sometime after the casket was lowered into a green-turfed hole, in
the dark hours before the long drive home tomorrow, you pace
through Saeeda's house, self-assured as a stray cat. Remember this? It
is night or it is morning.

You settle in a shabby throne in the center of my grandmother's
kitchen, at the breakfast island. A navy blue bathrobe pools around
the base of your chair, and the marble countertop is littered with all
the usual implements of your boredom—plastic hand mirror, nail

polish bottle pebbled with red lumps, cup of tea. Also, a stack of pita bread and a series of bowls containing olives, cucumbers, tomatoes, feta cheese, oil, and za'atar for the bread. So much salt.

To be clear: you and my grandmother held hands for the entire funeral. You drove her to the lunch, consumed nothing but cigarettes, and in twenty minutes had gotten a round of arak into everyone and galvanized the table with an implausible story about getting held up at gunpoint at the wig store, and convincing the kid he'd gone to the wrong address, and being given a free wig for saving the day, but a taloned bird had snatched it right off your head on the way to the car. No one believed a word of it, but by the time they were daytime-drunk, they all agreed in their various taxis back to their hotel rooms that Nuha Rummani had not lost her sparkle, even though she was looking frail these days, and perhaps Saeeda Rummani's hospitality wasn't really so meager.

"Alternative diplomacy," you mutter to Saeeda from this natty throne, as close to an apology as you are ever capable of giving. "I think it went well. If we're serious about a trip to the old country, you better get used to talking to your family again."

Saeeda has been awake. She leans on the counter, blearily answering condolences on social media. There's a clatter in the hallway, and you put one elbow on the back of her chair and see Tashi stumbling out, hunting for the TV remote.

"Help yourself to breakfast, habeebti." You light another cigarette. Drop the match into the coffee cup.

Tashi frowns. "It's four a.m." She finds the weather and mutes it.

"I'm up. So is your daughter." You take a puff and blow it toward the window. Unstated: *So are you. So is Saeeda, and we are both very curious about your choice to share a bedroom with your ex-husband.* The smoke eddies three feet into its journey and disperses against the ceiling. "Only Adam can sleep at a time like this, it seems." You wave at the clock above the sink. "I thought to myself, What good are you in this world, Nuha Rummani, if you do not make yourself useful? I'm good company for insomniacs."

I climb up from the air mattress and pluck an olive from the bowl. Then tear off a chunk of bread and scoop out a nugget of cheese, and shove it in behind the olive the way you taught me. It is all so much salt for the middle of the night. You cough, pick up the mug, turn your back to me, and spit in it. Then hold out the coffee mug. For the olive pit. I eject it into your palm and you dump it into the mug, like we still have an understanding after all.

"Good kid." You knock ash on top of it. A fresh cord of smoke rises between your knuckles and circles your head like a crown. You break it with your hand and point the cigarette at my mother. "She has a good appetite these days."

My mother sinks onto the couch arm. "Auntie, I mentioned not smoking around Elspeth a couple of million times. And not ever in my mother's house?" She glances at Saeeda, but my grandmother seems to be beyond caring. In fact, the whole house feels unfamiliar. There had been a hospice bed, and now there was not.

You shrug. The butt hisses out when it hits the sludge formed by the olive pits, ash, and wet tea bag.

"It's good you are up. Away from her father, I need to tell you. You will not put this child in school." You reach down and push one of my curls behind my ear, confident as a queen. "You saw your own family barely holding their tongues. Imagine other children. You need to teach her at home. Or let me take her to the old country. America kills brain cells. Ya habeebti, come here." You scoop me over to yourself, away from the bread, with an alarming smile. "Did I tell you the story of the one-eyed ghouleh that lived in the hills east of Ramallah? Looked a bit like your cousin Hilwa. I will tell you about her . . ."

Even though you soften your voice for me, that crooked spine of stubbornness cracks the middle of it. You murmur in my ear, wheedling these little hints directed at Tashi about all the terrors that wait for me at school.

Ask your mother what it's like.

Bullies. Pranks. Pull your hair.

She couldn't stand it, either.

She still has the scar along her wrist.

To be fair, my mother's head throbs with the idea of me in school. Of going anywhere but between these few houses of safety. She wants to sneak me back to the apartment and dig in the leaves and dirt behind the building until she can find a kind of fertile silence in which she can finally clear her mind.

"Pay attention," you tell us both. "I'm giving you a real warning."

Tashi shakes her head. Looks down the hallway toward the spare bedroom. "Elspeth's best chance is just for her to get on with her life. We'll see how it goes."

"Is this so?" You whip the robe tighter around your torso. "How is that know-it-all ex-husband speaking through your face right now? You do not believe this. You sat in that very chair weeks ago, crying your eyes out." My grandmother is finally paying attention. "Do you believe this? Betty, do you?" You ignore your walker and huff over to the teakettle, then crank the flame to high. "Answer me, somebody!"

My mother drifts up, hands hovering about my ears in case there is more to say about my father. In the soft roar of the gas flame and the tick of heating metal, no one speaks. The hallway to the spare bedroom is open like a throat, and the bedroom door a gateway that goes yet deeper. One body in the whole house is slumbering easily, and still, my mother declines to answer. Saeeda declines to answer. The open bedroom door doesn't need to speak to confirm that yes, I will definitely be going to school in two weeks.

"Betty." You brace the heel of your hand on the counter, leaning over as though to talk to me in private.

My mother pulls me closer. "Auntie, I swear. *I'm* talking to you. Not her. Look at me. Don't pull that trick."

"A trick, she says?" Your eyes drill into me. There were these times when I was almost afraid of you, when you could burn on the wick of an idea that went all the way through you. In this hour that is night and also morning, your eyes shine with danger, almost enough to illuminate what it is that we should fear.

"Betty, have your mom and dad told you the story of the silver gazelle who tricked a girl into leaving home—"

"Nuha, khalas." My grandmother slaps her laptop shut. "Khalas, no stories now. Listen to your niece. You see she loves her uniform. She's excited for school. Make us all some tea and forget it."

The way you straighten, you seem to be squaring up to the firing squad.

"Well then, mumtaz. I will forget it. You all already have. Let us see what the boring world thinks it can teach our little salt blossom."

On the drive to Oregon, my father hummed in the driver's seat. My mother half-napped in the back, snuggled up to me as though my aunt had put a little chip of ice in the center of her that would not dissolve.

I watched a distant mountain creep along behind us.

"If my grandad is dead now, do you think he'll get wings?"

"You mean like an angel?"

"No, like that baby. The one that died."

"Oh. That." My mother's face was unchanged behind the twin black disks of her sunglasses. "No, I don't think so."

"Is Aunt Nuha mad?"

She let out a burst of a laugh, but it was not the kind of joke that seemed to make her happy. Her smile was rigid as she said, "No, honey. She loves you no matter what. That's real."

No matter what. The angry thing inside me rustled, stirring fear as well. At the next rest stop, she sat in the passenger seat. And at some point when I woke from a restless nap, her hand was on my father's knee. Whatever her doubts, they were buried in a place where I could not find them or her.

Another car scene just a few weeks later: an asphalt lane leads our vehicle through a humid curtain of pine boughs. Past an iron gate, it finds its end at a gravel circle, in the shadow of a whitewashed chapel.

Other buildings cluster, a network of damp single-story structures with red tin roofs. A cafeteria, a lower-grade building, and an upper-grade building are swarmed with half-sized people with backpacks, dressed exactly like me. The only structure as big as the chapel is the gymnasium, which hunkers among a wall of rhododendrons at the edge of the parking lot. A chilly wind filters through the trees despite the sunny morning, and it fills the whole memory with the smell of wet fir needles.

Where did they think I would end up? The point is that there isn't a magical school. There is no secret society. No other special option. As you feared, this is just the world. My father has stopped the car in front of St. Catherine's Joint School, tuition a crisp $23,000 per year, and sits with his hand on the steering wheel. My mother is beside him in the same pair of round sunglasses. It has been three whole weeks since she misplaced anything tangible. I crane between their shoulders, trying to understand if this is the correct destination for my silver-threaded clothes.

A woman approaches the front bumper. Gusts pluck at her jacket and lift her lapels. Her braids are two ropes twisted into the teeth of a massive spring-mounted jaw she's clipped against the back of her head. The implement looks like the mouth of a carnivorous fish.

My father rolls down the window and says my name. I think of the story in which the peasant chased away djinn by invoking Allah. He says my name again, but the woman only peers over my father's shoulder at me, her face betraying nothing.

My mother turns around in her seat, her face full of real panic. Low, rushed: "We don't have to do this."

We are already sitting in the mouth of the future. We all know what comes next. I swallow my alarm and hold down, with everything else I know, that growing nest of secrets called *self*, and unbuckle my seatbelt.

My father shrugs and says to the woman with the fangs in her hair, "Go on. We'll bring her inside."

PART III

——·—·——

Ink

(Ages 6–9)

A funeral is happening two rows up. A motorcade comes and goes, a crowd. None takes notice of me, opening the plastic bag of your inky journals.

Folded in one is a ticket for a flight you never took, dated the day after my birth. No one thought twice about Nuha Rummani flying to Jordan in the middle of a war. But the flight was actually to Greece, where you were to meet Cecilia for a month of touring. Had you gone, my adoption would have happened.

On another sheet of loose-leaf paper, brittle with age, is a column of nothing but *Nuha Rummani,* as if you were practicing your signature.

Your bones are underfoot and whatever animated you is gone, but these Arabic letters—the hook of kaf and 'ayn, the cup of nūn and ya—are little vessels of mystery. Smeared and degraded, they hint at what was really going on in your heart, but it is hidden among grocery lists, the electric company's toll-free line, bits of poetry (ghazals, sonnets), and the telephone number for the U.S. embassy in Tel Aviv.

It's late in the afternoon. At dark, I am meeting my beloved, having promised to come down from this hill carrying an answer to our future. You chose family over love—but, as it turns out, not always.

Epistolary

———·———

If my mother is feeling beneficent when she recalls my first year in school, she says you were busy helping Saeeda settle the Second Husband's affairs. I'm more familiar with the versions of your absence my father variously dubbed the I Told You So Gambit, or the You'll Miss Me When I'm Gone guilt trip, or a snarky chapter of ancient history called "The Fossil Goes Underground."

And then the kingdom rejoiced, he would mutter, and I'd light up because I was still too young for sarcasm. The fading cadences of your storytelling were so much grander than anything I would ever hear in a first-grade classroom.

The school was not only for girls, nor only for Catholics. It was for human children called the Oregonians, sprites of the West Hills suburbs who smelled of shampoo. But on this first day, we are all the same: twenty small innocents settling in a circle on the rug, hugging backpacks, scouring one another with our eyes. Faces turn toward me on the pale stalks of their necks. It is a kind of pause, a breath cradled at the back of the throat, when nothing can stop me from staring back—taking in the dark eyes, blue eyes, hair curly and straight and short and long, even a few other pomegranate-red backpacks, all of us goggling around in the hush.

There must have been a moment long ago when all the earth's souls looked up at the sky and felt the first raindrops on their cheeks. A warm tap of water on the brow, a shiver of wind. It was the beginning of the end of the world, but for that moment, it must have felt like a pleasant change in the weather.

Tashi and Adam deluged the pretty, young teacher with bribes. Following a plan he had devised, Adam sent a fruit basket for her September birthday and gift cards for the classroom every month, and cooked a homemade dinner set against a backdrop of candles and a soundtrack called "Dinner Party/World." He made it clear that he and Tashi only wanted her to protect me at school, and that I was an extraordinary case. Miss Grace let herself be plied. She created lots of pair activities in class, because the students were kinder to me when they couldn't clot up in groups; heaped praise on my intelligence in the teachers' breakroom; acted as the kind and judicious eye that reported everything to Adam, who was smug enough to believe he had outsmarted ten thousand years of our species' instinctive social warcraft.

Did I make it easy for myself, Auntie?

Me, in a typical pair activity: *You be the Damascene merchant.*

Other student: *What?*

Me: *So the ghouleh doesn't chop my head. You have to save me.*

Because it was Partner Coloring Time (or Snack Break or Quiet Directed Activity), there was no wandering off to someone funner. So they asked, *Is it paint on you?*

"God made her that way," Miss Grace said. At a parochial school, anything could be ascribed to divine mystery.

It's because my family makes soap, I'd explain when we were alone again. *I'm special.*

Soup? A final, damning smirk.

Authority always fails, as you taught. And if you confuse people too much, eventually they throw a toy at your head when no one's looking. While my parents placed their faith in good alliances, you knew that the last defenses were to be either invisible or confident—which meant I had no choice but to wear my skin like an imperial robe and master the various seductions. But charm, trickery, and the manipulations of desire would require another ten years or so for me to even understand.

Meanwhile, other students mastered the low arts of bullying: preying on gullibility, blackmail, the various humiliations. Increasing amounts of violence. One day near the end of our first year, boys were kicking a ball around the fur of grass. They decided my shoes looked dumb and tried to push me down the stairs into the forest, but when they hurled themselves at me, they bounced off my back and shoulders and landed on the ground. It was how they discovered that I was not only blue but as heavy as the marble statue of the Virgin outside the chapel. Anyway, when I pushed back, there was a great deal of blood.

I was taken to the gargantuan nun in the front office, who announced herself as the disciplinary head of St. Catherine's. She looked much older than the head of someone who had been decapitated at eighteen, but the folds under her chin were soft and disappeared into a tight white neck-sleeve that—of course—must have kept the head from rolling away.

Saint Catherine stood up and assessed me, for I was too short to be assessed sitting down. It was an appreciative scrutiny, the way my father looked at his bookshelf when he was thinking hard.

"Miss Rummani, you were violent today. What am I supposed to do?"

"It was a misunderstanding."

"How am I meant to understand"—she checked a folder open on her desk—"two bloody noses, a stoved finger, and bruises?"

I had not spent five thousand hours overhearing my father's legal work without intuiting the relationship between selective language and a favorable revision of history.

"The monitor wasn't looking. They wanted to hurt me. It's not my fault."

More flapping papers. It worked in my favor that the recess teacher had been careless, a possible liability issue. Also that one of the instigators, a boy named Felix, was a budding sociopath.

"I can't hurt anybody. I'm too small. I'm sure it was an accident."

"I see."

"I forgive them," I said quickly. "They know they did wrong. I just want to move on."

"I do see." She closed her reading glasses on the side of her breast and dropped them into a fluted white vase that stood on her desk for that purpose. "You think you're clever. Pride is a sin, as you would have learned if we'd made you begin school with the younger children in kindergarten."

"Yes, ma'am."

"Maybe the B class is a better fit for you. Lots of clever ones like you, including Felix. That will be your group all next year, no more Miss Grace to play favorites. And because forgiveness seems to be so important to you, I'm sure you'll find a moment to seek it from your classmates today while you do extra chores."

By the early summer, when first grade was still a fresh wound, a U-Haul van parked in front of my father's house. My mother had rented it when he was not at home because he was not a man who wanted her to carry boxes alone, but neither was he a man who could carry them well himself. I lingered on the porch steps in full view of the street, making sure nobody bothered the van while she was getting this half of her belongings indoors. This wasn't a clean break from her hilltop crow's nest, which she would keep for almost two more years, but it was as close as our household had come to looking like the other families at the school.

I stood on the top stair and wiggled my feet backward, shoving my heels against the backs of the shoes my classmates said looked dumb. A while ago, my grandmother had bought me a pair of five-color sneakers that reflected light in the dark, just like my father's grown-up ones. Now the shoes were stained beautiful from grape juice, winter mud, food dye, pink ink, and the problem of being manufactured for children a quarter of my weight. I didn't complain, because that would have sent my mother folding into herself for days. But now I was seven and my toes were poking through a tear in the mesh.

My feet had grown.

My ankles were sticking out of the bottoms of my blue jeans. An alien excitement washed over me. I could finally ask for new everything. New shoes that matched my classmates'. A certain backpack, a certain smart-looking pencil box. Next year in the 2B class, I would become stylish and unremarkable. Maybe invisibility was an option, after all.

As you had feared, I had begun to grow into the world.

My new, morose second-grade teacher could not ignite a love of letters in us, so one Monday I found my rear-corner desk moved to the other side of the room, and in its place a tower of milk cartons. She had decapitated all of them and bound the remains together in a rigid matrix of duct tape. Our 2B class was sixteen students, and there were sixteen cubbyholes.

"We are going to play post office," she announced, "and I've given everyone your very own mailbox."

A little updraft of excitement caught me, something to do with the automatic anticipation of receiving a gift. I understood that mail was what I got from you on holidays. But then I remembered my actual situation. You were busy planning a pilgrimage to the homeland with

Saeeda, and you probably didn't have my address at school. I guessed I would be the only one with an empty box.

The teacher wasn't finished. "Ms. Howard's third-grade class has kindly agreed to join us in our correspondence project. You will have one secret pen pal and one assigned pen pal whose name you know." My stomach sank. "You and your two pen pals will exchange one letter a week."

I said nothing, as always, and began to plan. I would sneak things into my mailbox—pebbles, feathers, the pretty bits of green glass I found behind the gymnasium—and say they were from my new friend. Because surely when people found out who I was, they wouldn't write to me. I slumped in my back-row desk, wishing to dissolve into the coats behind me. Then it got worse: in the commotion of questions that followed, Felix and his friend came back one by one to "get a pencil sharpener from their coat pocket." The friend twisted his eraser into my shoulder so hard it sent a little chip of my skin flying, like a bullet hitting a stone wall. While I was reeling from the burn of it, Felix passed behind me, wiping a piece of paper across the back of my neck. It left behind a wet streak. The wetness began sliding down my skin in a slow, rolling walk. Near tears, I realized it was a whole gobbet of snot.

I was too disgusted to touch it and too proud to be seen wiping it away. I decided I hated my mailbox already, the gross invitation of it. And I hated school.

Monday-morning letters were the anonymous ones we got from the third graders; we didn't have to write back until Tuesday. The whole thing was starting on a good note because I would get a letter written by someone who didn't know who I was—it seemed likely to help my invisibility project. At that time in my life, reminded often that my body was nothing but a source of problems, and with no inkling of its pleasures, conducting a relationship through the window of a blank sheet of paper sounded entirely comfortable. The flutter of excitement returned.

When we came back from lunch, inside the milk-carton boxes was a new collection of soft gray shadows, a flock of folded sheets of paper whose edges caught the light from the windows. We couldn't retrieve our letters until the end of the day, and I couldn't wait to read whatever was in mine. I got my coat on fast and was the first to pluck my letter from the cubby—a tight wad of paper—and escaped with it while everyone was still surging around the teacher.

It was so lovely I didn't want to unfold it. The writer had made a paper chrysanthemum small enough to fit in my fist. I hid it in the folds of my coat as my mother drove me to her apartment, now just a workspace. I kept it from her eyes as she helped me out of the car seat, and even waited until she'd spread herself out at the six-foot folding table in her bedroom, opened her red computer, and begun muttering about doing homework for her therapist. Once a week she'd go in there and close the door, speaking on the phone for a while, then sitting in silence. It usually took a couple of hours, and I never knew what they talked about, but she looked me sternly in the eye before each one and said that total privacy was the rule: uninterrupted time with her San Francisco oracle was the only way the week ahead could be bearable. So, it was my time to play whatever I wanted. I liked privacy, too.

Hello

I unfolded the first five petals of the paper flower, each one a single letter of greeting.

Then I took myself away from the flurry of words coming out of the bedroom, out to the cold porch. I didn't get hot and cold like other people, so the slanting, velvet-wood porch was my favorite place, even when it was raining. Like being perched on a ship's deck or a princess balcony. The air was always a bit humid because we were right next to the hillside forest, another site of promise. As I peeled open my letter, it made no noise.

My name is Anna.

It was supposed to be anonymous, but okay.

> *My sister showed me how to fold this.*
> *We like to dance, but she is better. We have lessons on Tuesday. Do*
> *you like to read? Do you like big trees? I saw the Virgin Mary far away,*
> *in a cutout between the trees on the hill across from our house. My sister*
> *does not believe me but I hope you do.*
> *Write back with your favorite saint and food.*
>
> *Love, Anna*

I couldn't pick Anna out in the cafeteria, so all I had was her name and the thrilling things she had told me about herself. All those stories about enchantment, the hero who follows a gazelle, the gazelle who is a djinni princess—they gained new color. I wished I could impress her by moving a mountain or slaying a monster, or at least delight her with a letter in fancy folds, but trying to make a flower like hers was impossible—try pushing a baby back into a womb, try pushing a leaf back into its bud—so all I could offer was the baroque vocabulary I'd learned from you, Auntie. Anna became the blueprint for every sort of seduction in my life to come, from the innocent to the later, surprisingly joyful ones. The only trick was to make myself visible in the planes of imagination, a realm of words, my native land.

But still only seven, seized only with some limited premonition, I practiced a draft in the living room all evening. I asked my mother, "How do you spell *cannibal*?"

She barely lifted her face from her red computer as she spelled it out for me.

When I sat down for reading class on Tuesday, others heaved themselves into their slow task with chubby colored pencils. I wielded a Ticonderoga as though I were the very patron saint of writing, sponsor of the excellently formed letter, benefactor of the properly sized period and the appropriate exclamation point, savant of sensible paragraph breaks.

Dear Anna hi!

You and your sister know alot. I want to know how you do it with the paper.

I never saw the Virgin Mary in the trees. I live by the woods so I will look for her. Once I saw a mom coyote and her twins. Did you ever see them? My favorite saint is Francis because he lives outside and my favorite food is macaroni.

Miss C wants us to write a question we are afraid to ask anybody else. If you take Communion, does that make you a cannibal?

goodbye

Your friend

———— // ————

Hello friend.

I never seen a coyote but I like macaroni too. The Blessed Virgin has not been back because it is windy at my house all the time. I like Saint Francis! Do you like Saint John the Baptist? He lived outside and ate bugs and was the cousin of Jesus.

I do not know if we are cannibals. My sister wont answer so I have to ask on Sunday. Communion does not taste like meat. You will practice with wafers that are not blessed so you can see what it tastes like. Dont worry.

Love,

Anna

P.S. My sister says "a lot" is two words unless you have a pet called Alot. I don't understand. Do you have a pet?

P.S.S. You know my name. What is yours?

———— // ————

Anna,

They took Saint John's head and buried it by the town where my family lives in Filasteen. My aunt says the church is just rocks today. Also the friend of the dad of Jesus is buried down the hill from their old house.

I like your notes better than notes from my class. I got a box of mints with cat poop Thursday. But I like getting mail from you. I still want to learn paper flowers. My dad says it is called the art of Origamo.

Love,

Your friend

PS.. I am not Catholic. I do not get the crackers.
PS . . . I do not have a pet but the coyote came back and howled. I named her Alot.

———— // ————

Hello,

My sister asked who gave you cat poop. She is popular and will get them in trouble. Everybody is nice to us because she is a ballerina. Where is Filasteen? My sister and parents never heard of it.

My parents are Swedish. Do you know about Ingrid and Bridget? After Bridget got sainted the pope sainted Ingrid too because everybody already prayed to her. But somebody mixed their heads up in the grave, and now everybody prays to Bridget's skull but it is really Ingrid's. Isnt that cool?

I love you and Alot,

Anna

P.S. That is okay you are not Catholic. I am adopted. Tell me your name!

—————

If only she had stopped demanding my name, this could have been the one long-distance relationship in the history of the human species with a bright future. Even now, in the present day, when my beloved unfolds some new convolution of her heart to me, some insight or minor occasion from girlhood, our intimacy has the same glitter as that first fascination.

At first I was too scared to tell Anna I was the one everybody hated. Buckled into my backseat plastic throne, I considered the problem as my mother drove me home from school. In the fine rain and road mist, we passed a school bus whose sides glowed like an emergency. On the other side of dark glass were my classmates, hooligans at rest. They didn't know it was me down here, seeing them. This was the thrill of that first correspondence: as the fear of discovery faded, relief took its place. Anna was the only person on earth who knew me but didn't care how I looked, because she didn't know me. I was invisible.

I knew her, though.

The sister she'd mentioned was famous. Summers she went to New York, and during the school year, she did youth shows with the Oregon Ballet. Except for Anna's descriptions, she was all exterior: a figure swanning through the upper-levels building, trailed by a bitchy crew of ducklings. But little Anna was something else—a square-faced girl with a thin, beaky mouth and a tangle of slippery white-blond hair. She had a clique, but she wasn't at its center. I suspected she was telling me the truth about how her sister's reputation sustained her; she wore the same nice clothes, laughed at the same whispered jokes, and got to stand in the same tight ring at the corner of the playground, but somehow I knew she was the unmortared one. When you look at a wall, you can just sense which brick is loose.

But what does a seven-year-old actually know? I'll say this: you would have understood, had you been there. I lived for writing back to Anna. I had no friends. I had two grand talkers in my life—my father and you. He built elaborate arguments, arguments with spires and ramparts and spindly turrets. You built for the love of building, going up and up into the sky in mad, delighted proliferation. He was an architect; you were a cancer. And Anna was an opening. I wanted to dig at Anna. I wanted to scrabble at her with my fingers and pry the brick of her loose from the people around her and show her the forest from my mother's porch. We could look for Alot and listen to your tumbling stories on the telephone and hunt for the furry spider behind the broken grout under the sink. I sank into catatonic daydreams of her, put myself to sleep thinking of her, woke in the apartment or my bed at home still thinking of her, teaching my imagination how to love. It is no wonder that the word for *story* in English is the same one as the word for the floor of a building; we layer thoughts on thoughts until we are a tower of ideas, even if it means the whole unstable structure is shot through with the lies we tell ourselves and others. But when I sat at one end of my mother's bedroom desk and tried to find each letter of every word of each wish in my brain, each one a single-minded shape of want, the alphabet turned as shallow as the dimples of my watercolor set. Here are eight colors—reproduce life.

Her notes were always a little longer than mine, because she was in third grade and I was in second.

> Hello
>   Our cat is named Gertrude after Saint Gertrude the patron of cats and the recently dead. She died in 659. Do you know about her? Her parents tried to make her get married when she was only ten but instead she wanted to be a nun and died when she was old like my mom.
>   She is white and orange and has curly whiskers. (Our cat.)
>   Do you still have to write letters to that person since they gave you cat poop? My sister says that cat poop is gross and I think your pen pal is bad for giving it to you again.
>   I wish you would tell me your name so we could meet after school.

———— // ————

Dear Anna

My aunt says Saint Gertrude was alive when our home city Nablus got named. It was Neapolis before that. It is the cousin of a city called Naples because the Romans used to call Naples Neapolis too.

That is confusing. I do not understand why names are so important. I am your friend even if you do not know mine.

Time passed, and I must have said Anna's name too many times at home.

"Did you ever think of getting your friend a gift?" asked my father. He'd begun enforcing family dinners three nights a week, mainly to get my mom to eat good meals. Otherwise she would help cook our food and leave immediately for the lab.

"Who, cannibal girl?" she asked.

"She's a Catholic," I said, but my father still looked blank until my mother explained about my Communion questions. He had a prim way of smiling at me when he was about to tell me about a thing I had to do to get along with the world better, so I headed it off. "She likes macaroni, Dad. Can I bring her a bowl of macaroni and cheese?"

My mother let out a laugh—a real one.

"If it is something the post office wouldn't deliver," said my father, "it probably shouldn't go to school. How about a pencil case?"

"Mom ordered mice last week. Can I give Anna a mouse?"

She and my father exchanged a look that they thought I didn't understand. "The mice are busy working in the lab," she said, which meant they were already dead.

"What else does she like?" he asked.

"She wants my name."

"A name is a powerful thing," said my mother, at the same time my father shrugged.

"It is supposed to be a secret," he said, "so you are within the rules.

You never have to break the rules for anyone. Just because she broke them doesn't obligate . . ."

Mama's foot nudged mine under the table. My father took my moral education seriously, given the amount of money he had spent on his own graduate degrees, but my mother had even less patience than I did for the way he slowed the clocks and began mortaring together another verbal rampart—this time against the imaginary onslaught of the bad influence of good intentions. Mama's nudge was the hall pass, the secret door, the ever-rarer puff of magician's smoke. I hated school. She knew it, and she tried to make evenings feel like anything but school.

Last month, my bedroom window had sprung a leak and made a fissure of wet drywall that fed into a rash of bubbling paint, and my mother and I found ourselves just sitting there, poking at the crackling surface together. Later, Dad found bats in the attic. But before his irritable spackling of the drywall, before the grim weekend during which we all stayed in Mama's space while the exterminators killed the bats and she worked eighteen straight hours in her university office, these were not household disasters. They were interesting, and my mother cared so little for the integrity of a rich man's house that she sided with me in peeling off the bubbling wall paint, for the fun of it.

I nudged my mother back. She kicked my knee. I burst out laughing. My father came to an offended halt, but she sprang up and tackled me out of my chair, dragging me down and over to the living room, where she pretended to be you pretending to be an ogre, tickling my tummy and saying how good it is to munch little-girl fingers and little-girl toes.

She tickled until my father stated that things were "getting too crazy," with all the shrieking and panting. My mother sat back on her heels, black curls wild, fleece jacket off one shoulder. Which one of us was he talking to? I loved it when she was easy with her loose, gasping laughter here at the house—the happiness was bigger because there were so many rooms for it to fill up. But my father was slumping a little at the table, fork abandoned on his plate as he watched my mother drag me off the edifice of his well-meaning, colorless advice.

Mama looked over her shoulder and tugged her fleece back into place. Her smile settled into something like a consolation.

"Your friend. You could invite her over to play someday?"

"Then she would know my name, because she would have to tell her parents where she is going." I followed my mother as she returned to the table, my head thrown back, wanting her attention again, but she was now in adult mode. "The rules say my name is supposed to be secret. Dad just said I shouldn't break the rules—"

He picked up his fork as my mother sat down at the table. Something had shifted. Lately, they had this way of turning into boring adults together, sliding me out of their focus. It was an inaccessible place, complete with a silent language only they shared.

He sighed. "It's just a small rule, honey. Do what you want. Finish your spaghetti, both of you, please?"

Mama dug into the noodles, frowning. "Habeebti, are you going to write her letters forever? The school year won't last forever. If she finds out who you are and doesn't want to be friends, then she doesn't deserve to know you. It's better to be lonely than to wait for approval from a jackass."

My father nodded once, as if she had just set a door on its hinges, adequately completing the verbal structure he'd been building for me.

Nothing changed immediately, but my mother was right. The school year would come to an end, one that crept closer each week. Anna still stood in the ring of girls on the playground. Her sister still swanned, toes out, through the buildings. Anna still pressed to know my name, and my classmates still pressed to see me humiliated. She promised to avenge me if I would only tell her my name or, just as revealing, the name of my tormentor.

I tried so hard not to care. But even our teacher laughed off the pranks as a joke.

"God loves a sense of humor," she said, packing up her planner, "more than he loves a tattle."

My teacher was the most humorless person in the school. It occurred to me that she had made the rules of anonymity, and since all her other rules were dumb, so was this one. As her keys jingled and the final bell rang one day, I slipped away from the bus line and dared to imagine inviting Anna home with me. Tried to imagine Anna still liking me even though no one else did.

It is such a petty drama, I know. Does it please you, hearing a story of love and revenge? You would understand if you were here, because your stories had already built a world for me.

When I got home I wrote, *Cat poop boy is tall Felix, like Saint Felix the patron saint of spiders. (Saint Felix is from Naples! Mom says that is a c-o-i-n-c-i-d-e-n-c-e.)* And by then, I'd learned through imitation how to fold a note into a blooming square, the sort of pile of little triangles that once you started unfolding, the sheet of paper seemed to bloom and bloom into a kaleidoscope of creases, expanding beyond what seemed to be the right size of a piece of paper. A sense of order into chaos, like the churning under my rib cage. It felt like I was asking for the world, so at the last moment before bed, caving in to terror, I got my father to help me tie the paper flower to the top of a square of my mother's Nabulsi soap. If it was pretty enough, it might feel less like the beginning of a disaster.

I slipped the gift into my blazer pocket and waited to see if I'd have the courage to mail it.

Possibly, she wouldn't identify me at all. My name was not on anyone's lips.

Harassing outsiders was still good fun, but it had been a while since anyone had jabbed me with *Go home, A-rab*. Children have short memories, and somehow it was like they'd forgotten my name.

I gave no one a reason to use it, kept to myself, never raised my hand.

I think forgetting has more in common with cruelty than with forgiveness. But I can't pretend this was all.

When they looked at me, all they saw was the shock of my skin. The frank cluelessness of it, like I somehow possessed the world's ugliest dress and insisted on wearing it day in and day out, oblivious to the rules of peer shaming. The ribbing, the jokes, the shoves, the gawping, the giggling . . . these were the little bumpers that guided other children along the treacherous course toward safety and assimilation. So in their eyes, when I just kept showing up blue, ignorant, they treated my body as an aggressive refusal to conform. *Elspeth Rummani* became only a string of letters on the classroom roster, a piece of information that was nowhere as exciting as everyone's own new language for me: Blue Thing or Hey You, Pisscake. Even the other grades of St. Catherine's Joint School knew who Ugly Blue was, heard it every day, the singsong music of it cutting through the lunch line, the recess crowd, the hallway, spun into a high melody of four to six syllables.

As I reached out and deposited the note for Anna in the teacher's collection box, I ignored the sound of sniffing around me. That was the joke now: I was always getting an excremental smear inside a card, a pebble turd wrapped like a Tootsie Roll, a whole scoopful of brown logs in my raincoat pocket, so Felix and his friends laughed that the smell was me. I wanted the privacy of never being seen. I wanted to close like an anemone.

But the privacy of anonymity was pleasant, too. I unhooked my words from my body like Christmas ornaments and settled them behind Anna's eyes, and yes, I wished I *could* go on doing that forever. But First Communion was over, and school ended in a month. I had just propped open a door in telling Anna about Felix and his horrible shitting cat, and there was no closing it now. My name was what she wanted, and I didn't want her to discover my person and have nothing to call me but Ugly Blue. That was why I'd signed my note with my father's good pen: *Love, your friend forever, Betty Rummani*. Like you had been saying forever, Auntie, Rummanis always found a way to suffer for love.

It was a long wait for the return-mail day.

My mother had spent the weeknights with my father. When they were at the house together, sometimes for mornings in a row, she looked more solid, as if the light from the window above our kitchen sink no longer shone straight through her. The feeling between my parents had grown as cheerful and tense as the skin of a balloon: bright, colorful, and threatening an explosion. She spent less time paying attention to me, more of it conversing with him, or working, or on the phone with Saeeda and you as the travel plans for Palestine formed. After the first year of cleaning out the house, there had been shorter trips to nearer branches of the family, so many that you seemed to be stalling the greater pilgrimage home. But on these long calls, Saeeda had begun talking about where she wanted to spend her last years, and it was a conversation so boring and interminable that I had to fight to get you to come to the phone.

"Auntie, did you hear about my new hiking boots?"

You blew a raspberry. "Boots? This is the good news?"

"And a hiking backpack."

"What a shopper you are turning out to be. When I was a teacher, my students learned the difference between Umayyads, Abbasids, Mughals, Safavids, and Ottomans, but mumtaz, you mastered the REI Memorial Day sale."

I had begun to understand sarcasm enough to feel foolish.

"Then tell me a story, Auntie! I love your stories!"

I could almost hear you roll your eyes on the other end of the line. In a somewhat flat voice, you began, "There was once a girl and a silver gazelle. They met in the hinterlands between sea and mountains, west of Nazareth, in a hilltop village built near a dusty old Roman temple. The village called itself—"

"No, slow! Like you mean it!"

But my mother pried away the phone and said to let you get back to your visit with the L.A. relatives, and we were late ourselves. Every Friday night my father drove us to the crow's nest, time my mother guarded jealously.

The crow's nest was no longer unclean, and my father seemed to approve of the amount of food in her fridge, the presence of sheets and matching pillowcases on both small beds, and the refill counts on my mother's orange prescription bottles. She kept her hilltop aerie not because she didn't love him, but because she would never trust him in the same way, and she needed a place in her life where it was okay to put a six-foot folding table in the bedroom or her wet boots in the bathtub or have four stacks of journals twice my height—a place, in short, that was becoming more like your old apartment every year and whose clutter felt, to her, like a refuge.

Tonight he was programming her new wireless router. They were both in adult mode, and my mother sloughed off my request to call you back to finish the story. She knew it by heart but feigned ignorance and told me to play outside. She poured Coke for herself and a Coke and Crown for him.

I sat outside under a peach sky, staring into the tree-murk. Daytime lingered till almost bedtime, and the coyote was slinking out of the gulley, carrying a new pup from this year's litter in her mouth. She headed across the hillside—flash of red shoulder here, sweep of pale fur a moment later, then gone. The coyote had transferred one pup, then the other in absolute silence. Dad had guessed she had more than one den in the park and moved her family around to keep it safe. My heart hammered for her to come back. It was impossible to write to Anna about everything I thought; easier to imagine that restless creatures understood a misfit like me, shuttled between homes.

"Alot," I whispered between the wooden porch rails, wanting to summon her for one last sighting, but the name felt as loose and irrelevant as my own. Inside the glowing rectangle of the kitchen window, Mama stood at the counter with a peanut butter and jelly sandwich. She fed a piece of it to my father and said something that made him look up from the instruction sheet and briefly squeeze her leg.

I showed up for school that day vibrating with excitement. I have to admire myself as a child. It never once occurred to me to expect an empty mailbox on that particular day, much as it doesn't occur to you to expect a piano to fall from the sky. After lunchtime, sure as the law of gravity, Anna's letter would be waiting.

I mention my innocence only to marvel at it, the way you once marveled over old photographs of yourself. *Not a wrinkle, not a blemish!* Not a hiccup of bitterness in me back then as I steered my precious love through the swamp of a day, uncomplaining.

The lunch bell rang and our teacher waited for the chattering tide of students to fill the hallway; then she led the line of us out into the human river toward the cafeteria. I always took rear point in any queue: out of sight, out of mind. I could hit back with my heavy hand if I needed to, see what was happening, and once we were through the doorway, be safe in the view of whatever teachers were leading classes from rooms farther along the hall. It gave me a diaphanous sense of control, but not enough to hide how dwarfed and anxious I felt during room changes. Lunch was even worse, and I would have found a way to stay hidden in the classroom except for how much I enjoyed eating—the from-scratch Pasta Mondays, in particular. The odor of meat sauce tumbled down the hallways, along with the soft, sticky humidity of the kitchen. It was enough to make us children forget, for a thirty-minute eternity, who we were and who we hated and what the score was. Truce by lunch tray.

So, my mind was on macaroni when tall Felix paused to drink from the hallway fountain and someone shoved him into it, groin-first. The tan fabric of his slacks darkened and clung.

And a small, strong voice said over the clamor: "He just wet his pants! I saw it happen! Felix wet his paaa-ants!"

That's all it took to set off a hallway full of people who were not, strictly speaking, very long out of diapers themselves: a boy in wet-fronted khakis, red-faced and protesting.

Another voice: "And he brings cat poop to school!"

"So gross! Felix plays in toilets!"

"Felix wets his pants!"

This responsorial came in girls' voices from near the fountain, somewhere in the third-grade line, repeated two or three times more as the news of Felix's bladder shot back through the ranks. A wildfire of disinformation and rumor blazed. By the time I was seated in front of my macaroni and meat sauce, at least three separate students in the upper classes were insisting that they had caught Felix up to his elbows in the boys' room toilet. *The kid was obsessed.* And he was a bed wetter, according to his sleepover friends.

From where I sat at the end of the table, I could watch the full weight of ecstatic storytelling land on Felix. He hardly ate anything. Like a chameleon's skin, his ivory cheeks reddened. His eyes pinked, and he cried. His upper lip pushed out and he sat there with his hands in his lap, tears coming down his face, hair damp with sweat. The ecstatic storytelling shot around the cafeteria in circles, above his head and out of reach, shuttling around him like a filament of spider silk, engulfing him like an insect.

Maybe lunch could have gone on that way, until the wobbling feeling of recognition in my chest spilled over into pity. He'd gone to take a drink at a fountain, and a piano had fallen on him from the sky. Maybe my pity could have ripened into kindness and I could have picked up my plate of macaroni (almost gone now) and moved myself into one of the chairs that had emptied around him. Maybe I could tell you that this was exactly what happened, how we forgave and forgot, but I am determined not to lie very much.

What happened was that two teachers came over, moved his hair out of his eyes, draped an arm around his shoulders, murmured something soft in his ear, and escorted him to the nurse's office to help him dry his pants and call his father. Felix was the youngest son of a lo-

cally famous basketball player, and when he was transferred to another school at the end of the week, it was a much better one attached
to a fancy prep school.

I wiped at the meat sauce with my bread, full but not. Something
in the teachers' interruption left me grasping, feeling like I was after
a word that kept slipping away. The hurry of their approach, the gentle shelter of their exit. Was that it? The scooped arm across his shoulders, the way his shoulders convulsed with a sob?

No, his tears were the thing that bewildered me. So many of them,
over so little.

> Dear Betty,
>
> Thank you for the soap. You didnt need to give me anything to push
> Felix into the water fountain. I think he will leave you alone. My friends
> say to tear up this note and not tell.
>
> My sister says also to tell you the truth: I knew your name. Nobody
> else is from that part of the world and I already heard about the cat
> poop. I wanted you to trust me. Now we can be friends for the rest of
> school.
>
> Can I come see Alot? Where do you live?

Anna would be my first and most steady friend that summer and for
years. She was my secret stone, my loose brick among her own group
of friends, the only one who ever let herself be seen talking to me.
Yet I loved her so much that I found excuses for us not to speak, and
to continue most of our friendship by email after the school year had
ended. The distance was a relief for us both. She was shy and busy
with dance lessons. I, sick with nerves, was too quiet to navigate a
conversation. Our peers wanted to be doctors, veterinarians, paint-
ers, and pilots, but I had trouble imagining anything for myself
beyond tomorrow. Maybe I could grow up to be one of those mid-
century switchboard operators my grandmother had told me about,
a disembodied voice courteously splicing voice into voice from the

solitude of a basement, overhearing and silent. I wanted to be a me-
dium, not a self; I wanted to be the walls of the room but not its
occupants. Career Day offered no suggestions, for it was unsurpris-
ing that our teachers had overlooked the toiling, unglamorous work
of the archivist when showcasing futures that might deliver the
American dream.

My correspondence with Anna edged into the summer, once every
few days, and went through an account my mother checked. It was
evidence of a friendship, and she and my father were cheerful about
it, as if I were a spinster finally being courted for love. Both of them
distrusted the other's relationships—my father's affair had started
with a workout buddy, and my mother had a tendency to be swept
along by outsized personalities—so of course they took too much
interest in mine.

"Invite her over," my father said. "It's polite."

My mother was uncharacteristically firm about it. "Your father can
set up his telescope on my porch and show you both how to look at
the moon. The next full moon is in"—she checked an app on her
phone—"five days."

In summertime, dusk at our latitude came late. Anna and I crouched
along my mother's porch railing, facing the forest, out of things to say.
Please, I projected into the trees. *Hello. Let us see you.* I had not spotted
the coyote for weeks, but Anna had been so happy for this visit that I
couldn't pretend to be sick. Now her desire to see the animal gave off
an electric charge. The moon was rising, and my parents hovered in
the kitchen, doing a poor job of pretending to ignore us.

I felt a question coming before she asked it. "You really live here?"
she whispered.

"Yes."

"You told me you live in a house."

"I do."

"Are your parents divorced?"

"Sort of."

I kept the answers short and my eyes on the trees to avoid self-incrimination. The silence was Anna's struggle to ask the right question, the one, I thought, that would explain what made me such a poor fit everywhere. I heard the questions whispered at school: Had I always been this color, what did it mean, was it sickness, was it taboo? *What is wrong with you?*

Anna tugged a loose hair off her lips. "Why does your dad have one hand?"

"Oh." I hadn't thought about it much. "His motorcycle squished it a long time ago."

"My sister says when you get really famous, sometimes you have to sign a contract not to ride motorcycles. Like if you play the piano or dance. I'm never going to ride a motorcycle so I don't get hurt."

"Me either."

I could feel her looking at me, waiting for more.

"Promise?" she said.

I thought of falling, cracking, the dust of me everywhere, and doctors saying what they always said: *I don't know.* Or, worse, *Stone-cold normal.* Sometimes words weren't just a vessel; they were a prison. A swirl of uncommon fear caught me up, as though I were already falling with no one to help.

"I promise. Yes."

She extended a hooked pinkie finger. I'd seen her friends do it at school, and before she could change her mind and retract her hand, I caught her finger on my own. Her skin was cool like mine, delicate like my mother's.

"I promise," I repeated, meaning *everything forever.*

The silence settled again, easier but still disturbed by other questions on pause—a curiosity that had slipped further away, like the sun behind the hills. She shifted her body toward the forest and said if I unfocused my eyes sometimes I would see the ghosts of saints walking in the trees, and we sat there with our faces hanging through the bars, practicing an attentive thousand-yard stare. The kitchen faucet hissed on for a moment, stopped, and then came my father's baritone in the living room over the opening music of a show my mother liked to watch on his laptop. They were the sounds of my parents' boredom with us, their friendship with each other, the sounds of the blue half hour before the full moon crested the trees, of the hum of crickets in the grass, of everything in the long twilight awaiting beauty, love, entertainments—a summer season of the heart. I wanted to tell Anna everything I knew, from blue soap till now, but my tongue was still. I couldn't bear to interrupt, to impose the ticking clock of a sentence on the shared quiet. It would have disturbed the symmetry of our waiting. We were out there together, and no one was watching me.

Story Hour with

Interrogating Soldier

———•·•———

Imagine my body in another country tomorrow night, poised at a desk just inside the border. Imagine the sheet of Plexiglas between me and a uniformed immigration officer. Imagine our faces superimposed on my reflection there, but because this bureaucrat sees the phenomenon a hundred times every day, the overlay of human faces is drained of its metaphorical potential.

I've thought about it every sleepless night. The moment when I step off the airplane and up to this booth window, I will have stepped into a new identity as a foreigner. For ten years of my childhood, at least, I felt stripped naked. It took time to learn to wear my body, to find the balance of invisibility and pride that helps me get by in the only country my feet have ever touched. I'll abhor feeling like a child again, a fringe individual who has a skin condition, who is possibly a threat, and this struggle will become a large part of my life while I petition to stay with my beloved in her country and learn not only a new language but daily psychic survival. Would I endure this for her? She says she already does it for me here, but it makes me doubt that she really understands what she's asking me to do. There are a lot of

Felixes in the world, and in every iteration of the tale, one way or another, he always hurts me.

The easiest thing to do is stay home. But my mother told me she's not an invalid, and she has said many times how glad she is to have raised a brave child. She says not to fear starting again, being unhinged from the familiar. It's a new experience and yet the same exile you knew so well. So the second-easiest thing to do would be to follow my heart, go with my gazelle as she bounds back to her home country, and let the bullying bureaucrats turn me away with a rejection. Instead of a resident card, I'd get a brief tourist visa, a stamp in my passport, a month to say goodbye, and then I would return to my family, my job, my few friends, and Mama. In this scenario I'd have no real power, but I'd get a taste of two futures superimposed on a single month of my life, and then, oh well, declare my loss and come home. My beloved and I have discussed the conveniences of such a planned failure, but here's the thing: I am not interested in tricking myself into thinking I made a choice, nor in letting bureaucrats hold all the power. You gave me my pride, and I am an auntie, too. I have an example to set.

If I go with her, I'm going, and I'm going to fight to stay there.

But *if* is a very small word, soft as a breeze.

This is what I've come to ask you, Auntie: When you ran away for love, did you know you were abandoning everything? Did you know that you'd become just a girl in a story? Would you have gone, had you recognized the *if*finess of everything you'd once recognized?

In your little cardboard notebooks, your writing is so haphazard even my grandmother struggled to read it. Some years ago, after months of pressure from my mother, Saeeda started a translation of what you wrote, but even though she outlived you by a decade, she left the task unfinished. The work was tiring, and she'd found it uncomfortable and difficult and often boring. You were not a linear person, preferring to stuff your discomforts and difficulties inside eddies and convolutions, so the little notebooks held grocery lists, birthdays, phone numbers, directions, fragments of fact, and then the occasional blood-spattered grievance ejected onto paper in a jagged whole, like a bullet tweezed from your heart. My grandmother translated these brutal self-surgeries in short summaries, as embarrassed as if she'd caught you naked, then shoved them into the attic box where I found them a few days ago.

It is more than luck that your notebook containing material from the 2011 Palestine trip survived, the one whose first pages held an orange California poppy and whose last pages held a red one from home. I think you left it out for Saeeda to find at the house, maybe to get some distance from it, or to make sure the truth wouldn't be lost. It is this notebook that I have open now, a messy, dark green artifact with Saeeda's reluctant annotations pinned to the cover on a folded leaf of yellow paper. It tells what happened in scribbled impressions from the plane trip home, forcing me to imagine flesh on the bones of fact. The grave usually gets the last word. But I am a professional resurrector, as well as an auntie who can recognize the truth when I hear it.

And that was the purpose of your and Saeeda's trip back to Palestine, too. To be courageous—though it had taken you almost three years to gather that courage, once you had promised Saeeda on Kelly's deathbed to accompany her. You and my grandmother would confront what you recognized in yourselves and what remained of the Rummani soap factory. All you'd had to go on for years were those few photos: halfway up a wall, a blue doorway. On the floor, the ceiling. One story after another hiding beneath what was left of the roof, leaving everything that used to be there to the imagination. Against the profound fragmentation of your life, you wanted resolution, even if you had to invent it yourself.

Why, I asked one day, did the Rummanis come to America?

"Your auntie brought us all from Nablus," said my mother. "I don't recall the details."

I pictured you—legendarily the most cavalier woman to come out of 1950s Nablus—getting off a plane with all of the Rummanis tucked in a package like a carton of Marlboro Lights. It would be a long time before I actually understood how we were your doing. Also, Nablus, the factory, and the family you brought to life in your stories—all of this was, to some extent, an invention—it would be my grandmother who, in translating your notebooks many years later, created the English-language evidence.

Fact: You never set foot in Nablus until 1948, when you were twenty-seven.

Fact: You came to America in 1954, a married impostor.

Fact: You had returned to Nablus only once, in 1959 for Saeeda and Jibril's wedding, months late. When the remaining family erected a stone for Jibril twenty years after that, you had not been allowed across the border because of problems with your travel documents.

You had spent a lifetime telling the stories of a city you had lived in for fewer than seven years. You'd been a cavalier woman who came out of Nablus the way people come out of a roadside rest stop, merely passing through on their unguessable journeys. And that year of the new millennium, at the border once again, you sat in the car, softly nauseated with dread.

"It always hurts to come home," my grandmother murmured. But when the car reached the barrier, and the fees were paid and bags surrendered and American passports presented, and the nephew who had driven you turned the car around and headed back toward Amman, the border guard read each page of both passports and then put them in his pocket.

He pointed down the hallway to a waiting room.

"Someone will speak to you about your visit."

You had always known this day was coming.

I want to be clear. The interrogation was not my fault. My photograph did not matter until the second hour. The problem first arose with the

Rummani last name, and grew worse when the guards understood
that their quarry was heading for (of all the Palestinian weekend get-
aways) the recalcitrant, scarred, undying city of Nablus. So even then,
even with the American passports, the border might have been a
problem—except that one of the Israeli officials marched back into
the hall and confronted you with a surprising accusation.

"Madame, our system informs us you are dead."

You laughed. Then coughed to cover the offense. "It must be a mistake."

The fine-boned man sliced his finger through the air, excising
humor. "Your identity is not valid because Nuha Rummani is dead.
You need to explain."

"Yaani, I'm aging well for a corpse. Or else your system is wrong."

"Madame, you will need to come with me. This is a big problem for
you."

"Nobody takes my beating heart as seriously as I do, let me assure
you. But if the wise computer system of Israel says I am no more, even
as I live and breathe, well, this might be one for the philosophers. Or
a computer repairman." You were speaking so loud that Saeeda
cringed and other travelers looked over at you. Two guards in the
doorway touched their machine guns. The official tensed himself like
a man about to escalate a bar fight.

"The Israeli screening system is the best in the world. Are you
against Israel, madame?"

"At the moment it seems I'm crushed against it like a lover."

The other travelers looked away. The official was one of those square
youths who never know what to do with extravagant people. He actually shuffled his shoes on the waiting room's dull tiles before addressing himself to Saeeda.

"Madame, this is a problem for you as well, traveling with someone
who has been dead for many years."

"Is that right?" Saeeda's aloofness swept across her features like ice
creeping across the surface of a pond. It was the same expression my
grandmother had been giving bullies since her childhood. She had

the brutal patience, in other words, of a woman who had put two husbands into the ground and still planned to live many years. If Israeli security wanted to turn them away, she would calmly summon the nephew and wait for a ride back to Amman.

But the official was afflicted with a contrary optimism of his own, and he said, "We will need to detain you until we get to the bottom of this. Come with me. Someone will speak to you about your identities. Everything has an explanation."

Inside the terminal holding room were what looked to you and my grandmother like an impossibly young staff of officials, haranguing the two dozen or so travelers with stupefying questions. These interrogators were dressed in lightweight bureaucratic uniforms but projected a more hostile, soldierly air. Because their system insisted Nuha Rummani was dead, they took you and Saeeda to a smaller office deeper in the building.

An American passport should have been helpful, but not today, not with the ponytailed, cheerless teenager who seated herself next to a computer and proceeded to shake her head grimly at the log-in screen. You folded your hands on your cane, having both dreaded and expected this sort of performance since airport security in San Francisco. Your pulse beat in your neck, and you worried about Saeeda, even though it had been Saeeda reassuring you all the way here, saying you both would eat something in Jericho. But as in Zeno's paradox, each step had gotten you only half the distance to a food vendor, and now you were starving. Your bladder was full. What a pair—old ladies, a real threat to the nation. The officials regarded the two of you like a pair of land mines forgotten under the back garden for half a century, still theoretically dangerous.

The barrage of questions began anew: Nationality? Then why do you speak English like an Arab? Why didn't you tell me the truth the first time? Where did you get this passport? Do you feel more American or more Palestinian? If you didn't want to live in the Palestinian territories, why are you here? What organizations in the Palestinian territories do you belong to? You will need to write down the names of everyone you know who is still in the Palestinian territories . . .

You could always make yourself sound as boring as a wet sandbag when you needed to. "American. I was not born in America. I applied for it from the government. I am alive. You can see in my official document that my nationality is American. I don't understand, I am alive. I feel like an auntie, and most of my grandnieces and nephews are American . . . What, organization? In Palestine?"

"There is no such thing as Palestine!" The official made the word sound like a disease. Her eyes sharpened behind her glasses, steel-rimmed librarian frames that drew subtle attention to her heart-shaped face. She belonged on an advertisement for an optometry practice, but seemed unaware that she was out of place in a desert interrogation room. "What Palestinian websites did you visit before your trip?"

You stifled a sigh of irritation. Only someone brainwashed by bureaucracy could assert that the living were dead and, moreover, sit on the border between Jordan and Palestine and declare that the territory just beyond it did not exist. The remark deserved nothing but a blank-faced look of confusion.

"In California? I don't use a computer. I don't have children . . . I don't remember . . ."

"Arabs always have children. Why don't you have children?"

"I gave it everything I had, but two wrongs cannot make a right."

She only looked puzzled. "Jokes will get you nowhere."

"What jokes, I only said—"

"Write the names of your family members. Everyone you can think of—there must be more than that. Write, write." The official flagged another woman over to the desk, who came spidering over on a wheeled office chair so they could both watch you hunched over the pen and paper as you wrote down the names of all the Rummanis buried in the Nabulsi cemetery. At the top of the list was my grandfather Jibril. The official began typing, then snapped her tongue against her teeth. Family who *still were living* in the Palestinian territories.

"Since I am dead, should I not start in the cemetery?"

"Have you ever been to prison?"

"Excluding this office? I am just trying to get through without anyone calling me dead."

"You didn't say that," said the first official. "You said you are visiting family."

"I did not. I am just writing their names like you told me to."

"More funny jokes. Nuha Rummani died forty years ago in a prison in Judea. What is your real name? I will need to see your phone—calls, texts, everything."

You put your hand to your little string purse and covered the zipper. "Why? I'm an American, not a Palestinian."

"Jokes, jokes. The joke is you expecting to see the other side of this border."

"I saw Palestine from the road. Your eyesight is terrible for someone with such flattering glasses."

"If you were innocent, you would not be so hostile. Show me your phone. Who are you in such a big hurry to meet?"

You rolled your eyes. "John, then."

The official lifted her eyebrows a millimeter and shook the paper in the air. "John who? You left that name off your list."

"I need the john then, I said. Are you listening? I am an old woman. It is urgent."

"Sit there and hold it," the official said. "If you soil Israeli property like a dumb dog, I will treat you like one. You need to cooperate to clarify the facts. Tell me again, the truth this time, where you were born, where you acquired a false passport, and who you are here to meet. Also, you must agree to have your phone searched . . ."

There was once a girl and a silver gazelle.

They met in the hinterlands between sea and mountains, west of

Nazareth, in a hilltop village built near the white bones of a Roman temple. The village called itself Maaloul. It had a church and a mosque and a spring. It lay in the long morning shadow of Jebel Tabor, the mountain where, people said, a long time ago, the boy Jesus jumped to the ground.

Who remembers if it really happened? There is no truth but in old women's tales.

The girl took the long way to the spring twice a day because her stepmother was too stupid to count a handful of almonds, but she ruled over the house and her husband's carpentry shop like an occupying bureaucrat. It wasn't the family the girl wanted, not the family where she belonged, but her brothers were bones in the dirt.

And it was there, a ways off from the clear water, that the lonely girl visited an animal she had never seen before: a silver gazelle. The creature was in a circle of colorful tents, and was advertised as the singular specimen in the land, able to tell your future.

Now, the girl herself was a fine specimen of *Homo sapiens*. Her black hair was long enough to tickle her feet and she wore it in a crown of braids. Her arms were white as a peeled cucumber, more curves than a mountain road, smart eyes. Her family was counting on a good bride price because they still did weddings that way, although by then televisions existed in the world.

But there, where the light tilted through the trees, changing everything, stood this young gazelle. Her legs were slender and strong as saplings. Liquid black eyes. They were so wide that this gazelle, she seemed to be looking into the back of the girl's soul, as if they had known each other before in some other place. Her coat was the color of ash, and she had a round, strong breast like a bird's. She stepped on delicate feet along the carpet of grass toward the girl, unafraid.

The gazelle's coat glittered with the dust of other horizons, promising the future, intoxicating the girl with desires she hardly recognized. The gazelle got closer, and the girl reached. She wanted to touch the pretty gazelle's long neck, to run her hand over that soft curve and over her muscular flank.

Do you know what it's like to be bewitched? Your mind bends. Your entire life shrinks to the size of a small room. The imagination is a fever. You can't stand it. Nobody can stand it—that's the point of falling in love. The reckless thought occurred to her that she might fling both arms around that neck, draw her body onto the creature's back until she could smell the perfume of open air, and let her run wherever those slender, strong legs might take them. No second-guessing, none of this waffling that will infect the generations after her.

And so she went. Away from Maaloul, away from its spring and the holy mountain, away from the colorful tents and Roman ruins, away from the graves of her brothers, who had died in the revolt, and of her mother, who had died from grief. The gazelle ran to the setting sun, to purple twilight, to the whispering white sea. The girl loved the gazelle for taking her to freedom, and so long as they were together, so long as they belonged to each other, the girl was blind to everything else. Love is forgetting.

But this time, in this version, the gazelle ran to the enormous port city of Haifa.

"What school did you attend in Haifa?"

You hesitated. "The French missionary school."

"Which one?"

"With all due respect," you said, "there *was* one. You cannot tell me what my eyes saw."

"I asked *which* one," the interrogator said. "The name of your school."

"I'm very old. It was . . . on Mount Carmel. Look it up in your best-in-the-world computer system."

"What year was this?"

You flicked your hand at the question, which buzzed around your head like a blowfly. "I don't know. Twenties, thirties—I thought you people didn't care about anything that happened between ancient Babylon and 1948."

Weariness and anger trembled through the tendons of your neck and hands. Having been bullied into turning over your phone, you watched yet another official enter with two documents. One, a picture of me that had been printed from the phone's photo library. Bright blue and inexplicable, comprehensible only in the present framework of suspicion. The other paper's contents drew a lift of the official's eyebrows, but he laid it facedown for now.

"Explain this costume, please," the official said, offering the photo of me.

"This is not a costume. This is my niece's daughter—"

"We need to know why she is the color of the Israeli flag."

"She is no such color."

"She is Israeli blue," the official insisted.

The remark landed exactly where it was aimed. "The Star of David is not the same blue," you said. "Even a color-blind person can see that."

"What would you compare her color to, then?"

"This is irrelevant, she is—"

"Cornflower? A blue sky in the Alps? Lapis lazuli? Or holy blue?"

"Lucky me, interrogated by a painter."

"We will stay here all night until you answer. Cornflower? A blue sky in the Alps? Lapis lazuli? Holy blue?"

You shut your eyes against an ice pick of a headache. "Fine. Holy moly."

The official snapped the paper onto the desk. "The blue Star of David represents the blue of our prayer shawl. This girl is the color of the Star of David on our flag. How can we believe anything you say?"

You glared. "That sounds like it should work in my favor, then."

It was like glaring at a brick wall. "Keep talking and you'll wish you were back here, chatting with me, after you see where they take you."

You lowered your eyes, fighting a stab of pure temper.

My face would sit for some hours on top of a stack of documents next to the computer, smiling between red backpack straps and a pair of pigtails. The shift changed. The guards left. New ones arrived. Each one looked at the other piece of paper but made no comment. Your heart hammered as you tried to imagine what it might reveal.

The interrogation was consolidated, and Saeeda was brought in, looking equally threadbare. She took the seat and settled her hand on yours. A warning, a placation. My face smiled up from the desk, but you were trying not to see the flag of your captors. It was peculiar, how fear made you perceive my strangeness anew.

"Let's try again," said the officer, a new one, a youngish man with a strawberry-blond beard. He was slower with his questions; he was pacing himself. "Now. Your passport says you were born in 1923. You claimed to have finished primary school in the twenties? You were a very precocious student, or your story has a flaw. Or it is not the truth."

"The 1930s, then," you said, frowning. "It is all the same anymore. What is five years more or less? It was not as important as the fact that we lived. I am old. I am tired, and you give me all these numbers to confuse me."

"So you made an inaccurate statement about your education a moment ago. Now we are getting somewhere. Can you"—he turned to Saeeda—"identify this woman?" He picked up the piece of paper that had been facedown all these hours. It was an older photo, perhaps from the 1960s or 1970s, judging by the masculine cut of the woman's blouse collar and her chin-length, curly hair. She was a stranger to you both: gaunt, with long, prominent clavicles and a narrow, strong jaw. The person glared into the camera, holding a number and standing against a bare wall. Her hands were dirty and her nails broken. Most startlingly, the photo was a mug shot, printed from a database.

Both women responded with stillness. Your attention was directed at the officer, but something behind Saeeda's eyes withdrew. Recognition seemed to wash over her—as it washed over you. The person in the photo resembled Jibril Rummani. She resembled kin. She did not, however, resemble you.

But my grandmother had not survived a cunning family for so long by being foolish. She folded her hands, gazing serenely at a point three inches to the left of the interrogator's ear.

"Bismissalib, the years have been unkind to us. This was so long ago. My sister-in-law has gone through sicknesses and decades and grief. This woman in the picture bears a resemblance to Nuha here, many years ago. Anyone would forgive you the mistake. But my sister-in-law was busy with her teaching job in California in these years. This person in the picture gave you a false name, surely."

The official seemed, for the first time, amused. "Has she shrunk by half a meter and gotten a new face, too? Does a camel turn into a crooked little pig as it grows old?"

Saeeda settled her hand again over yours.

"My sister-in-law came from Haifa in 1948. I met her after her schooling was finished, and she has been my constant friend for over sixty years. She immigrated to the U.S. when she married. Not everyone here puts the correct year on a birth certificate, so? Or gives a correct name to the police? You must know this. A dead prisoner with her name—we know nothing about it. Rummanis are everywhere. Let us go now."

"But," he said, addressing you, "your origin story is coming apart, and so is your stated purpose of visiting family 'at home' in Nablus. What schools and trainings have you attended, in what countries, and in what years? What about your husband's family? Begin again."

"Mills College in California. I got a teaching degree in 1965. Before that, I attended primary and secondary school in Haifa, in the French missionary schools, like the rest of my family there. That was in the twenties and thirties, yes, before we were chased back to Nablus, by you people."

"So you speak French." He switched from Arabic to French, said something while pointing at the two pictures on the desk, and waited for a response.

"Stop pointing your finger at my niece."

"He asked what subjects you taught in school, after you were a teacher," Saeeda said, her voice pitched low and urgent, before you could make this any worse.

"Oh." You folded your hands over your crocheted purse and sat up straighter. "I taught history. *Histoire*," you added, pronouncing the *H* and rolling the *r*.

The officer pressed his fingertips against the corners of my picture, the very edges that were white and without ink. "History. You don't seem to know it very well, either." The moons of his fingernails were purple in the hard air-conditioning. He seemed about to remark on me, on my picture lying on the desk, or else he just liked the way the two women leaned forward in their seats whenever he stared too long at the side-by-side faces of the child and the prisoner.

He smiled at you and Saeeda.

"It would be much easier if you gave me your real names. Let's begin again. Haifa."

No discredit to Haifa, mind you. The city was full of wonders, which worked their way into what used to be a familiar story about a pirate heading out to sea. Now other objects entered, adding something new to the story the final time you told it, long after you had returned to America. It just took me this many years to hear it with the right ears.

In this other version, there were British jeeps with chugging engines. Metal-sided ships. Radios in coffee shops. Officers' wives in tight-waisted, slithery dresses; in fine traditional embroidery; even a few in military stripes. Shop after shop, each with an expansive front window made of a single, flawless pane of glass. Streets were thronged with people, more people than the girl in your story had ever seen in one place at any one time in her eighteen years on earth. Yet even so, a girl riding a silver gazelle would be strange. Our girl slid off the gazelle's back and walked beside her, behind her, not even touching that tempting soft coat as the crowds in the streets thickened.

And then she lost sight of her beloved creature. The gazelle slipped away from her and disappeared, almost as though it was ashamed of her: embarrassed by the girl's country ways, her fellahin accent, her gawp-jawed surprise at anything big. Or maybe the city shocked them both, and they each got lost on their own paths. The girl wanted to believe it was all just an honest misunderstanding—so she ran through the streets, night and day for three days, shouting, "O gazelle! O beloved!" until she was a laughingstock for every dockworker, every washerwoman at her well, every merchant in his fancy automobile. But the gazelle did not come back. The girl was stranded and broken-hearted, and her long hair was dirty, and she was very, very hungry.

Here is where she usually goes to the docks and boards a ship.

But this time, her nose led her through an alleyway, up the stairs, across a terrace, down into a canyon of narrow streets, in whose belly burned a mountain-load of hot coals and dripping meat, crusty bread, steaming rice. Men and women forged through the marketplace, stopping to crowd around the braziers and eat and talk among the jungle of wares, rugs, pots, camera film, shoes, paper, tobacco, scarves of slippery fabric. Objects for every need. The girl lay down at the edge of the terrace, behind a wall of wooden crates, wondering if God would forgive her if she stole some meat. If she repented for letting herself be led away from where she had promised to stay. Repented every strange wish that cluttered her brain. How had she gotten here? Was there no road leading the other way, no way of reconciling her life?

How strange it is for nonspecific shame to surface in one of these old stories, making it new. What prompts our characters to decide to do what they do? The same private fires and fears as anyone's, it turns out.

During this very hour, as she looked down on the market and con-templated all the ways in which she was an error, she saw—not the gazelle, alas, but a boy climbing along the opposite roof. He was nine, maybe, a handsome boy, rich clothing, bare feet for stealth and grip. He seemed intent not on the shelf of fine cameras and watches, but on the table of little knives and old Ottoman bayonets. The trinket

vendor's back was turned. He was inspecting a necklace for a cus-
tomer who was feeding a sugar cube to the man's donkey.

The boy's foot slipped.

He caught himself, but a piece of broken tile plummeted. It struck
the donkey, and the donkey leapt back, startled. Its leg hit a bucket of
hot coals at the neighboring stall, the briquettes tumbling everywhere.
People lurched away, knocking into flimsy tables, racks of swaying
scarves. One thing happened after another, but it was a box of camera
film that ignited first.

The nitrates in the film all but exploded. A hundred little fires
danced to life at once. The market was chaos. More coals tipped from
a grill, and a leaking kerosene stove lit up rugs and draperies like kindling.

And the boy was trapped. His face was bleeding from a piece of
flying debris and his eyes were stupid with fear. So for no good reason
at all, he leapt into the flames. Why and when does a person choose
death? Maybe he thought he could run through the canyon of fire.
Maybe he didn't realize how hot it was, or maybe he knew he couldn't
stay where he was and he should end his pain quickly. The girl knew
he would die if she didn't come to his rescue. He was already a flailing
silhouette in the flames, lit strangely from every side.

She can't remember how it went. Later, she was sure it was her
braid. She unpinned it and lowered the fat plait from her high perch,
and miraculously, it grew and grew until it was long enough to touch
the ground. The boy clung to it, and she raised him to safety even as
the strands of her hair shriveled in the heat.

That's the way of it: you get the future that falls into your lap. It's
never the gazelle you asked for. It is usually a boy on fire, and then you
just have to deal with him.

He was badly burned. His face was a ruin. He sobbed. The fire was
all his fault. But the girl in this version of the story knew something
about shame, knew something about brothers dying too soon, and she
made a promise that she would keep for the rest of her life. She was
bound to this never-to-be-handsome, mortified, unlucky little boy. In

the years to come, she would save his life again, she would lie for him, she would steal for him, she would march across Palestine and then the entire world for him. She believed he was a project from God, a reason to belong nowhere in the world but where she was needed, a chance to put her idle hands to better use.

The girl walked out to the city's main street, cradling him in her arms. Her hair was singed from her head. Her hands and feet were blackened. She held against her breast this wounded child in his princely clothes, and the women cried out and wrung their hands and pointed up the road to a kingly walled house.

And suddenly she was being pulled indoors and told that the boy was the son of Hakim Rummani, of the banished Rummanis of Nablus. "The boy's name is Jibril," they said, "and he is burned to an inch of death's door."

I should be explicit here. The answers you were giving to the Allenby Bridge Terminal staff were not quite the family stories. They were not quite your own stories—I am substituting the ones you told me, and filling in from what I read in the notebooks, mortaring some holes in the family memories using the archives, resurrecting the truth bit by bit. Then shocking it to life with my surprise.

But at the time, you answered their questions as succinctly as possible. The interrogators learned to interrupt if you spoke more than a few words at once.

My photograph, however, still lay on the desk next to the other one.

If you hesitated to give an answer, one of them would graze the papers with his fingertips. As you grew tired, as you forgot what you'd said a moment ago, as you felt that you were withering inside your skin with cold and hunger and confusion, the essential blueness of my smiling face began to float off the page, stroked by the hands of pencil pushers exposed since birth to the casual dislike of *Aravim muloukhlakhim,* dirty Arabs. The silent stranger in the other photograph seemed to know this bigotry even better than you, and her eyes accused you of being a conspirator. Called you a traitor and a thief. And meanwhile, there I was, a grin between two pigtails. Dressed in a school uniform and with a red backpack over my shoulders. Everything as it should be for a girl of seven except that indelible mark. And was it a journey so different from your own? It all began to seem illicit.

Under questioning, under the sort of skepticism you had not faced in sixty years, you wondered whether it would end this purgatory just to tell the truth, and admit that it had been so long since the beginning of your own story that you no longer remembered how it went.

Winter 1947. The girl was twenty-seven years old if she was a day, but we'll keep calling her a girl, for narrative convenience.

By then, she'd been a servant in the house of the Haifa Rummanis for nine years. She still wore her hair in a crown of braids, but since the fire, it had grown in as a voluptuous red.

She bought chickens and trussed them for the pot, fussed over the winter kitchen garden, and scrubbed wet laundry up and down the washboard until the muscles in her forearms twitched with fatigue. She liked it best when the pretty cook, a widow with heavy eyelids who always looked half-seduced, tasted her saffron rice and made that low, intimate noise of approval. She was good at eliciting that sound from the pretty cook—one way or another. The girl's household talents, however, were best applied in the market. She was a demon negotiator; she could stretch the week's budget like rubber, even if it meant catching game birds from the edge of the forest herself and weaving the household brooms by hand.

The widower Hakim, the head of his house and the proprietor of a seventh-generation shipping business, eventually noticed the surplus and lumbered down from his office and into the kitchen garden. He chewed at his heavy silver mustache as if it were cud. He was an unlucky man, people said, because he'd lost his eldest child, a daughter named Nuha, who had run off with a Turk in a boat. But he rerouted his paternal feelings toward his kitchen staff, and he admired the servant girl, he said at last, because she was the only person in this god-forsaken city who was carrying on with life with any measure of sensibility and calm.

"No matter what happens, you will stay with my family as though you are one of our own."

He rasped out the compliment as though shaving it off a marble slab. It both awed her and left a cold shard of fear lodged in her breast. She wasn't afraid of her boss—when his children were not around, she called him *djeddi*, grandfather, for he was kind, and in his dignity and indulgence he reminded her of her village elders. But in spite of these qualities, or more likely because of them, she was afraid of his fear.

The house that had become her home was built of cool buttermilk-colored stone. Its architecture was square, heavy, tight—built in 1918 to attract the admiration and business of the British, who by 1947 had overstayed their welcome by a few decades. In January, old Hakim moved the Sparton radio from the drawing room and put it in a for-bidden room of the house, the one that had belonged to his daughter, locked up with all the other bad news he didn't want to think about. The girl retreated to the shade of the courtyard arbor in the evening, needing to escape the distrust and unease of the streets. On Epiphany night, she drifted asleep out there to the nasal clang of an out-of-tune piano. Hakim's youngest son played it, and only when he was upset.

Yes, poor Jibril, her boy on fire. He had struggled his way to seven-teen. He was lanky and sullen, and his face—oh. Slippery burn scars crisscrossed it like worm trails. When he blushed at the pretty cook (not that she blushed back), the scars stood out white against his skin. He was the third of three sons, never to inherit the family business, so he lurked over his math problems and dreamed of college abroad. One day, he confided in the servant girl that he wished he had run away with his sister, Nuha, when she'd gone. Being too young at the time, he couldn't remember her clearly, except that she was tall and strong.

"She was probably like you," he said one evening. "Fierce enough to walk through a fire and not be ruined. Smart enough to find a way out of this city before the Jewish militias take over and expel us."

The rumors in the house were that his father was looking east, to the mountains, and dreaming of escape. The British were ceding their thirty-year control over Palestine so that the new Jewish nation could be born into the world, combat boots first. Its military would shock the country with a careful display of violence, scare Arabs rich and poor from the cities, and roll outward to confiscate land and property as their own. Being the territory's only deep-water port, Haifa was valuable and would fall soon.

Old Hakim wasn't a coward, but he wasn't a fighter, either. Whatever retreat he chose, it would have to be the graceful, profitable retreat of a businessman.

He chewed his mustache to a frazzled yoke of whiskers, weighing options. The tensions between the British overlords, the locals, and the flood of new immigrants had complicated his business. It added time and expense to every task—especially transporting his chief export, prime Nablus soap, from the inland mountains out to the port cities. The roads were full of jumpy gunmen, jumpy soldiers, and wary locals, to whom the transportation of soap was the least of their problems. Beyond the sea, the postwar European markets were in smithereens, mourning sixty million dead and in existential need of steel and engineers. In these cracked hands, a cube of olive oil soap had become a joke.

Meanwhile, the other Rummanis, the usurper Rummanis of ancient Nablus, grumbled over their ledgers. They accused everyone of theft, from the lowest farmer picking olives to the highest-born businessman in the seaports. They drank tea for heartburn and brooded on the future, too. And it was there, in the dawn of 1948, that they received an offer, delivered by kin they had not spoken to in decades: the widower Hakim and his youngest son, Jibril. For the price of the factory, its warehouse, its olive oil contracts, its orchards, all of their outstanding debts, and the benefit of a family discount on storing and shipping the soap from Haifa, the scar-faced Jibril would marry their only child, a daughter with black ringlets and a taste for sweets. She was Saeeda, and she was not quite six years old.

Jibril's father argued that the factory was a business, and it belonged in the hands of real businessmen. Especially during such dangerous times.

The wedding would wait almost eleven years, but all of the family's Nablus assets would go immediately into a profitable trust and revert back to Saeeda only if Jibril perished before their future children came of age. It would be her trousseau in an otherwise unremarkable marriage contract. Gone, forgotten, was the bitter feud over blue Alissabat and her three blue daughters, the role of tattooed ogre-pirates, unworthy trollops, death by hot olive oil, and murder soap.

Because lawyers and bureaucrats drain the fun out of everything, don't they?

They do. And so does war.

In April, one month before the founding of the State of Israel, Operation Passover Cleaning mortared Haifa's neighborhoods, shot hundreds of men, and sent soldiers house to house with the threatening news that every Arab in the city was now a foreign criminal. It was a cleaning only in the sense that the new army thought of the city's inhabitants as dirt. When soldiers arrived at the buttermilk-stone house, however, all they found was a pile of cold ash in the courtyard, where the girl and the pretty cook and the rest of the servants had followed Hakim's orders to burn everything they couldn't transport to Nablus. They'd left a month ago, taking their money, clothes, important papers, and the Sparton radio. The girl had torn up the garden herself. By Operation Passover Cleaning, all that remained in the warren of bare corridors was one of the girl's hand-cut brooms: a sheaf of dead branches and uprooted grass.

"She is a threat to national security."

"My sister-in-law," said Saeeda, "is right here. She is a retired teacher and has not spent a day of her spotless life in prison. You must be mistaken."

Three other officers crowded behind the new interrogator, some sort of boss, a thick man wearing a black sweater over his white uniform shirt. He had an owlish way of looking around, moving his head but not his wide eyes. He seemed rushed, only perched on the edge of the desk, but had been asking questions for almost an hour.

"You cannot come into the country with a fake ID," he said.

"I am not dead, and that is not a fake ID," you said. "I am Nuha Rummani."

"Nuha Rummani of Haifa, by our records, was arrested for political activities and died in a desert prison." The stubble on his neck grated against his shirt collar. "What is your opinion of the Israeli army?"

You goggled at him. "This interrogation is nothing more than harassment. It is dark outside and we haven't had any food. I don't care what your computer says. Some dead prisoner told you once upon a time she is me? Look at my passport!"

"If you do not want to cooperate, I can hold you until you do."

"Then hold me." You shut your eyes. "Let me fall into your arms. My husband was gay as a three-dollar bill, and besides, he's the one who's dead."

Saeeda no longer sat with a straight back, and she was so tired she was on the edge of tears. Her hard reserve was thinning. The boss's stubble grated again as he spun his head all the way around to address one of the subordinate interrogators: "Get them each a cheese sandwich and some coffee so we can stay focused." His head swiveled again, and when you opened your eyes, you blinked: you were sure the stubble on his neck was actually a coat of pinfeathers.

He sent the other two officers out. The room felt bigger, colder.

When the door had closed, he situated his bottom on the desk, dangling his black sneakers.

"Your problem," he said, "would not be so bad except for your mouth. And you keep denying everything when it is already in the record. I'll offer you a favor." He leaned back awkwardly and pulled open a drawer. Plucked out a pen and paper. "If you don't want to tell us the truth, this will be the shortcut. A formal reason for denying your entry. If you each sign one, I will return your passports right away and personally see you on the first bus back to Amman. The reason for rejection, as it says here, is illegal entry with intent to disseminate anti-Israel propaganda."

Saeeda, the guardian of unimpeachable conduct, shook her head. "Propaganda?"

He searched around himself for a moment, picked up the picture of me, and shrugged.

"You have to be joking," she said. "If this is how your records get made, no wonder we have this problem."

"Then tell me the truth about your friend here." He set the papers aside. "That is an option. Her details are inconsistent; you didn't meet her, your own relative, until she was an adult woman. She is ideologically attached to this blue person. If you assist us in filling in some blanks for the sake of national security, maybe I could get you through. If you wanted to eat your sandwich in a separate room and think it over, I could arrange that."

Silence. Your sister-in-law seemed to be actually thinking it over.

You smacked your palm on her chair. "Saeeda!"

"I promise," Saeeda told the man. She shoved a tissue under the lens of her eyeglasses. "We will leave if you let us see our city one more time. We don't mean any harm. Just let us go. It is all a mistake. Innocent, this picture of the girl—she is only in costume for American Halloween."

You forced yourself to stop speaking. Saeeda wouldn't abandon you. She wouldn't sign some farce of a paper just to stick it to you after all these decades. It had to be a final bit of theater. You kept on telling yourself not to worry, hurling *had to be an act* against the rising tide of anger—right up to the moment when subordinates returned with two cheese sandwiches and two cups of coffee, and the boss directed one of the meals to be taken into the next room, and at his invitation, Saeeda stood up from her chair and followed him, tissue in her fist and purse under her arm, not looking back.

It takes an unnatural power to create an entire family. Only now, when I'm facing the end of my own life in America, do I imagine my nephew and young cousins, in short all the children in my life, living their lives in a future when in all likelihood I will be a distant memory, a blue auntie, the improbable figure of a childhood dream, the way we all sometimes remember things that did not really happen— and they, in turn, will also be less real to me, even though we will all have gained a degree of immortality for one another. Who will dry their tears? Who will wrap their arms around my legs? And my mother, will she try to take my place with them, just to sate her loneliness? We will just be ghosts, rattling around in our separate versions of what we thought happened. You, however, had spent more than sixty years of your life keeping everyone's story straight, especially your own.

Yet the smoother a history runs, the more likely it is to be full of holes. You put all your faith in this: the human tendency to mistake smoothness for beauty, like the draw of a young woman's cheek. And now those sacrifices had their cost.

For a while, the interrogators left you alone in the office. They took the laptop—the only valuable thing in the room—and departed. Locked the door. The plastic sandwich wrapper crinkled once in a while, balled in the trash. The coffee was undrinkable. The windowless room was bright and timeless, and you slouched back in the chair and counted holes in the ceiling tiles till your eyes watered. Then the lights went out.

Darkness permeated everything. It was as though your eyes had failed. The primal lack of light made the silence seem total, too, and in a moment of panic, you thought maybe it was true: this was death.

"Hello?"

The question bounced against the walls and died.

"Yoo-hoo?"

Gradually a pinstripe of light appeared beneath the door as your eyes adjusted. They had forgotten you, or wanted you to think they'd forgotten you. Although you knew it was probably a trick, Saeeda's abandonment made all of your doubts keener. Feeling around, your fingertips brushed against the coarse upholstery, the cold arms of the next chair, the greasy edge of the desk. Found the blotter and the picture of me.

A photograph in the darkness is just another piece of paper.

My face seemed to rise, dimensional, off the surface of the desk. It hovered, not quite visible, but more than something imagined, and a tangible presence nonetheless: the footprint of the elephant in the room, which had been there for sixteen hours. It was like you could fit your own self into my contours, if you only leaned forward somehow— not with your body, but with the more slippery shape of yourself that you carried in your chest and that did not age. Pressing close. Your heart hurt and your skin felt as delicate as wax. Something inside you was bubbling to the surface and trying to leak through the hours, the days, the years of layered anger and exhaustion—a softer person, someone as soft as cloth.

Tell the truth, Auntie, the one you'd scribble in a notebook later:

I don't know Nuha Rummani. Nuha Rummani ran off with a Turk in a boat. I don't remember the name I was born with. I served the Rummani family since the day I rescued a boy from burning. I was a girl, as common as cloth, and my name has unraveled from me.

The panic returned, the stacking of one breath on top of another.

"Help!" You clambered to the door and banged on it with the flat of your palm. "I am dying! I am having a stroke! My heart is stopping! I have gone blind! It is an aneurysm!" And for an eternity it really did feel like you were standing on the ceiling, shouting through a door on the floor.

Saeeda sat on a steel bench in the hazy apricot light of a Jordan Valley sunrise. For January, the air was already warm. She glanced up when you appeared in the doorway, blanched and unsteady. On the front of your blouse were a few brown freckles of blood; it looked as though you'd given yourself a nosebleed. But Saeeda was serene, a cool point in the morning, wielding knitting needles. All the suitcases were at her feet, and the tang of diesel drifted from a bus the color of the stains on your shirt. Without speaking, you boarded for Jericho.

Who knows why bureaucrats get bored? We'd have to assume they were interested in the first place. You had pounded, and the door opened. You were given your passport and met with a shrug when you asked for Saeeda. For all that, you were through.

Now you and my grandmother sat next to each other on the bus.

"Is it true?" Saeeda asked.

"You tell me, you stinking collaborator." It was supposed to sound regal, but it only sounded cranky. Beyond the window, a date plantation rushed past. The ease of the highway was a steadily unfurling pleasure after so long being stuck.

"I ate my sandwich," Saeeda said. She held a row of stitches closer to the window. "And I made myself finish that cup of goat-piss coffee and made sure to smile when I did it, and he said I could go. Then I might have mentioned gifts for his children and forgotten some of my cash on the chair, but it is hard to remember, since I was so tired and it was all very stressful for an old woman. But khalas, he let you go, too." She resumed knitting. "End of story."

The remark pulled a dry, angry chuckle from you.

"So is it true?" Saeeda asked. "The problem with your identification?"

The second question had the reserve of euphemism. The sharpness of a knitting needle, too. Saeeda was carefully not looking anywhere but at her work.

Your hands stirred in your lap, a kind of shrug.

"It's true. A long time ago, I was somebody else. But I'm no less of a Rummani." You studied the side of Saeeda's face for evidence of disgust, revulsion, anger—but your sister-in-law remained a still point in the neighboring seat. "You really have nothing to say?"

Saeeda gave a terse shake of her head. "Jibril talked when he drank. I already know who you are."

You spent years hiding in plain view. After your passing, Saeeda created the English-language evidence from your notebooks. But then she put it all in a box, those many years later, and taped it shut without telling anyone what she had known all along.

As of 1947

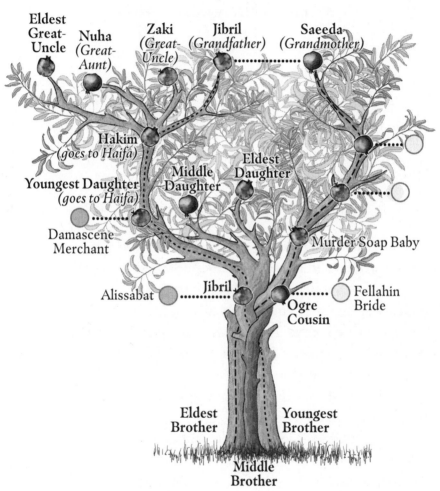

Eldest Great-Uncle
Nuha (*Great-Aunt*)
Zaki (*Great-Uncle*)
Jibril (*Grandfather*)
Saeeda (*Grandmother*)
Hakim (*goes to Haifa*)
Eldest Daughter
Middle Daughter
Youngest Daughter (*goes to Haifa*)
Damascene Merchant
Murder Soap Baby
Alissabat
Jibril
Ogre Cousin
Fellahin Bride
Eldest Brother
Youngest Brother
Middle Brother

The Skin and Its Girl

————•—►——

The factory and house no longer belonged to my family, of course. The former Rummani properties belonged to one of the city's charitable boards, so the news that had reached us over the years was tattered by hearsay. Completely demolished, some had said; just the upper story, said others. That was why, once in Nablus, Saeeda led you to the intersection at the far end of the meat sellers' market and halted. She spun once, puzzled. There was morning sky where no sky had been before; light where filtered privacy once reigned; an open street where there had been closed archways.

"Is it possible we're lost?" you ventured, for the first time not hiding the fact that you'd never known Nablus all that well. Not as well as Saeeda, for whom it was the first city of her life.

A youngish man delivering groceries to his mother's apartment across the street saw the two of you, marooned-looking women, figures he didn't recognize. He stopped, skeptical of your bare heads but not wanting to be rude.

"You see? Look at what they've done," he said, half-hoping Saeeda might be a foreign correspondent. If so, he'd leave the groceries in the doorway and lead her around the damage.

But my grandmother said, with a local accent, "I'm looking for the old soap factory that was here. Am I in the right place?"

He thrust his hand at the open space. The gesture rustled the plastic bags of bread and tobacco hanging from his wrist.

"A grave site, Aunties! Are you visiting someone?"

Saeeda turned her back to the broken stones and bits of garbage, because she never could bear to see a thing so naked. "Your mother is Umm Ala', yes?"

His expression softened. "My brother Ala' was martyred when they bombed the prison. Would you like to come upstairs? Our poor mother doesn't get many visitors. Tfaddalu, please, she would be honored to welcome . . ."

Saeeda said their names. His face lit with a complicated expression, one you both would see many times while in Nablus. Something like reunion, if it also reflected a betrayal. The Rummanis had not helped— they had pulled away when they were needed most. Some would say they were deserters. But Umm Ala', when she welcomed you in her apartment, apologized extravagantly for her poverty and praised the family for their wisdom in selling the factory, reminding Saeeda that her husband had once worked for the Rummanis in better days.

"Wallahi, the late seventies was the last good time for the soap factories—akeed, you must have gotten a good price. What could you do? You had to educate your children, or they might have ended up like my Ala', ya ibni, ya habeebi. Bombed in a cell. Martyred. Ya Allah. You saw his picture on your way in?"

His face was among the framed portraits around the rooms of her apartment, but his mother insisted on taking them to see another one. Umm Ala' was younger than Saeeda but eased herself down the stairs in a frail way, watching her feet touch each stone step, grazing the wall with the outside of her hand, until she'd brought you both to the antechamber off the street. She unbolted the metal door and stepped over the doorsill to the pavement, and stretched both hands to something on the façade.

"My Ala' was so handsome."

A poster, stuck to the wall with paste, was faded and peeling. Once it was an image of her son, but he was not the wild boy under a mop of black hair from long ago. He had been what—four? five?—and riding a handcart downhill, ecstatically imperiling everyone in his path. The face that glowered from the martyr poster was transformed—sure, by a white keffiyeh, by the Photoshopped Masjid al-Aqsa in the background—but mostly by his thin, solemn mouth, the almost purple shade of his lips. He'd grown up, but he'd also grown into someone shaped by specific grievances.

The posters were everywhere throughout the city. Some fresh, some brittled by nine years of weather. It seemed like an entire generation had been pasted on the city's stones.

"You see? Look at what they've done," she said. "Mujrumin, they were going to blow up our house. They put him in prison for trying to save a cat before the engineers detonated the explosives. I thought he was lucky not to get shot. But they carted him off and blew up our house anyway, and when they invaded—later in the intifada, you know—they blew up the prison and everyone in it. This is our situation. But inshallah we survive."

She ran her hand over the scaled paper, whispering to the image. Saeeda recoiled and turned away from Umm Ala', but there was nowhere to look but the ruins of the soap factory. A pair of cats, orange and black, slid under a slab of broken stone and disappeared. When the visit ended, she would slip money to the surviving brother on her way out, giving all the polite entreaties for his mother's life and health.

But by the end of their days here, Saeeda would admit to you that the city no longer felt like home. Selling out the family had bought her this estranged safety. You nodded absently, but later, smoking a bad-tasting cigarette in the hotel lobby, you felt that the nature of your involvement made it harder for you to disentangle yourself from Nablus. One of Saeeda's strengths, as well as her main weakness, was her profoundly literal mind. She had sold the factory, it had died in an air strike, and now she had confirmed her divorce from the entire place. Her privilege allowed her to heed the crawling sensation that had overtaken her as she'd toured the ruined properties. But as I'm learning: if you've taken responsibility for knitting people and places together in the imagination, what does it cost to disentangle yourself from that? You'd clothed yourself in the grand Rummani story, just as you'd clothed me in it. I wasn't just a blue child; I was blue *because* I was a Rummani. You'd written it on the blank page of my body since those chaotic years of the second intifada—but I see now, it was a truth not far off your own. Saeeda had sold the building, and the army had brought it down, but the story of it still mattered. Not only had you given your word to keep it alive, but you had skin in the task, too.

This story continues, wending in a way I'd never imagined, not until I dared to imagine myself living inside a new life. Our bold heroine— the girl who loved a gazelle and ran away to be a servant in Haifa— she found herself in Nablus at an interesting time. Isn't that true, Auntie?

Did you already know how long it takes to walk the Road of No Return? If you leave from the port of Haifa and walk inland to Nablus, it takes one week. Maybe twelve days if you try Nazareth first, and you are carrying all your valuables and traveling with children. Less if you hitch a ride. More if you get routed through Jordan, or try living for a few months in one city but find no job. Twenty thousand walked that road and all its tributaries, and the first arrived in Nablus by the end of May 1948.

Looked like ants to the girl, at first, because they came to the valley in a swarm of black dots. In the city and among the goatherds on the hills, everyone squinted through the sun and dust and shaded their eyes. These people were carrying rolled mattresses on their shoulders. They were carrying heirloom wooden chests of clothing. These people were carrying babies and jugs of oil and wearing fine, dirty shoes. Men in suits, men in traditional coats, women in their grandmother's embroidery, children dressed in four layers so that their arms were free to carry the pots and pans. Old women on donkeys, a hulking gravedigger who slung his shovel on his shoulder and batted dirt from his knees. Some carried nothing at all.

As the people watched, sullen figures filled the valley by the hundreds, followed by crows and dust. It was one week since the declaration of Israel, and the goatherds took off running down to the city, their donkeys galloping, dogs barking at their heels, to tell everyone the refugees had come.

In a few days, the church and mosques and schools overflowed with people, and then tents went up in the rocky orchards and in the old city. The well at Al-Yasminah almost ran dry with all the new washing and so many new throats. You couldn't go outside to buy sugar without seeing somebody crying against his sleeve. There were funerals without bodies. The priest barely slept; his church, whose walls and rafters usually held the quiet like a drum, was now as cluttered as the market and smelled like many bodies. These people, they carried so little with them, but they took up so much space, filling all the city's mosques.

At the Rummanis' ancestral house, old Hakim's Sparton radio was on around the clock, broadcasting either the news or some play or other. Distant relatives and strangers slept shoulder to shoulder among the pillars of soap; the boys stole cakes of it to give away in the camps, until lurking Jibril caught them at it, and then he sent them with three cartloads of it to distribute at the church and at the medical tents.

In chaos, you can be anybody.

Jibril, he became bigger. The acceptance by the Nablus Rummanis thickened his blood, and he stood up straighter. He avoided his future bride, the child Saeeda, as much as possible in the crowded house.

Hakim Rummani became old. He had the girth of a horse: his whole life through, he denied himself not a single bite of supper, nor let languish one sticky bite of kanafeh on his plate, lest he disrespect

his ancestral city; for his mother, who had been the only one of Alissabat's three blue daughters to survive, had told him in her final years,
when only the faintest trace of blue dye lingered around her mouth,
like death, that this dessert for which Nablus was famous was an antidote to forgetting. But now he was sick with grief and horror. When
his ancestral city flooded with these pathetic castaways, he refused all
nourishment. He nibbled at his own mustache. By the time the orchards of his new domain were heavy with olives, and a tent city obscured the ground between them, his skin hung from his bones like a
costume.

As for the girl, Hakim had given her a strange gift on the day their
household departed for Nablus. It was a suit made of skin.

The skin buttoned up the back, and he instructed her on how to
slide her arms and her legs into it for the best fit, and how to smooth
it over the planes and curves of her face and around her eyes. To go
with it, he had given her a chest full of clothes suitable for the eldest
daughter of a Haifa merchant: dresses, new shoes, jewelry, even a mirror and a silver brush. He instructed her on how to care for the skin:
she must not plunge her hands in hot water, must not hurry, must not
let the broomstick or trowel handle wear at its delicate finger pads.
She must wash it in rose water and oil, and keep it out of the sun. She
was to treat the gift like his grandmother's own embroidery: to respect it, in other words, as something she was not capable of having
created on her own, nor might ever hope to repair should it become
damaged in her care.

The skin fit so close that each morning she sat in the gray sunlight
at the foot of her bed, stiff and still, smoothing her silken shift across
her knees like a pet cat. It hurt to lift her arms. It hurt to smile. She
turned down as many visitors as Hakim would permit in the first
weeks of her arrival in Nablus, and she felt especially afraid of the
servants. They couldn't *not* see through the milky outer membrane,
underneath to the real calluses and freckles. She twitched with restraint when food was brought out from the kitchen, wanting to grab

the empty platters and carry them outside to wash, and simultane-
ously wanting to grab at the handfuls of bread and meat and stuff her
face—for the food tasted so much better because she hadn't lifted a
finger to prepare it. But in those moments, the skin would seem to
shrivel taut, pulling her elbows into her ribs and curling her hands
into useless fists.

She should not have been so uncomfortable, having lived among
this family for so long. But, you know, when people say a servant is like
one of the family, it only means that they have made a cozy place in
their mental house for a certain person—not that this person can just
leave the laundry for someone else to do and call herself a Rummani.
She had saved Jibril from fire and protected him in one hundred other
ways from his bullying brothers, and she trusted that Hakim was true
to his word; but she had no illusion that anything else but this starving
old man stood between her and a violent ripping away of her new skin.
The eldest brother pretended that she was invisible, and so did the
wives. But the middle brother, Zaki, summoned her before dawn or
while she was smoking with the other Rummani women, and he talked
to her like the lowest servant. One morning, he burst into her room and
threw two pairs of scuffed shoes on the floor and demanded to know
why she had stopped polishing them. She raised her chin and said to
him, "It is the servant's job, brother." And he sneered and grabbed her
through the front of her blouse, squeezing her breast as if juicing an
orange—and through his gritted teeth he said, "Call me that again and
I will make you kneel down and learn your place in this house."

When she folded down her brassiere that evening, the delicate new
skin above her nipple was rent open an inch, showing the darker,
older skin beneath. No needle could repair it, just as Hakim had
warned. It was as if the girl had never understood the Rummanis'
language until now, and hearing it through new ears, she realized that
her employers of nine years were a family of jackals.

In the meantime, Jibril studied the creation of his new sister with
interest. Even though he was betrothed to one of the larger soap fortunes in Nablus, and his eventual wealth might make his brothers'

shipping inheritance look like an ice-cream allowance, he was still hideous. And if there was any sin among the true Rummanis since their long-ago exile from Nablus, it was the sin of getting more than you seemed to deserve.

"Dogs can't eat from the good china, I've learned," Jibril said one day, on one of their walks outside the family compound. He had a droll, mumbly way of speaking—bowing his head into his chest, hiding his scars. Their conversation felt private, even in the street. That month, the Iraqi army had quartered some soldiers in the city, and today they'd brought their cars out for the refugees to wash. Through the crowd, Jibril and his new sister carried blankets and soap, bundles of thyme, and her old servant clothes to give away at the Christian school.

"I served food on that china for nine years," she muttered back to him. "If djeddi says I can eat from it, I will."

"He is not your grandfather, and he is starving himself to death. You are playing a very dangerous game."

"He gave me no choice, Jibril. If the rest of the Rummanis learn that I'm not who you and your brothers and father agreed to say I am, the family will kick me out in disgrace. No house will hire me, not here, not now. Look at all these people searching for work. It is worse outside of Nablus. Djeddi chose this fate for me."

"You could have refused."

A jagged feeling shuddered through her chest. "Do you think I would have stayed in Haifa and left you here alone? I love you. And you aren't safe in that house till that little girl is old enough for you to marry and the only names on the soap factory are hers and yours. Your brothers' wives are already scheming how to get the biggest share of djeddi's business deals."

Jibril's mouth twisted. "*Our* brothers' wives, then. *Our* father, not your boss. Stop worrying about me and start worrying about keeping your story straight. And pay attention to that fellahi accent of yours. *Jeddi.* Soft. Not *djeddi.* But just call my father *Baba,* for crying out loud, like the rest of us."

But she was worrying about her village, Maaloul. What had happened to her own people? Were they here in this very city—had they already spotted her? She was a fool to be out here like this, thinking that her red hair and expensive clothes concealed her. Anyone could see straight through her skin to the cloth underneath. But when she passed people she'd known in Haifa, other servants, teachers from the school, none of them recognized her in the new skin.

When she and Jibril reached the school, the Orthodox priest was overseeing donations, and Jibril bent and kissed his hand. The girl followed the example, even though she'd been raised Muslim.

"Thank you, sister," said the priest. "I have seen you before, but I can't quite place you. Remind an old man?"

You warthog. You've seen me every Sunday sitting under your greasy snout, and one time you even grabbed my ass. But her skin pulled her hands and wrists close to her body, folded demurely at her waist, and her mouth stretched into a polite smile. "My father owns one of the soap factories. I am Nuha Rummani."

And he blessed her and Jibril both, and he accepted their donations on behalf of two hundred homeless children. "With your family's permission," he said as they left, "come back on Monday. The teachers need your help with the children, Nuha Rummani. As ever, we appreciate your great family's patronage."

You can be anyone in chaos, and the tricky thing is, the closer you look at life, the more chaotic it is. From hour to hour, day to day, the girl had to keep but one fact straight in her head: her name. But it was all she could do to prevent that fragile suit of skin from snagging on a wrong word and ripping off like a sheet of wet paper.

I can hear you now, those times in your stage whisper or your voice that was too big for every room, reminding me that no one is honest all the time. Especially not the girl in this story. She was used to keeping parts of her life a secret; she would grow up to speak in parables and sayings, ensuring that certain facts cast a double shadow. How can I put this? I know now that sometimes, a gazelle is not a gazelle—it is desire itself. It is a young woman who read palms in the back of the tinker's shop, the one who cradled our heroine's hand a moment too long, stroked the line at the base of her thumb and across the inside of her wrist, and said, *A long life and many journeys. Is this what you want?* as her eyes added, *Would you want it with me? Let's go.* Our heroine, she was not the virtuous maiden she had made herself out to be: the feet and shoulders she had followed out of Maaloul nine years ago were no gazelle's, but smooth as her own. Our heroine learned the freckle on the side of a toe and the curve of a hip in her hand; she learned how soft a woman's lips felt, and how many shades of warmth and coolness she could find when she ran her hands through another woman's unbound hair. And for as long as she lived, she would never forget how it felt to hide—and to caress that fine, thrilling line between the fear of being discovered and the ecstasy of discovering.

Hiding one's true desires, day in and day out, was a type of skin. But in the old country, our heroine wore it out of habit. She knew no other way. There would never be any taking it all the way off. But now that she was buttoned inside yet another new skin, she felt like she was wearing two winter coats. And with Hakim's vaunted name wrapped around her in flashing lights for everyone to see, she felt both stifled and naked all of the time. Her hands were in constant motion: rolling cigarettes, tugging the hem of her sleeve, brushing at the front of her blouse and straying to the hidden tear where Jibril's elder brother had grabbed her breast and sneered.

She tried to be loud, tried to be cheerful, so that no one would have time to react to anything except what she showed the world of herself. She acted like a caricature. The children at the school and the church loved her. She told them stories of gazelles that flew from Baghdad to China and back. She told them of the djinn and ogres who lived in caves (other caves, far away! not the ones where their families were living now!), and of pretty sisters rescued from wells and married to handsome princes. She got these tales to dance in the air like wooden puppets, colorful and dead.

And when she came home in the afternoons, she retreated to her bedroom and stripped off all her clothes. She curled up into herself, eyes closed, and lay wide-awake for hours—blank with a kind of grief.

"What is the matter with you?" Jibril muttered through the door.

"Get lost."

"I need your help with my university application."

This coaxed a flat laugh out of her—our heroine, she was hardly literate. Jibril was the only one who would bother to teach her to read. Now he leaned against the door, whistling badly. She rose and put on a sweater and a long woolen skirt and a pair of embroidered slippers. Jibril said nothing until they were on the roof, where they could be out of sight from the inner rooms, and out of earshot from the servants. She discovered that even here, high above the city's tight streets, the day was dark and cold, and snow was beginning to cover the mountaintops like ash.

"It looks like the ash that goes into the soap," Jibril said at last. He was taller than her now, but when he was cold, he still had a way of leaning into her side like a boy. "Have you seen the vat on the factory floor?"

She shook her head.

"Let's go have a look tomorrow."

They stood awhile longer, exchanging news of the whispered plans and plots in the household, and whether Hakim had allowed himself to eat some soup that afternoon. Their words clouded and vanished. And the next night, they made their lonely trip to the soap factory. The guard unlocked the chain for them and then bid them good night.

"You can't be a Rummani unless you feel the history in your blood," he said, his voice echoing on the six-hundred-year-old stone walls. The floor gaped open around a low, wide vat that was three times as deep as Nuha was tall. The stone was scaly with mortar, and soot blackened the vaulted ceiling. A kind of wooden oar rested beside the empty vat, smooth and waxen to the touch. The fire pit was cold, but the place smelled subtly but powerfully of the best Nablus soap. If

Nuha had a child, which she never would, she would want to name her something that cradled the senses the way this place did. A smell with an inscrutable life of its own, like a comfortable silence.

As Jibril moved in the dim light, his face and hands turned the color of olive oil, and his scars the color of soap. He was both at home and reverently apart, like a priest in his sanctuary.

He said, in a loud, clear voice: "I am named for a boy who lived and died a hundred years ago, and first made blue soap out of this land's indigo and oil. This is my family's industry."

And he told her all the tales again, breathing life into them this time: of Alissabat and the wedding, of the tattooed corsair and how the factory had fallen into Saeeda's ancestors' hands, of the murder soap, of the crooked priest, and of the merchant who had rescued one of Alissabat's blue daughters—she was Hakim's mother and Jibril's grandmother. These stories had been part of the household on that day nine years ago when a boy on fire had leapt from a rooftop and into her life, drawing her into his household and its imaginary landscape, both of which were, by now, almost more familiar to her than her own memories.

"This is you, too, Nuha. You are *my sister*, ukhti. This is *your* history. Memorize it and tell it to everyone who will listen."

She felt the name trying to crowd out what she remembered of Maaloul and her own household. Even now, with the rest of her land, the memory was fading. Who she'd been was fading, suffocating to death inside this new skin. The stories you can only whisper to the walls become like ghosts, doomed to haunt your sleep. She opened her mouth to speak, but her throat was empty. She rushed out the big steel doors and stood alone in the street, gasping for air.

But from that day forward, you told the Rummani stories to nieces and nephews and to little Saeeda. At church and at the school, Nuha Rummani was loud and loved like a favorite buffoon. The words of the stories sealed her in, as airless as they were timeless. On the day two years hence when Hakim went to his eternal sleep, the children's adoration of you was what kept you safe from Jibril's brothers. They had all grown used to you by then, and Palestine had bigger problems. And when Nuha Rummani lay down to sleep, you saw that the inchlong tear above your left breast had healed. The skin had closed around it until all that remained of the wound was a scar like a shut eye: dreaming of all you had and would never have again.

How am I doing, Auntie? The truth always flaps just out of sight, shading everything. It's like the big picnic blanket my parents often shook out over my head in the backyard.

Meanwhile, another story had been swelling up out of the dark at night, giving my mother her feral restlessness. One night when the raincoats were dripping dry in the laundry room, and another December shower trickled down the gutters, and Anna was sleeping with me in my bed, and our mud-stained jeans were in the washer, and Adam was sleeping like a figure on a sarcophagus, Mama lay in the slatted shadows, alert. So she got dressed and sat on the top step of the front porch, gulping the frigid damp.

The pavement had been whispering all day, trimming the hiss of wind in the branches into words of a language she didn't know.

But still, a point in the center of her body felt like a restful happiness, like a closed eye.

She'd felt such a thing before.

She struggled to remember when.

Ah, yes.

She'd felt it when she was pregnant with me.

"I'm going back sooner than we'd planned," Saeeda said.

You opened your eyes. The twin bed next to you was made, and Saeeda was in makeup and sitting stiffly on the green coverlet. Her suitcase was zipped at her feet.

"To Amman?"

"Back to California," said Saeeda. "I'm going home because I'm just wasting time here."

You groped for your cup of water and sat up. "Esh sar? What happened?"

You two had finished your peacemaking visits but had still planned to make the most of your hard-won entrance visas and see a few more towns. If Saeeda was canceling, you expected a complaint about your fickle company or, more likely, the draw of my mother's pregnancy. For the past days, she'd seemed ill at ease, ever since Tashi had phoned with the news of her latest ultrasound.

But Saeeda said, "I need to sell my house. It's worth almost two million."

"Is this a joke? This is what our visit has done for you? Make you want to sell some valuable real estate for old times' sake?" You couldn't help it. You fell back into the pillow and laughed.

"It is not a joke." Saeeda plunked a wad of unspent shekels next to your purse. "I did not make a mistake selling the factory, and I am not making a mistake now. I see what I want: a house that does not remind me of eight terrible years of illness. And my children's children need their inheritance. If you want to laugh, go ahead. I know how to find the bank through my tears."

Breathless, unhappy, you said, "I'm not laughing at you, sister. I'm laughing at . . ."

But you couldn't be sure. For three days your sentences had trailed off like this. You had both gone around the stalls and homes finding people you recognized, finding out who had died, drinking liters of tea, and showing pictures of the family children. It had come out on a macabre tour of the old part of town, the second day in Nablus: how the collapse of the old factory had claimed two lives. It was supposed to be deserted, but two strangers had taken refuge that night among the heaped junk on the old factory floor, and by the time workers dragged their remains from the rubble many months later, they were unidentifiable. It was why the brother of Ala' had called it a grave site, this place that had once been the center of everything. Now all that was left was a crumbling divider wall, and high up, where a floor had once connected to it, was a door spray-painted blue. Its separate stories were blasted open to the air.

It bothered you and Saeeda both. All sentences kept trying to find a way to this particular subject but getting lost. A deadness at the center of the map, a ruin instead of an origin story.

"I'm laughing," you said, not even smiling, "at your ease with moving on."

Elspeth Rummani and the Mystery
of the Red Chandelier

hrough winter evenings, while Saeeda and Nuha were in Palestine, my mother patrolled sidewalks behind her growing belly. Round as a fruit, it carried the next Rummani. After I had snuggled into bed to write a note to Anna, the squeaky spot by the shoe shelf creaked. From the crack of my door, I saw my mother jackknifed forward in the apartment doorway, huffing and tugging the laces of her scuffed duck boots. Her nose still bore pink divots from her glasses, which came off only when she was about to go walking in the rain. Her expression was engrossed in the task of her hands—distracted, serious, annoyed with the awkwardness of her emerging belly. This irritability only showed up in the apartment, away from my father, when the freedom of her time most reminded her that she was, once more, a tenant in a body owned by a fourth-month fetus.

I understood what pregnancy was. Precocious Anna had explained about the secret dance, how it must be done with all your skin showing, which signaled the fetus to start growing. I imagined an infinity of babies within us, tiny and patient until summoned to grow. I had once seen a frog expel its eggs into a puddle, and at first, I expected this of my mother. In her fetus hid millions of babies, a gauzy cluster she would expel into the world sometime in mid-July. *No, "fetus" means the baby,* my mother had corrected me, almost sadly. *There will only be one. You have to be ready to be a good big sister.* My attention tilted toward disappointment—not at the arrival of a solitary fetus, but at the absence of its millions of others.

My mother straightened, buttoned her black wool coat over the expanding sibling, and flipped her deep hood over her curls. She tromped down the wooden staircase to the street, sounding a hundred pounds heavier than a nauseated woman who barely ate two meals a day.

My mother walked most when she was busy with work. These walks were a keystone of her personality, and she had recently shared their secret with me. She used as mnemonics the rooms she saw and liked best. The method didn't make much sense to me, but it seemed vital during periods in which she was reading a lot. There was a house in my father's neighborhood she had shown me, for instance, on the lower slope of Mount Tabor, with a dining room that took up three front windows. Through her orderly magic, she transformed the memory of its deep-cranberry wall into a mental color code for a new paper in the latest *Journal of Neuroscience.* From there, she pointed out how the room's sideboard became a container for the methodology, along with the matrix of hanging wineglasses and flash of someone lifting a lightbulb toward the wall sconce. The primary author's name was He—"Like the chemical symbol for helium, and the light fixture is big and round like a balloon. So now I won't forget it, no matter what." I didn't understand yet, but she gave these invisible parts of herself to me and to no one else, and as she spoke she held my hand in both of hers, as if it were a bird, and I loved that. Later it would matter more, because a storyteller must remember things for everyone; you hung it all on the family factory and house, but the children of exiles have to depend more and more on imaginary landscapes.

And imagine what almost thirty years of mental rooms must look like. Tashi had never stopped collecting interiors all these years: Houston sunrooms, Boston fireplaces, Oakland windowsills full of succulents and spider plants, Pacific Heights dining rooms, Eastside Portland hothouses and wide Craftsman living rooms. Colleagues, otherwise alarmed by her messes, admired her near-perfect memory, for they knew nothing of the byzantine imaginary that supported it or the way she roved after dark, pushed along by her cellular-level estrangement toward something she knew she'd recognize if she saw it. From these rooms, she had assembled a whole lifelong tower of warm spaces observed from sidewalks. A whole mental palace of science, culture, news items, my grades, and even some workaday shopping lists ... all of it growing around the family tree and a whole private ossuary of times she had nearly gone under. It was her most private place, and she made it as beautiful as she could.

Below our living room window, the streetlamp illuminated a silver glaze of rain on her hood as she reached the bottom of the stairs and turned downhill to begin her walk. Then only the flash of white fur at the tops of her boots suggested a living presence in the night rain.

I expected to find the usual mess of binders and printouts and computer cables on the kitchen table. But it was blank except for a dish with an abandoned slice of cheese. Her prescriptions sat on the sink, the new ones they'd put her on since pregnancy. She'd left her phone, and it opened to a medical app. More and more, she used her crow's nest to stew, not work—refilling herself for the health performances she enacted for my father. *I'm getting my hair done today. Let's go to yoga. The coffee shop in the medical building has the best salads. Why don't we take a walk along the river?*

During the first pregnancy, with me, she had found one way to feel in charge. She'd decided to grow this baby for a pair of women who would take it away, knowing she was built for motherhood physically but in no other way. In other words, she had been fulfilling a duty that was supposed to end at the delivery ward. But now, what was this other thing? This risk of building a human of blood and cells, at the cost of her sanity all over again? Her returning tread on the stairs was heavy with the weight of the future—hers, ours, its. I suppose the future was a sort of room, too, one whose walls were squeezing in from all sides.

The next week, I overheard her telling all this over the phone to her shrink, that oracle whose name I had learned was Kim. The Friday appointment required her to rush me home from school in Nuha's old car. She shut herself in her room and thought I couldn't hear her saying, "I just keep focusing on the red chandeliers. It's all I think about—the longing." I wondered what it was she was trying so hard to remember.

Adam had private recesses, too. My mother was just more deliberate about hers.

"Can you keep a secret?" he asked me.

You, Auntie, were a clearinghouse of idle family gossip and had taught me the value of collecting shards of other people's lives, ones they didn't want flung around. You had survived by capitalizing on what was most delicate, most vulnerable about people's conduct. Although you didn't say so, I assumed that this was why another word for money was *tender*, because what could epitomize the underbelly of a good secret so well? It was, as you called it, the universal currency: an economy of the ear. A secret didn't discriminate on the basis of language, nationality, sexual orientation, gender, skin color, or, in my case, age. I was an aspiring bank vault, so I told my father I could keep his secret.

So he said, "I keep thinking about making your mother a special place of her own." Leaned in close. *"In the garage."*

I giggled.

But he meant it. At the end of our short, buckled little driveway was a freestanding shed that was too crooked to be trusted with housing his luxury SUV. Instead, it was a long-term storage unit for a bunch of grim furniture: his in-kind inheritance, he said, from the childhood house he'd shared with his mother and grandfather. The clutter would have had some value as antiques if he'd stored them better, but when he opened the shed doors and stood in its slow cough of dust, the sun revealed armoires and dining chairs and headboards that were covered in a golden-gray pallor.

"It has good bones," he said.

I wasn't sure if he was joking. Even emptied, the garage shed was leaning on its laths. Spiderwebs furred its rafters, and the floor was concrete. By the door, some other child had pushed their hands into the drying slab sixty years ago. Across the back wall, under a wafer-thin windowpane, was a built-in workbench that sheltered a brace of tools I'd never seen my father touch.

But he said, "A big Turkish rug or two. Clean this stuff out. Maybe a power wash, a coat of paint. Good electricity."

A lot of work, in other words. My father was generally a writer of checks, which he dispensed with a fake, swaggering joviality to the people who did tasks a one-handed man could not. And only five minutes ago, we'd been eating Saturday breakfast, just the two of us, when he'd stopped scowling into his own thoughts and dragged me out here, alight with something I'd never seen before. Now his whole live-wire body sparked with something only he could see, and he observed his secret vision with little gasps of amazement.

"Betty," he said, "do you think your mother would finally give up the apartment?"

The crow's nest was a beloved part of her life. She'd only just begun to experience it as an organic extension of herself, making it feel as comfortably grotty as your Oakland apartment had been. "Her work is next door to the apartment. She likes it."

"She's going to change her tune. Walking through the rain all the time? Driving in a warm, dry car would take her the same amount of time. And it's safer, right?"

He was debating with me, but no adult had ever asked my real opinion before. The interrogations I was familiar with came from the classroom, the whole humiliating Socratic exercise of it, knowing I was being led along just so everyone could bask in my stupidity. But

when I didn't respond, my father asked me again what I thought—
really.

"Mom hates traffic. She likes walking."

"I'll drive her. Or we'll buy her a car of her own. I don't care about that."

"She'd ride the bus. Or walk. She likes walking . . ."

"She's not going to want to go up and down those bad wooden stairs with a baby." He'd stopped listening to me. "Yes, work might be farther, but her family will be here. Your little brother or sister will be here." He had recently begun saying *your little brother or sister*, as if the thing in my mother's belly was anything other than a fetus. *A neon-pink alien covered in a coat of downy fur,* my mother had explained. She, at least, was honest about what she was growing in there. But my father had an imaginary plane of his own, even if it had taken us longer to wonder about it. That submerged coldness at the center of him had melted off, baring a more vulnerable affection. That first night he had seen her in Haight-Ashbury fifteen years ago, an enigmatic neighbor sitting on the forbidden fire escape, a new room in his mental house had appeared, and he was happier since he'd admitted that this old fascination still had a pulse.

"Christmas lights," he was saying. He waded into the old furniture. "A lamp. Soft, dry heat. A few more bookshelves, a pullout couch. She could come out here when she needs to work. A better door so she feels safe at night, or if she wants to lock us out, ha."

I tried to see it the way he did. The wood was a cozy, blushing brown. If you sat at the workbench you could see the backyard grass, the neighbor's fence, and snarled berry canes through the rear window, and through the window on the side, just a glancing slice of the patio. It could be nice, this illusion of a house alone in a meadow. But I searched it for anything that would make it appealing to my mother, make it a place worth collecting.

"A red chandelier," I said.

"Excuse me?"

I repeated myself. "She always talks about it on the phone with

Kim." Uttering her shrink's name invited my father's full attention. He stood there sweating into his T-shirt despite the cool air, holding a dusty mirror against his leg.

"What else does she say . . ." *In therapy? About everything?* He knew he shouldn't ask, but I saw the question in his posture as clearly as the pair of handprints in the concrete. His curiosity was a desperate slow tugging that would have paid any amount for the information— would have magnified my worth by whole kingdoms.

"I'll help you clean," I said, "if you buy the chandelier and let me make it red."

It was too low a price. He was already locking up the garage again and patting his jeans for the car key. There was a junk shop on lower Hawthorne; he sometimes entertained you and Saeeda there, and we were both thinking of its maze of rooms full of everything in the universe under a layer of sticky dust. You could buy ten chandeliers there, probably a whole house, a whole dynasty, piece by piece.

"Is she doing okay? Do you think?" I'd never experienced this side of him. As he backed us down the driveway, his attempt at affable detachment sounded like it had a mushy spot right at its center.

I said I guess she was *doing okay.* But did that mean, I wondered, my prying into the medical apps on her phone? Was this a trick question? And anyway they were both adults, and as adults together they were reliable, like the radio coming on when you turn the dial. My mother, around my father, was just another grown-up.

He put the car into gear. "Now about what she might like in her hideaway," he said, "a chandelier . . . Are you sure? She's not really the ballroom type. She does like red . . ." It was like he was trying to figure out what else it could mean, whether there was a catch, but was afraid to reject what amounted to a free glimpse of my mother's unreachable interior. A free way to delight her.

What *had* she said on the phone? I watched house after house slide past the backseat window, all those rooms obscure in the daylight. The memory escaped me, but I wasn't about to let him know that the currency in my hand was just a speculation.

"She said she thinks about red chandeliers all the time. She must really want one."

How much did he know, this man with educations in law and medicine? Did he know my mother was the one-woman resident of a tower of strange rooms?

He did have that knowledge. They met during her postdoc. They were neighbors. He was charmed by her walking. She was charmed by his attention. He knew it existed, this anthology of rooms, because she told him something about her private self, but neither she nor he could explain how important these rooms were to her or why—those thoughts were only for her therapist, later. They thought, at first, that they knew enough about each other because they both had passports to the land of lost fathers; and though they never had the words to unlock every last door of every last room of each other's interior, for a long time, the sense of parallel rooms was enough. The intimacy of two people knocking on either side of a wall.

Also: How well do we know anyone in our lives? Do we trust what they tell us? Are knowledge and empathy mutually assisting or mutually distracting?

My father had the knowledge that my mother had left him while I was still orbiting my umbilical cord, and she'd hidden me from him for a year and then only ever halfway returned to him. It didn't matter what color the chandeliers were in the home of her heart. He just feared her leaving the house again during this new pregnancy, even though he hadn't looked at another woman in years. As for her, she knew he'd cheated once; betrayal had left a dent. On some level, though, they'd come to need each other around and care for each other's company, and at some point, like an image seen through a pair of lenses, their separate views of the future had converged around the new baby. They were excited about it almost in the same way, he thought.

It is easy to lose track of what is dangerous when there is so much else to pay attention to, like in the old game where you would put a button under one of three little coffee cups and slide them around and around on the kitchen table until the true location of the button almost wasn't what mattered anymore.

Anna liked it when I lay on top of her.

I was very heavy, over a hundred and thirty pounds and growing. When she stretched out on her back like a scarecrow on her bedroom rug, I could be face-to-face with her while my socks only grazed the knees of her jeans. She lay there flushed with laughter, somehow pleased by the feeling of being pinned to the earth. And no, it wasn't what it looked like, not really. At the time, I took such a delicate position as routine. I was almost nine, and it was the second year of a friendship in which Anna slung her arms around my waist or did backflips off my shoulders into her pool, or we blew raspberries on each other's arms, shared a sleeping bag at a winter campfire in the backyard, napped in the grass on the first good day of spring, tickled each other in the car's backseat on the way to her sister's recitals or to see Christmas lights or waiting in the car at the ice-cream stand. I had learned to pretend that friendship and touch were as natural to me as they were to her, so that after so much time together, Anna had a thoughtless comfort with my physical being and yet no idea of how helplessly I craved her.

"Maybe I was an error," I said.

She rolled her eyes. "God doesn't make mistakes, Betty. Just like he wouldn't make me want a dog if I wasn't supposed to get one."

"God doesn't care about what pet you want. Listen." I stopped talking until she finally turned her face back to me. Our noses were almost touching. I could smell that she'd stolen some of her sister's French face cream. "My mother says it's covered in soft fur. Did you ever hear of that?"

"It's a fetus, not an animal. And she should know by now if it's a boy or a girl."

"She doesn't care because it will be a monster."

Anna wrapped her legs around me. "Don't call the baby *it*. You have to be a nice big sister no matter what."

"No, I don't."

"You do. My sister is a bitch, and I don't want you to ever be like her." At school, the joke was that Anna had gotten so skinny because their parents starved her to spend the money on her sister's summer lessons in New York. I knew this to be untrue but basically accurate.

"Don't worry," I told her, "I'll pity it. It's going to be even uglier than me."

This was another trick I'd learned—self-deprecation as a lure for Anna's reassurance.

She held me tighter in her legs. "Betty, no. And if your parents don't want the baby, we'll raise it as our own. We'll take it and run away." Squeezing me harder in her excitement, she unspooled a whole vision that she was having just now, us together, with a house of our own that had a dance studio downstairs and a nature park in the back for Alot, and how we'd have this baby, this miniature person with perfect arms and legs and hair and toes, what a wonder this child would be because of how much love we felt, how perfect, how beautiful, how everyone would knock on our door to say so. Our happily ever after, out there in the world, while all the other girls we went to school with were still stuck here imagining their someday weddings to boys and being boring.

What startled me—nested in this overheated tangle of hers—was the idea of being responsible for someone so small and helpless. I was my own biggest project. I knew nothing about keeping things alive except myself, being, as I was, a bullied child raised by four people who already had one hand in the grave and having returned from death myself. It was my first experience in realizing that relationships begin to fracture when two people look into the future and see two different worlds, even though by your definition, we were in love: liking and needing each other equally.

———————

My mother was holed up for an entire weekend training a student who kept accidentally ruining her cell cultures, so my father and I got two days to turn the garage into a place that she was supposed to like better than her apartment. My bad mood from the conversation with Anna had carried across days, underlining the certainty that a sibling was not just an intrusion but a life-ending chore—or something just as bad, on the suspicion that a happy road was dividing into a thousand murky tributaries. I wished I could visit you until those roads converged again in brightness and verdure, but you were still very far away in Palestine, as far as the dark side of the moon. I sulked on the porch steps as my father tried to drag out an armoire, which was supported on his back. He yelled at me to assist.

He'd hung on to these pieces of his childhood so long that they had desiccated. They were an endorsement of neglect as a strategy for starving nostalgia to death. He'd loved them once, these artifacts of his family, but all that he kept now were his old wooden aeroplanes and the pair of colonial cannonballs—one of which Tashi had launched through the front window when he'd told her, years ago, about the affair. They seemed like bad luck, but he wouldn't let them go.

We were outside, my father standing in the yawning crater of the garage, explaining adzes to me as he pitched the tools into the wet grass, when his back pocket buzzed. He hitched up his jeans on his bony hip and held the phone between his shoulder and sweating cheek. It was the junk shop owner, saying she'd searched her warehouse and found a crystal chandelier in the neoclassical style. Would we like to come look at it?

Oh, yes. Our chandelier. It was hanging there, waiting for us, when we opened the shop door, suspended in dusty light. Thousands of ice-white surfaces, like the glinting eye of some ghostly snow insect, seemed to watch us from behind the counter. Inside that giant fascicle of quivering pendants, a silver stalk emanated countless silver branches.

"This great dame," said the shop owner, "is the genuine artifact. She's hung over governors and titled royalty. She'll be a bit dear, I'm afraid."

My father didn't haggle. He bought me a paintbrush, mineral spirits, and a half dozen vials of cherry-red model paint.

"Your job is to turn crystals into rubies," he said at home, not really joking. "And you need to work fast, before your mother gets home tonight."

He hung it at eye level for me next to a work light in the garage and gave me nothing but the advice to *be surgical*. I took the one step up onto a painted stool he'd saved from his haul, and I peered down into the gently clinking mass. It seemed a shame to cover seven hundred dollars' worth of crystal teardrops with a light coat of paint. I hesitated, but he reminded me that this had been my idea in the first place. I understood that he was probably having doubts, too. Had I been lying about the red chandelier? Was this another one of my *romances,* as he called them? Lying was an annoying habit I'd learned from Anna, and it had worsened in the two months you had been traveling, especially in the few weeks since my grandmother had returned without you. He stood in the garage doorway with his arms crossed, watching to see if I'd cave, debating whether he was really going to hang his gambit with my mother on the testimony of an eight-year-old.

He'd even bought her a ring—another, even bigger diamond, the magic by which he hoped to turn their half-anchored love back into a marriage.

How do we know what we know? I knew what I'd heard of her conversation with her therapist. I knew about her rooms. I knew they were elaborate and made her happy.

I dipped brush into paint.

What membrane runs between brain and blood, throughout the whole human race? Where is the border between imagined and real? I had heard something I wasn't supposed to, but I thought I was the only one who knew that my mother lived in a world no one could see, an invisible tower of collected memory rooms.

I just keep focusing on the red chandeliers. It's all I think about.

A fat teardrop hanging at the bottom tempted me to begin. The brush's bristles fanned over the crystal. It was like painting your fingernails, all hard angles. Under the hot work lamp, the paint dried quickly, a red shell. I sat back from the first strokes, assessing my work. That single bottom pendant now dangled like a garnet, like a pomegranate seed, like a fleck of blood in a porcelain sink. I should have stopped right there, but my handiwork compelled me.

I am a patient person. I can work for hours at a thing, whether it's separating the pages of an old book or transforming a chandelier. *It's all I think about.* Time slides away. Noxious, mouthwatering paint clings to the brush. I probe the center of the jingling mass. The light trembles in it as though it is a kind of expensive gelatin. Its wires and chains and branches and beads become one system, daubed at, holding on to the paint, gradually becoming a core of luminous pink. *Like a fetus.* The thought floats up on the fumes. Flashes travel, singing, around my hand and coolly along my wrist. It's like I'm reaching into a whole mind, blessing each facet of a thousand little thoughts with this dizzy-making color. Objects have memory. They do. *Governors and titled royalty,* the lady said, but with my face pushed into this jungle of light I feel something older and still present—from before the jeweler cut the crystals, from the time when the crystals were a slurry of hot sand. Out of darkness comes light. Under my brush, the paint runs and dries unevenly. My work is methodical, prickling redly outward. Some of the facets are the pale pink of blood in the water, others dense and striated. Bristles cling like eyelashes. The chandelier grows ever more organic, its memory ever more muddled, more of a red glass injury. Morbid, like a thousand bloodshot eyes. Its sound flattens, becoming the clatter of bugs in the wall. I have doubts.

"Almost finished?"

My father stood in the doorway.

The sun in the side window said it was past dinnertime. He'd been working behind me all this time, and now the walls were clean, a rug covered the floor, the couch was in place, and he'd added some other comforts for warmth and better electricity. A small lonely palace for my mother, the best gift he could give her.

"It's looking good," he said as he finished attaching a plug. On his face was real admiration, reflecting none of the queasy dread in my stomach. "You were deaf to the world for hours. Let's plug 'er in."

A buzz excited the filaments, and there we were, bathed in a harlot-red glow. In a fever, I'd even painted the bulbs. It looked like a slaughtered cow.

"That's a nice, warm light," he said, refusing to drop the smile.

He had me help him tie a good knot in the rope and twine the extension cord around it, prepped to be hauled upward on the pulley. The thing swayed and lurched.

"Once it's on the ceiling, the color will even out," he insisted. "She'll be home in twenty minutes."

I'd worked hard. I'd stayed out of his way for hours. This was, presumably, the thing my mother thought about all the time: a red chandelier. We give each other the gifts we are capable of understanding.

He hauled on the rope, raising the red mass to the ceiling.

Anna had an easy mother—gentle, kind, on time. Hers and mine had met on many occasions, but they were stuck at politeness, each feeling judged by the other. For Anna's mother, it was a condition of not having received enough education for her intelligence before her first daughter was born. For my mother, it was that her discomfort with motherhood felt like her own fault, and she was always failing at it. She was uninvolved in my school. Clumsy with manners. Reclusive. Foreign. Her cousins had given birth and mastered the art of showing people what they wanted to see. But she had learned from the Time of Feuding that there was no satisfying people who were trained to hate your mother, and that if your own family could be so poisonous, the rest of the world had to be worse. She was simply herself, a mess, saddled with a difficult brain, one that filled her skull with horrors that might belong to her or might not. Living was doubting—a mantra that fit more or less well enough with her job, with me, and with the loss of her real father, her wider family, and several homes. Had she been better with children, she might have been more like you. But she was not, and would never be an easy mother.

What did I know about my mother's death wish? Did I sense that inside her losses was a magnetic force that drew her mind toward annihilation? That for thirty years, everything that felt *right* aligned with bridge railings, open veins, bullets, and bones? That she'd survived this long only by resisting anything that felt too right?

I didn't know anything at all.

But I felt dread as she stood up from the car that night. Horror at not being able to rewind and do something else. My father was telling her to cover her eyes. Smiling, he led her toward the garage.

She settled one hand across her belly. "I don't need to be surprised," she was saying. "I spent the weekend cleaning up surprises. Can we just eat?" My father led her forward anyway, making promises.

The doors swung open to a red glow.

"Now!" he said.

At first, her face showed recognition. It was a warm room. Antique brass and books adorned the workbench and shelf. Then her gaze floated upward. She took in the bloody chandelier with a sort of relief, as though someone had finally spoken the right word aloud.

Here it was: the cone of glittering red, suspended as though blown upward through the roof of her skull.

And in front of her, my father was holding out a square velvet box. He said nothing, waiting for the look of recognition and relief to land on what he was holding. But her gaze was locked on the nightmare that my hard work had dragged across the membrane between imagined and real. She was beginning to understand that this was no accident. The wrongness grew into revulsion.

She spun around and rushed back toward the car.

". . . the fuck," I heard her say before the engine swallowed even the sound of my father calling her name once, twice, before they both looked at me.

Their voices downstairs, in some middle-of-the-night hour. The microwave beep had woken me.

Red chandelier. She must have overheard . . .

It's . . .

No, I didn't want to tell you. I'm fine.

But what . . . ?

"It was none of her business!" My mother's voice, clearly.

I crept halfway down the stairs. They were on the couch together, her knees drawn against the side of his thigh. Teacups on the floor, his feet in socks. His tone was coaxing—then a waiting silence.

She said, "When I am angry, or when I, if I don't or can't . . . be right. It's not *my* thought. But it feels better than I want it to . . . You don't need to hear all this."

My father's murmur, too soft to make out.

"Adam—please."

A firmer coaxing, something that might have been a gentle ultimatum.

"The thought," she said, "you don't want . . . Don't say I'm crazy. Do you promise?" A long pause. "Fine. The chandelier. If you think about putting the barrel of a—of a gun under your chin. The thought of, you know, ejecting everything from the top of my head. All of it, the skull, the brains, the moment when everything I hate about myself is suspended in the air. Like a red chandelier, before it splatters the ceiling and—there's some relief in it. Okay? That's one thought. The meds don't work, and I think of my brains in the air, maybe forty times a day, and I don't think I can do this for seventeen more weeks. Hence the therapist. And *red chandeliers.*" A hard double click of her tongue against her teeth, just like you did when you were irate about something. "She was a little shit to eavesdrop."

I waited on the stairs, hoping that someone would clarify that the *little shit* was the therapist, not me. I listened after my father got up. I listened as the teacups clinked in the metal sink, and as the side door creaked, and until after I heard the grumble of the trash bin wheels in the driveway. I could only assume the complex *thwack* that followed was the ruined chandelier landing inside the bin's four plastic walls.

Meanwhile the fetus grows, gathering cells to itself. Busy like mold, epiphytes, algae, accruing matter. Growing fingers. Eyelids. Genitalia, male. A brother, then. My mother shows me an online video of a fetus turning slowly in a red world, but the ultrasounds on the refrigerator are static—grainy black-and-whites, more of what you'd expect from a bomb crater.

While we wait, let's call up some gray-toned ghosts from the First World War, in particular, photographs from General Allenby's Palestine campaign. Stranded between the ghastly trenches of Europe and the better-known fight for Baghdad, observe: the smug slant of an Englishman's helmet as he smiles up from a grass-lined trench outside Beersheba, a row of Australian cavalry sabers planted in the Gaza sand, the toadlike howitzer crouching in the Nazareth countryside, the line of Ottoman prisoners trudging through Nablus.

Not pictured: blasted animals in their speechless agony, corpses in the monastery.

Archives are interested only in scenes of triumph.

Yet even with all this evidence of victory, it is hard to believe that after thousands of years of armed visitors, it's these pasty Englishmen who are the ones to tame it with their weapons and ledgers. Is this what victory actually looks like—the ability to divide and count and capitalize upon? Judging by all the talk of a forty-week pregnancy and the volume of baby-oriented consumer goods colonizing our home, maybe so.

———

You had announced a campaign of your own by then. Given the success of the family visits, you were going to round up Rummanis for the arrival of my brother into the world. Something had happened, you wouldn't say what, but your voice on the speakerphone was angry. You spoke of a particular checkpoint, the settlement on the hill, ever-present trash and rubble in the old city, a certain despair that thrummed behind Nablus's characteristic hospitality. But even this testimony had the feeling of a deeper evasion.

"What else?" I harangued you from the background. "What else, what else?"

"What's that noise? Where are you? Do you know how much I'm paying for every minute of this call?"

My mother turned off the speaker and put the phone to her ear. "Sorry."

But I could still hear you, shouting at your normal volume: "Never mind. I'm just telling you, the children need family. The children shouldn't grow up without a sense of history."

"I'm not traveling anywhere. Not for a long time."

"I am not asking," you snapped. "For now, yes, stay home, rest. You bring them later." With a shock, I realized that I didn't like the word *children*, nor how I disappeared into it. "I'll be there for the birth, inshallah," you continued, "and I will bring everybody. A hundred of your kin. Your mother agrees with me that things can change for the good. We will bring everybody. All your blood! Right there under your roof!"

Some men are galvanized by heroism. None more so than my father. Tashi moved into the home Adam made for her, at least as much as my mother was willing to inhabit anything. He moved her red computer and nest of power cords to the workbench and pinned all her charts and reminders to the wood around the window frame. The space heater hummed, warming her little cavern with its breath. And over the next weeks, he helped her empty the crow's nest, exposing its tracts of mottled white paint until I could turn around in the middle of the living room as though marveling at the inside of a giant's hollow skull.

When the rooms were almost scraped clean, we spent a last night up there. She attacked the empty drawers and shelves with the hand-held vacuum. Spiders, crumbs, hairs were sucked into a plastic womb and thrown from the porch—a tempting idea. But my task was using a stick of gritty white paste to fill the nail holes, which I worked at until I noticed her putting on her sweater. She had her laptop.

"Where are you going?"

"I'll be back in twenty minutes." She twisted the horn buttons through their holes, and they bristled down her belly like a row of spines.

"Can I come?" The friendship with Anna made me crave touch, and sometimes, my mother would put my hood up and take me with her, holding my hand through her silent walks.

She stamped her feet into her shoes. "Just be done patching when I get home."

Off she went, into the warming spring night, dissolving at her edges. My sibling inside her, leaving me behind.

When you had lost your apartment, the prints of your life marked the walls and floors. Phantom pictures, phantom rugs, a phantom headboard against the bedroom plaster. For twenty years you had ex-uded smoke like a church censer—ensuring that once you had swept up the stray coins and tacks from the empty rooms, and left those doomed spaces behind, the record of how you had used them was still inscribed on the building's very skin and bones. Only by wrecking and covering can we erase a domestic story. My mother, to my new surprise, was no exception. She had lived in my mind as a presence that was barely physical—an aura I was always welcome to linger in, but by nature on the move, unstable, sort of like a sentient plastic bag, spinning around on every eddy of the wind. But as I filled the tack holes behind where her desk had been, brushed my foot along the stained nap of the living room carpeting, I read her domestic story here, too. A heat stain from her mug on the wooden table. Lone coils of her hair on the bathroom floor, a constellation of her spit and toothpaste on the mirror, a certain sponginess to the paint on her bedroom windowsills, remembering the thousands of nights she had slept with the windows cracked to the sound of rain. And there were the small graves at the verge of the forest: all those holes she'd dug in worse days, containing decaying bits of paper and coins that, if we were to press for her state of mind in those years, radiated sickness on a long half-life, because you can bury a memory but it can still speak from the dirt. Her peculiar prints were everywhere.

And they always had been. My mother was a human like any other, after all. The weight of her body wears a divot in the world. Her body bears a sibling in the night streets, on the way to the hospital chapel, which has Wi-Fi and quiet, and when she returns her tired bones will make a heavy sound climbing the stairs.

That night, before the key turns in the door for the last time, she will step inside the apartment and slide her back down the wall until she is seated on a clean patch of carpeting where the couch used to be, and she will cup my cheek and say, "Good Lord, you're almost nine," and pull my head onto her lap. She'll begin to fold around me in one of those deeply protective embraces, as if I am still an infant. And yes, in this memory I am still almost nine, and you are almost as old as you'll ever get in this life, and what I still know of my mother's body is how it yields to the weight of mine. How I am never cold, and how she will gradually curl herself around me, until it happens that my ear is against her belly, hearing the thudding swirl of a growing sibling.

We are not alone.

He has been turning in a watery room all this time. Red ceiling, red walls, red floor. All this time my mother has kept herself alive for him, moving toward the blank walls of his future, still unwritten and clean as soap. And meanwhile here I am, almost nine, so heavy, holding our domestic story on my very skin. If he is soap, then I am ink.

As of the present day

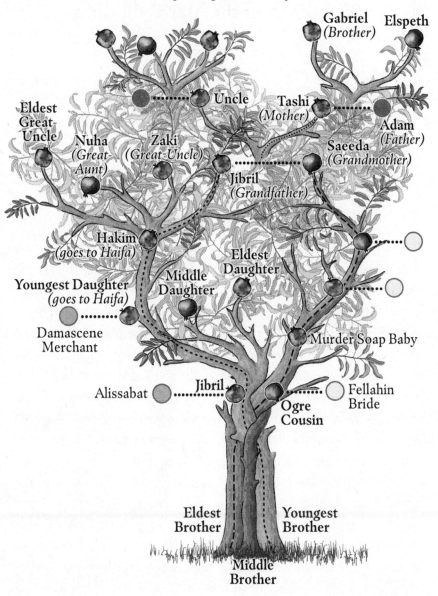

Gabriel *(Brother)*

Elspeth

Uncle

Tashi *(Mother)*

Adam *(Father)*

Eldest Great-Uncle

Nuha *(Great-Aunt)*

Zaki *(Great-Uncle)*

Saeeda *(Grandmother)*

Jibril *(Grandfather)*

Hakim *(goes to Haifa)*

Eldest Daughter

Youngest Daughter *(goes to Haifa)*

Middle Daughter

Damascene Merchant

Murder Soap Baby

Alissabat

Jibril

Ogre Cousin

Fellahin Bride

Eldest Brother

Youngest Brother

Middle Brother

Sing, Poet, of the Married Bones

Your notes say you traveled alone for weeks, observing apathy toward an Arab Spring in Palestine. You reported this to the Rummanis, who met it with tired equanimity. You told them what Umm Ala' said about the deaths in the factory collapse. Even old Zaki, Jibril's toad of a brother, grunted over the phone, "Better we don't have strangers' blood on our hands. Somebody would have sued us." Cool Hilwa, who was in Amman for good, said, "Nushkur Allah, the evil eye blinked and missed us." You also called Cecilia several times, the number you knew by heart, simply to hear her mild, familiar voice on the other end of the line asking whether you'd fed yourself with anything besides those awful cigarettes.

Now, on the smooth northward highway west of Jerusalem, in the middle seat of a sherut whose exhaust fumes leaked into the cab, you noted and appreciated the median strip full of hollyhocks. They were superior to the view of cement factories. Passover was close, and so was Easter, all these people telling their different stories over similar kinds of bread. You thought of how other people began and ended these tales: putting the blood-smeared doorways and crucified young

men in the blooming season of new life. If religion had gotten anything right, it was this. The embedded disappointment, the expectation to end in the heart of a beginning.

Ask any outsider—it's a native form, this rhyme between promise
and loss.

The sherut unloaded in Afula. While waiting for a bus to the forested
village near Migdal Ha'Emek, you observed a group of schoolchildren. It was their singing that made them unusual in the crowd of
distracted travelers, and since you were already bored, you left the
shade beside the station and worked your way over to their gathering.
Just outside the ring of them, you leaned assertively on your cane. But
no one even glanced at you as their teacher led them off. Each of
them left a stone atop a memorial plaque. It was rough and gray,
carved with Hebrew letters that looked contemporary, and it stood
directly on fine beige gravel inside a concrete berm. The flanking
roadway offered no clues, and the buses grumbling past felt danger-
ously close, so you made your way back to the station's shade.

The laborious journey had drawn the attention of another woman.
Buttoned inside a long aqua windbreaker, she stood guard over the
little wheeled travel bag you had left standing against the building.

"You should not do that," the woman said.

"Do what?"

The woman indicated the security guard who was now loitering in
the doorway. "Leave your bag. Anyone could take it. And anything
could be inside it."

She revealed that the stone was a memorial marking an event that
had happened during this month in 1994. A young man had waited
until a group of schoolchildren boarded their bus, and then he'd detonated a car full of grenades. The attack was, as they all were, retaliation
for an earlier offense. Many had died, and in the scene of carnage, the
bodies of young and old, Israeli and Arab, had been scattered every-

where. Limbs and bones, unmarried from bodies. Because of this, and for security in general, station employees preferred travelers to remain with their luggage.

Despite her fine windbreaker and her dyed black hair, this woman had a slightly pockmarked, straightforward face with heavy features—like an almond in its shell, and basically friendly.

"You are going to Timrat alone?" The woman had moved her jute bags to the pavement beside your suitcase, establishing a brief alliance. "The stop is two and a half kilometers away from the town. I will help you get down from the bus."

"No, one stop past there." You said the name of the stop. "It's no trouble. Please don't bother."

"But anywhere is a very, very difficult walk for you. I will find someone to drive you. You have your bag." She went on, imploring you, saying that it was safer to go by car, insisting on the ease of calling a friend's son who lived in the town: he was not busy, he was a good young man, and her niece was recently single. She had many reasons to talk to him.

"Thank you," you said, "but I'm going to a place that is no longer there. A car won't make it all the way. I need to walk no matter what, and I'm in very good health."

"What? Where are you going? What is this big mystery?" Her features lit up with chiding.

As we know, none of your inner roads were direct. Answers about anything deeper than an opinion were impossible. You fiddled with the torn foam on the cane's handle. This pilgrimage had to do with the names you'd forgotten, and a gazelle with her mouth full of desires, and having chosen to follow a love that felt honest but was also a torment, an invisible irony that had plagued you since earliest memory. And since these answers stuck in your throat now, you spat out the one that was less odd for an old woman to admit to a stranger.

"I'm here to see the town where I was born. It is under the forest. Maaloul."

The woman's face clouded, but to Nuha's surprise, she didn't with-

draw her kindness. "People repaired the church last year. Cyclists go
to the park." It wasn't the right thing to say, and she seemed to reconsider. "How long since you were at home?"

In the growl of the approaching bus, you said, "The town was
standing when I left it seventy-two years ago."

You and the companion rode the bus in periods of silence, long
enough to calculate various numbers. If this month was seventeen
years since the bus bombing in Afula, it was nine since the bombing
in Nablus by fighter jets and the soap factory's destruction, as well as
my ninth birthday. (Indeed, a few weeks before, you had called the
house for ten minutes and spent only four of them talking to me.)

The bus rolled over the smooth pavement and dirt, rushing over
the layered bones. There were lost towns just under the surface, not
even a century out of reach. Yet on the bus were tourists in search of
lost biblical sites, as though the dirt beneath their feet was only a
distraction on the way to other truths.

"Our stop is here." A soft tap on your shoulder, and the woman
lowered the bags from the overhead compartment.

Outside the bus was a smooth slab of concrete, an island in good
repair among the rocky hillsides. Above was a disorienting blanket of
scrawny pines that had not been there seventy years ago. As the bus
pulled away, you were questioning whether your memory was already
wrong. The woman pointed out a white Škoda in the departing veil of
dust.

"Just there, you see? The village is in this forest here. He will take
you."

The friend's son did not smile much. He was effusively helpful,
however, in positioning the little suitcase in his trunk and getting his
passenger settled in the front. All this for a journey of absurd brevity,
across the highway and a mere hundred meters along a dirt road to a
lot beside some modern-looking water tanks.

He was a part-time cabdriver and penned several names and phone
numbers around the text on his card, making you show him your
phone, promising to come as soon as you called. "Ten minutes," he

repeated, "ten minutes and I come." And in the many repetitions he sounded almost Arab, piling on his sincerity. He meant it. His mother's friend, the woman with the aqua windbreaker, added her phone number to the card, too. And with that, their part in our story comes to an end; perhaps the boy married the woman's niece, perhaps they worried about you that day and later, perhaps by delivering a relic of a woman to a village under the forest they felt a new, faint pulse on their map of home, the sort of pulse when a fact ceases to be theoretical.

You had expected people to be unkind, but you had not found any unkind people today. Without an enemy, and therefore in solitude, you walked up the hill alone. The wheels of your carry-on suitcase left parallel tracks in the dirt.

I am here on the precipice of leaving your grave site forever—leaving, I mean, the sort of life that allows me to visit this stone in this patch of grass whenever I want. The time you returned to the place you had started your journey more than seventy years before, when you set foot on the path that had led you away, did your body recognize home? Did all the swarming stories of your life finally roost? Or had you, having gone along the millions of forking paths of your life, become a stranger to the past? I reach the center of the problem: in all the crossroads real and imaginary, there is no Road of Return. It is possible to come back to a place, but there's no undoing the transformation that happens once the heart has chosen to leave.

Maybe I'm not as sound as I thought. I think I hear your voice now, traveling alongside mine. It's that language-before-language that feels true in the bones. I inhabit you in a dozen ways even now, but this is new. There is so much I didn't see. Is this what recognition is? When the subject of one's story has something to add?

So speak, Auntie, speak again. Make the clock run backward.

Weddings in our culture, Betty, they are more inevitable than dying. The joke went something like this: "Wallahi, my friend, I was walking to my auntie's to celebrate my twenty-eighth birthday, and on the way, I got run over by an army truck. The bystanders and the driver crowded in. My bones were all over the road, and everyone was crying, 'Oh, oh, look at this, this is just terrible! She is twenty-eight, and she has no husband!' And then the doctor comes and he kneels and listens to my dying heartbeat, and he shakes his head. 'Summon the priest,' he says. 'I recognize the driver and I know that he is a widower!' And then the priest comes with his holy book and pronounces us man and wife, and then my parents and every other idiot in the city throw candy at us and go dancing. I am dead, but hamdullah, my friends, at least I am married!"

This is what Yacoub and I were dealing with in the summer of 1953 in the city of Nablus.

Yacoub was Jibril's best friend. They had a friendship of convenience; they were both very rich and of the same age, and our families both made soap, and neither one of them invested much of their free time in courting girls. Jibril was already engaged to Saeeda, who was only eleven and a half years old. Yacoub was very handsome and very charming, but also a little mean and stringy, with cupid lips and too-small ears and the neatest hair you've ever seen outside of the Egyptian film industry. They hiked together in Sebastia and on Ebal, where there was no water and the caves were empty. They drank a lot of wine and complained about their problems.

Jibril's problem was that he'd applied to an engineering program in the United States and had finally been accepted. He was technically a Jordanian citizen, because of political winds far above anyone's head, but his student visa had been declined. He wondered if he was truly a citizen of anywhere.

Yacoub's problem was that he spent day and night at the cheap coffee shops, among old men and refugees, looking for men who knew why he was there, and who were brave enough to return his gaze. Yacoub and Jibril, they were both stuck in a city they wanted to leave.

And one thing led to the next and then I, Nuha Rummani of the two skins and stolen Rummani stories, was getting married to Yacoub Abdul-hadi of the little ears and good hair. Our wedding day was as ridiculous as you can imagine, under an arch of stupid roses, with me in a dress as big as a drilling platform, but maybe let me back up a minute and focus on why it seemed like a good idea at the time.

My husband, Yacoub, and I, we each knew what the other one was, at least.

Jibril had gotten it out of me a few years before. His father had died regretting not having been able to get me married off, and the week of the funeral Jibril and I were drinking on the roof and he said he was sorry for not finding a good match, for it made the whole family embarrassed. I broke down and confessed that I was not embarrassed. And then I confessed my loneliness. And then I confessed about the lanky, beautiful girl I'd followed down the hill from my village of Maaloul and west to the sea—she, the gazelle I had been chasing in Haifa the day I'd rescued him in the burning marketplace, the boy on fire. For a second, right before I was sure he would throw me off the building, I could breathe. Then I thought, *It's the last breath I'll ever take.*

"Ah." He just looked at me. "And the cook in the old Haifa house?"

"Very much so."

"Ah." The scars on his forehead stretched and furrowed—making what I recognized as a frown. "I thought it was just because I look like this."

"Habeebi, no." And thanks to the wine: "She was widowed and she used grief to make people leave her alone. No one suspected—it wasn't just you."

His mouth twisted. Whenever he smiled, the corners of his lips pointed down. "But I really embarrassed myself. Surely she had great fun laughing at me."

"Oh, my little brother. She thought you were adorable."

He was easy to talk to, this man afflicted with sadness, especially when he was drunk. Although he was smart, he only pointed his mind at things with edges—rocks, chemicals, facts he could find in a book. People were too slippery for him. I'd talk and he'd absorb, but he had almost nothing to say. Never judged. The first time I came to America and saw a lava lamp, this blue blob dancing its slow ballet in the water, I realized what we all looked like to him.

Yacoub trusted him, too. Jibril endeared himself to every kind of self-hating misfit in Nablus, but because Yacoub was so rich and well-respected, everybody assumed Jibril had taken responsibility for his sister's honor and was seeking a betrothal. My other so-called brothers certainly didn't care about me and had dropped the matter before their father's body was cold. Still, the yammering for single people to be married, and married people to have babies, and parents to marry their babies to one another—it's water torture. Drip, drip on your forehead till you'll sign anything. Hypnotizing even Jibril.

Yacoub and I, we were two different species. But Jibril made the mistake of thinking we were different in the same way.

Jibril's arm snaked into mine as we left church. It was a Sunday near my official thirtieth birthday—the summertime one, the one on Nuha Rummani's birth certificate in the family's safe.

"I have a present for your special day, ukhti," he murmured in my ear. "Come to Sebastia with me."

"There are fifteen people already at the house. If I don't help—"

"We'll be back by the time the uncles wake up after lunch. Just come."

He steered me past the priest and all the children before they could break loose from their families and ask me to tell them a story, to look at their trinket, to tell their sister to leave them alone. Jibril rushed me away, down the uneven street, into the next quarter, into a neighborhood that felt like a journey all the way through the underworld because I was wearing tight, thick-heeled shoes. He took me up a steep alley, to a door to a private courtyard. In that city we all knew which family was Christian or Muslim as we knew what day it was, and this was a Muslim house, one far richer than ours and which was called a palace by some. In the archway beyond the tiled fountain, a servant was at work, polishing the headlights of a coffee-and-cream Humber Hawk.

"Do you like it?" Yacoub asked, striding out of the carriage house. "My father bought it from a British supply officer on the sly and had it redone for me."

I knew of Yacoub. His family, the Abdulhadis, had already sent relatives to Jordan to make friends in the government of mad King Talal, before he'd lost his throne. Remember, Jordan was our occupier in those years—they said it was to protect us from the new State of Israel—but Yacoub's family was rich enough to have a couple of dogs in that fight, too, hoping that when all the blood washed away, they would end up either with a place in the Jordanian administration of Palestine or else with a lifeline out of the region entirely, if things got worse. But Yacoub styled himself a black sheep. He bought and read the firebrand pamphlets trickling out of Cairo and Beirut in those years, repeating all their nonsense about the refugees being proletariat heroes, about how all the Arab nations could sew themselves together like a big Frankenstein monster and show the West that the Middle East was great without any help from America or Russia.

I thought of the families still living in caves on Jebel Jarzim. I thought of the snow last winter, and the old ones who had frozen to death, and the Nakba widows who cooked for the church. While these people were weeping in their bones for their stolen farms and houses, Yacoub was having his toy car painted. Now he stood in front of Jibril in oxblood suspenders and a driving cap.

"I thought I'd have to drive through the church doors and rescue you," he said. "Or that you'd given up on our treks, and I'd have to drink our Sunday wine alone." He had a languid, formal way of talking, but I saw his eyes—anxious around Jibril. A constant measuring of himself against perfection and the possibility of failure.

The servant swiped a chamois across the silver grille and slipped away. Jibril walked once around the bumpers. I knew we were thinking the same thing: of how the car had looked with its original camouflage paint and an armored chassis. It was a war vehicle, of the kind that had made appearances around our home in Haifa leading up to the invasion. This one had new tires and that dapper new body, and a leather interior as soft as the feathers of a desert bird. I was wondering how many times you had to change a thing before it stopped being what it was.

"Lacquered cedar trim, new brightwork, and restored Connolly leather on the seats. Wait till you hear the engine." Yacoub was all but standing on the balls of his feet, following Jibril's eyes and shoulders and breath. "Well?"

"Sorry, Yacoub. Your car's pretty. I'm blown away. I'm speechless in admiration."

"All right then! You sit in the front." He opened the door for Jibril and skipped around to the driver's side. I stood outside like I wasn't there at all until Jibril saw me and conferred with Yacoub, whose eyes made a swipe at me over the arc of the enormous steering wheel. He jerked his chin at the backseat.

The gate swung open and the motor hummed in the seats. It was noon of the hottest day of summer, and the valleys between the buildings and the walls filled up with sunlight. The gloom lifted, carried up into the sky with the last moisture in the shadows. Yacoub's shoulders uncoiled and faded into the seat.

"Just how far do you think we could go on forty-five liters of petrol? As far as Beirut, where people are happier?"

He turned his face toward Jibril, and I saw Jibril ignore the look in Yacoub's eyes.

They bought their wine from the Samaritans; then we motored into the valley again, now in the opposite direction and past the ruins of twenty civilizations at least, even as new factories were going up around the quarry outside of town. We went as far as the Humber would carry us, climbing the spine of a mountain that led to the ruins of ancient Sebastia. It bears repeating here that the West Bank is one of the oldest places in civilization. In Nablus, the bible isn't the Bible, it's a community anthology by a bunch of local writers. But these boys were running around Jacob's Well and the church where Saint John the Baptist lost his head like a pair of teenagers in the Hollywood Hills. One of them, I was pretty sure, was getting crushed under love for the other. I knew exactly what it felt like, and so I couldn't quite despise Yacoub.

"Every day a good party," I said, "like every day is the wedding of some-body important." I climbed out of the car. The track ahead was alive and fresh with untrammeled grass and wild okra.

"It'll soon be your birthday," Jibril said, "and you are well past thirty, and you finally deserve a present to reverse all your years of bad luck."

"Are you mad? I'm not thirty yet." I cut my eyes to Yacoub.

"Don't worry about anything," Jibril said.

I didn't know how we'd get back in time for dinner. "How about we save that wine for later, to celebrate your brothers not murdering me for disap-pearing?"

"They won't mind that you're gone, I promise."

Yacoub stood with his fists in his pockets, cheek to the wind, squinting over the valley. "My money paid for that wine. You're not taking it any-where."

"I'm wearing heels. I can't hike on these rocks."

"I thought you said she was willing to do this." Yacoub picked up the two bags so that Jibril could hike unimpeded. "Shut the door, please. I don't want dust on my leather. Now, can we go?"

Somebody once said that if you can understand another person's pain, loving them is inevitable. I've encountered turds that are less full of shit, but I will say, empathy can get you at least through an hour-long picnic. I shut the door, thinking, *Tongue, fold your hands and behave*. I pried off my shoes, squinted at Yacoub's back, and set them on the Humber's hood with a clunk. Barefoot, I picked my way through the scrub to catch up with him and Jibril as they climbed a lattice of shade beneath the olive trees.

The bags held wine and also a picnic blanket, bread, pickled vegeta-bles, a ball of cheese, and some water. After we were all settled and look-ing out over the hilltops, Jibril reached into the second bag and pulled out a folio of papers.

"You're to get a passport," he said to me.

I laughed. "We don't live in a country."

"And I was never a captain in the Jordanian army," Yacoub answered, "but now is not the time to bore each other with honesty." He pushed the wine against Jibril's chest. "We care about Jibril getting his science degree in America."

"What country is this? There is no country here. You have to be from somewhere to go anywhere." The thought of leaving Nablus was absurd. It was its own world. If I left, I would be erased—as out of place as any of the refugees living in caves across the valley. I thought I could hear their occasional shouts even now, their distant voices echoing through the afternoon, bouncing between the cliffs.

Jibril rubbed at his eyebrows. "Just look at the papers, will you?"

There was a two-page passport application, visa papers, a medical form, and a letter from the U.S. embassy in Amman, Jordan, that was addressed to Yacoub, confirming an interview appointment in two weeks. The United States had given Jordan a boost by opening an embassy there some years ago, and now Jordan was definitely in charge of us—at least on the map and in the offices of bureaucrats around the world. But we weren't Palestine-the-political-entity yet. There was no word for us as a place of our own, a people of our own. Just as there was no word for me, and no word for Yacoub. All of us simply existed, with our lives and habits and loves and relentless progressions of days.

Yet I was slow to understand, because I was afraid that I understood exactly what they were proposing.

"This letter says the appointment is with Yacoub Abdulhadi . . . and his wife."

I was stranded. Yacoub had finished an entire bottle of wine while I'd been reading, and now his lips were dark blue from the wine and curled down at one corner, enduring a lingering acidity. His eyes were on Jibril, begging him to say out loud that he understood and appreciated that this plan was a nearly suicidal gesture of love. That here before Jibril were two people who had nothing in common but the fact that they would do anything for him, get him to another country, get him into an engineering program, all so he might enjoy a shred of the independence that was so impossible for either of us. But we were just these two slippery blobs to Jibril.

My stomach roiled, my head spun, and my thoughts moved too fast to pin words on them. I was aware of my hands shaking, but for the first time in my life, the silence of who we were and the impossibility of a future overtook me, smothering out anything I wanted to say.

"There's talk that the rules are changing," Jibril was saying, "that I'm going to need a relative to sponsor me for my student visa, and then after that, I want to stay in America. We can all stay there. I'd have a shot at a good job. And right now, you're the only one who can go, but only if you marry Yacoub. You hate it here! You said. We can't live in Nablus forever and make soap in a broken factory— Nuha!"

I'd drawn my arm back; before he could stop me, I hurled the other bottle of wine down the hill and took off.

I already knew I would do it for him. I knew I deserved it, for all my lies. I also knew he deserved my anger.

When he and Yacoub finally made their way back to the Humber, I was sitting on a boulder in front of the vehicle's bumper, facing into the wind so that my tears dried before they could fall. In the sun and wind, my hair was extra red, extra a mess. Jibril stretched his drunk self across the back-seat. Yacoub leaned on the grille and stared at my shoes, still on the hood, and then hooked them by their heels and lowered them gently to the ground beside the front tire. He opened the door and slumped behind the wheel, glowering over it at me. He looked like he wanted to drive over me—but what good would it do us? As the story went, hamdullah, at least we'd be married.

No, before that. Go back. To earlier enemies.

Bones under bones under bones. In some ways it seems life did not begin until this body was called Nuha Rummani, born adult into a family of rich troubles and overbearing history. But the body precedes the name, and the bones inside it wake to this other place as they did not in Nablus.

Maaloul. It is the name of a spring that fed a productive hillside village. Now the site is a sloping, airy pine forest: empty, but there's a trammeled artificiality that is hard to pinpoint. Maybe it's the road. Although the feeling is subtly forbidding, no one is here right now to stop a traveler from climbing up and looking for ruins.

Once upon a time, the streets had been terraced, like the stories of a tower. They rose to two hilltop churches and, on the way up, met a plain stone mosque whose imam climbed a ladder to the roof to chant the azan. It had been a village of Christians and Muslims and a few godless kooks. Its people shared a pasture with the kibbutz on the next hill. Peace, of a kind.

But memory is cobwebbed with gross nostalgia—if it had been so good, why leave paradise for Haifa?

The only sound now is the crunch of dead grass under the new spring blades. Find the stones. Put hands to them. Troublesome cemetery of a town, whose house was this? A keen eye finds another toppled wall in the scrub, its limestone bones poking up like the tops of skulls. The government has since planted a forest over this place to cover its army's many sins, as though hiding a corpse by pulling a sheet over the carnage.

A massive, gnarled prickly pear reveals itself behind a scrim of distracting pines: the shape and age fit. This very plant once grew at the corner of the carpentry shop. Appreciate its slow, vegetable patience, like the famed tortoises, hatched when Napoleon's heart still beat for Egypt and Josephine.

The old house is uphill somewhere. Climb, and try to breathe without wheezing. The village, what's left of it in the weeds, is almost as unintelligible as a forgotten language. The grammar of it had something to do with betrothal to the mason's son and acting happy about it; but that girl doesn't exist anymore. A language begins to peel away the moment it encounters an unsayable thing—going to the well one night, for instance, hearing a little plash, finding a forbidden young woman washing. Traveling with a caravan, she said as she wrung out her hair; water dripped from her elbows. Only in tales did it make sense, a magic door appearing in the side of the well. Once you think of going through it, you are already gone.

Hot now. Sunlight evaporates the last coolness out of the grass. A lizard scrambles out of the leaves and bobs its head on a rock. The hillside mutters to itself in its own simple words. The only familiar thing is the suitcase, which waits a little ways downhill, a bright aubergine cube of fabric, standing by the trail with its handle in the air. It is like the gazelle of that long-ago evening, alert and out of place, waiting for nothing but an excuse to depart.

Stop. Permit this foreign tree to hold you aright for a spell. Wheeze.

Why leave paradise for a gazelle? Because there is no paradise. Because the body is alive and wants the future. Because places have no self-knowledge; they are only known by others. Because life may or may not be long. Because the world is wide. Because time spills forward. Because promise always beats like a pulse inside certain disappointment. Because that woman's mouth fit against yours. Because she wanted a life with you in other cities, among strangers. Because recognition is rare. Because the layer of skin between one rib cage and another still feels like the only thing in the world that prevents two hearts and their branching arteries from growing wild, locking around one another like the limbs of neighboring trees astride the broken-down fence of two bodies.

In 10B, the woman who emerged from this journey was stuck in the middle seat of a transcontinental flight.

One-third of the way around the globe, another Jibril was soon to be born. His name was spelled *Gabriel* in the phonetic habit of his English-speaking parents, but it was still the name of his forefathers. Gabriel, bringer of tidings from the heavens, holy revealer, shit stirrer of the ages.

To forget about the elbowing ogres in seats 10A and 10C, you worked out a guest list in your little cardboard notebook. Names crowded all four of its corners, and the page was now limp with ink. Why not? It might be the last time in life to see so many Rummanis together. The Time of Feuding was done, after so many visits had restored their shred of goodwill. You imagined, for the first time, how it might actually go—gathering them under Tashi's roof to make them recognize how the U.S. Rummanis had really come to America. To tear off the false skin and show them the common-as-cloth woman beneath it. The woman whose name time had forgotten.

Or maybe the age of cinematic melodrama had passed. Maybe it was better to let them carry the tidy story they already knew. Inviting people's judgment, especially evil Zaki and his grabbing hands, seemed to be tempting fate. There was something one of the Israeli interrogators had said, late in the questions, when the anger under your tongue might have gotten away from you. "You know," the man said after a silence, "Israel is very good to homosexuals. We treat you better than your own people do. That's a little ironic, don't you think? They say you should be put off the face of the earth. But tell me if you still love *Filasteen*."

Now, hesitating, you wiped a glob of ink off your knuckle; you noticed a tiny tear in the skin.

It was late to rip everything away. People would have too many questions for an old woman. To be so honest would feel like that moment on the tiles beside your old bathtub, being discovered in no clothes. But it was not too late for sly truths, if they made you happy. You penned Cecilia's name on the list, because why not? If they even realized who she was to you, well, it was never too late to electrocute life back into people. At least they'd have the story to bring them together after you had gone home.

Humans Versus Monsters:

A Ballet

———•·•———

My favorite moment from Anna's sister's well-received performance in the talent show that autumn is the one where Hades dips her back into an exaggerated arabesque, just before he abducts her to the underworld. Her left toes are planted on the stage, en pointe, while her right leg passes beneath his arm and straight up, into the lights and rigging. She is so flexible that the pose is both beautiful and disorienting: ankles, calves, and thighs drawn apart like the undulating curves of a longbow.

The effect, as Hades holds her to his chest, is of a young woman transformed into something else by splitting her down the middle.

Ballet was therapeutic. When I was nine going on ten, I entered a period of vertiginous empathy complicated by the secondary symptom of remembering the future. It was like being an oracle except I was still a kid menaced by bullies everywhere.

My ear, nose, and throat doctor speculated that my problem was puberty.

"You could try activities for balance," he said.

I swung my legs from his table, squinting into the blurred image of myself through his eyes, and told him he had a child in Panama. Or perhaps he would, if he traveled there in the future.

When I was in the bathroom, my father told him, "We're expecting her brother soon. I think she's acting up." Being an only child himself, Adam assumed that all new siblings were crises. The doctor typed the information into my chart, which would be coded that evening by his billing department:

ICD-9-CM Code V61.8: Other specified family circumstances

ICD-9-CM Diagnosis Code 259.1: Precocious puberty, not elsewhere classified

ICD-9-CM Diagnosis Code H81.399: Other peripheral vertigo, unspecified

The office referred my case to a child psychologist, but my mother preferred the sound of "activities for balance." Saeeda said I was turning into yet another graceless American, and all three women, including you now that you had returned from Palestine, thought of trust in medical doctors as akin to raising a lamb among wolves. They enrolled me in little-fairies ballet at Lida Maria's Dance Studio on advice from Anna's mother, since the school talent show was coming up.

In my mind, the talent show had already happened and it had been a disaster.

But no one cared about that. We were awaiting the any-day-now birth of my brother. Although I also reported that the delivery would go well but that he'd be engulfed in flames, you hissed and sent me to sweep my mother's garage workspace and dust its new chandelier.

"I'm not a liar," I said, draped against the kitchen counter, making my body into the manifestation of a whine. You turned fully around from the plate where you were peeling cucumbers, and you looked at me. Or, really, skewered me and lifted me off the floor with your eyes.

"This is a game? Very good. Call your mother in to hear it, too. Entertain us. Or is this not a game, and you would rather do your chores like a good girl while your mother rests?"

I dangled there, unsure. That morning, I'd lain in bed before the alarm, aware of the room's temperature and the sound of the house, yet I'd also felt snared in the filaments of a dream—an infant swaddled in flames, although peaceably asleep. It had happened the previous morning, too, and the one before that. But your attention frightened me, and I had not yet learned to temper my fear into a steel spine. I had also not yet heard the story of the boy whose hair was fire, and now I wonder if you wanted me to say more, after all—to prove something about the tributaries of imagination and memory and their secret, common source. But I had a child's fear of disturbing my pregnant mother, and went outside with a broom and rag.

I already knew we'd miss the birth—fast, uneventful. When it happened I was in dance class and not at the hospital. Saeeda had dropped Anna and me off for an hour and a half of leg lifts and swanning arms with other girls who were three years younger than us and profoundly interested in my appearance.

The studio, insofar as our project is concerned with architectures imaginary and real, was part of a strip mall uphill from St. Catherine's. Adjacent to a corporate coffee shop was a brilliant window, tantalizing with its golden studio floor and concentrating children. Mothers drank lattes and watched. It was the eye of Miss Lida Maria Gravina's enterprise, pressed against the glass, though the studio's body snaked back through hallways lined with locked trophy cases and other practice rooms. The front studio was to advertise entry-level dance classes to suburban parents. The back studios, as Anna's prima donna sister told us, were for the dancers who actually knew what they were doing.

Saeeda parked in front of the coffee shop. "Do you girls have lots of water to drink?"

I did not. Anna rolled her eyes and stuck her bottle in my gym bag. This is what passed for a détente between us, since she had cursed and screamed and finally been bribed to come to her sister's dance studio with me, as an ally, despite being three years of ballet classes ahead of me and insisting that Miss Lida was the actual Satan.

In the locker room, I steadied myself on Anna's shoulder as I struggled with the many-tentacled slippers.

"Girls! Hurry up!" someone yelled from outside.

Anna muttered, "I wanted to practice walking on hot coals, for the record. That would win the talent show."

"That's a terrible idea."

"We could be practicing with charcoal from the grill right now."

Outside the door: "Sixty seconds and I want you out on the floor! Sixty, fifty-nine . . ." The teacher's purred *r*'s and overripe consonants were Mediterranean, but the accent was somehow more astringent than Nuha's. She punctuated the command by rapping something metallic against the door. As we rushed out to the barre, we saw that it was a tap shoe.

The middle C hammer struck inside the studio's old upright.

"I am Lida. Maria. Gravina. You are my new level ones." Her voice was deep and dry. Anna gave me a *told-you-so* glare as the room quieted. Miss Lida named everything in the room and all the things we would do here today—the barre, first position, plié, revelé—while her eyes scraped over the row of us. She was an eagle over a box of mice.

"Weak girls come to me. When you leave my class tonight, you will be a little less weak. And each time a little less, until you are no longer a girl, but a ballerina. My school is not for girls who wish to have fun. If you are in the wrong place, leave now."

One girl vanished into the locker room, where she'd sit for the next sixty-five minutes, lip trembling with disappointment. I decided I did not want to be a ballerina, either; nor did I care about winning anything in the school talent show. I stayed, however, because Miss Lida was terrifying, as severe as an overplucked eyebrow. She felt like family.

"Your name?" she demanded, stalking down the line of pink-slippered girls.

Rosa. Charlotte. Brie. Mackenna. Kendra. Sam.

She arrived at me. "Who are you?"

"Betty Rummani, Miss Lida."

She was not a tall woman, but she gazed down at me. Her orange eyes sliced through my hair and clothes and took in the whole of me. People startled by my body usually hid their surprise—sidelong glances, fake compliments. But Miss Lida stared in silence, taking it in. This body: it knows where the muscles go, what bones should be long and what bones should be short. It has patterned its genetic mosaic after the Rummani side—the long fingers and toes, the wide ovals of my nails, the sharp edge of my jaw, the sleepy-lidded eyes set close to a nose whose bridge bears a family resemblance to Babylonian ramparts. And lately, breasts. Strange flights in my dreams, like lifting off, a tower so high that its upper stories lost the encumbrance of gravity. Yet I could not be considered apart from what is most obvious about me. From those stunted years away from you, Auntie, I was smaller at nine than the statistical American average, yet from the mortar in my cells, I weighed a hundred and fifty pounds. And I was the blue of a talisman in Miss Lida's culture and mine.

Miss Lida's gaze settled on my braided hair. "Your mother's work?"

"My aunt's, Miss Lida."

"Reasonably well-done." She passed to Anna, then over her. "I already know your sister. You will have to unlearn everything they taught you at that joke of a studio if you want to be half as good as her."

For the rest of the class, we pressed our heels together like the tip of an ice-cream cone, pointed our toes like holding down a mouse by its tail, dipped at the knee, reached for the stars. All without music, without any noise at all except the soft taps of ballet slippers on the floor and hiss of fabric as girls obeyed Miss Lida's commands. Anytime someone stumbled or fidgeted, she lashed out with a sharp "Pay attention!"

As I slid my foot outward again, my black slipper seemed to creep across the wooden floor like a caterpillar. The more I remembered the future, the more absurd it seemed: my own foot under my body, heavy and solid as a sandbag. I saw it stepping not on the studio's bamboo floorboards but a metal stair, only in a boot, crossing a bright gap that seemed full of distance and strange air. My balance started to tilt and I grabbed the barre.

"Again! And try!" Miss Lida shouted, clapping her hands once.

Anna looked furious, but for me, it was a relief to be treated no worse than anyone else. At the end of the hour, Miss Lida clapped one last time and sent the class to the locker room. "Some of you, good riddance! The rest of you, my assistant will see you next week! Bring locks for your lockers—and practice!"

Mothers gathered in the lobby and on the sidewalk. Cars waited, sending exhaust fumes tumbling into the red glow of their own tail-lights. Saeeda was out there, too, hunched over an antiquated little cellphone, learning of my sibling's uneventful birth. In the fumes she looked like a red apparition.

Gabriel was not engulfed in flames, at first. While I lay in bed with vast headaches, my parents plied me with a useless heating pad and began reassembling the crib in my room, which they now called the nursery. They say that, as I lay there that first summer of my brother's life, I often predicted what would become of Palestine, but no one could make any sense of a vision of flying—soaring past a blue-glass tower that reached to the sky—or of one human face superimposed on another as if in a thick pane of glass. These mysteries undermined any use in warning them that their infant would be on fire by October.

As for me, it felt like my head had been bored open like a well, and all the universe had come flooding in. The space between my ears was alive and deafening, as if all the speech of the seven continents and the high seas poured directly into my brain. A future written in a flood. But the neurologist only repeated the advice of other specialists and prescribed more activities for balance. I lay awake half the night, hearing everything and nothing. I heard two soldiers harassing an old woman along the wall, heard my mother and you singing Gabriel to sleep, and felt your relief to be doing this in clean rooms, a paid-for house, for an innocent who had come into the world dragging no strange problems, no strange gifts, or so you thought. *Blessed* was the actual word you used.

Who was this blessing?

When my parents had carried him across the threshold for the first time, the whole city had jolted with an earthquake. The antique cannonballs had rolled off their shelf, leaving a divot in the hardwood. Now the cracked floor was toothy with splinters, which I peeled out of the grain and used to needle the bottoms of his feet. He didn't wake, so I needled harder.

I was alert, unsteady, and resentful. I gripped his crib railing and pondered, needling one toe at a time, what the letters of his name could tell me about this thing that had fallen into my bedroom.

G is for the glow of pink-white skin in the streetlight.

An *A* for alabaster eyelids, closed until morning.

Brother of mine, looking nothing like me.

R for the bit of rosacea around the left side of his mouth, which you and my mother daubed with olive oil despite my father's saying *contraindicated*.

Little *i* for his dot-sized fingernails, or how much like the letter his skinny body looked on the mattress.

E for everything about him being pathetic, though decades from now, he'd become angelic and severe and consistently heroic.

L for let him cry a little longer in the middle of the night, because his privilege stretched before him wide as a highway, and tears might teach him humility. Also, my parents might lug themselves out of bed and shuffle down the creaking hallway, without my having to go shake them awake.

Gabriel, harbinger of future tidings, was here to stay. Perhaps it was his nature I heard in my skull, the whole chaotic future, buoying this baby on top of it. So I felt, that summer, no pang of concern as I saw him burning like a torch in a wild column of sparks. I wondered about magic, this fragile seashell of a boy in my old blankets. He was so well wrought in his diminution, so at ease in his body and its comforts, that perhaps he was a wrong turn in a family of stories. With his echo of a name and fragile skin and hidden Rummani blood, he seemed not so much to be hiding but to be playing a trick that fooled everyone but me. You even called him Adonis when I wasn't in the room.

I bored the floor splinter into the skin right between his first and second toes, and his eyes shot open, and he kicked and wailed.

"Maybe a rash," said my mother, all attention the next morning. She ran the pad of her index finger over the raised dots in the center of his footprint, and then went for the olive oil.

"Maybe so," you said from the chaise longue. You were wrapping a Band-Aid around your pinkie finger, patching a torn piece of skin, but looking straight at me.

The talent show was scheduled for the end of October. The whole school had known about it since May—Saint Catherine had declared it a tradition, a place to showcase how we'd improved ourselves over the summer holidays. We didn't have to do it, but it got us the academic version of an indulgence. I didn't need one, but Anna could never get anything better than a B. Tests made her nervous, and she was worried about not being placed with her other friends in the upper school classes next year.

"But isn't the talent show a kind of test, too?"

"No, it's different," she insisted, kicking her locker door to make it latch over her mess of books, dance gear, and other random junk she seemed to regard as necessary. The latch popped open again.

I already sensed how the show would turn out, and I could have just stepped on her foot and broken a few toes, but my father had trained me to use peaceful methods. "I think *Swan Lake* is a real ballet," I said. "Like, a hard one. You really want to dance to it?"

Her other friends, for instance, were dancing to Top 40 songs or throwing batons.

"My sister is doing her big, leapy dance from her *Persephone* rehearsals. I'm just going to steal some of the choreography. She'll dance after me, so there'll be a whole forty minutes when people think I'm a genius. I've been working on the routine every day."

"Instead of your social studies report?"

She slammed her locker again. "I need you to believe in me, *Elspeth*. Dance classes were your idea."

I was reconsidering the broken-toe plan, especially because I also remembered a future in which she asks me, in the same tone of voice, *What are you? What exactly do you call yourself, anyway?* But as my head swirled, she was already stalking off to math class.

Whole days passed when I didn't remember the future. Then I'd wake with a steady reel of déjà vu, such that even turning left or right out of the bedroom felt like walking through a trick mirror. Downstairs, I'd wonder why my father didn't have a beard today and remember, *Oh, the gray beard comes later.* I'd have a bright notion of walking all the way to the cemetery and picnicking at a headstone, and break off in confusion at such a morbid idea, and realize the cemetery itself was a figment. That particular day, I sat in the backseat afflicted with a crushing dread that stemmed—I couldn't quite tell— either from living through a future in which every major avenue of every city in the world has emptied overnight or from simply knowing that today was another day of fourth grade. I went through the week, jolted each time the future folded into the present like a zipper.

It didn't help that you were living with us for a while. Saeeda had sold the Palo Alto house, as she'd threatened to, and was nearly ready to move out into the new one she was building farther north. Unhoused again, you moved in downstairs with your craft supplies and books of Arabic ghazals and baked us cookies and applauded Anna as she filled our driveway with her crooked leaps and tipsy pirouettes.

The choreography Anna had stolen from her sister was just too hard for her. In her froth of sibling envy, she couldn't see it. But when I tried to point out that she was going to hurt herself, you whipped around and said, in Arabic, that with enough practice, even a donkey can learn to read.

Plans, these prayers to the future, are always double-edged.

Anna would get attention at the talent show, just not in the way she expected.

That year, I thought there were only endless middles. Yet the friendship with Anna felt newly fragile—an ending lurked, despite my future memory of a letter from her in the brass mail slot of a flat I would inhabit, many years later, alone.

"Everybody changes at your age—that's all it is," my mother said.

"I'm not making it up. I know."

She laughed absently. She was enraptured by the trust in Gabriel's face as he let her feed him from his bottle. Enraptured, too, by how much easier it was this time around—every condition of her life was better, she had returned to the medicines that worked, and there was confidence in knowing that she had already survived one child's infancy and could do so again.

She said, "You'll know everything until you're about twenty. Enjoy it."

Disgusted, I tried taking refuge in your room downstairs. It neighbored my father's office and the snacks he kept in his drawer. I could hide out there the whole weekend if I wanted, as long as I didn't tattle when you cracked the window by the ceiling and lit your ten o'clock thinking tobacco.

You had grown truly old since returning to the United States. Your skin seemed papery, and you crept around the house as though you were tearing at the seams. You preferred to be still, planning Gabriel's baptismal party. You turned the furnace up too high and kept your commentary almost to yourself. Yours had never been a neutral presence, but now you got to work over a desk of fabric and sewing supplies, glasses limned from the gooseneck lamp.

Fingers covered in Band-Aids, you sewed baby clothes and wrote invitations to Gabriel's baptism in chaotic Arabic script and shaking English letters. You shouted into your phone, making sure the importance of the occasion arrived intact across continents. I was old news by then, counting down the months until I was ten, blue as ever—so what? No one cared about the three blue-soaped daughters of blue Alissabat and her smitten Rummani boy-husband, Jibril. They only wanted to hear about the baby, what food they could expect, what the weather in Portland was like. The last marks of the past seemed to have been rinsed away, leaving me, for the first time since birth, blank.

"Tell me about the blue soap," I said. "Or the silver gazelle."

"No, I forget."

I protested, sensing a game.

"They have flown like birds, I'm sorry."

I lay down in protest and hung on her ankle. "Aunnntie . . ."

"Hush. I'm tired of repeating myself. A lifetime on repeat. And you are too old for this nonsense behavior. Stand up and help me." You squeezed the good scissors and snipped into a bolt of lofty white felt. It was soft, fussy. Only the best garments for my sibling, clothing him for his special day.

"Don't bother," I said. "He's going to burn up with everything else."

You looked at me more fully than anyone had in weeks. But this time, the look was full of concern.

"You are not to speak like this to your parents, not never. Do you hear me? You are not about to follow in the footsteps of your mother. I am not going to leave this world worrying that you'll go through the same story as she did. Not happening."

"Auntie, I saw it in my dreams. I'm not crazy and Gabriel is on fire."

She seemed to reconsider, then said, "Dubbi Isanek, not another word. You heard it in the story of your grandfather Jibril. That is all. Everyone is well."

But the house taunted me. I could not open a pantry without seeing the door wrapped in flames or climb the spacious stairwell without charred abscesses opening beneath my feet. The whispering vents carried odors of woodsmoke to my nose in the middle of the night, and when I looked over at Gabriel, he, like me, seemed entranced by the flames snaking across the ceiling. My father's house had many fine rooms, and the more committed my parents grew to the fiction that we were now a normal family, the more the imaginary house inside it collapsed into conflagration.

I didn't know how the debacle would happen. It was like remembering a dream. The bits and flashes I gathered over the weeks of dance class and our lunch trays gave me enough of an idea that the talent show would not go well, but I couldn't figure out how to stop it. Once, I could have told Anna the mystical truth—that I *just knew*—and she would have shuddered and taken my word. But this new Anna was coarser, ready to fight with anyone.

So on the appointed day, when one of the school's major donors decided to attend, and we arrived at school that morning, and her sister Greta and the boy dancing Hades were asked to go onstage first to begin the show with a flourish, and Anna found this out because she overheard the principal's request on the curb beside their mother's car, and she came to me vibrating with shock, and the future snapped into the present with a fraught congruence, I still didn't know what to say.

"Break her toes?"

"Don't be a monster," she said. Her face was the color of gelatin. "I was supposed to go first. Now I'll look like a copycat. I have to think."

"No, you have to dance. Just do your best."

"Fuck you, Betty. A good friend would actually believe in me."

During our dance classes, maybe it was true that I spent too much

time watching and worrying about how Miss Lida constantly corrected Anna. But it was only because I wanted Anna to magically
improve.

"I am your friend. I'm saying just don't worry about anything else.
Go out there and do your best. Your practice was looking better."

She ripped her gym bag taking it out of her locker and whimpered
with rage. "You're lying. You think I suck." Her eyes welled with tears.
"What are you? What exactly do you call yourself, anyway? *Friend,*
sure."

This was what a typical fit of nerves looked like on Anna—operatic,
brief—but the familiar words landed like a slap. The questions seemed
to interrogate what business I, strange in every way, had in the lives of
anyone around me. I grasped for words, but she left me in the hallway
as she headed to the bathroom to change into her frilly sequined
getup. In her wake were a sea of turning heads, tracing her tantrum
back to me the way sharks sense blood.

I imagined myself elsewhere, in a place with no future and no people, living in a household where they treated blue women like queens.

"Matthew teaches us that to hide your talent," Saint Catherine con-
cludes into the microphone, "is to give in to damnation. Good luck,
everyone."

She is not in her habit today, just a plain civilian suit, which eases
her journey down from the podium onstage to the front row of auditorium seats. The lights fall dark. Set change: heavy fabric tumbles
from the rigging, making a deep rustle that whispers through the
noise of two hundred bodies. A recording from Igor Stravinsky's *The
Rite of Spring* rises—an ethereal bassoon, stirring two radiant figures
into motion, demonstrating to a roomful of short attention spans
what is possible with the good education each of our guardians has
bought for us.

A *talent* is an ancient unit of weight and money. It is the heaviest
one, worth about three thousand shekels. It is the root of the word

that came to signify, in most of the languages ancient Phoenician ships could encounter, a human being's unique gifts. The broader idea that gifts can be measured in money has a strong footing in a world where everything costs, and judging by the brief opening performance of Anna's sister and her partner, they have every reason to expect they'll get paid for their dancing in years to come. Ironically, they demonstrate this value by seeming weightless.

I've seen all these movements before: degraded on my driveway, the living room floor, and Miss Lida's studio for beginners. I can still feel it to this day, Anna's dread emanating from behind the curtains. Applause fills the lofty shadows, and Saint Catherine and the wealthy donor stand in the front row, triggering an ovation that washes across three hundred parents and students.

As it drains away, I force myself to be seated with my homeroom cohort. Anna's performance will happen however it happens. Our friendship has a better chance if I don't get involved. I know this. It's the old battle royale between heart and mind, a force strong enough to split any road in two. A contrary impulse writhes in me, and one after another, third graders play lullabies on recorders, fourth graders sing a song from an animated movie, and a fifth grader uses magic to force an entire box of cereal out of existence and then vanish himself in a puff of smoke. Behind its painted walls, the auditorium's bones and wires are set for this exact performance: an eternal lineup of bad violin solos, wavering voices, bully egos, a daring flash of leg, a few redeeming cameos by upper school students, all of it bookended by the remarks of a bored administrator. Its integrity of purpose over time is palpable—it was the same way fifty years before today, and fifty years in the future the bodies in these seats will sit in the same lofty shadows, watching a variety show of children with so-called talents. People like Anna's sister are the anomaly; everyone else gets credit just for trying. Any other day, I'd take pleasure in the earthy, digestive churn of the school's life.

Perfume, the flat citrus-blossom kind from the mall, wafts down the row. During Anna's long walk to the middle of the stage, a soft ticking punctuates the quiet nearby, someone picking at a hangnail. Behind me, there's a hiss and flip of a necktie being redone in the dark. A talent or just a skill? My uniform blouse brushes against the backs of my arms with each breath. My sweater emanates the smell of laundry soap, and my braid hurts the nape of my neck. As my friend steps into the disk of light, my attention keeps spilling back into my own body.

Here I sit, human miracle, blue queen, at a school assembly in the American suburbs. All these skills I've learned for blending in, and I still know exactly how singled out she feels. This empathy can only hurt me.

Anna's normal friends scream and whistle from the seats and the wings. As she halts on the elevated stage, she still seems uneasy with her body after its recent growth spurt, unsure of what to do with her arms.

In a wobbly voice, she says her name.

"I'm in ballet, and I'll dance to music from *Swan Lake*."

She is shaking in the hot quiet. The music is taking too long to start. Fair-skinned under normal circumstances, she glows like an undersea creature in the greater blackness. Rawboned, leggy, her body stretches the fabric of her leotard too high in her hips and too tight in her crotch.

I have seen her fail at this dance a hundred times. And as the music begins and she takes her first steps, it's obvious why this won't work. She's stolen the choreography from another ballet to different music, and not only that, it's supposed to be a dance for two people. One mercy: it is unrecognizable as the weightless dance of her sister.

The first hum of ridicule flutters through the seats.

Her knees shake. Lanky, her arms and legs have grown inches since spring. She comes down from a crooked jeté and springs up into a wild pirouette, now tilting on her axis. I cease to recognize the sequence. She's improvising because she has already forgotten how it goes. Steps and notes jumble. I will her to give up and run offstage, but she stays up there for several reasons, I know. She wants the extra credit, wants to get placed with her friends in next year's classes. Plans, futures, grades, measurements, categories—what she'll endure for the promise of fellowship. And down in row six, in the fifth-grade section, those friends sink in their seats, laughing into their hands. Teeth and eyes glint in the lights.

Fierce, insecure Anna, not even trying to smile anymore. She knows it's hopeless and throws herself into another leap anyway. Her leading foot hits the slippery stage too far behind her weight, and the satin slipper shoots straight back, throwing her facedown to the floor. Her chin hits the boards with the full weight of her body, approximately the weight of one talent, and the music goes on but she does not.

Her pale fingernails curl under against the dark boards. Her knee slides a few inches sideways, the one with the playground scar. Her breath is gone, but by the trembling of her back, I can tell that she is trying not to cry. I know her body almost as well as my own.

I remember just a scrap of the future, and it says that the bond between Anna and me depends on my staying seated. To keep my talents in my chair, because they are worth nothing in this moment.

But that's the thing: in every language all over the world, the word people use to signify *us*, the group of ourselves and the people we love, corresponds to the word for *human*. Whatever I am—I am human. And Anna is one of mine.

Because of that, I get up and go to her side. The carpeted aisle passes in a blur even while it becomes a hundred miles long, this trajectory to the steps beside the stage. It is like I've never walked before in my life—the shock of doing what isn't allowed alive in my feet, the miraculous improbability of standing up from the audience and approaching the front. My fear is so strong that I can only push it into a cold, flat stubbornness and keep walking. The stairs pound like timpani under my shoes. It takes a minute for people to realize that the figure now onstage is not part of the show.

I reach down and offer my hand to Anna. Music still plays over the sound system, not loudly enough to cover the drawback of silence that pulls the air from the room. The spotlight is even hotter up here.

And beyond its substantial glare is a cavern of shadows. Out in the audience, glimmers of light ricochet off glasses and jewelry. People see me, consider me. Ask their children whether I am in some kind of makeup, whether this is part of an inscrutable act. A mortified laugh leaks from one of her friends: *Oh my God . . .*

Having committed to this plan, however, I seal my shame behind the hard fact that I am already up here.

"Anna, get up!"

The light continues to find us, over and over. Her torso rises with one clear breath. She's goggling at me as if she's never seen me before. Here I am, here we are, in the middle of her nightmare.

"Anna, are you okay?"

My voice gets lost in the sound that has begun rushing into the auditorium. But as soon as her shock wears off, Anna's body comes alive with decision. She scrambles up and says, "Get away from me," as she runs offstage.

Past, present, future.

Last night I shared a bowl of almonds with you. I really remember this. You asked me what had gotten into me and I said, "How come everyone hates me?"

"Oh, Her Majesty has breaking news for me!" you muttered. "I don't love my favorite grandniece! Truly, I dislike her so much that I am not making her help me with seventy-seven yards of mindless handicrafts." Your embroidery needle made another circuit of the bamboo frame. "Lucky girl, so bored. America, land of overstimu- lated, underutilized child monarchs . . ."

"I hate everything," I said. "I hate all humans."

You adjusted your grip on the needle, awkward because of the ban- dage on your finger. "Oh, chickpea, no. You don't. The whole problem is just a broken heart."

I said, "Ew," and shoved the whole handful of almonds in my mouth.

You shrugged so neutrally your hands didn't move. The triangle pattern you were embroidering on Gabriel's baptismal blanket was traditional, meant to ward off the evil eye. But all I could do was chew with my face burning, as if you hadn't seen straight through me. Here I was, with prickling armpits and small lopsided breasts and this terror that the stone of me was gradually being overtaken with soft moss, splitting apart from the inside, as though whatever I was meant to become was somehow compromised by a process meant for mortals. And here you were, saying I had the softest of all human problems. The most shameful one, such that you had flung it from yourself whenever anyone had suspected you of having it, like that time you told my mother I had almost been adopted by perverts. But it was fear, always and only fear, that the world had put into you of yourself and that softness. And in this comfortable room of your old age, sitting beside the bookshelf where Cecilia's wooden gazelle watched over your bed, you imagined all my futures and spoke of the kindest one. Gifting it to me as if you could give it to your past self, the village girl who had not yet seen anything of the world.

"Of course you will not listen, but take it from a nobody." You stuck the needle in your sweatshirt cuff and reached for the spool. "Love whoever you want. But if you can, love a good person who will love you back, unless you want your heart to cry like a gazelle cornered by a hundred lions. But whatever way your heart takes you, just go. Pick up the pieces later. And drink some water before you choke on that mouthful of my snacks."

And the next day, I would be holding my brother in a hotel room, because no one listened to me when I said everything was about to end. What unites us, besides the universal word for *human*, is our tendency to universally ignore warnings when our nature pulls us toward what feels right—or at least toward something that feels better than the truth.

————

Forgetting the future is easy. When I stopped telling myself stories about it, I lost the habit, and it withered.

When Anna sent emails, for instance, I stopped thinking about what to write back to her. I stopped imagining plans, such as what color beads to put on the bracelets I was making. The plastic pearls would melt in their drawer, anyhow. I stopped wishing my brother would be adopted, and that night, the flashes of his incredible future stopped poisoning my sleep. I gave up planning my meals and clothes—my mother was a lifelong testament to the gross pointlessness of minor plans, anyway—and in a snap, the déjà vu dried up. Like an animal, I had never been comfortable imagining what lies very much ahead, and the career counselors had never extended themselves for mysteries like me. I felt myself becoming an overnight success, in that I could say there was only a short interval of my life during which I had let my mind make a home in the future. After I stopped dwelling on a time that did not yet exist, I ceased to be haunted by portents and ghost houses. It was the same advice my grandmother Saeeda might have given to any of us about her relationship to the past: one quick pull of the knife, and what once encumbered you drops away.

Saturday was a good day. We went to the zoo.

The weather feinted at summer. Inspired by a case of parental indulgence, Adam and Tashi decided that I deserved an excursion without the baby. They dressed up. I rode the light rail. I ate a chocolate bar in the long line to enter. The sun lit up yellow-and-white striped umbrellas along the zoo's food court. At an iron table in the shade, I dug through foamy layers of whipped cream to the sweet, grainy hot cocoa underneath, and called myself an anteater as I sucked it up through a tiny black straw. Tashi glanced around, but Adam winked at her to relax. And it *was* fine. One or two varicose-veined tourists, always in shorts and always yoked with a heavy camera, asked in fake-polite terms if we wanted our picture taken.

Adam's response: "Of course we do."

And why not? There we were, as if already framed: the neat, hale father in jeans and a crisp gray shirt (no one noticed that one sleeve was empty at the end) and, in a white A-line skirt and Prada sandals, his striking wife, whose eyes, when she pushed her sunglasses to the top of her head, added sincerity to her awkward smile. Nothing bad happened.

"Do the gazelles ever get to go home to the mountains?" My head lolled against the backseat window, full of favorites.

"They are in a zoo because they can't." My father was driving us home, tense from too many people. "It's like a special home for the gazelles. They have it better in the zoo than in the wild, where they have to worry about getting sick or people shooting them."

"Maybe *better* is a stretch," my mother said. I pretended not to see my father's glance. For the most part, they got along, but this new quirk of always correcting each other seemed to be an outlet. You couldn't stand it, and neither could I.

My mother sighed. "Slow down. You're driving like a madman."

He eased off the gas, but only because we were at the last big intersection before our neighborhood. By the lurch of the car a few moments later, and a distant horn, I could tell that traffic was bad.

"You know what will be better?" he said. "When we get home and put our pajamas on." He cursed. "You really think this is the fastest way right now? It looks like fire trucks up there."

"Oh, for crying out loud, Adam, next time we'll take a helicopter. But we're stuck in the car tonight."

My father sat in irritated silence for a long moment. Then something in him came loose and he slumped into a slow chuckle.

"A helicopter. I wonder if I'd need a parking pass." He swore and blew his horn at the car in front of him. My mother's mouth knitted into a seam.

"And when Betty gets old enough to drive . . ."

"I'm back here and can hear you," I said, "and I just want to be home."

"That's all I've been trying to do," my father muttered, "get to the pajamas," and then that was the end of the conversation. The charge in the car wasn't directed at me, but it hurt my feelings. My parents sat in rigid silence as traffic crept through the intersection.

They made the turn off the thoroughfare, sitting upright in their seats at the same time.

On our street the lights were red and flashing. It was coming from down the block, at a distance that felt familiar, because it was the exact distance between the intersection and our house. My father brought the car to a stop at the police barricade. Ahead, a tanker was spraying water into sky-high gouts of flame. The water scrawled meaningless letters in the sky.

Yes, it was our house on fire.

Ghazal on Fire

———•ı•———

In one night, our roof ejected ten years of our lives in ash mangled by exile.

Flames translated every file and folded counterpane to the language of exile.

Like locusts, like bombs, like a fearful god or an indifferent president, the fire that began downstairs consumed the entire house. It ate the mild-mannered floorboards and swallowed the bite-marked crib. It smelted the cannonballs to a red syrup that splattered in the foundation. It carbonized your wigs into stinking powder and reduced my mother's computer to a twisted mark on the workbench. The new chandelier's glass flesh trickled away to a brass skeleton. Tashi's books burned. Your ghazal collections and history texts burned. Anna's notes burned in my schoolbooks. Adam's wooden shelves and leathered encyclopedias gave way like a corpse, burning the archive, shedding kindling across the filing boxes. And then the fire gasped in a great breath, tearing open its prize.

Those orange fingers had found reams of loose-leaf pages, agitating a whole decade of paper:

. . . uncertain medical needs beyond the scope of the clients' resources . . .
. . . well-being of a medically sensitive child . . .
. . . deserted General Pedro de Ampudia's army before the rout at Monterrey . . .
. . . waiver undersigned by an authorized representative of St. Catherine's School . . .
. . . H81.399: Other peripheral vertigo, unspecified . . .

But just before the floor collapsed, the front door opened and you stepped across the melting welcome mat. A riffle of night air scooped up the burning evidence of my life and flung it to the sky: embers gleaming, spangled in exile.

Maybe there had been a cigarette left on the basement sill.

Maybe it was a surge in the wiring of my mother's workspace.

The documented cause would come later. For now, the possibilities were a cyclone of embers, each one storming the night air. You had once looked down from a terrace in Haifa and seen Jibril Rummani set a market aflame, and you'd lowered a rope of your hair to save him; so when you first opened your eyes in the chair by the living room's tamely crackling hearth, you heard a baby crying and believed you were seated in that long-ago alley. In that moment of inexactness and uncertainty, all things were true at once: you were yourself and someone else, saving Jibril or someone else, climbing the burning staircase to the nursery. The flames rolled up the walls and poured from the ceiling.

As you climbed the stairs, the only heat that touched you was through a tear on the skin of your pinkie finger. You were pleased but not shocked to find Gabriel unhurt and asleep.

You scooped him from the burning crib.

Wrapped his sleeping form into a blanket.

Stacked his smoking clothes into a bag.

Kissed his brow at the hairline.

Whispered that it was time to go.

The roof vomited flocks of burning paper and wood against the sky, turning the windows into bores of fire. The front door came off its hinges, and a stooped and gently limping figure stepped from the inferno. In one arm a baby and in the other a suitcase, the baggage of exile.

The Rummani tales sound, yes, like annals of doubt.

But I, of all people, have to begrudge my brother his miracle.

The pale limestone of the mountains around Nablus has properties that our grandfather Jibril would have known from his work as an engineer and as a native of his own city. Fine, pale, workable, the limestone made good walls, good ovens, and good soap vats. Gabriel came out of the house fire somewhat heavier than before, clouded with denser patches of grayish-white skin, like marble. Inheriting the blood of stones doesn't make you invincible; surviving fire doesn't make you strong; but after you carried him out of the burning house, he was briefly famous. *Lucky,* the evening news called him. *Brave,* they called you, but when they asked you questions, you spoke to the cameras in agitated Arabic until they left you alone.

While the handfuls of burning paper were still looping on the updraft, the authorities sought to pencil the miracle into the boxes of their paperwork.

"Were you smoking?"

Steaming, sparking, a bucket of coals . . .

"Where were the flames?"

Consuming the market, burning wool . . .

"Where did it start?"

You pressed your hand to your forehead, disoriented. Where *was* the beginning? Gabriel, bearer of old names, took the flames over his body like earth in a kiln. No matter how far you felt from yourself, your story still held you tight as a skin. Years, strangling in exile.

———

My parents loved me, sure, but it was Gabriel's night to evade death.

New moon, strange magic, who knows why some Arabs get to live.

What I remember is how my parents came alive together, alight themselves, finding the common spark that has less to do with love than the discovery of a shared fear. Funny, when all that knowledge burns away, there are two people hurling themselves at the barricading arms of officers, shouting to firefighters, clawing for a steaming, unburned son who was too hot to touch. You put him in my arms. It was the first time he felt like my brother, despite all that separated us. He watched the flames with the puzzled seriousness of a philosopher. Years from now, he would be handsome, and no one but his lovers would suspect that the opaque striations in his torso were a kind of stone.

My mother lightly held the back of my neck and my father had my arm, both of them gripping me as the closest thing to Gabriel, anchoring themselves in a gale of professional advice:

"Take him to the hospital."

"They need to get evaluated."

"Standard procedure."

"The only responsible thing."

"It's a liability issue, too."

Like the flames that had washed over their son, the entreaties washed past our parents. Tashi looked at Adam, ready to concede, but he was staring at Gabriel and me as if for the first time. He said, "They're fine, love. Let's just find a hotel where we can wrangle with exile."

On November the twentieth at two P.M.
we request the joy of your presence at a baptism.

This steadfast invitation flew to Jerusalem, Amman, London, Miami, and West L.A., and the many tributaries of migration on the heels of the terrible news that had preceded it. Adam and Tashi would host the party at Saeeda's new home, where they were staying for now. The official story was an electrical fire in the rewired garage. But mechanics are the least interesting part of a tale; what drew a rush of viral attention were reports that you had carried an infant out of a burning house, walking as calm as a spring morning. The elder relatives—Jibril's toadlike brother Zaki and cool Hilwa, their cousin—weren't wrong to feel déjà vu. They knew you'd always had a propensity for reaching into flames.

Across the many continents, the Rummanis slid their fingernails under the flap of the invitation's envelope, and then dialed each other to dismantle its news.

"Nuha always exaggerates things."

"We don't think this is possible."

"But the child is unburnt, hamdullah."

"Should we go? It's in wine country."

"Saeeda owes us a lifetime of hospitality."

This latter remark carried weight. It's not that any of them would have lived in the old city again, given the chance; but understand, the half-life of dreams and grudges will last till the end of human time. Rummanis booked their flights, eager for this banquet of exiles.

Saeeda built her hilltop house from a developer's plan on a plot bought cheap.

At the end of a burn-scarred lane, it overlooked a valley and a root-choked creek.

Far north of the city, on a burnished hillside studded with live oaks and olive trees, the view from her patio reminded her of Palestine—the way rock erupted ungoverned from the grass, sheltering snakes. The rain came before the Rummanis arrived for the baptism, so when the many airplanes touched California tarmac, the landscape was awash in brilliant green growth fed by last fall's ashes. Her rooms filled fast: You and I on a pullout in the den, my parents and Gabriel in a downstairs bedroom. The two upstairs went to Hilwa and her daughters and to Zaki and his wife from Miami. One London nephew flew in with his boyfriend, who'd been promised wine tours. Then there were no more rooms.

She knew they had come to scoop food from her platters and lick their fingers and handle her things. Fine. In Nablus she'd been young and powerless, but here she was the master.

Front yard, a tiled garden thick with herbs.

Bedrooms also tile, full of intricate furniture.

A sunroom, secluded like the women's courtyard.

Rugs, colorful lanterns, family icons on the walls.

Limestone pillars, checkered faintly like towers of soap.

Her architect had echoed the memories she cared about, and the rest was modern, sound, and still smelling of paint. It had taken a flight of decades to get here, and now the family was coming. A house could ease, if not defeat, the anguish of exile.

"Wait, what kind of story is this, anyway?"

"It is the noble syntax of a dying gazelle. Listen."

You were in turns exhausted and eccentric—exhausted by living in Saeeda's house, by the party preparations; eccentric in the number of domestic hills you chose to die on, and in the startling number of Band-Aids that now plastered your fingers and arms. The fire had done no other damage except make you too jittery to sleep. I often woke to the light of your phone in the middle of the night, with its billboard-sized font, as you poked out texts to someone who made you chuckle. When you saw me, you'd swing an arm over my back and set your phone on the nightstand, and we'd listen to the rain sluicing the gutters. Then you recited some poetry in Arabic, untranslated, mysterious.

"It doesn't sound like a creature about to get eaten," I said, but you turned my hand over and traced some of the lines you saw there. You told me my palm said I needed more culture.

A ghazal, the poetry of distance and longing.

In Arabic, the word's root also ran to flirting.

And to pain, and tale-telling, and, yes, gazelles.

Repetition, a tightrope across chasms.

Leave it to me to bastardize anything.

The sound got in my ear, as did the hypnotizing thrum of the rain against the window. Your phone blinked; I felt you wanting to reach for it. You kept Band-Aids next to the bed. I made a production of peeling one open and holding your hand still so I could bandage the exile.

The future is not so different from a myth:

outside of time, ripe with promise, a vessel.

The day after my birth, you were to fly to Greece with your beloved. Buying that flight at the beginning of a war, you foresaw yourself barefoot on an island, the horizon an unbroken hoop, a woman beside you, grasping your hand as your heart fell open to the air. Overhead, the bowl of sky. And I dare imagine it too: putting on my boots and boarding a plane over the unbroken waters, picking up a long migration. I know what you'd tell me, auntie to auntie: *What is the problem, your plane only goes in one direction? Is it a journey to the moon? Yaani, even the man on the moon was allowed to come back—stop imagining the worst and go.*

Maybe freedom is just this: a path forks right and left, and the wrong direction costs next to nothing. The future needs possibilities as a hand needs separate fingers.

Your ears aren't down there in the grave.

I can talk to you from anywhere.

The children all have cellphones.

I want to see a new city.

I want to see it with her.

The sun is sinking toward the water and we haven't found our way home yet, stalled in Babel's long shadow. So a moment more with your stories, words I'm packing for exile.

Here is a story, a Babel remix, past and future.

The water rushes in, the flood we know about.

Like rivers of myth, it travels underground for a while, passing through caves in many lands. As the seas slosh higher, higher, over the continents, all the humans of the world move their cities to the mountaintops. But the flood bursts from the mountaintops too, spilling down through every street and alleyway. It's how the holy waters of the Ganges drown lifeboats in Pittsburgh, and how the Mississippi sweeps away Amsterdam. Jerusalem sinks into the mingled waters of the Pacific and Lake Kivu. They say that every human being on earth carries one molecule of Julius Caesar's dying breath in their lungs. It's like that, how the soap vats in Nablus will become cisterns holding every river from the Yangtze to the Po.

When all the waters of the world have run together again, everyone is a citizen of the same land—their cries reaching over the unbroken water like long fingers.

"We need to build higher than the tide," some say.

"We don't have time," say others, uncomprehending.

"What do we build with?"

"Where do we find land?"

"How do we begin and with what?"

They don't realize that their languages have begun to sound alike again, for the first time in untold millennia since the cleaving at Babel, for they are speaking our language of exile.

And the birds of the world return to nowhere, circling the floodscape, until one with flame-red feathers spies a branch and foots itself there, breast heaving, to take in this vantage on exile.

The Bird of This Aggravating Tale

———·—·———

"Come here, chickpea."

I'd thought I was the last one moving around, but a light was on in the far corner of my grandmother's sunroom. You were just sitting. No cigarette. No tea, no book. It was like you'd been waiting for me, but then I noticed the tissues wadded in your shirt cuff. I folded myself onto the wicker sofa and laid my head in your lap.

"Do you remember the time you lived with me?"

I did, a little—I had a memory of being carried through a mass of watchful rooms.

"Do you remember all the people who helped us when I hurt my knee?"

Voices late at night, waking with the sense that knots of tension had been massaged out of the apartment's very air. But the people? I shrugged the shoulder that was sticking up, feeling too groggy and restless to make any other answer. You worked your hand into my hair and I felt the snag and scrape of Band-Aids.

"Cecilia had a dove named Red. You used to make yourself hiccup with laughter—Red walked his feet up and down your arm and nuzzled you under your ear. Cecilia wanted to take pictures, but your

mother was so strict about it. We were talking about my old apartment today, and we had a good laugh about you and that dear little
bird." You began tugging at my ear the way I liked, an odd thing to
want, but the sensation had a soporific power over me. It almost didn't
occur to me to wonder what you were saying.

"Auntie?"

"Hmm?"

"Who's Cecilia?"

The wicker seat creaked. A moth stuck in the sunroom beat itself
against the glass.

"Oh, chickpea, I guess you could say Cecilia is my girlfriend."

In the days leading up to Gabriel's baptism, you had been compliant
with all of Saeeda's preparations. You sat in the sunroom extinguish-
ing half-smoked cigarettes in a flowerpot. You left the baby to my
parents. With boundless patience, you helped me pick out a sweater-
and-jeans combination that downplayed my appearance, because I
was nervous about the people I'd heard about my whole life but met
only once, in front of a casket.

My grandmother rolled cabbage leaves, frowning. "You look beautiful in all of it, habeebti."

You said, "Your grandmother doesn't remember the family's sixteen
lawsuits and all their opinions. But it is okay. No matter what you
wear, I will make sure they are more worried about me and not about
you."

Saeeda lifted the pot of malfouf to the stovetop. "You do not *need*
to be worried about their attention at all. It is a party for your nephew."

You pinched up a few grains of uncooked rice and licked them
from your finger. "You know, Cecilia is flying in."

Saeeda peered into the pot again. "If we Rummanis are so terrible,
how unkind of you to inflict us on your friend." She seemed more
concerned with the position of the stacked malfouf in the pot than
with the sideways slant of your gaze.

What to do with this thread, which has a whiff of another beginning? I worry that you prefer to hear about the actual Rummanis, what they thought of me, what they are doing now, because that story is broadly relatable and holds more potential for an ending. But what is there to say? The Rummanis are humans, as they always were. That day, they barely recognized my mother. They saw me and pitied her. They asked me tired questions about school and activities, and I answered them, saying that I enjoyed reading, and no, I did not dance or play sports. When they saw in my eyes that I was smart, they folded their opinions away. Even Zaki, Jibril's middle brother, who had tossed his shoes at you in 1948 and grabbed your breast and torn the skin his own father had given you to wear, looked at me with the beginnings of dementia and slipped me one-dollar bills like I was any other grandchild.

His quivering hand is all you need to see. The ones who remembered the past were all so old. And you feared that with them, the past would die.

The younger ones, Hilwa's daughters or the London cousin with his expensive T-shirts and precise facial hair, remembered cracked pieces of the tale but had never set foot in Nablus. The daily price of scientific wonders and professional doubt had hypnotized almost everyone into seeing not ghosts, not miracles everywhere, but normalcy. I had a birth certificate, I was part of the school and medical systems, I returned high fives on my way to the fridge for another deviled egg. I kept almost everyone under their spell of a baggy present tense.

It is on this day of my brother's baptism that I will learn about hiding whole elephants in plain sight. For instance, when my family arrives at the church in their Sunday best, a woman with a veil of silver hair sits in the third pew, as promised.

She stays behind after the liturgy is over, stretches her legs with the rest of us, and resumes her seat when the priest rolls the marble font to the center. Her old-peach cheeks crinkle in sympathy for my naked brother as the priest hoists him, howling wet, into the embroidered baptismal cloth. She is there in her cozy sweater to offer congratulations and give Tashi a lingering hug of real affection and pride. So they (a) assume that she is somebody's aging mother-in-law; (b) conclude that she is known to everyone else and it would be insulting to ask her name; and when the murmured inquiries about her identity all lead nowhere, the outer Rummanis (c) figure that she must have arrived in the family constellation during the Time of Feuding. That seems to be right, because if asked, she will volunteer anecdotes about Nuha Rummani's renown as a teacher, beloved of students, nemesis of administrators, outsmarter of micromanaging parents. So no matter what, she must also be your good friend, requested by Saeeda, here to keep you on good behavior so my brother can be the day's center of attention. As I said a long while ago, Rummanis claimed a confident authority over matters in which they were ignorant—you had always known this, all the way back to your days as a servant in Haifa. And Cecilia knew it, too. She felt no urge to clear the confusion of the struggling, deceived Rummanis whose naïveté had created so much heartache and secrecy in your life.

Afterward, she is behind the wheel of a scratched electric vehicle that shuttles the both of you back to Saeeda's house. She adjusts a fruit basket on the kitchen counter to better display its bow and distributes serving spoons in each of the bowls—helpful! maternal! Rummanis wander into the dining room with their sectioned styrofoam plates of malfouf and kibbeh and salads, and see that this silver-haired woman sits beside you in a seat of honor and will not yield the chair.

It is the only irritating thing about her.

"If a person has finished eating, she should leave the table," an elder cousin mutters to Saeeda in the sunroom. She balances her plate on her knee with the help of a designer heel, which is hooked on the crossbar of her stool. "So rude."

Saeeda drops another dirty plastic cup into the garbage bag. "But

Nuha has not finished eating." Her face is empty of the requisite irritation.

And so the one remark that is said with enough friction to elicit a deflection accrues into a very small pearl of recognition. The cousin goggles at Saeeda for confirmation (oh, those halfhearted Arab attempts at subtlety), but Saeeda lets her errand carry her out of the room without yielding more.

Why would my grandmother be surprised? Long ago, in the Time of Feuding, on an unremarkably humid Houston evening, in the tract house she newly shared with the Second Husband Who Was Not a Rummani, Saeeda already had her suspicions. Visiting, you sat with slippered feet out on the grass, swatting mosquitoes under a tree full of whistling grackles. You were, in fact, midway through issuing a complicated challenge to the insects, daring them to discover how much chemotherapy still coursed in your veins.

"Ukhti?"

Smack. "Hmm?"

"How is Cecilia?"

You lifted your eyes from the smudge of blood on your forearm. In the damp blue twilight, a string of small memories hung between the two of you. The quiet, unobtrusive friend with a cascade of salt-and-pepper hair who had been present at so many treatments. Folding laundry while you were pale and retching at home. Slipping behind the closed bathroom door to sit with you by the toilet. Teachers together, sure. The tiniest flicker of alarm appeared in your eyes, and then you stifled it and grinned.

"Oh, all of us biddies are raising funds for the revolution again, one crappy T-shirt design at a time."

Saeeda decanted the last of the coffee between their cups. "Well, send my regards to her."

Counting between that humid Texas evening and my brother's

party, twenty-nine years is more than enough time to get used to an idea. Our exile taught us to get used to anything.

"Are you upset to know all this about your aunt?"

Sleepily, I shook my head. It wasn't what bothered me. I'd seen the future once upon a time, and I knew what tonight was. I wrapped my arm around your knees and hugged them, wanting nothing but to fold myself into smaller and smaller halves until I could fit inside your thighbone, like the djinni that hid its spirit in a tiger's leg to escape being destroyed.

"Then what is it, chickpea?"

I couldn't think of how to begin. Instead I asked where Cecilia, your girlfriend, the woman with the veil of silver hair, had gone.

"Back to the city, to her family. Today was a big day. You are a good girl to keep me company so late. Look at us—here we are together, alert as a pair of owls."

I stared over the ledge of your knees at the tract of floor between us and a shelf of miniature roses. The single bright gardener's lamp found thin patterns of shadow along the cement—troughs and ridges, arcs and intersecting lines between the colorful Armenian tiles Saeeda had paid the builders to embed. The longer I stared, the more the finish looked like faces, like fields, like everything swirling together and apart between the intricately painted squares. I wanted to stay here clinging to you forever.

"I'm not like any of them," I said.

"Of course you are not. You belong half to them, half to me, and half to no one at all."

"That's three halves, Auntie."

"Yes, so?"

That was part of what bothered me. But you had raised me on the promise of a narratively endowed family, and I kept coming back to my great-uncle Zaki's trembling hand and blank gaze and the thread of dental floss he'd hung on his shirt button after dessert.

"I don't feel anything. They're just a bunch of people."

The wicker couch made a snickering sound as you laughed. "What did you think? We all come together like the plastic pie in Trivial Pursuit, then a disco ball drops out of the ceiling?" You rubbed my back, and I felt the tickle of your fraying finger bandages on the back of my arm. "Of course they are just a bunch of people. And if you go back far enough, everyone on the planet is family to each other. One big dysfunctional family. Welcome to the human race, unwholesome and irritating and selfish and backstabbing and tiny-brained since the day the Tower of Babel fell."

One of your bitter moods, then.

"You know what, Betty? You're exactly right. I kept everyone in your family a little bit happy for seventy years, performed wonders so that they all could grow up with the privilege of being just like everyone else. To hell with everybody. Everybody but you. And maybe one or two others. I wish I—"

"Can we walk down the hill?" My restlessness came on in a rush, bringing a need to feel the air on my skin, a fear that at any moment my mother would fill the doorway and tell me it was past bedtime. The possibility filled me with panic; her authority would close like a hand over the half of me that belonged to family and drag the rest of me with it—the rest being, as you had said, the other two halves that did not belong to kin. And I was terrified of running out of time.

"Down the hill now?" you asked.

"To the orchard," I said, "while the moon is out. Sitti said there's an owl's nest."

"I suppose we could go look for owls at this hour." You pushed me off your lap and heaved yourself to your feet, though in those days you couldn't have weighed more than a hundred pounds. "It sounds like a lovely idea, going to visit wild beasts in the dark of night with who knows what else. Do you know that owls have been known to kill people? The corpses turn up with little feathers stuck in their heads. Not to mention the possibility of cougars, ghosts, and unspecified ogres. But Your Majesty, my lifelong city dweller, knows best when it is time to go walking in nature . . ." On and on with the protest, as you put on Saeeda's long goose-down coat and found the switch for the porch light to illuminate the stone stairs, and got your sturdiest cane from the foyer, seeming more and more to relish the idea of departure.

Here in the cemetery all these years later, the marine layer is coming in. The wind starts smelling like the sea and leaves a trace of moisture on the skin, so I slide your journals back into their plastic bag to preserve them. All this history, it takes up so little room—small enough to fit inside a shoe. It's an indistinct hour, not quite twilight, when the clouds are edged in pink from the setting sun. This is the view I will remember. Downhill, the headlights of the cemetery's security vehicle sweep along the pavement, beginning the evening circuit. On the next hill, along the gray staircase, two women fold a picnic quilt into a stroller. A birder in the valley between us aims his camera into a cedar tree, while from the grass, his dog picks up its head at the sound of the vehicle's approach.

So many years on, I still cannot remember exactly what you were telling me that night. The stairs down from the patio of Saeeda's house were, as I recall, made out of pale slabs of limestone that glowed in the moonlight. We didn't need a flashlight. When we got down to the orchard, it went on forever, these regular round islands of moon shadow and a smooth grid of grass between them. There were no leaves on the ground, no sticks or rotting windfall. No roosting starlings, no mice, no owls.

The night was primordially silent as you described memories at random, so that soon I felt like I could find my way around a hillside on the other side of the world, the ghost of the village of Maaloul, without ever having been there. At some point we seemed to be standing by an ancient cactus under the night sky, and the apple trees were gone, and beneath us were low, terraced roofs receding down toward the spring.

"Tell me a story," I said.

"I thought you were looking for owls."

"I can do both things at once."

"Famous last words from Emperor Napoleon, but okay," you said, setting your cane one step at a time in front of your feet. "I am getting overheated again. Carry my coat, and I will give you a story."

Once upon a time, there was a woman with long silver hair who lived by herself in an enchanted wood. She taught children how to sew. They were her only company since her baby had died, and after she traveled the whole world around, she brought all the threads of all the continents to her house and made garments to flatter the queen of the djinn. Her fame spread far, and one day a stranger came to her door with a complicated problem.

The stranger was losing her beauty.

"But I am a seamstress," the woman with silver hair said, "not a magician. And beauty isn't a woman's prime asset." Yet she had to admit that the stranger was magnetic—graceful as a gazelle, hair as red as flame, skin that glowed like porcelain—but the edges of her face were veined with a thousand small cracks.

"What you do not understand," said the stranger, "is that I *want* to lose my beauty, once and for all. It is not mine. But I am trapped inside it, watching a stranger age in the mirror. I need you to undo this skin garment."

The woman said, "Show me?"

That is when the stranger demonstrated her problem: on her left breast was a seam, healed like a closed eye.

"If you can flay me," said the stranger, "I will be yours forever."

The woman was uncompelled by love, but in truth she was so talented that her work had become boring—the queen of the djinn had wanted nothing but rompers, long out of fashion. So the challenge intrigued her.

She ordered the stranger to undress. Once the red-haired woman was standing on the wooden stool, illuminated by a plane of raw sunlight, her predicament was clearer. Every curve and joint of her body was encased in a suit of sturdy skin. First the seamstress chose a seam ripper. She cupped the stranger's breast and sank the metal tooth into the flaw, expecting the suit's construction to reveal itself.

"I've tried that already," said the stranger. "You have to flay me."

But the seamstress was not brutal, and she chose from her kit a pair of silver scissors, a gift from the jackals of a faraway desert. Surely these would loosen the skin. She ran her fingertips along the nape of the stranger's neck and pressed the tip of the jackals' scissors along the bottom of the scalp. Still the skin resisted.

"You have to flay me with a knife," the stranger said, "or it will not work."

"I am no butcher."

"If you can't help me undress, I will throw myself into the river."

The woman no longer wanted the stranger to leave, and she was also very stubborn, so she went to the sink outside and got the curved knife she used to skin rabbits. She dragged its tip lightly along the woman's hip and over the base of her spine, but at the stranger's encouragement, she pressed harder, until the razor-sharp blade plunged all the way through the false skin. The stranger cried out, and the woman dragged the knife all the way up to the base of her throat and began scraping the skin away. It slipped to the floor in folds, and the sunlight pierced the space where the stranger had been.

"That's it?"

We have walked so far that the horizons are black velvet. The only light in any direction is the moon. We stop in the silver cross of light between four apple trees.

"I'm very tired, and this is getting so heavy." You are leaning on your cane, catching your breath. The night is cool, but I am sweating from carrying the down coat. The only noises are the low rasp of its fabric and the higher rasp of air in your throat. "But let me see . . . Oh yes, the sunlight streamed over the empty suit, yada yada. But standing in the folds of the skin suit was a brilliant red bird the size of a parrot with a flowing tail like a peacock. Our bird flew straight out the window and roosted in a tree on the property, and she became the woman's devoted familiar for thirty years."

You poke the cane into the grass.

"There, the end, and if you look just above your head I think you'll be pleased."

Confused, I tilt my head back and gaze into the gnarled apple limbs overhead. On the stoutest branch sits a barn owl. Its pale face and twin eye pits seem almost humanoid, yet also alien—what a soul might look like. For a moment I'm transfixed. Then its wings open in a white slash of feathers, and it leaps into the air, making no sound but the chatter of leaves. With the barest whisper of air over its body, the owl flies into the dark space between the boughs.

And when I look down I'm alone in the orchard.

On the ground, spotlighted in the grass, is a pile of flesh: sleeves, suit, the hood of the scalp, folded neatly in a square and tied in a strip of cloth. But though I call out, she keeps going, away from her skin, as the words of her story hang in the air, connecting us for a while.

Give me something to imagine.

Tell me a story.

That next morning, when I woke to a commotion, Nuha Rummani was sitting on the wicker sofa with a smile on her face. Her lips were parted enough to show the edges of her teeth, and her wig had slipped. In a life of many complications, one of them was the persistent, ambivalent relationship my aunt had had with her dignity. So—no matter the collective distress, no matter the sort of phone calls the

Rummanis had begun making—the body's clownish final posture struck me as a problem.

When everyone had gone out front to watch for the ambulance, I gripped the wig with my fingertips and removed it. I'd gotten a scarf from the little aubergine suitcase, and now I pressed its folded edge smoothly against the body's brow and made a proper knot. I brought the body's hands to its lap and moved toward the sunroom door. Never had this familiar face been so compliant or so papery around the eyes, yet I kept waiting for the life to show up behind it and wink.

If anybody ought to defy death . . . But on second thought, that had been me. My brother, too. And my mother. And my grandfather and all the Rummanis who still walked around in the stories, heads high, alive in me. We were the ones who had cheated death and gathered under Saeeda's roof for a baptism and ended up planning the final itinerary of this abandoned body, which sat straight and still in the morning sun, in a room overlooking a valley of apple trees.

To this day, many years later, I embellish your death, Auntie, when the children ask about it. Sometimes, lately, I say that when fire burns through the hills every autumn, its path parts around Saeeda Rummani's house, which now belongs to my mother. Other times I say that a red bird makes its nest on the roof or that indigo flowers grow out of season in scandalous excess around this gravestone. I might be lying, but it's important to give the next generation something to imagine.

I informed Mama of my plan to drive down to the cemetery this morning, and she described an encounter she'd had only five years after the funeral, when a work event had brought her to Oakland. She'd skipped the final day to visit the cemetery. As she drove along the matted and muddy grass, water gurgled in culverts and flooded the reservoirs. At the section that was her destination, a scratched Prius sat at the berm. A figure loomed at the headstone in an overcoat and wellies, leaning on an old ski pole for balance in the wet: Cecilia, who was, in all ways that mattered, your widow. Her daughter had driven her up but stayed inside the car, engrossed in her phone's glowing rectangle.

"Cee, I'm embarrassed!" Tashi got out with a wreath and solar lights in a bag. "I should have called to say I'd be in town." She slogged up the slick hillside. The other woman's face had aged into a natural smile, but at the moment, grief had distilled it into vacancy, a raw afterthought.

"I'm sorry. I'm intruding," Tashi said. "Would you like some time alone?"

Cee shook her head. Her cheeks were wind-scalded. "Happy Solstice. What did you bring your aunt—" She stopped, and something complicated settled around her eyes and brow: the rest of a question she would not form into words. Only decades later did Tashi think back and hear the rest—what did you bring your aunt *for her birthday, the real one, which is today?* But on the hillside that afternoon the meeting was only a coincidence, and the moment was awkward in a puzzling way, and Tashi quickly opened the bag on her arm.

"Just a little holiday bling." She pulled out the holly wreath. The ribbon was clownish and sequined, and she hoped that the obviousness of the occasion and the attention-getting bow would hurry them past the strange hesitation. Tashi felt Cee watching as she pressed the prickly wreath into the mud on its little stick and then inserted the two solar lights, so that they flanked the stone like stage footlights. When Tashi stood up, Cee's attention had settled into amusement.

Tashi said, "It looks okay, right?"

"That ribbon is gaudy enough to be Mrs. Claus's date-night thong. It's perfect." She pulled Tashi close with her free arm, into the damp wool of her coat, into its dog hair and colored fibers and crumbs from her grandchildren's snacks. She smelled of crayons and a potting shed, a fragrance from Tashi's past so imprinted that it overpowered time, forgetting, and loss itself. In that moment, it seemed that the two of them had survived very much indeed, and might survive to the very end of time, since they had already managed to outlive the immortal whose body had gone to rest here beneath their feet. Cee said, "She was so proud of you, Tashi. You're the toughie, the only one of the lot of them with her spirit. It's not a strength that's inherited. She'd want me to remind you of that."

Mama was bewildered, tried to laugh. "You have me mixed up with someone else."

Cee refused the joke. Instead she hugged Tashi closer and said, "She raised you in strength, and you raised your daughter in it, too. Don't let other people's fear confuse you. Nuha was a tough old root, and she'd want me to tell you this: there is no truth but in old women's tales."

I trust that my mother related this story for a reason, a letter of recommendation to carry against my heart, a strength, as I travel onward.

This, too, is true: imagine a city of towers, a grave on a hill, acres inside a gated fence. A woman in a high-collared coat shoves a bag of notebooks into her pocket, preparing to go.

The security guard asks, "Who are you?" and I say nobody.

"The gates are closing for the night. And you must be cold."

"Very well," I tell him and head for the cemetery exit with your words in my pocket. I pull the skin a little tighter around my throat, passing through the gates in time to walk down the avenue as the marine light casts the city in an even, lustrous blue.

ACKNOWLEDGMENTS

The care and generosity of many helped me research, write, and share this book with readers. I give special thanks to my extraordinary agent, Adam Schear, to my keen and unfailingly kind editor, Chelcee Johns, and the entire hardworking team at Ballantine Books, and to publicist Kathy Daneman, for their collective and wholehearted belief in this story.

For their vital and practical support of my craft when I needed it most, thank you to Beth McCabe of the Rona Jaffe Foundation and Debra Allbery of the MFA Program for Writers at Warren Wilson College, where I wrote most of the novel. I owe special debts of gratitude to those faculty members who worked closely with me on early drafts, especially Nina McConigley. Other organizations and literary communities have provided essential energy and support: the Northern California Writers' Retreat, the Oregon Writers Colony, GrubStreet, the Elizabeth George Foundation, and the Creative Capacity Fund.

For publishing excerpts and earlier portions of this manuscript as stories, my gratitude goes to the late Jon Tribble of *Crab Orchard Re-*

view as well as the editors of *New Ohio Review* and *LEON Literary Review*. At the *North American Review*, I'm especially grateful to Jeremy Schraffenberger, whose exquisite generosity has helped me along the way and who models the sort of literary citizenship I aspire to.

For expanding my knowledge of traditional storytelling and soap production in Palestine, I found initial help in innumerable secondary sources, including Beshara Doumani's *Rediscovering Palestine: Merchants and Peasants in Jabal Nablus 1700–1900;* Ibrahim Muhawi and Sharif Kanaana's *Speak, Bird, Speak Again: Palestinian Arab Folktales;* and Michel Khleifi's short film *Ma'aloul Celebrates Its Destruction.* I found later help while in-country from so many people, especially Mohammad Barakat and everyone at Green Olive Tours; they made moving between Israel and the West Bank much easier for me than it is for the 130,000 Palestinians who have permits to work in Israel and its settlements but who do not have the privilege of predictable travel that I had as a white-looking American citizen with my father's Anglo surname. I am grateful to the Mahmoud Darwish Foundation for granting me permission to translate and use the epigraph, and to translator Nada Sneige Fuleihan for her assistance and contributions throughout the final stages.

Thank you to my communities from Pittsburgh to Portland and the Bay Area, as well as points elsewhere; and to so many early readers and dear friends, among them Laura Stanfill, Dr. Barbara Pope, Emily Manice, Dr. Laurie Rosenblatt, Meghan and Michael McLitus, Dr. Heather Fowler, Chaney Kwak, Mackenzie Evan Smith Sajan, Maddie Oatman, and especially forever-mentor and friend Professor Jane McCafferty. Thank you to Dr. Mihail Iordanov and many others in Portland who provided vital insights into the scientific life. Thank you to Dr. Leena Akhtar (for so much), Dr. Hatim El-Hibri, Dr. Odeese Ghassa-Khalil, and others who shared their knowledge and experiences of contemporary life in Arabic-speaking cultures.

Thank you to my family, all of you, who cared about this project in direct and indirect ways over the years. You are in this effort in more ways than I can name, and for all you've done to help me make a life in the arts, this book is yours.

And, most of all, to Erin, my love, my person, my North Star in everything.

ABOUT THE AUTHOR

SARAH CYPHER has an MFA from the Program for Writers at Warren Wilson College, where she was a Rona Jaffe Fellow in fiction, and a BA from Carnegie Mellon University. Her writing has appeared in the *New Ohio Review*, *North American Review*, and *Crab Orchard Review*, among other publications. She is from a Lebanese Christian family in Pittsburgh, Pennsylvania, and lives in Washington, D.C., with her wife.

sarahcypher.com
Twitter: @threepenny
Instagram: @sarahcypher

ABOUT THE TYPE

This book was set in Caslon, a typeface first designed in 1722 by William Caslon (1692–1766). Its widespread use by most English printers in the early eighteenth century soon supplanted the Dutch typefaces that had formerly prevailed. The roman is considered a "workhorse" typeface due to its pleasant, open appearance, while the italic is exceedingly decorative.

14 day   4-23

cv

EMMA S. CLARK MEMORIAL LIBRARY
SETAUKET, NEW YORK 11733

To view your account,
renew or request an item,
visit www.emmaclark.org